TRUTH
OR
DEMON

TRUTH
OR
DEMON

KATHY LOVE

BRAVA

KENSINGTON PUBLISHING CORP.
www.kensingtonbooks.com

BRAVA BOOKS are published by

Kensington Publishing Corp.
119 West 40th Street
New York, NY 10018

All Kensington titles, imprints, and distributed lines are available at special quantity discounts for bulk purchases for sales promotion, premiums, fund-raising, educational, or institutional use.

Special book excerpts or customized printings can also be created to fit specific needs. For details, write or phone the office of the Kensington Special Sales Manager: Kensington Publishing Corp., 119 West 40th Street, New York, NY 10018. Attn. Special Sales Department. Phone: 1-800-221-2647.

Brava and the B logo are Reg. U.S. Pat. & TM Off.

ISBN-13: 978-0-7582-3197-0
ISBN-10: 0-7582-3197-0

First Kensington Trade Paperback Printing: March 2011
10 9 8 7 6 5 4 3 2 1

Printed in the United States of America

For Kate Duffy—

This is the last book I sold to you.
But not the last book
I will write with you in my thoughts.

ACKNOWLEDGMENTS

I want to thank my new editor, Alicia Condon. Thank you for making this transition so easy and so positive. I'm thrilled to be working with you.

Thanks to my wonderful agent, Amy Moore-Benson. I'm excited about the future now. Thank you.

Thanks to Beth Ciotta for introducing me to the fabulous Amy. I love you, girl!

Thank you to the Tarts—otherwise known as Kate Dolan, Christie Kelley, Janet Mullany, and Kate Poole. Love you, ladies.

And thanks to my family—especially, Mom and Dad. You help me *so* much. Love you.

Oh wait—And of course, to my Emily. I love you, Boo!

CHAPTER 1

Killian knew his screams.

As a demon from the First Circle of Hell, he'd heard plenty of them. Screams of terror. Screams of agony. Even screams of ecstasy.

But he'd never heard screams like this. Really, it was more like squealing. High pitched, nearly deafening, like a sound that should only register in a dog's hearing range. But unfortunately, *he* could hear the piercing sounds, and he could hear they were tinged with something. Some emotion. Almost . . . delighted horror.

He blinked again, disoriented. He had just walked into the darkness of his dwelling. Tired from a day of hard work. Escorting damned souls to their appropriate places in Hell wasn't easy. Just the pleading alone got to him, never mind the ones who thought they were going to make a break for it. Where did these pitiful souls think they were going anyway? There wasn't any escape. They were in Hell—that was tighter lockdown than Alcatraz times five.

Anyway, he'd been beat.

He'd just gotten home, had poured himself a drink and was heading to sit down and relax, when *bang!* There'd been a blinding flash and a dizzying whirl and now he was . . .

He blinked again, his eyes finally coming into focus, and

he realized he was in a living room. A living room that wasn't his, and he was surrounded by . . . young girls.

He frowned. Was this some trick? Demons did have warped senses of humor.

"Who the hell are you?" he demanded.

His question was answered by more squeals and a hailstorm of flying popcorn and . . . red candies shaped like fish?

"He's real," one of the girls cried.

Well, yeah, he was real.

"It worked," another said. She didn't look as frightened as the other two. In fact, her dark eyes flashed with excitement, and a bemused smile curved her lips, revealing a row of silver braces.

"This isn't good," the third girl said. She was armed with more popcorn, ready to attack if he made any abrupt moves.

"Who are you?" he asked, then winced as more popcorn hit him in the face. Apparently she considered talking as attack worthy as a sudden movement.

"Who are *you*?" It was the one with no fear in her eyes who asked. She actually stepped forward.

He noted, out the corner of his eye, the others had renewed their ammunition. Pretty brave, he had to admit. Or foolhardy.

"I'm Killian O'—"

But Killian didn't get to finish his sentence, or find out what the hell was going on. For the second time that day, a blinding flash blocked out his vision. But this time it was accompanied by a sharp pain to the back of his head. Then everything went black.

Poppy stared down at the crumpled body of the man now unconscious on her mother's Persian carpet. There was another thud, and she realized she'd dropped the silver candlestick holder she'd been gripping. Another heirloom from her parents.

"Are you—" She had to pause, struggling for air. Fear stole her breath. Oh, my God, who was this man and what had he intended to do to the girls? Awful thoughts raced through her head like a vivid horror-movie trailer.

"Are you okay?" she finally managed.

The girls all nodded in unison, their gazes on the prone body in front of them.

Poppy gathered herself further to step around the downed man and usher the girls away from him. She considered taking them to the kitchen, where she could call the police, but then changed her mind. Better to leave the apartment altogether.

"Hurry," she whispered, herding them ahead of her, glancing back at the man to make sure he was still down.

They'd reached the door when the girls seemed to snap out of their daze and start talking all at once.

"We can't just leave him," her sister, Daisy, said.

"He could be dead," Madison said, looking as distressed as Daisy.

"You can't kill a demon, can you?" Emma asked, cocking her head to the side as if considering her question. Then she shot the other two girls a pained look as if she realized she'd just said something stupid.

"Demon?" Poppy asked, shaking her head, positive the girls were in shock after all. "What are you talking about? Demon? He's just a man. A strange man who broke into our apartment. So let's get out of here."

She tugged on the doorknob. The door was locked. She went still. The dead bolt was locked too.

How did the guy get in here? They lived on the fourth floor, and the only other way inside was the fire escape, which was outside her bedroom window. He hadn't come in that way—she would have heard the warped old window scraping open. So how . . . ?

"Did you let him in?" she asked as she turned to face her little sister and her friends.

Daisy made a face not unlike Emma's just moments earlier. "Kinda."

"Kinda," Poppy repeated. "How do you *kinda* let someone into our apartment?"

"Well—" Daisy started slowly.

"I let him in," Madison said quickly.

"What? Why?" Poppy asked, but the girl's answer was interrupted by a groan from behind them.

All heads turned toward the sound.

The man shifted, then fell silent again.

"I've got to call the police," Poppy said. She wanted answers from these girls, but right now that was the best course of action.

"No," Daisy said, then to Poppy's surprise walked back to the man. "You can't do that."

Poppy watched in amazement as Madison joined Daisy. Only Emma lingered with Poppy.

"Okay, explain why a stranger is in my apartment," Poppy said. "Now."

All the girls answered at once.

"He's not a stranger."

"We all let him in."

"Don't call the cops."

"And what if he's really hurt?"

"Demon? I didn't say demon."

Poppy raised a hand, overwhelmed by the rush of remarks. She joined them and they stood in a circle, all staring at him.

"One at a time," she said slowly. "Who is he?"

There was a slight pause, then Daisy said, "He's Madison's cousin."

Madison's head snapped in Daisy's direction and something passed wordlessly between them.

Then Madison looked at Poppy and nodded, her gray-blue eyes wide. "Yeah, he's my cousin."

"Really?" Poppy knew something here didn't add up. But why would they let this guy in otherwise? Daisy and her friends had never been the type of kids to do dangerous or stupid things. Well Madison . . . maybe. But overall, even she was a good, sensible kid.

Poppy glanced at Emma, who stared down at the man like he was in fact a . . . what had she called him? A demon?

"He texted me," Madison said slowly, but then picked up speed as she talked, "to let me know he was here and to get the keys to my place. You know, because Mom's at work."

Madison's mother was divorced and a nurse. Poppy knew she was working night shifts this weekend, part of why Madison was spending the night with them. But it seemed strange Madison's mother hadn't mentioned a family member coming into town.

Poppy glanced from girl to girl. Daisy nodded in agreement with Madison's story. Madison nodded too. And Emma looked from the man to Poppy, then back to the floor. She toed a candy gummy fish with her fluffy, rainbow-colored slipper.

The man groaned again and this time flipped over onto his back. Emma squealed, and all the girls jumped back. Including Poppy.

But after the initial movement, he fell motionless again, his eyes closed, his arms flung back above his head.

Poppy stepped closer, for the first time really seeing the man. He was quite amazingly handsome, even lying unconscious amid popcorn and candy. His hair was shaggy, with a slight unruly curl to the tips. In the lamplight, it shone somewhere between dark blond and chestnut. His lashes were several shades darker against his pronounced cheekbones. And his mouth was perfectly sculpted, with the upper lip bowed slightly and the lower one just a little fuller.

She managed to tear her gaze away from his face to survey the rest of him.

For the police, she told herself. Although why she'd have to identify a man who was out cold on her floor didn't make sense. But that was her excuse, and she was sticking to it.

His tall body was covered in dark clothing. Strange-looking clothes. Almost old fashioned in their cut. Poppy was reminded of movies like *Sense and Sensibility* and *Pride and Prejudice*. And though he wasn't wearing a velvet waistcoat or pleated breeches, she just got the impression of that era. It was a costume of some sort.

Poppy found herself kneeling down to inspect him closer. "Where is he from?"

The girls were silent, and she turned to look up at them. Again Daisy and Madison exchanged looks. Emma continued to poke at the candy with her toe.

"Sweden. He's from Sweden," Emma suddenly said, beaming at her friends. Neither girl smiled back. In fact, Daisy looked confused, and Madison frowned, the gesture laced with something akin to disgust.

Emma's smile faded.

"Yeah," Madison said after a moment. "He's from Sweden."

Nothing in the girls' agreement made Poppy believe any of them. But again, why would they lie?

"Where—where am I?" a husky voice said from beside her.

Poppy started, whipping back from the man, nearly losing her balance in the process. And making eye contact with him didn't help her equilibrium. If she'd been aware of his good looks while he was out cold, she couldn't begin to fathom how handsome he was now that his eyes were open.

Amazing eyes. Heavy lidded. Liquid gold like firelight flickering through a glass of whiskey. Intelligent eyes, despite their languor. Despite the current confusion there.

"You're in my house," she finally managed to tell him.

"Who are you?"

"Poppy Reed. The sister of your cousin's friend."

"My cousin?"

Poppy pointed to Madison. "Your cousin, Madison Cobb."

Madison waved at him, offering an awkward smile.

Awkward, Poppy was sure because of the current situation he was in. Lying on a stranger's floor, wincing at the knot on his head.

As if to validate her thoughts, Madison's cousin gingerly touched a hand to the back of his head. He glanced at his fingers and, thank God, there was no blood.

"What happened?" He moaned slightly as he struggled to sit up.

Poppy looped an arm around his back to help him. He stiffened slightly as if he was surprised she was touching him. She was surprised too—he was still a stranger in her home.

She braced under his weight, and with the help of Daisy on the other side, they got the man on his feet and to the sofa.

"What happened?" he repeated, again touching his head.

"I'm sorry," Poppy said. "I—umm, I hit you on the head."

"With what? A battering ram?"

"No, a candlestick holder. And to be fair, I thought you were an intruder."

He nodded, seeming to ponder that.

"I don't think I'm an intruder," he finally decided. "I was—asked here."

"Yes. By Madison." Again she gestured to the girl.

"My cousin?"

Madison smiled at him, but Poppy noticed the gesture looked wan at best. God, the poor girl was probably terrified that her cousin was badly injured. And he might be. Suddenly, Poppy felt terrible that they'd just left him lying on the floor. Unconscious, no less.

Although she *had* been a little consumed with finding out why he was here in the first place.

"Maybe we should take you to the doctor," Poppy said.

"No!" both Daisy and Madison cried.

Poppy frowned. "Why not? I think it's better to be safe than sorry."

"My mom will look at him. She'll be home soon," Madison said. "And she'll be mad at me, because—because I was supposed to leave a key to our apartment in our mailbox. And I forgot. That's why he texted. You know, then came here."

"And *we* let him in," Emma added.

"I got that," Poppy said, frowning. Why were they all acting so strange?

"So I'll just bring him to my apartment now." Madison stepped forward.

"Maybe he should stay here until your mother's home." Poppy wasn't going to let him leave. Especially with the girls. She still didn't know for sure who he was, and now he was injured. The whole situation was pretty strange. Definitely a first for her.

Madison straightened and looked at Daisy.

"I think we should go see if your mother is home. And get him that key," Daisy said.

"Good idea," Madison instantly agreed. Emma nodded too.

Poppy watched them closely for a moment. Something wasn't right here. Then she noticed the man rubbing his wounded head again. But they were asking to go see Madison's mom. So he must really be their relative.

"Okay," Poppy agreed. "But leave . . ." She realized she didn't even know this man's name. "Just come right back."

She watched the girls go. Normally, she wasn't too nervous about the girls running back and forth between their apartments, even this late at night. But, well, she was shaken tonight.

Once they disappeared, she turned her attention back to her strange houseguest. The cousin.

"Maybe we should put some ice on that bump."

He shook his head. "It's fine. Just sore."

Poppy nodded, clasping her hands in her lap, feeling uncomfortable about what had happened and unsure of what to do now.

"So, Madison didn't tell me your name," she finally said, when it became clear he wasn't going to say anything.

He frowned, as if thinking, then said, "Killian. Killian O'Brien."

"Poppy Reed. But I guess I told you that."

He nodded, then winced.

She sighed, shifting slightly on the other end of the couch. She hoped Ginger Cobb was home. She could look at this guy's head and take care of it. And he'd be out of Poppy's house. She hoped he wouldn't be too irritated at her.

"So Killian O'Brien," she finally said after several awkward moments. "That doesn't sound Swedish."

CHAPTER 2

"Sweden?" Daisy said to Emma as soon as they were in the hallway with the door firmly closed. "Couldn't you have picked someplace like Worcester? Or someplace in Connecticut even? Why Sweden?"

"I'm sorry. I was just looking at all those Swedish fish on the floor, and it popped out."

"It doesn't matter where he's from," Madison said in her usual dry way. "It matters what the heck we're going to do with him."

Madison stopped outside her apartment. It had a cream painted door with ornate molding to make it look like the fancy front entrance of a colonial mansion rather than just a door in a six-story apartment building. She slipped off her key, which she kept on a black cord around her neck. When they stepped inside, the place was dark and silent.

"She's not home yet," Madison said, flipping on a light. They all herded into the little eat-in kitchen and slid onto the café-style stools around a small round table.

Daisy looked at each of her friends, for the first time really letting what had happened sink in.

"We have a freakin' demon in our control," she cried, setting all her giddiness free. She grinned. Craziness.

Madison smiled, but not with the same glee. Madison was

too cool for that kind of emotional abandon. Well, except for when Connor Martin asked her to go to the movies, but he was a senior and by far the best looking guy at Cambridge High. Definitely worth a little giddiness.

Although, personally, Daisy thought this was even more amazing than Connor Martin.

"A demon," Daisy repeated.

"I don't know," Emma said. She winced, worry clouding her bright blue eyes. "Demons are bad, aren't they? How do we know we can really control him?"

"The book says so," Daisy reminded them.

"But the book is fiction," Emma said.

"Obviously not," Madison said. "The spell worked."

Both Daisy and Emma nodded.

"But we still do need to figure out what to do with him," Madison said. "My mom does work a lot, but I can't get away with him staying here."

"No," Daisy agreed.

Madison's mother was often at the hospital, taking extra shifts because she was the sole support of Madison. But the woman was too savvy for them to sneak a rather . . . *noticeable* man into her apartment.

Heck, Madison hadn't even gotten away with the Connor Martin thing. Her mother figured that one out fast and ve-toed the date. Because he *was* a senior and the cutest boy at Cambridge High.

"Well, Poppy won't let him stay with us," Daisy said. "As it is, we're lucky he isn't in a coma or on his way to prison as we speak."

Poppy was a great sister. And she'd been wonderful after the deaths of their parents, taking on the role of both mom and dad, but sometimes Daisy wished she wasn't quite so up-tight. Couldn't she just go with a strange man/demon staying with them? Geesh.

"Well, I would have clocked him too," Madison said confidently.

Daisy seemed to recall that Madison had screamed right along with her and Emma. Sometimes she was all talk—most of the time, actually.

"What about you, Emma?" Madison asked.

Emma was shaking her head before Madison even finished the question, her blond curls bobbing against her cherub cheeks.

"You know my parents. My mother notices when someone nudges one of the knickknacks on the end tables out of place. And remember when she yelled at my brother for putting his boots away in the front closet with the left one on the right side and the right on the left?"

"She'd totally notice him," Daisy agreed. He'd be pretty hard to miss, even if her mother was half-blind. And she wasn't half-blind. If anything, that woman had the second sight.

"Plus your dork brother would so narc," Madison said.

Emma's little brother, Harrison, lived to get Emma in trouble, which wasn't easy, because Emma was darn near perfect. She was actually a lot like her mother—of course, she'd throw a hissy fit if anyone said that. And Daisy would give her the benefit of the doubt—she probably wouldn't rearrange the shoes to be matched by left and right.

Not that shoes were the point, Daisy reminded herself. The point was, Emma's place was totally out.

"Well, we have to figure out something," Daisy said. "Because if all the other stuff in that book is true, he isn't going anywhere until he fulfills the wish."

"You know, if I knew he'd really appear, I would never have gone along with your wish," Madison stated to Daisy. "Not that I don't like your sister or anything. But wishing for him to find your sister a boyfriend. Really? Can't she find one for herself? Totally lame."

"What would you have asked for?" Emma asked.

"To get my mother to let me date Connor Martin," Madison said as if that were perfectly obvious.

Daisy supposed it was. But wasn't she wishing for a boyfriend too? Apparently, it was not such a lame wish when applied to herself.

"I'd have wished to pass French Two," Emma said.

That was obvious too—at least for Emma. But Madison rolled her eyes.

"You think Connor Martin is more important than good grades?"

Now it was Daisy's turn to roll her eyes. Honestly, didn't these two know each other?

"We still need to find a place for him to stay," Daisy said, raising her voice to get them back on track.

The table fell silent.

Then Daisy straightened. "What about Mrs. Maloney's apartment?"

Madison leaned forward, her eyes glittering with excitement. "That's perfect."

The two girls turned to Emma, who didn't appear nearly as thrilled about the idea. She crossed her arms as if she were cold. Her shoulders hunched. "I don't know."

"But it's perfect," Daisy said.

Old Mrs. Maloney went to Tampa, Florida, for six weeks every year, and Emma took care of her fat, cranky, one-eyed cat, ridiculously named Sweetness. Which meant she had a key to Mrs. Maloney's place. And Mrs. Maloney had just left last week. That gave them plenty of time.

"I don't have the key with me right now," Emma said, giving them a "see-that-won't-work" look.

"It's on the key hook right by the front door in your apartment," Daisy said.

Emma's mom was even tidy with keys.

"They're all asleep."

"Exactly," Madison said. "I'll sneak in with you. If someone wakes up, just tell them you came back for . . ."

"Your teddy bear," Daisy said. Emma still slept with a worn bear she'd had since birth.

Emma pulled a face at the mention of it, then reluctantly said, "My mom would never believe that. She knows I never forget Mr. Jellybelly."

"We'll think of something." Madison stood and tugged on the sleeve of Emma's fleece pajama top. Halfheartedly, Emma allowed herself to be pulled to her feet.

"Be quick," Daisy said, once they were in the hall. "You know Poppy's going to be full of questions."

"So have you been living in the U.S. for long?" Poppy asked the man who sat beside her.

"I—I—no." The Swedish stranger shook his head, clearly not sure of his answer.

Poppy glanced at the clock on the fireplace mantel. Twenty minutes. Where were the girls? She'd attempted conversation with the man, but all his answers were vague, and she could see flashes of confusion in his amber eyes.

His muddled answers and looks could be due to the hit to his head, but she liked to think it was because he was Swedish and everything was just new to him here in Boston. That way she didn't feel quite so bad about whacking him so hard.

And to be fair, the girls had been screaming, and Poppy was terrified out of her mind.

"Why were the girls screaming?" she asked suddenly.

"What?" More bewilderment clouded his eyes.

"The girls? They were screaming like crazy. Why would they do that, if they knew you?"

He shook his head, but before he could give Poppy an answer that likely wouldn't make any sense anyway, the apartment door opened.

Poppy rose to greet the girls, anxious to have this all-around unnerving guy out of her house.

But only Daisy walked into the living room.

"Where are the other girls?" Poppy asked.

"Still at Madison's."

Poppy glanced at the man, who, even despite his confusion, managed to lounge on the couch like he owned the place. Then she asked Daisy in a hushed voice, "Is everything okay?"

Daisy nodded. "Madison's mom is just annoyed that she forgot to leave the key for him. And she also got in trouble for texting—"

"Connor Martin," they said in unison.

Poppy nodded. That sounded like Madison. That girl could be so boy crazy. Once upon a time, Poppy had been boy crazy too. Such a waste of thoughts and energy. Now she knew there were more important things in life than romance.

Things like her little sister and keeping her safe and fed and healthy—both physically and emotionally.

"Well, I'm glad you are more grounded than Madison," she told her little sister. "No crazy antics to get the attention of a boy."

Daisy's eyes flicked toward Killian, then back to Poppy. She smiled. "No, no crazy antics for me."

"So is Madison coming to get him?"

"No, I said I'd bring him down."

Poppy frowned. She still didn't like the idea of this guy alone with her little sister. Not that he'd shown any signs of anything—well, anything but confusion.

"Maybe I should walk with you," Poppy said.

Daisy shook her head. "Nah. You know what I would like?"

Poppy tilted her head, still debating going along, but her sister must have taken it as a gesture to continue.

"I know it's late and all, but I'd love some of your famous hot chocolate."

Poppy didn't answer.

"Please. We'll only be ten minutes, and then the girls will all be back. Hot chocolate would be nice."

The warm, milky beverage might be just the thing to calm everyone down after a wild night.

Poppy glanced at Killian, who still sat there, although now his eyes were closed, his head leaning back against the couch's overstuffed cushion.

She was beginning to wonder if this poor guy did need medical attention.

"Okay. But only five minutes. Or else I'm coming to find you with the candlestick holder," she said loud enough for Killian to hear too.

Daisy smiled. "Promise." She turned to the man on the couch, then paused as if considering something. Then she said, almost tentatively, "Um, Kill—ian?"

The man opened his eyes, looking more confused than before, if that were possible.

"I'm going to take you to where you'll be staying."

He frowned, but slowly unfolded himself from the couch. It was like watching a giant stand inside a miniature apartment that was decidedly feminine and delicate.

Poppy thought Daisy looked a little hesitant to leave with him now, and she started to say she would go along after all, but Daisy stopped her. She waved and promised five minutes again.

Poppy watched as tall, broad Killian followed petite, skinny Daisy from the room. A weird feeling tightened her chest, but she didn't think it was dread. Or fear. It was more the sense that something was amiss.

"Five minutes," she murmured to herself as she went into the kitchen to make cocoa.

Killian followed the girl in front of him, trying to make sense of what had been going on. But he couldn't. He wasn't even sure who he was, or how he got here.

Well, he knew his own name. Or at least he thought he did. When the tiny woman with the disheveled hair and baggy sweatshirt and even baggier flannel pants had asked his name, Killian O'Brien had popped into his head.

That could be from anywhere, though.

And he was Swedish? Now that he had no recollection of at all.

"I'm from Sweden?" he asked the girl.

She paused in her determined trek through the hallways of the building.

"Yeah," she said, sounding no surer than he felt.

"So why am I here?"

The girl started to open her mouth to speak, then hushed voices from around the corner drew their attention in that direction.

Two more teens came into view.

"Did you get it?" asked the one he thought he'd heard . . . Poppy call Daisy.

A dark-haired girl dangled something in front of her triumphantly. A key.

"Piece of cake."

All the girls surrounded a door a few feet away.

"This isn't going to work," the curly-headed blonde said.

"It will," the darker one said, her voice filled with exasperation.

"Just open up," Daisy said. "Poppy said she'd come look for us in five, and knowing her, she's actually timing it."

The dark-haired girl unlocked the door and pushed it open. Then they all looked at him expectantly.

He frowned in response.

"This is where you are going to stay," Daisy said, gesturing to the open apartment.

His frown deepened as he stepped closer. The place was dark, except for an old-looking lamp creating a dim pool of light around a hall table. The place smelled. He sniffed again. Like old age. Old books and the menthol of arthritis creams and mustiness and cat.

He looked at the kids.

"I'm staying here?"

They all nodded, wide-eyed.

"You have to," Daisy said.

Killian thought about it, wanting to say "no, I really don't have to." But he found himself nodding and stepping inside the apartment.

"Don't let anyone know you are here," Daisy said once he was inside.

He was supposed to be staying here, but no one could know. That didn't sound right. But again, he found himself nodding.

"We'll check on you tomorrow."

He nodded again.

They nodded back as if they were silently closing some secret pact—and maybe they were. Then the girls left, enclosing him in the dim light of this strange place. He listened to their footfalls hurrying away, back to Poppy's apartment and her famous hot chocolate.

Just leave yourself. Surely this wasn't right.

But his feet remained anchored to the spot.

Eventually, he turned and surveyed the fussy, frilly, floral room.

He was stuck *here*. What in hell was going on?

CHAPTER 3

What the hell?

Killian blinked up at the unfamiliar ceiling—a dingy white ceiling. Not the crisp, new white of his ceiling at home. Nor was he in his own bed. This one was decidedly feminine, covered in a ruffled bedspread plastered with pink and red cabbage roses. Nothing like his black silk sheets.

He glanced to the right to see an antique nightstand. On it, in its full flowered and beaded glory, sat a lamp that looked as if it came from a yard sale circa 1959. An Agatha Christie was opened, facedown on the doily-covered surface. Several medication bottles were lined up beside that.

Great, not only was he in a strange bed, but it appeared to be that of an elderly woman.

He glanced to his left, hoping he'd see something that would make sense to him. He definitely needed an explanation for this predicament—and why he didn't seem to recall how he got here. But instead of some clue, he found someone staring back at him.

It was the ugliest, mangiest cat he'd ever seen. It stared at him with its one good eye. An eerie yellow eye. The other was stuck together into a crusted black line. The cat's long, white fur—or at least he thought it was white—had a matted, gray tinge as if it had rolled in ashes. Damp ashes.

Maybe Killian was still in Hell. But he suspected that even demons would throw this thing back.

Keeping his movements slow and subtle, Killian levered himself up onto his elbows, concerned that even the slightest move would set the beast into attack mode.

The cat hissed, its back arching and its tail, once broken or maybe just as naturally ugly as the rest of it, shot up like a tattered flag at half-mast. It hissed again, louder, its lips curling back to reveal a splintered fang and some serious tartar buildup.

Killian braced himself for what appeared to be an inevitable fur-flying assault, but instead the feline monster darted over the chair and disappeared under the bed, surprisingly fast for such a massive creature.

"Great," he said, peering over the edge. Now he felt like he was stuck in some horror movie where the monster under the bed would lunge out and grab him as soon as he set a foot on the floor.

He fell back against the mattress. The scent of musty pillow, masked only slightly by some kind of stale, powdery perfume, billowed up around him.

Where the hell was he?

He lay there, searching his brain, but nothing came back to him. His last memory was getting off work and going home. But he was clearly no longer in Hell. This place was very definitely the dwelling of a human. Humans had a completely different energy from demons.

Had he gone home with some human woman for a little nocturnal fun? Not his usual behavior, but not unheard of either.

He glanced around the room with its flowered walls and damask curtains. A pink housecoat was draped over a rocking chair in the corner.

He cringed at the sight. Not unless he'd suddenly developed a taste for the geriatric set.

"At least let it have been the hot granddaughter," he said aloud. The monster under the bed hissed in response. Probably not a good sign.

He remained there for a moment longer, then decided he couldn't stay trapped in this sea of frills and flowers indefinitely. He had to figure out where he was—and more important, why.

He sat up, steeling himself for his next move. Then in one swift action, he swung his feet over the edge of the bed and gave himself a hard push against the mattress, vaulting a good three feet across the floor.

The dust ruffle quivered, then a paw with claws unsheathed shot out and smacked around, hoping to connect and maim. Finding nothing, it snapped back under the bed's depths. The bed skirt fluttered, then fell still.

"Ha," he called out to the animal, feeling smug. Then he just felt silly. He was a demon who'd managed to outsmart a cat. Yeah, that was something to get cocky over. Especially since he was a demon who had somehow managed to forget where the hell he was.

He stepped out of the bedroom into a small hallway. Directly in front of him was a bathroom that revealed more flowers on the shower curtain and on the matching towels hanging on a brass rack. Even the toilet seat cover had a big rose on it.

To his right was another bedroom. A dresser, a nightstand and a brass bed—and, of course, more flowers.

He frowned. Would he really hook up with a human who was this obsessed with floral prints—very *bold* floral prints? He didn't think so, but anything seemed possible at this point.

He wandered to a living room with swag draperies and ancient-looking velvet furniture. BenGay, hand lotion, Aleve, a crystal bowl filled with mints and a box of tissues were arranged on another doily-covered table beside a tatty-looking recliner. A crocheted afghan was draped over the back.

"Let there be a granddaughter . . . let there be a grand-daughter," he muttered, even though he'd seen not a single sign of youth so far.

He crossed the room to a fireplace, looking at the framed photos crowded along the mantel. Only one woman kept reappearing in the pictures and she didn't look to be a day younger than eighty. But he didn't recognize her. In fact, none of the people in the pictures jogged his memory.

"Maybe I don't want to remember," he said, grimacing down at a picture of a group of elderly women on what appeared to be adult-sized tricycles beside some beach.

Then his own shirtsleeve caught his attention—or more accurately his cuff link, deep red garnets set in a charm of a ferry boat: the symbol of his position and job in Hell.

He set down the picture and inspected himself. He was still dressed in his standard work uniform, a white shirt with a tab collar, a black vest and black trousers. He'd taken off his greatcoat sometime during the evening, but he was relieved to see that the rest of his clothing was intact.

A good sign nothing untoward had happened, but it still didn't give him any hint as to where he was or how he got here.

"Just get out of here," he told himself. He could just as easily contemplate this bizarre situation in the luxury of his own place.

He closed his eyes, picturing his ultramodern dwelling with its clean lines and stark colors. Not a single flower to be found anywhere. He visualized the living room with its black leather furniture. The bedroom with its king-size bed and dark red walls. He especially visualized his black granite bar and the bottle of Glenfiddich sitting on it.

A nice glass or two of fifty-year-old scotch and a little Xbox 360 on his big-screen television seemed exactly like what he needed after all this strangeness. There was nothing like expensive liquor and Modern Warfare 2 to get him calmed down. Then maybe he'd recall his lost evening.

Let there be a hot granddaughter, he added again.

Then with his creature comforts affixed in his mind, he willed himself away from this odd apartment and back to his own world. . . .

Except nothing happened.

No whirring sound, no sense of whisking through space and time. No—nothing.

He opened his eyes to find himself still surrounded by flowers and the scent of old age.

Pulling in a deep breath, he closed his eyes again and really focused. But this time he noticed something he hadn't the first time. It was a sort of weighted feeling as if leg irons were around his ankles, keeping him in this dimension.

He released the breath he didn't even realize he was holding pent up in his lungs. What was going on? Why shouldn't he be able to dematerialize out of the human realm?

But then he realized *shouldn't* wasn't the right word. He felt like he *couldn't*. No, that wasn't exactly the right word either.

For the first time since he woke up in this place, a sensation akin to panic constricted his chest. He forced himself to ignore the feeling, chanting over and over in his head that there was a reasonable explanation for all of this.

"Just go to a bar here," he muttered to himself. "Have a stiff drink—and relax."

Things were bound to make sense if he just calmed down. How could he expect to think clearly surrounded by floral chaos?

Just then the cat from the bedroom leapt up onto the recliner, the springs creaking under its massive bulk. It peered at him from its one good eye, then hissed.

"Yeah. I'm outta here."

He left the living room, striding toward a door at the end of another small hallway. It had to be the exit. But when he reached the door, he stopped. Everything within him told him to just grab the doorknob, turn it and leave, but again something stopped him. Told him he had to stay right here.

"Just go," he growled.

But he couldn't bring himself to move. That was, until he heard the rattle of the doorknob, jiggling as if someone was inserting a key from the other side.

Killian glanced around, trying to decide what to do. He noticed the kitchen to his right and sidestepped into the narrow little room, leaning against an avocado-colored refrigerator as he listened. He heard the whoosh and creak of the door opening.

"Where is he?" a female voice said. A young female voice. The granddaughter?

"He's got to still be here," another female voice said.

Hmm, he hadn't considered there might have been more than one granddaughter. That certainly made things more interesting—and worth remembering.

Killian decided there was no point in hiding. After all, they were expecting him to be here. At least, he thought they were talking about him, and they were the ones who could likely offer him the information he wanted.

He stepped out of the kitchen to see three young girls. And *girls* was definitely the operative word.

Dear Lucifer, was there *any* middle ground here?

As soon as they saw him, in almost comical unison, the girls screamed. And with the familiarity of that piercing sound, all his lost memories rushed back. The screaming girls, the flying snack foods, the thwack to the head.

Killian raised a hand, frowning down at his, for all practical purposes, abductors. Surprisingly, his gesture silenced them.

"Why did you bring me here?"

If his memories of the night before were any indication, he needed to get an answer as quickly as possible, before another candlestick-wielding woman appeared.

He shot a quick look over his shoulder, just for good measure.

The girl with a smattering of freckles across her nose and the dark brown eyes moved out of the doorway, waving to the other two to join her. The other dark-haired girl joined her inside the apartment. Only the cherubic blonde hesitated behind them. But finally, and clearly against her better judgment, she followed, although Killian noticed she didn't release the doorknob.

Ready for a speedy escape. Smart girl. He was not in a good mood. And he was a demon. Never a great combination.

"Who are you? And why did you bring me here?" he demanded.

The girls all shifted, nervous.

Then to his surprise, the freckle-faced one straightened to her full height—maybe a whopping 5'2"—and met his gaze directly.

"I'm Daisy."

Killian tried not to make a face. Of course, *more* flowers.

"This is Madison," Daisy said, gesturing to first one girl, then the other. "And Emma."

Madison surprised him by meeting his eyes too. She sported that ennui that all kids seemed to master as soon as their age hit double digits. Killian was tempted to point out to her she hadn't looked quite so bored just moments earlier when she was squealing, but he remained silent. Emma still clutched the doorknob, managing none of her friend's cool boredom. Quite the opposite. As soon as his gaze moved to her, she tensed as if she was ready to dart—or pass out. Her blue eyes widened and seemed to eat up half her face.

A twinge of sympathy pulled at him. He ignored it.

"I was the one who conjured you," Daisy said, her expression neither blasé nor frightened. This girl was simply direct and calm.

A girl with a mission.

"We all conjured you," Madison corrected her, giving Daisy a pointed look.

"Yes." Daisy acknowledged her friend, but remained undaunted. "We all did. But we conjured you to fulfill my wish."

"Which we should have negotiated," Madison muttered, collapsing against the wall in a perfected slouch of disgust.

Daisy didn't even glance at her friend this time. She stayed focused on him. "We called you to—"

"Do something impossible," Madison interjected.

This time Daisy did shoot a censorious look at her friend. Then she said, "No. It might be a little tricky but not impossible."

Madison rolled her eyes. Emma swayed. Apparently passing out was still an option for the silent friend.

"What is this tricky—possibly impossible task?" Killian asked, growing tired of the teenage bickering.

This wasn't his usual thing. Hell, he'd never been conjured before, and he had very little experience with teenagers. But even with his admittedly limited experience, he wasn't prepared for what the earnest girl in front of him said next.

"I want you to find my sister a boyfriend."

CHAPTER 4

Killian blinked. Then he blinked again.

It was pretty rare for a demon to be speechless. Hell, he considered himself a rather talented talker—part of his job requirements—but . . .

"Boyfriend? For your sister?"

Yeah, that was eloquent, all right.

"Yes," Daisy said, frowning at him as if she'd decided maybe she'd made a mistake conjuring him, after all.

Which she had.

"See," Madison said. "Lame idea."

Daisy frowned at her friend, then looked back at Killian, some of her doubt replaced by something akin to hope.

"Totally lame idea," Killian stated, his tone not all that different from Madison's. "I'm a demon, not a matchmaker."

"But the book said that you have to grant us our wish," Daisy said.

"What book?" he asked.

"*Jenny Bell, Demon-Hunter*," Daisy said.

"Which is fiction," Madison said.

Daisy threw her friend another look, this one fully exasperated; then she gestured to Killian. "Obviously not all fiction. Hello. He's here, isn't he?"

That was true. But Killian was more concerned with how the hell he was going to get out of here.

"So what exactly does this book say?"

Daisy turned back to him again. "It says that once the demon is conjured, he cannot leave until the wish is fulfilled."

Killian shook his head. "Oh, no. No."

There were so many reasons this was not good.

He stepped toward the door, and the one called . . . Emma squeaked and stumbled backwards away from him and to huddle in the corner.

He started to reach for the knob, but again got that feeling. That strange, strangling sensation that he couldn't go.

Shit. This girl was telling the truth. He couldn't leave. That's why he hadn't been able to simply materialize away. Hell, it seemed that he couldn't even leave the apartment on his own two feet.

This had to be fixed and quick. The big boss man, and yes, he was referring to Satan, wasn't going to be pleased when Killian didn't show for work. Satan definitely didn't adhere to the "happy employees make a more productive workplace" philosophy of management.

He twisted back to the girls. They all watched him as if they were uncertain of what he was going to do.

He wasn't even sure himself. All he knew was he was pissed. This was unbelievable.

"I'm not some kind of goddamned genie," he finally said, deciding not to reveal the fact that he was trapped here, by their mandate. Best not to let the teenyboppers know just how much control they had.

"Okay," Daisy said, smiling slightly as if she was already aware of the power she had. "But you still have to grant this wish."

"I don't have to do anything," he said, taking a step toward her—fully intent on intimidation. "I'm a demon. That makes me the one in control here."

He saw a flash of uncertainty in the girl's eyes. Then, to his surprise and dismay, she actually smiled. Her lips quivered slightly, as if the gesture was strained—but it was a smile nonetheless.

"You won't hurt us. In fact, you can't hurt us."

He stopped stalking forward. Damn it, this book revealed far too much. They already knew they could control him, even if her quivering smile revealed that she wasn't sure she should trust that fact. And she shouldn't. She didn't realize what his special demon power was—a very handy one to have at this moment. Killian focused on Daisy, holding her gaze. "Really? Can you be sure?"

He answered for her in his mind—that she wasn't in control and he could go without fulfilling the wish. Words she'd say back to him as if they were her own idea. Just like Obi-Wan when he manipulated the guards in *Star Wars*. She'd be surprised later, after he was gone, that she'd decided to let him go. But that wouldn't occur to her until after he was far, far away, and she'd never realize he was the one who'd made her do it.

His power was as practical as it was cool. Very handy when one of the damned panicked, refusing to join him on his trek into the depths of Hell.

Oh, Mr. Jones, there's no need to be so upset. Hell isn't nearly as bad as all the literature makes it sound. Really.

He'd gotten many a sinner to his or her proper destination with his little mind tricks. And he'd get himself out of here the same way.

But instead of the confused look he expected, Daisy just shook her head.

"Yes. You can't hurt us. Because I've just told you that you can't. Just like you can't leave until you find my sister a boyfriend. That's what the spell says. That you have to do whatever we say. Then you can leave."

Killian stared at her, unable to believe he hadn't been able to control her thoughts. She didn't even seem to notice that he was trying to influence her.

"Damn it," he muttered, frustrated, running a hand through his hair. Was he really powerless here? He'd used his powers on humans in their realm before. What was different this time?

"You might as well just go with it," Daisy said, her tone irritatingly reasonable.

Killian dropped his hand, glaring at his pint-sized puppet master. "Is that so?"

She shrugged. "The quicker you do what we ask, the sooner you can leave."

He gritted his teeth. Did a mere teen have to be so equable? And right?

Anger rose in his chest, and he considered advancing on her, intimidating her, but again he couldn't do it. Not only because she'd told him he wasn't allowed, but because bullying young girls went beyond even his dubious moral code.

"Fine," he said, ignoring the fact that his tone sounded almost as petulant as any teenager's. "What's your plan?"

"First, you have to befriend my sister," Daisy answered without hesitation.

She'd given this matchmaking idea a whole lot of thought. She'd been awake most of last night, trying to figure out the best way to pull off this crazy scheme. Poppy wasn't exactly open to strangers. Not that she wasn't friendly. Her older sister was very friendly—and once upon a time, she'd been very outgoing too. Until their parents' deaths, when she'd gotten full guardianship of Daisy.

In the past four years, Daisy had watched her sister put all her own interests on the back burner and focus everything on Daisy. She'd lost more than just their parents in the car crash that took their lives. Poppy seemed to have let go of all her hopes and dreams too.

Daisy might be a self-absorbed fifteen-year-old at times, but she knew what her sister had given up to see that she felt safe and loved.

Now, Daisy wanted the same for her sister. And well, who didn't want a boyfriend? Duh.

"Okay," the demon said, giving her a doubtful look. "How do you propose we do that? In the shortest time possible."

She'd thought about this too. "Since you're supposed to be here from out of town—"

"Sweden, to be exact," Madison interjected in her usual wry way.

"I said I'm sorry about that," Emma mumbled. "And we fixed it by telling Poppy he's been in Connecticut."

"*Since* you're from out of town," Daisy repeated, "then you are going to ask her to show you around."

The demon frowned. "This doesn't sound quick to me. I am busy, you know." Then he muttered something about Satan, and he was clearly pretty agitated.

Daisy hadn't considered that. But she supposed being evil did take up quite a bit of time. And she was counting on this guy . . . this thing? Whatever, she was counting on *him* to find her sister Mr. Right?

"Maybe this was a bad idea," she said to her friends.

"No—duh," Madison said in her usual helpful way.

"It isn't one of our best," Emma agreed.

"Well, since we are finally in agreement on something," the demon said, "why don't we call this whole matchmaking scheme off and let me get back to my world?"

Daisy reached behind her and pulled the book that had started everything out of her back pocket. She flipped the dog-eared pages right to the exact spell she wanted. She scanned the spell that she knew nearly by heart. Shaking her head, she offered him a pained look over the top of the open book.

"It says this spell is binding until the request is fulfilled. Nonrefundable, nontransferable."

She jumped as the demon snaked out a hand with blinding speed and plucked the book from her grasp.

"Hey!" she said, but watched as he read the passages she'd just perused, then snapped the book closed and scanned the cover.

He made an irritated noise low in his throat as he read the author's name aloud, "Ellina Kostova. I should have guessed."

"Do you know her?" Emma asked, excitement raising her voice an octave, a fan-girl moment clearly overshadowing her fear. That was until the demon glared at her. Then she shrank back to her place in the corner.

"I know of her," he said. Obviously, he *wasn't* a fan. He looked at the book again, then held it back out to Daisy.

"So what was the exact wish?" he asked.

"Well, I asked that you find my sister her true love. Someone who will stand by her, make her laugh, inspire her, understand her, and . . ." Daisy hated that she could feel herself blushing. "And you know, make her toes curl."

The demon frowned. "Make her toes curl?"

Daisy shrugged, feeling more heat creep into her cheeks. "You know . . . make her feel all giddy and excited and . . ."

"Get her off," Madison said.

The demon shot the girl a surprisingly parental frown. "Are you old enough to say things like that?"

Madison rolled her eyes.

The demon ignored the look and turned back to Daisy.

"And why would I be able to find this person for her? In fact, what do I know about all those things? Except the last one," he said quickly, holding up a hand to stop Madison, who'd started to speak. "I know how to handle the last one."

Madison looked doubtful.

Daisy only half-registered the exchange, considering why she did think this guy—this demon—could find such a person. Surely the spell had brought forth this particular demon for a reason. It wasn't like they'd had their pick of demonic entities. He was just the one who came. He had to be the right one.

"Do you have any special powers?"

He didn't answer right away, and Daisy got the feeling he didn't want to share that information.

"Tell me if you have any special powers," she said, putting as much authority in her tone as she could.

He gritted his teeth, but then said, "I have the ability to control thoughts and feelings."

"Whoa." Madison actually looking impressed for the first time since entering the apartment. "See, we totally could have gotten him to convince my mom to let me and Connor date."

This time it was Daisy's turn to roll her eyes. "Next time."

"Next time?" The demon shook his head. "There isn't going to be a next time."

Daisy didn't argue, since she wasn't even sure he could pull off the current wish.

"So that's it," she said instead. "You need to find my sister her true love. Then you are free to go."

He sighed and that muscle in his jaw ticced, but he nodded.

"Fine," he muttered. "Let's get started."

CHAPTER 5

Poppy had just flipped the last pancake when she heard the door to the apartment open.

"Daisy? Girls?" she called. "You're just in time."

She turned from the stove to see Daisy and her friends filing into the kitchen. But it was the tall figure trailing behind them that caught her attention.

The man from last night. She stared, taking in his sleep-mussed hair and the hint of five o'clock shadow shading his cut jawline.

"Madison brought her cousin," Daisy said, even though her explanation was totally unnecessary. The man seemed to eat up all the space in the relatively large kitchen, even before he was fully inside it.

"You know my mom," Madison said. "Nothing but some breakfast bars and skim milk. I hope it's okay?"

Poppy started at Madison's question and realized she was still staring at the man. *Manners, Poppy*. Especially after last night.

"Of course," she said, nodding—perhaps a little too vigorously. Which she could only hope was distracting him from the blush burning her cheeks. She was blushing, of course, about the events of the last night. Certainly not because she'd been gaping at him like a mesmerized schoolgirl.

She gestured to the table, an old country kitchen piece that had been her mother's. Then she busied herself with gathering plates and silverware.

Last night, over hot chocolate, she'd talked to the girls about this man. They hadn't provided much more information than they had while he was prone on the floor. He was Madison's cousin. From Sweden. But he'd lived in the States for several years. Apparently in Connecticut. And he was here for work—although she didn't know what that work was.

The girls had been all fidgety and restless, which she'd chalked up to the crazy events of the evening and copious amounts of soda and candy.

She placed the platter of pancakes in the center of the table, looking at the girls now. They sat around the table, watching the man who remained in the kitchen doorway. And they didn't look any more relaxed. In fact, they all stared at him like he was a creature from an entirely different world.

She glanced at the object of their attention and supposed she understood their reactions. He was unusually attractive, like he'd tumbled out of an ad for Calvin Klein or some other world where men were tall and muscular with brooding, pouty good looks.

She glanced away from him, busying herself with getting juice glasses down from the cupboard, knocking two of them over as she set them on the table. She didn't look back at the man—Killian—because well, she was just trying to get the food on the table before everything got cold.

She could definitely see how daunting Killian could be for these young girls. But nothing so earthshaking for a grounded, grown woman such as herself.

She rummaged around the fridge, searching the shelves for the maple syrup.

"Can I help you with anything?"

Poppy started, banging her head on the handle of the freezer as she snapped upright.

"Ouch."

Hand pressed to the back of her head, she turned to find Killian directly in front of her.

He didn't smile or offer sympathy, he just regarded her with those sleepy golden eyes. In fact, Poppy got the distinct feeling he didn't care about her bumped head. Then again, she *had* hit him last night. Maybe he figured this was a bit of poetic justice.

Then he held out a hand. "I'll take that for you."

She looked down, realizing the syrup dangled in her loose grip.

"Um, thanks," she said, her eyes returning to his. Those almost hypnotic golden eyes.

He accepted the bottle, without a smile. His gaze held hers for a moment longer, then something strange and unreadable flashed there. Something she couldn't quite understand, though she had the impression he wasn't pleased.

He strode away, placing the syrup on the table and taking a seat with the girls. Poppy blinked, gathering herself. His odd gaze had left her feeling a little confused, a little unsure of what had just passed between them.

Did he dislike her? She got the feeling he did, and who could blame him after last night?

She joined the others, taking a seat beside Daisy.

"How are you feeling, Killian?" she asked, realizing she probably should have asked that as soon as she saw him. Maybe that was what that look was about

"I've been better," he said, his tone dry.

Oh, no. Had she really injured him?

"Did Ginger think you should see a doctor?"

"Who?" He frowned, then glanced at Daisy.

"My mom," Madison answered, and smiled at Poppy.

"He's always calls her Gin—Ginny. It's a childhood nickname."

Poppy nodded, her attention still on Killian. "So what did she say?"

Again, Killian looked at Daisy, just a quick glance, then he met Poppy's eyes. "I will be fine."

That wasn't exactly the definitive answer she'd been looking for, but she nodded. She lifted the platter of pancakes and offered them to him.

"You should serve yourself first. It's the least I can do."

"Yes, the very least."

Poppy blinked, surprised at the animosity in his voice. "I'm truly sorry I hit you, but I would hope you can understand that I was a woman alone with three teenage girls. And you were a stranger who, as far as I knew, wasn't welcome."

Killian speared several of the buttermilk pancakes and slid them onto his plate, all the while meeting her gaze, his expression none too friendly or understanding.

Poppy did feel bad, but she also thought her reaction was justified, given the information she'd had at the time.

"It's really my fault," Daisy said, her gaze moving back and forth between the two of them, landing on Poppy. "I should have woken you up to tell you he was coming."

"That would have kind of ruined your big plan, now wouldn't it?" Killian muttered, slathering butter on his pancakes as if he had a grudge against them as well.

"What plan?" Poppy was confused. "What was your plan?"

Madison suddenly started coughing, reaching for her glass of juice and knocking it over in her fit. The orange liquid splashed everywhere, but most spattered all over Poppy.

Poppy jumped up, and then the table was abuzz with activity. Madison reached to right her glass. Daisy hurried to get a towel. Emma moved the platter out of the wet mess.

"I'm sorry," Madison said.

"Don't worry," Poppy assured her, tugging at her T-shirt, which clung, cold and sticky, to her skin. "Accidents happen." She couldn't stop herself from giving Killian a pointed look.

He was the only one at the table who remained where he sat. He took a bite of his pancake, watching them as if nothing had happened.

"Go change," Daisy urged, mopping the juice with a dish towel. "We'll clean this up."

Poppy nodded, hearing her sister even over the whir of irritation in her head as she watched Killian continuing to chew away, oblivious to the rest of them. He acted as if they were nothing more than the hired help.

She was beginning to feel pretty glad she'd clocked Killian O'Brien. In fact, she kind of felt like doing it again now. She should have known a man that good looking would be a real jerk.

"I'll be right back." She tugged at her shirt again, shooting the perfectly blasé Killian a look, which also went unnoticed. She left the room for a dry shirt and a moment to calm her growing temper.

"What are you doing?" Daisy asked as soon as her sister was out of earshot.

Killian finished chewing his pancake, poured some juice, took a sip, then gave the girl his best innocent look.

"I'm eating breakfast."

Daisy braced both hands on her hips. "You're supposed to be making friends with her, not arguing with her."

Killian sighed, affecting his best bored look. "I tried. It's not going to work."

"You didn't try at all," Madison said.

"I did," he said, giving a significant look at the bottle of syrup. "I helped."

Daisy rolled her eyes, then continued. "There's no point in being difficult. You're stuck here until the wish is fulfilled. So rather than being a jerk, why don't you just get to work?"

Killian stared at the girl. Her tone, her speech pattern, sounded remarkably like her older sister, although he wondered how, after such a short time in Poppy's presence, he could recognize that. He narrowed his eyes, but then returned his attention to his pancakes.

As much as he hated to admit it, the girl was right. He was stuck here, and making Poppy hate him was really defeating his own purpose. But he was having a hard time not showing his aggravation. He did not want to be here. And he hated being controlled by young girls.

And to make matters worse, he'd discovered another very irritating fact. He couldn't control Poppy's thoughts or emotions either. He'd attempted to do so when he'd offered to help her while she was at the fridge. But nothing had happened. She was as unaffected as the girls.

"We need a more detailed plan," Daisy decided, tossing the orange-juice-soaked towel into the sink. "You need to hang out with her. Just the two of you."

"Are—are you really going to trust a demon alone with your sister?" Emma asked. She glanced nervously at Killian.

"He can't hurt her," Daisy said. "He has to do whatever we want."

Killian gritted his teeth. Did they have to keep repeating that?

Smug smiles curved both Daisy and Madison's lips. Damn, this was the most frustrating situation he'd ever been in. Killian couldn't think of anything more humiliating than being controlled by teenage girls. This was hell—much worse than the Hell he knew.

"I still don't think we should trust a demon," Emma said.

"Demon?" Poppy came back into the kitchen in a new

T-shirt, this one sporting the Superheroes, in their full retro glory. She also had changed into a pair of jeans that showed off the subtle curve of her hips and slight build.

Killian frowned, wondering why the innocuous change of clothes would suddenly draw his attention to her figure. Especially when he had much bigger concerns to take up his thoughts.

"What is this about demons again?" she asked.

"Oh—um," Daisy looked around at the other girls, "we were just talking about . . ."

"His career," Madison said. "Killian is a paranormal investigator."

Killian fought the urge to roll his eyes. Paranormal what? Really?

"Really?" Poppy said, her tone intrigued, despite her obvious dislike of him. She turned to him. "Wow, you don't meet one of those every day."

No, you didn't. And she hadn't now either. But he simply nodded, not sure what exactly to say about this newest lie. Couldn't these kids come up with something even remotely normal?

"He's actually here to do research," Madison said.

Okay, he could probably work with that.

"He has his own paranormal show," Madison added with one of her smirky little smiles.

Okay, now they were just getting silly again.

"Your own show? Like one of those ghost-hunter type programs?" Poppy asked.

"Umm, yeah, sort of like that," Killian said, not sure what exactly she was referring to.

"He's quite a celebrity in Sweden," Madison said, clearly enjoying this storytelling a bit too much.

"Madison's actually getting a little carried away," Daisy said, obviously agreeing with him. She shot her friend a warning look, then turned to Killian. "Weren't you saying that you are just here to get ideas for a show?"

"Um, yeah. Just ideas." Killian forced a smile. If they were expecting his help, then they were going to have to let him make up the fake life for himself. A paranormal investigator/pseudo-celebrity from Sweden? Teenage girls had strange ideas of cool.

"That's pretty impressive," Poppy said, although he couldn't tell if she was impressed or not. He supposed it didn't matter as long as she was actually buying this load of nonsense.

"In fact," Daisy said, "he was hoping to have a look around Boston today. You could do that, right, Poppy?"

Poppy shot her sister an irritated glance, then gave Killian a feigned look of regret. "Oh, I don't know. I have some work to do today."

"It's Sunday," Daisy said. "Surely even you can take a Sunday off."

Poppy shifted, her discomfort with this idea clear on her face, but reluctantly nodded. "I guess I can join you."

"Great," Daisy said. "He wants to walk the Freedom Trail. There's plenty of ghostly stuff there. Plus, I'm sure he'd like to just see the city."

Killian nodded. What he'd really like to see was his own place, but to do that, he was going to have to find this waif-like woman in her superhero T-shirt true love. Which was going to apparently involve ghost tours too. Joy.

"Okay, well let me just run to my office and check my e-mail and grab a sweater. Then I will be ready to go." Poppy hurried out of the kitchen as if she'd rather just go hide and avoid their plan altogether.

He didn't blame her. How was he supposed to pull off this cockamamie scheme anyway? What did he know about matchmaking? Or true love, for that matter? He'd never experienced such a phenomenon. In fact, he didn't actually think such a thing existed. In his world, people were usually coming to him because they'd been involved in acts and deeds that had not a single thing to do with love.

"Okay, so here's what you need to do," Daisy said in a hushed voice, shooting a furtive glance toward the kitchen door. "First of all, be nice. I mean you're pretty hot"—Killian raised an eyebrow at that—"but you need to work on your personality."

He frowned at that. Work on his personality? Whatever.

"Poppy's not the type to warm up to someone quickly," Daisy told him. "So you're going have to work it."

"You need new clothes too," Madison added with a disdainful grimace at his uniform.

Killian looked down at himself. "What? This is classic. Dashing."

"It's gay."

"I kind of like it," Emma surprised him by saying, even though she immediately avoided his gaze, toying with her syrup-drenched pancake.

"Well, you like those Johnny Depp types," Madison said in a way that made it clear she did not.

"He is a paranormal investigator," Daisy said. "I think he can pull the look off. It makes him interesting."

"Because the life you've invented for me isn't interesting enough," Killian said wryly. "I think maybe I need to invent my own background from now on."

Madison smiled, smug as usual. Emma bit her lip, sheepish as usual. And Daisy nodded.

"Fine. But remember your task. And try to be someone my sister would like. Well, not like like, but, you know, hang out with."

"I get it," he said, finding it rather terrifying that Daisy was the only one who seemed at all sensible.

"And no telling her that you are a demon," she added. "That won't make her like you at all."

"I hadn't planned on it." Actually he had thought of it earlier, but that definitely wouldn't get him home any sooner to his comfy bed, Xbox and expensive scotch.

"Okay," Poppy said, walking into the kitchen in a black cardigan that looked like it had been around since the sixties. "Are we ready to go sightseeing?"

All three girls stood then.

"Oh, we aren't going. We have to help Emma's mother," Daisy said.

Poppy frowned. "What?"

"We're helping Mrs. Wills—" Daisy looked at Emma.

"Clean," Emma said automatically. "We're—helping with the annual spring cleaning."

"So you two have fun," Daisy said, waving as she hooked the other two girls' arms and dragged them from the kitchen. The apartment door slammed shut before Poppy even managed to snap her gaping mouth closed.

Slowly Poppy turned to look at Killian.

He smiled, perhaps his first real smile of the past two days. "I guess it's just the two of us."

CHAPTER 6

Just the two of us.

Poppy was still trying to figure out how she'd ended up alone with this man, even as they stepped off the T and headed toward their first stop on the historic Freedom Trail.

If Killian's silence on the subway trip was any indication, she suspected he didn't quite understand how he'd gotten here either. But the truth was she had knocked him unconscious with a family heirloom, he wasn't from the area, and she had agreed, even if misled to do so, to show him around. And while she still thought he was a jerk, she was polite enough to make an effort to show him a few of the sights.

"I'm taking you to Boston Commons," she told him as she led him down the sidewalk toward the park. "It's the oldest public park in the U.S.—and supposedly hosts a number of ghosts."

Killian nodded, looking around him, and she couldn't decide what his opinion of the city was thus far.

They walked silently for several moments; then she decided it was going to be a very long day if they were both mute the whole time.

"How long have you been into the paranormal?"

Killian looked as if he was startled to discover her still in

step beside him. Probably he was. He seemed like a pretty
self-absorbed kind of guy.

Be nice, she told herself.

"Oh—" He seemed to consider the question for a second,
then shrugged. "My whole life, really."

"Really? Was your family into paranormal research too?"

He nodded. "Yeah. Really into it."

"Was that—strange?"

Again he was silent for a moment, then another shrug.
"Not really. It's all I've known."

"Yeah," Poppy said. She kind of felt like the past four
years were all she'd known too. Sometimes it was hard to remember a time before her parents were gone.

As if he was somehow aware of what was on her mind,
Killian asked, "So your sister lives with you?"

"Yes."

They walked through the park entrance before Killian
spoke again. "Why does she live with you?"

The question caught her off guard. Most people she dealt
with either knew or assumed the reason. Or they didn't ask
at all. It actually felt really strange to say the words aloud
to an utter stranger. To share the most pivotal event of her
life.

"My parents died four years ago, and I've been raising
Daisy ever since."

Killian didn't offer the condolences she expected. Instead
he said, "That must be hard. To go from sister to mother."

She glanced at him. He offered her a slight smile, and suddenly she felt something in her chest relax. Like a screw that
had been drilled in too tight had been loosened, just a little.

She pulled in a breath, considering his response and her reaction. Most people said they were sorry. That they were sad-
dened by her and Daisy's loss. But people rarely said the
words about how difficult it had been to not only lose her
parents but to have to become a parent—all at the same time.

"It has been hard," she said. "But Daisy is a great kid. So we've managed."

Killian walked beside her, looking at the ground rather than at the beautiful sun-dappled scenery. Poppy found herself wondering what he was thinking. Why should she care, really? She'd just met him, and she didn't even think she liked him that much.

"I imagine it's doubly hard to handle things alone."

She glanced at him again. She tried to hear pity in his voice. She'd gotten pity before, and that was just as hard to deal with as hollow sympathy. Sometimes she just wanted someone to say they understood.

"Sometimes," she admitted, but then decided she didn't want to discuss her life with this man, a man she barely knew. They strolled along the park pathway past a sprawling flower bed overflowing with red tulips fringed in an orangey-yellow.

"Aren't they beautiful?" she said. "Like a sea of fire."

He didn't answer for a second as he followed her gaze to the flowers.

"They are considerably less dramatic than a sea of fire."

"Okay," Poppy said, not expecting that response. "I guess that's true."

"Oh, it's definitely true."

Poppy laughed, not sure what to make of this conversation and his adamancy. "I suppose, but they are still beautiful. In their own nonfiery way."

He nodded, and she wasn't sure if he really agreed or not. He was sort of a funny guy—funny in an odd way. But he was a paranormal investigator—that probably did make him look at the world in a different way.

"You must really resent it?"

She glanced over at him, not following. "Resent what? Your dashing my sea-of-fire analogy?"

"No." He cast her a look like she was just silly. "You must resent having to take care of your sister."

Almost instantly the screw in her chest that had released, even just a bit, twisted violently back into place. Tighter than before.

"No," she managed to say, even though she couldn't pull in a full breath. And without speaking another word or looking in his direction, she veered off the pathway onto the grass. Walking with no direction. Just needing to be away from this man and his awful words.

Killian watched Poppy stride away, realizing a fact about himself. The girls might have had a point. Maybe he was going to have work on the personality thing. He was considerably less charming without the ability to manipulate thoughts. Kind of a deflating realization.

But he'd thought getting Poppy to admit she was lonely and wanted someone to help with the burden of essentially being a single parent was a good way to segue into convincing her to date. Apparently not. In fact, he'd pretty much ruined the tiny bit of camaraderie they'd managed to build.

Ramp up the charm, buddy. Otherwise, he wasn't going to be able to befriend her, much less play matchmaker.

He started after her, doubling his steps to a jog until he was beside her. He touched her arm to stop her, to get her to look at him.

She did, and when her gaze met his, he could see the pain in her dark eyes, pain so clear and strong he could feel it radiate through him as if it were his own.

He dropped his hand away from her as if breaking physical contact would also break the emotional connection. It didn't.

"I'm sorry," he said automatically, stunned by how much her hurt expression affected him.

Her gaze roamed his face as if she was trying to decide whether she should believe him; then she just nodded. She pulled in a deep breath and pointed past him.

"There's the Central Burying Grounds. It's supposed to be haunted. I know some of the stories. Maybe they would be good for your television show."

Right. Right. The fake career. The fake TV show. And now it was time to create a fake friendship with this woman.

He smiled, pouring every bit of sheepish charm he could muster into that one curve of his lips. "That sounds like just the type of thing I was hoping to find."

He gestured for her to lead the way. She regarded him again for a moment, then walked past him toward a fenced-in plot of land, scattered with old tombstones, crooked from years of the earth freezing and thawing under them.

Poppy pushed open a wrought-iron gate, and a loud creak moaned through the air. But the sound seemed more out of place than eerie. With the bright spring sunshine warming their faces and new grass almost blindingly green around the weathered gravestones, it was hard to see the place as anything other than peaceful.

As if reading Killian's mind, Poppy said, "Maybe we should have waited to explore this place in the evening or on a rainy day. I'm afraid the stories will sound sort of lame on such a sunny day."

"That's okay. Tell me."

"Well, there are several tales surrounding this place. This cemetery is where the most unfortunate citizens of Boston were buried. The poverty-stricken who died from awful diseases and from wretched conditions—"

As Poppy spoke, weaving the spine-chilling tale of tormented humans who became tortured apparitions forced to walk the earth, tied forever to this one place, Killian lost track of the story. Instead, he found himself lost in watching her face. The widening of her deep brown eyes as she told him of something frightening. The drawing together of her finely arched brows as she talked of something sad. The little wrinkle of her small, pert nose as she mentioned something unsavory.

He nodded at the appropriate times, pretending the story held him captivated, but it was really her small elfin face that held his attention.

Despite his earlier assessment, Poppy was really quite cute. More than cute. Lovely, really. He'd have no problem finding a man who would be interested in her. Maybe if she put her hair up—and wore prettier clothes. He bet she'd look really nice in a dress. And heels.

"It's said that on moonlit nights the little girl appears. The girl . . . without a face. Killian?"

He blinked. "Yeah?"

"What do you think? Do you think you could make that work?"

He frowned. What work? The dress and heels? To get a man? Did she somehow know what he was thinking?

He shook his head slightly, not sure what the right answer was.

She laughed then, clearly enjoying his confusion. "Were you even listening to the story?"

"Oh. Yes. Yes, the story." He nodded his head. "I can definitely make it work. Totally."

She smiled, eyeing him as if she still knew he hadn't heard a word, but she didn't question him any further. Instead she began to wander around the tombstones, just meandering and looking at the inscriptions, or at least the ones that were still legible.

Killian followed. Both were silent. The city bustled around them. Cars' engines, honking horns, the sound of a busy metropolis—all seemed incongruous with their surroundings.

"Do you mainly focus on ghost stories?" she asked, her gaze on a headstone in front of her.

"Um, I do a lot with demons, actually. Damned souls. The different circles of Hell, that sort of thing."

"Interesting." She wandered to another stone. "How does someone become so interested in Hell?"

He shrugged, then moved to stand beside her. "Again, kind of a family pastime."

She glanced at him. "You really must have an unusual family."

He chuckled at that. "Definitely."

When he looked at her, he noticed she was not staring at the grave marker in front of them. Instead, her gaze was locked on him—his mouth, to be exact.

His smile faded as he wondered what she was thinking. Then she seemed to realize what she was doing, and she looked away, moving closer to inspect the stone.

He continued to watch her, but neither spoke as they looked at several more graves.

Finally, she directed her gaze to him again, but almost unwillingly. Pink colored her cheeks, but he wasn't sure if that was from the sun and spring air or from embarrassment.

"I'm actually getting a little hungry," she said, nothing in her voice revealing her true feelings.

"I can always eat," he said, which was true. He had a ridiculous appetite—most demons did. Gluttony was a favorite sin. Right after lust.

She pointed toward where they entered the park. "We can go to Faneuil Hall, that's another place along the Freedom Trail, and they have a lot of places to eat."

He held out a hand. "Lead the way, tour guide."

She didn't smile, and a pang of disappointment actually vibrated through his chest. She turned and began walking through the graveyard. He followed, and he didn't hasten his steps to catch up with her.

Lust. Definitely his first favorite sin.

Which, he assured himself, was the only reason he was lingering back, his gaze locked on the cute little curve of her rear end.

CHAPTER 7

"Do you like it?" Poppy watched with a slight grin as Killian dug into a huge cinnamon bun coated in extra frosting.

He took a bite, then closed his eyes, his handsome face the picture of unadulterated ecstasy. He moaned low in his throat, and Poppy tried to ignore the fact that his reaction caused little flips in her belly.

So he was quite amazingly beautiful. Good for him. He wouldn't be her type, even if she was looking for someone.

Even if she could get him, a part of her added, although she'd ignored that point until she noticed a tall blonde in designer jeans, a cute trendy top and killer high-heel boots staring at Killian as she passed, stalking him like a hungry, lithe cat. She even slowed her pace, clearly hoping he'd spot her. That was more his type.

But Killian was too wrapped up in his love affair with his dessert. Poppy picked at the remains of her falafel pita pocket, irritated she suddenly felt as awkward as the nerdy kid at the big school dance. Invisible to all the beautiful people.

"This is amazing," he said, regarding the dessert with an almost reverent expression.

Again Poppy's stomach fluttered. Could she even imagine him looking at her like that?

Good golly, she was comparing herself to a cinnamon bun. She glanced over to see the gorgeous blonde had taken a seat at a table just a few feet away from them, angled in just such a way that Killian couldn't miss her once he looked up.

Poppy made a face at herself, even as she ran a hand through her hair, annoyed that she felt self-conscious again. If she couldn't compete with a cinnamon roll, she sure as heck couldn't compete with a stunning Amazon blonde.

Not that she wanted to compete, of course. Just random thoughts, she assured herself. But before she even realized what she planned to say, the words were out of her mouth.

"Do you have a girlfriend?"

He didn't speak, his mouth full of pastry, nor did he look surprised by her sudden question, but he did shake his head.

Something that felt an awful lot like relief washed through her, but it didn't last, as her mind moved right to another thought: Maybe he didn't have a girlfriend, but rather a wife, although he didn't wear a ring.

Not that she'd been looking.

"No, no one," he said once he'd finished eating.

The strange relieved feeling returned. She ignored it.

"Not the type to settle down, huh?"

He immediately shook his head, which didn't surprise her. She suspected an amazingly good-looking man like him wouldn't want to limit his choices too soon.

A feeling an awful lot like disgust, which she embraced, helped push away that other, more disturbing relieved feeling.

"Actually I do want to settle down," he added. "You know, soon. Really soon."

Poppy blinked. Huh?

"But you don't have a girlfriend? Don't you kind of need one of those to settle down? Especially soon?"

"Yes, I do. That's one of the things I hope to do here, actually."

Again she couldn't hide her baffled look. "You plan to settle down? Here?"

"Umm, yeah."

Damn. He'd really just said all that? Settle down. Here. Soon. All of that couldn't be further from the truth.

Damn.

No, he told himself, this was a good plan. He'd convince her to go out and do the singles thing with him. Because he wanted to find a . . .

"Yeah, I'm looking for a wife."

Poppy stared at him like he'd lost his mind. He kind of wondered if he had too. But he was willing to go with any plan that might get her a true love and him back to Hell. Even pretending he wanted to get married.

"I've wanted to get married for a while now," he said with a nod of his head, trying to sound prosaic about it. "It's always been a dream of mine."

Did he really just say that?

"Really?" Clearly Poppy didn't believe it either.

But he mustered his most sincere look—*this would all be so much easier if I could just control her thoughts*—and he forced a smile, the gesture tinged with melancholy. He hoped.

"It's been something I've wanted since childhood. That special someone to share my life with, to raise a family with, to have as a best friend and lover. Forever."

He fought the urge to wince. Had he poured it on too thick? From the dazed look on Poppy's pixie face, he had. Oh well, it was out there. He was going to have to run with it.

"So what do you think? Do you think you could help me?"

She gaped at him as if he'd asked her if she'd be willing to give him a kidney. He tried not to be offended by her aghast expression. Did she really find his request so impossible a task? He was a good-looking guy, and he'd never had problems getting human women before. Her incredulity bothered him, more than he would have liked.

"I don't think you need *my* help," she finally said.

"Why not?"

"Look over there." She jerked her head slightly to the left. He did, only to discover a blond woman seated a row away, watching him. She smiled as soon as he met her eyes. A wide, inviting smile. A smile that all but asked him to come join her.

He forced a polite smile back, then returned his gaze to Poppy.

"I don't want her. I don't like blondes," he said, saying the first thing that came into his mind.

Poppy gave him another look of disbelief. "Well, I'm sure any number of brunettes or redheads would fall over themselves for your attention." She stood then. "I really should get home. I do have some work I need to get done."

She started walking away before he could even get to his feet. He gave a longing look at his half-eaten cinnamon bun, but left it behind.

As he passed the blonde, she smiled at him again; this time her look was filled with sympathy. She'd obviously seen Poppy's abrupt departure.

"Problems?"

He nodded automatically. So many problems.

"Well, call me if you need a sympathetic ear." The blonde had a business card out and pressed in his hand with the speed of a Vegas magician.

The woman's forwardness oddly disgusted him. Why, he wasn't sure, but he didn't bother to respond; instead he hurried his steps to catch up with Poppy, confused by her reaction and by his own.

*   *   *

The subway ride back to Poppy's apartment building was as silent as their first trip. Killian attempted conversation a couple of times, but Poppy was lost in her own thoughts and unwilling to do much more than give him a one-word response. Eventually he just gave up, getting lost in his own thoughts.

He still wasn't quite sure what had triggered this coolness in Poppy. They'd actually had a nice lunch, but once again, he'd said something that ended up pushing her away.

As before, he wasn't sure exactly what he'd said that had been so offensive. Relating to people was hard work.

"I hope you found some places to research today," she said as the old elevator shimmied and shook, taking them up to her floor.

"I did." He struggled to find something to say that would possibly smooth things over between them. But nothing came to mind. Damn, he wanted his powers back.

She nodded as if she didn't know what else to say either. The metal doors shuddered open and she stepped out.

"Have a good afternoon," she said with an aloof nod, and before he could think of what else to say, the elevator doors closed again, leaving him staring at his own bleary reflection in the scratched metal.

He remained that way until the elevator jerked to a stop again and the doors parted. Automatically, he stepped out, then stood there, trying to decide what to do next.

Was this even the right floor for the awful apartment he was staying in? He couldn't remember. He looked left, then right, and was trying to decide what to do when he heard voices coming towards him.

Seconds later, three familiar faces appeared.

"What are you doing back?" Daisy asked, surprise and then dismay flashing in dark eyes so very much like her older sister's. He'd seen both these emotions from Poppy too.

"Were you mean?" Daisy asked.

"No," he said, not quite keeping the defensiveness out of his tone. Apparently, he had been, although he didn't know how. "Your sister just wanted to come home to work."

Daisy gave him an unconvinced look. "If she had been having fun, she wouldn't have been thinking of work."

Killian supposed he couldn't argue with that.

"She's not that easy to befriend," he admitted.

"I told you that."

"Yes, you did," he said. "So what's the next move in this master plan of yours?"

Daisy looked at her friends. Madison shrugged with her usual boredom. Emma looked pained—a common look for her too.

"What did you say to her right before she decided she wanted to come home?" Madison asked, revealing that her lack of interest was feigned.

"I told her I was hoping to settle down."

All three girls looked at him as if he was mad.

"And I asked her if she'd help me meet women," he added by way of clarification.

"You do remember that you're supposed to be finding *my sister* true love? Not yourself," Daisy said.

"Yes," he said. "I'm well aware of that. I told her that so she'd go with me to meet people. I mean how else am I going to find this man for her?"

"It's not a bad plan, really," Emma said, then glanced at her friends to see if they'd reprimand her for agreeing with him.

"It's not a bad idea," Daisy said. "But what ticked her off?"

Killian relayed the story of their lunch and how well things were going until the moment when Poppy pointed out the blonde, who'd been watching them.

"And I simply said I didn't want that woman, because she was blond."

All three girls stared at him, speechless for several seconds.

Only Emma showed any emotion as she touched her fingers to her hair, clearly feeling a little self-conscious about her own blond curls.

"Wow," Madison finally said, shaking her head.

Killian frowned, still not sure why his comment was so awful.

"That is pretty bad," Daisy agreed.

He shook his head, waiting for them to explain.

"You kind of sound like a jerk," Madison said.

"And super shallow," Daisy added.

"That's rude," Emma said, her voice barely above a whisper, still watching him with large, wary eyes.

"Why?" he asked.

They gaped at him like he was an utter moron. He was starting to think maybe he was.

"Because now Poppy thinks you would not date a whole group of women solely based on their hair color. That doesn't make you very likeable," Daisy said.

"Why would she care? She's not blond." He still couldn't see why it should matter to her.

"Like Daisy said, shallow, dude," Madison said.

Killian considered that. He supposed it did make him seem a little shallow. Poppy definitely didn't seem like the type of woman to respect someone who was so superficial. Not that he needed her respect. That didn't matter. At all. The only reason her reaction was bothering him was because he needed her to like him enough to hang out with him.

That was the sole reason he was concerned with her irritation.

"Okay, so how do I fix it?" he asked.

"You don't," Daisy said, moving to punch the down button for the elevator. "You go back to Mrs. Maloney's apartment and let us fix this."

The elevator opened and the girls piled in, while Killian

just stood there, wondering yet again how he'd ended up in this ridiculous situation.

"Wait," he called just as the doors started to slide shut, "where is Mrs. Maloney's apartment?"

Daisy's answer was nothing more than muffled noise.

He looked around him again, pretty much back to the same predicament he'd been in before the girls appeared. He surveyed his surroundings again, hoping to recall something familiar.

Nothing.

Sighing, he plunked down into one of the worn, waiting-room-style chairs in the hallway across from the elevator.

"Great."

CHAPTER 8

"Why would the spell conjure this dude?" Madison said. "He's pretty much a tool."

Daisy shrugged. She was beginning to wonder that herself.

"He doesn't know anything about true love," Emma said, shaking her head.

No, he didn't. That much Daisy was very certain about.

"Well, he is a demon," Madison said. "It's not like anyone would expect a demon to know a lot about love."

Daisy had to agree with that too. And they were going to be stuck with this guy until he found a boyfriend for Poppy. At this rate, they'd have him here forever. This was not good. After all, Mrs. Maloney was going to be back in a few weeks.

"We have to figure out a way to make him more appealing to Poppy."

"If he'd keep his mouth shut, that would probably help a lot," Madison said.

Again, Daisy couldn't argue.

"He's so good looking," Emma said, her voice wistful. "You'd just think he'd be more charming."

All three girls nodded at that one.

The elevator doors opened, and they stepped out, staying in the little lobby area. Madison collapsed into one of the peach upholstered chairs. Emma leaned against the wall and Daisy paced.

"We need to come up with a story so that his stupid comment suddenly makes sense," Daisy said, thinking aloud. "A reason blondes would have a bad association for him."

"A bad experience with bleach?" Madison suggested.

"Highlights gone wrong," Daisy said with a giggle.

"What if a blonde broke his heart?" Emma said. "And left him afraid to love again?"

Madison snickered, but Daisy stopped pacing.

"That's a great idea, Emma," Daisy said, her mind already inventing a story. A heartbreaking story.

"He needs to be wounded just like a hero in a romance novel. Poppy will go for that."

"Hey."

Poppy looked up from her computer to see Daisy in the doorway of her small home office.

"Hey," Poppy said, welcoming the distraction. She'd been trying to finish up the last couple chapters of a legal textbook she'd been hired to copyedit. But her mind wasn't on the work, which was dry at best. Today it was downright painful.

Two more heads poked into her office; Poppy should have known Daisy wouldn't be alone. Her little sister was rarely without her friends.

"Hi, girls."

"I didn't expect you home this early," Daisy said, coming into the room and flopping down on the brass daybed.

Emma joined her, although she perched on the edge of the cushion, looking oddly nervous. She fidgeted, twirling one of her blond curls around her finger. Madison remained leaning on the doorframe, but even in her slouched position Poppy got the impression she was uncomfortable.

Daisy, however, lounged among the gingham pillows, picking at the chipped nail polish on her index finger with no worries on her face.

Poppy usually didn't mind Daisy's entourage, but this afternoon, she was a little frazzled. Time spent in the company of someone like Killian O'Brien was nerve-wracking on many levels.

"So why are you back so early?" Daisy asked again.

Poppy glanced at Madison. She could hardly answer Daisy's question honestly with the man's cousin—second cousin? whatever—with his family member here.

She looked back at Daisy. "Well, I did have some work I had to get done."

"You are a workaholic," Daisy said, not for the first time.

Poppy knew she could be, although the past half hour hadn't been an example of that.

"Killian's a workaholic too," Madison said, coming into the room. She nudged Emma with her hip, sitting on the daybed. All three girls lined up, looking at her almost expectantly.

"Is he?" Poppy asked, even though she didn't really want to talk about the most stunningly beautiful and frankly most tactless man she'd ever met.

Madison sighed. "Well, he wasn't always that way. He used to be quite a carefree, fun-loving kind of guy. Or at least that's what my mom told me."

Poppy shifted in her desk chair, not sure she wanted to hear anything more about Killian.

But she still found herself saying, "Really?"

Madison sighed again, this time the sound a little sad. "Yes. My mother said that was before he lost the love of his life."

Poppy shifted again, her attention focused on Madison. Waiting for the girl to continue.

"The love of his life?" Daisy asked, looking from Madison to Poppy, then back to Madison.

Madison nodded, her expression somber. "Yes. It was his high school sweetheart in Sweden. Agnetha Fältskog."

Agnetha Fältskog. Why did that name sound familiar?

"They were together for nearly eight years and were going to marry. And then the worst thing happened." Madison paused, shaking her head, clearly reflecting on the story her mother had told her.

Poppy hitched forward in her seat, wanting to ask, what? What happened? But she kept silent.

"Agnetha left him. At the altar."

Daisy gasped.

"That's awful," Emma said, her voice filled with sorrow.

Madison nodded. "Yes. She left him for the minister. They announced their love for each other while in the church."

Poppy gaped at the girls. That was beyond awful.

"That must have really affected how he deals with women in general," Daisy said.

"Definitely," Madison said.

"What did she look like?" Daisy asked, which Poppy thought an odd question, but she still found herself on the edge of her seat, wanting to know too. Despite herself.

"She was a tall blonde. Of course, I mean she was Swedish."

Well, that explained his comment about blondes today. Disliking all blondes still seemed like an extreme reaction, but then wasn't she still a little gun-shy of musicians?

"She also starred with him on his Swedish television show. And he ended up leaving that too, because it was too difficult to see her every day."

He'd lost his love and his career. Some of Poppy's displeasure with Killian faded. He'd probably just reacted today when he saw that woman. How would she react if she saw someone who looked like Adam? Probably not well, honestly.

Maybe they weren't so different. She understood both those losses—all too well.

"Well, we're off to work on our science project," Daisy said, jumping up from the daybed. She gestured for the other two girls, who appeared a little surprised by her sudden announcement.

"Oh, right," Emma said, standing too.

Madison joined them.

"Are you nearly done with that?" Poppy had forgotten about her sister's big biology project, which wasn't like her.

"Yeah, just writing up our data and practicing our presentation."

Daisy was a good student and a great kid, and Poppy rarely had to get after her to do her schoolwork. Still, she liked to know what was going on.

"Great. Where are you working on it?" Poppy asked her sister.

"Madison's. I'll be home for dinner."

Poppy knew she should have simply nodded, but her own curiosity got the better of her.

"Is Killian there?"

Daisy paused. "Umm, no. He went out again."

"Oh, okay." Poppy fiddled with a pen on her desk, trying to look not particularly interested and fighting the urge to ask more.

"See you later," Daisy said with a little smile; then she and the girls dashed out of the room. And Poppy heard giggles as they exited the apartment.

"I don't think we have to worry now about your sister befriending old demon boy," Madison said once they got in the elevator.

"She totally bought that story," Daisy agreed.

Madison's eyebrows shot up, then she grinned. "She did more than buy the story."

Daisy frowned, not following.

"She's totally got a little thing for him," Madison said, widening her eyes with disbelief.

"No, she doesn't," Daisy said, immediately shaking her head.

"She does."

Daisy looked to Emma. "Do you think so?"

Emma shrugged. "I don't know. But I kinda suck at the whole 'boy' thing."

Daisy shook her head again. "I really don't think so."

"It doesn't matter. He may be hot, but he's definitely not the true-love type."

The elevator jerked to a stop and the doors slid open, but before Daisy exited, she added, "Well, and Poppy would never be dumb enough to fall for a guy like that."

She turned to step out and nearly ran into one of the objects of their conversation.

Killian raised an eyebrow as he looked down at her. "Poppy wouldn't be dumb enough to fall for who?"

Chapter 9

Killian knew who they were talking about. But if he was expecting Daisy to hem and haw and fumble to find a suitably tactful answer, he should have known better.

"You," she said.

"Why would she be dumb to fall for me?" He hated to admit it, but he was a little offended.

"Well, first of all, you're a demon," Daisy said.

Okay, there was that.

"She doesn't know that," he said, most of his defensiveness disguised by the fact he was busy stopping the elevator door from automatically sliding shut.

"Still, you aren't her type," Daisy said.

Just leave it alone. He didn't care if he was her type, he didn't *want* to be her type. But his ego wouldn't let him remain quiet.

"I'm everyone's type," he stated.

"And that's exactly why you would never be her type." Then Daisy frowned and peered past him into the hallway. "Why are you still here?"

Did his ego need more bashing?

"I—" Embarrassment joined the displeasure in the pit of his stomach. He didn't like it. Not one bit. "I didn't remember which apartment I was supposed to stay in."

The girls exchanged glances, their shared expression one of unimpressed tolerance. Then Daisy stepped back, waving for him to enter the enclosed space.

"You are staying on the sixth floor," Madison said slowly, as if she was speaking to a simpleton, as she pressed the button labeled with a print-smudged number six.

In truth, he was feeling a bit like a simpleton. It wasn't like him to forget—well, anything. Of course, that hadn't been true here. Nothing he knew about himself seemed to apply here.

Without any further conversation, the girls stepped out onto the sixth floor and led him to the door of his flowery abode. Emma moved forward—not without giving Killian a wary glance—to unlock the door.

"You should give the key to Killian," Daisy said, and the other girl's face immediately collapsed into a worried frown.

"I don't know . . ." Emma glanced at him again, and clutched the small, silver key tighter in her fist.

"He's got to be able to come and go without us around. And you don't want to leave the apartment unlocked, do you?" Daisy said.

"What if Sweetness accidentally got out? Or someone stole something while Killian was away? Isn't it better that he lock the place when he's coming and going?" Daisy said.

Emma shot another glance back at Killian, twisting her lips as she considered Daisy's words.

"Come on, Em, we're already trusting a demon to stay here," Madison said, her tone much more impatient than Daisy's. "What difference does it make if he has a key?"

Killian supposed the girl had a point, but again he could have done without it sounding like another slight.

Finally, Emma nodded and held out the key to him.

Killian didn't really want the key, but he took it. Then he followed the girls inside the apartment, his nose immediately assaulted by the stale scent of old perfume, liniment and cat.

He grimaced as they walked into the living room with its fusty furniture and decorations. "Isn't there somewhere else I could stay?"

"No," Madison said, her nose wrinkling too. She didn't care for this place any more than he did.

"I can't stay here indefinitely." He raised his hands, gesturing around him. Surely he could sway them. If he did have to stay in Boston, there had to be nicer accommodations. Hell, he could pay for a five-star hotel himself. He shot a look at the plastic-covered sofa. It would be money well spent.

"No, you can't stay here indefinitely," Daisy agreed. "Only until you fulfill the wish. So I guess you'd better figure out how to do that."

With that, the girls trooped down the hall, leaving him in flower and doily hell. Just then the cat appeared, somehow managing to spring its amazing girth up onto the back of the chair. It hissed and swiped at him, missing.

Killian jumped back just as it lashed out again.

"I guess I'd be pretty pissy too, if this was my permanent residence."

"Oh, I'm pissy. But not for the reasons you think."

Killian stared at the cat, then blinked. He knew that voice. "Vepar?"

The cat cocked its head. "Yes, in the fur."

Poppy stared at the page of dry, technical writing, red pencil in hand. But she didn't mark any changes, nor did she really even see what she was reading.

Finally she dropped the pencil in defeat, watching it roll across the desk. Her work was pretty tedious on the best of days, but today, it wasn't holding her attention for even a paragraph.

She glanced at the clock on her computer monitor. Four-thirty. Rather early to start dinner, but puttering around in the kitchen was bound to be more distracting than the edits of *Milton's Business Law, Eleventh Edition.*

She pushed away from her desk, an antique piece made from mahogany, with carvings of swirls and ivy along the bottom and down the legs. It had been her father's, and she loved it. Even though she never really enjoyed her work, she did like sitting in the very place where her father had done his research, or corrected papers, or written his essays on great pieces of art and their artists.

Usually that gave her a sense of peace, but not today.

She wandered through the living room to the kitchen. The whole apartment was filled with things from her parents' house. Pictures, dishes, pieces of furniture, even her mother's pots and pans.

Poppy went to the cupboard where she stored those very items and pulled out the stockpot that her mother had used for her specialties like fish chowder and chili and her amazing lentil soup.

Lentil soup. That's what she'd make tonight, since she was starting dinner early enough. She began gathering the ingredients she needed, placing them on the soapstone countertop. Twice, she went to the pantry, only to stand staring at the stocked shelves, trying to remember what she'd been about to get.

It wasn't like her to be so preoccupied. Over the last four years, she'd trained herself to be task oriented, organized, to live on a set schedule. She'd had to have routines to create a stable, healthy environment for Daisy.

But since the girls had told her about Killian's disastrous love affair, her mind seemed to be skittering all over the place. To her own lost love. To losing hopes and letting go of dreams. She rarely allowed herself to consider what might have been. There was no point. But Killian's story had triggered those thoughts.

Yet, as much as she thought about her own past, she spent even more time thinking about Killian. Had his losses changed him? Made him the kind of callous guy he seemed to be now?

No, callous wasn't the right word. He was more tactless than outright unfeeling. Did that sort of thoughtlessness stem from hurt? She didn't have an answer, but that didn't keep her from mulling the idea over and over.

He could be quite nice, which made her think that maybe his moments of insensitivity weren't the real him.

And much to her dismay, all of her musings seemed always to return to one place. How good looking he was. His tall muscular build. His broad shoulders. His amazing golden eyes. His disheveled hair. His mouth, how it looked when he smiled, when he'd been eating that cinnamon roll.

She moaned in frustration as, yet again, his lips appeared in her mind, but this time, to her utter consternation she found herself imagining how those lips would feel against hers. Smooth and strong, moving over her.

She jumped as a clattering sound of something, many things, falling on the floor rained down behind her. She turned from the pantry and her heated imaginings to see lentils scattered all over the vinyl checkerboard floor.

"Satan is not pleased."

Killian stepped farther into the room, skirting the cat, which was still perched on the back of the reclining chair, but this time not because he was afraid the animal would attack. But because it was talking. With his coworker's voice.

"Vepar?"

The cat actually rolled its one yellow eye. "I thought we'd already established that."

"What . . . what are you doing here?"

"What are *you* doing here?" Vepar countered, the movement of the cat's lips somehow looking remarkably like the expression of the demon himself. Although, in his normal form, he was tall, lanky and had two eyes. But he did have bad teeth—so maybe that was it.

"It's a long story," Killian said.

The cat/Vepar lay down, arranging himself in a sphinxlike position. "Well, I'm here via a cat. I think I have time to hear it."

Killian nodded, then much to his humiliation shared the story of how he'd been conjured by a group of teenage girls and was stuck here until he could find Poppy a boyfriend.

Vepar sighed, which sounded remarkably like a purr. Although Killian didn't think in this case it was a sound of pleasure.

"So get this female mortal a boyfriend ASAP. And get your ass back to Hell. You've got damned souls backing up, and frankly I'm sick of picking up your slack. You know how Satan gets when his business isn't running smoothly."

Yes, Killian did. And there was a reason Satan was known as, well . . . Satan.

"I'll have this finished right away," he assured the possessed cat. Even though he wasn't sure how exactly he would accomplish it.

"Darn it," Poppy grumbled, realizing that in her preoccupied state she must have set the bag of legumes too close to the counter's edge.

Proof that she did not need to be letting her thoughts go in such ridiculous and inappropriate directions as the attractiveness of one Killian O'Brien.

She'd just reached for the broom when a knock on the apartment door stopped her. Picking her way through the mess, she went to answer it.

"You forgot it again, huh?" she said as she opened the door, expecting to see Daisy. Her sister was terrible about remembering her key.

But instead of Daisy, she was greeted by a tall, muscular

male. The object of her recent fantasy. And, she added, a wee bit irrationally, the cause of the current mess in her kitchen.

"I must have," Killian said with a slight smile, "because I don't seem to recall what you're talking about."

"Oh, I'm sorry. I just assumed you were Daisy."

He nodded and neither spoke. Then he seemed to realize he should probably say something just at the same time she did too.

"I was—"

"Did you—"

They both snapped their mouths shut. After a moment, they both laughed.

Poppy couldn't help noticing how deep and musical his laughter was. As attractive as the rest of him.

"I'm sorry," he finally said, "I just couldn't hang out in that apartment anymore. So I thought I'd come see what you're doing."

"Ah," she said. "The girls getting to you with their practicing?"

She suspected there was more giggling than practicing. Three teenage girls—there had to be lots and lots of giggling. And boy talk. And fashion talk. And hair talk.

Yeah—totally no man's land.

Killian frowned, confusion flashing in his golden eyes. Then he said, "Practicing. Yes."

She smiled at his muddled expression. "I know it's hard to tell, but they are getting some work done, aren't they?"

His brows drew closer together, but he nodded. "Yes. Some."

"Good." She stepped back. "Come on in. I can't say there's anything terribly exciting happening here, but if you are looking for some quiet, I can offer that."

"Thanks." He stepped into the room, his body not touching hers as he passed, but she swore she could feel heat radiating over her. Her body tingled as if her skin was finally feeling warmth again after being cold far too long.

Taking a deep breath and willing her silly body and mind to behave, she gestured toward the kitchen. "I was just making some dinner."

As he strolled into the room, she recalled the lentils scattered all over the floor like some makeshift booby trap à la *Home Alone*.

"Oh! Be careful—" she called, but it was too late. Before she could get out the rest of her sentence, Killian had not only walked into the legumes but also slipped, sliding on them like they were marbles rolling under his feet.

With a loud thump and a grunt, he landed on his rear end.

"Oh!" Poppy cried and hurried as quickly as the slippery mess allowed to his side.

"Are you okay?" She kneeled beside him.

He didn't respond for a moment, then to her surprise, he chuckled. "I seem to spend a lot of time on the floor in this place."

"I'm sorry," she said. "I was just getting ready to clean this up when you knocked."

"Sure," he said with another amused smile.

She braced a hand under his arm to help him up, but as soon as her finger connected with the warm, hard muscles under the cotton of his shirt, her body reacted, and she forgot what she was trying to do. All she could focus on were her nerve endings, each one sizzling to life as if every cell in her body suddenly became aware of him and only him.

Killian tensed too as if he felt that same strange sensation snapping between them.

She lifted her head, realizing just how close his face was to hers. The lips from her fantasy were just inches from hers. Instantly, she jerked her hand away from him, her sudden action causing her to lose her footing and slip too. She joined him in the scattering of legumes with an "oof."

But unlike him, she didn't stay down. Hopping right up, she tried to hide her awkwardness.

"I'd better sweep this up," she said, rushing toward the broom, slipping once, but catching herself before she fell again.

Killian watched Poppy busy herself with sweeping as he rose to his feet, bemused by her reaction. But more than that, he was mystified by his own reaction.

He'd had a totally visceral response to the woman's touch. An innocuous touch at that. Just her fingers curled around his arm. Something he'd have found impersonal from most others, but from Poppy it had been completely—sensual.

Hadn't his plan been to come down and charm her into trusting him? He was on a deadline here. But he certainly hadn't planned on being oddly charmed by her in return.

"Can I help?" he finally managed to ask, actually dazed by her touch.

"No," she answered, her tone and her movements both brusque. Was she shaken too? Then she glanced at him again, offering him a small, tight smile. "Just have a seat before you hit the floor again."

He smiled back, telling himself he wasn't noticing how cute she was in her agitation. Obediently, he took a place at the kitchen table, watching her work. She bent over to sweep the lentils into a plastic dustpan. Killian's gaze lingered on the way her jeans tightened to cup her butt. A perfect little butt.

"Is Ginger at work?"

He blinked, not immediately following her question. When his eyes lifted, he found her looking over her shoulder at him. He wasn't sure if she realized where his attention had been focused or not. Her expression revealed nothing.

"Umm . . . Ginger?" he asked. Shit, who was Ginger again?

"Oh, right, I forgot you call her Ginny."

Ginny? Ginny? That's right, his supposed cousin.

"Yes, she's at work." She could be, right?

"Well," she said with a sigh as she dumped the legumes into a silver trash can. "I guess I have to find something else for dinner."

She opened a cupboard, peering at shelves of canned and dried goods for several seconds.

"Do you like tacos?" she asked.

"Sure," he said. "Does that mean I'm invited to dinner?"

"Of course," she said, "unless Ginger— Ginny's going to be home and she's planned dinner for you."

"No," he said. There was no chance of that. "No plans here."

She smiled, this time the gesture more natural, less strained. And even more attractive.

"So," he asked before he thought better of it, "have you forgiven my bad behavior at lunch?"

CHAPTER 10

Poppy wasn't surprised by the directness of Killian's question. She'd known him less than twenty-four hours, but she already recognized that was just part of his personality. She was, however, a little startled by the almost flirty quality in his voice.

Finally, gathering her wits, she nodded. "Sure."

Now that she better understood his reaction to the blonde in the food court, she felt her reaction was over the top. Besides, what difference did it make to her if this guy had turned out to be genuinely shallow?

"I was in a mood, I guess," she said.

Somehow taking the blame seemed like the easiest way to apologize without saying too much.

He studied her for a moment, those amazing eyes of his roaming over her as if he was trying to read her mind. Then he simply nodded, although his gaze didn't leave her.

She suppressed the shudder, the overwhelming sensation that zinged through her body as if electrical pulses coursed through her. Breaking their stare, she looked back to the cupboard, not wanting those feelings. After all, what could she possibly do with them?

"So, tacos?" she asked.

"If you let me help."

She hesitated without looking at him. Working closely beside him—bad idea. But they'd formed a truce.

"Sure."

She pulled down a yellow box containing the taco shells and spices. Then she went to the fridge and got out ground turkey as well as tomatoes and lettuce.

Killian started to rise from the table, but she stopped him. Space was key if she was going to keep her silly hormones in check.

"Stay put. You are going to be the chopper."

She set the ground meat on the counter, then brought the veggies to him. He frowned, regarding the common produce with an almost wary expression. She smiled slightly, but she didn't say anything as she left to grab a wooden cutting board and a knife. She placed them in front of him, waiting to see what he would do.

Almost hesitantly he reached for the lettuce. Peeling back the plastic, he just stared at it.

"Cut it in half, and then just slice it fine."

He nodded, still regarding the vegetable like it was an alien life-form that might attack at any minute.

"Better get it before it gets you," she said with a laugh, then headed back to the stove to prepare the meat. She could have showed him what to do, but she didn't trust her body being that close to him.

After a minute, the knife began clacking against the cutting board, and she hoped it wasn't the lettuce that won.

"Killian O'Brien," she said, not looking at him as she spoke. "That doesn't sound particularly Swedish."

The cutting paused for just a second, then continued.

"No, it's not. It's Irish, actually."

"So your father is Irish?"

Again the chopping paused.

"Yes. My father. He's from, um, Dublin."

Poppy reached under the counter for a frying pan, keeping

herself busy as she talked. The tactic seemed to be working. Her wayward body was under control. Well, mostly.

"Where in Sweden did you grow up?" she asked.

The knife was silent again.

"Um, Stockholm."

Poppy got the impression there was almost a question mark at the end of his response. But she figured she must have imagined it. After all, why would the man be uncertain about where he lived?

"Is it very different to live in the States?"

"It is," he said, this time without hesitation.

"Do your parents still live there?"

"Yes."

Poppy nodded as she plopped the turkey into the pan and reached for a mixing spoon to break it apart.

"I can imagine it would be a big adjustment. Especially since you didn't want to leave." She nearly groaned when she realized what she'd just said. She hadn't meant to bring up anything about his reasons for leaving—and she definitely didn't want to reveal she knew the reason.

He didn't respond, and she glanced in his direction. He was turning a tomato over and over in his hand, a speculative look in his eyes. She wasn't sure if that tentativeness was truly directed at the red veggie or if he was considering her words. Remembering what happened to make him leave.

"I've lived in Boston my whole life," she said, deciding a shift in conversation might be the best thing.

She glanced at him again, and this time he was watching her.

"Did you always live in this apartment?"

She shook her head. "No, I got this place right after— Once Daisy moved in with me. I had a small apartment before that. But once Daisy came to live with me, I wanted a place that seemed more like a home."

"How did your parents die?"

Again she shouldn't have been surprised by Killian's straightforwardness, but the question still gave her a moment's pause.

"Maybe you'd rather not discuss it."

"No, it's fine." More surprising than his directness was her desire to tell him about it. She never talked about that day. Not even to Daisy. "They were killed in a car accident. Hit head-on by a drunk driver."

"That must have been devastating."

She nodded, staring at the meat sizzling and popping in the pan but only vaguely aware of it. Absently, she stirred.

"It was. It was the defining moment of my life. Everything changed after that."

"Tell me about it."

She paused, the spoon forgotten in her hand as she looked at him. He did have an amazing ability to startle her. She returned her attention to her cooking, her thoughts swirling.

What was the point of talking about it? That had always been her philosophy. She'd never seen any point to lamenting what could have been.

But for some reason, a sudden longing to share pulled at her. She wanted to tell this man about how she'd felt that cold day almost five years ago. A day when her phone rang and changed her life forever.

"Poppy."

She turned her gaze to him, expecting him to say she didn't have to share. Not if she wasn't ready or willing. But, instead, he just gazed back at her, his eyes golden and beautiful like a warm, flickering light. Drawing her in.

"I was still in grad school at BU—Boston University," she heard herself saying. "I was in my last year, working on a doctorate in children's literature as well as a minor in illustration. I had an apartment with . . ." With the love of her life, but she didn't say that. "With my boyfriend at the time. He was a music major."

Killian raised an eyebrow, but she didn't understand what that response meant.

"I was actually at the library doing some research for my thesis when I received that call. Sitting among the stacks as some stranger's voice told me I needed to come to Boston General. That my parents had been in an accident."

Killian rose from the table then, coming over to her, stopping just in front of her. He didn't say anything. He didn't touch her, but his closeness seemed to urge her on.

"I rushed to the hospital, praying, just praying to God, to any god out there who would listen, that they were okay. When I got to the ICU, I was told that my father was pronounced dead at the scene. Killed on impact.

"My mother lived for four days. Four horrible days when I held it together, telling Daisy we would be okay. Telling myself we would be okay. Telling myself my mother would be fine. She'd survive. And never quite believing any of it."

She pulled in a shuddering breath, all that pain coming back as crystal clear as if it had just happened again today.

"I'm sorry," he said, his voice low, his eyes searching hers.

Killian touched her then. Just a hand reaching out to capture hers. Her fingers burned, icy against the heat of his palm. Aching like warmth coming back into a frostbitten limb.

She snatched her hand away, not looking at him, staring down at her fingers instead.

She couldn't deal with this. She didn't want to feel this.

Pulling in a deep breath, she straightened. She braced herself, pushing the memories away. Pushing those emotions back, back to the recesses of her mind where they belonged. Where they couldn't hurt her.

"Oh, my," she said, her voice sounding far more calm and

controlled then she would have imagined possible. "The meat is burning."

She turned then, retrieving the spoon to tend the ground turkey, focusing all her thoughts on the task.

Killian watched Poppy for a moment. Man, if he thought he had the power to control thoughts and feelings, he had nothing on the slight woman in front of him.

He'd seen the anguish on her face. Pain that was so deep it cried out to him. And then, within the blink of an eye, she'd shoved the emotions away. No, not away, back inside, a wall coming up like some invisible shield keeping the world at bay and her feelings guarded deep inside.

He wouldn't begin to call himself an expert on emotions. Hell, he wasn't even a novice, but he could see that what Poppy was doing wasn't good for her.

Pain always needed an outlet. When angered, you yelled. When injured, you screamed. When heartbroken, you cried.

Instinctively, he knew she'd never done those things.

"So did you get the lettuce done?" she said after she rescued the meat from becoming a charred mess.

He nodded, knowing she wasn't going to talk about her past anymore. Not now anyway.

"Sort of," he said, returning to the table. "You did want it to look like mush, right?"

She shot him an alarmed look, then saw his smile and realized that he was teasing. Still, she came over to inspect his work.

"Pretty good."

He smiled wider, oddly pleased by her compliment.

She crossed back to the stove before she added, "It will still taste good—even as mush."

She shot him a quick smile, then turned back to her cooking.

Killian remained watching her for a moment, then caught

himself, returning to his work too. But he had to admit there was something about Poppy that intrigued him.

Maybe he was starting to see why Daisy had made this wish for her. Poppy did deserve some happiness. She deserved to let go of that pain inside her. To move on.

And he had to keep focused on finding her that. As quickly as possible.

"Hey," a voice called from the other room, and Killian looked away from Poppy just as Daisy entered the kitchen. But not before Daisy noticed the direction of his gaze.

Poppy turned around to see her sister, and a fond smile curled her lips. A smile she'd never bestowed on him. A smile that revealed a small dimple in her left cheek and made her dark eyes glitter with warm affection.

"Hi. Killian and I were just making dinner."

Daisy frowned, her gaze moving from her sister to him and back again. "That's good."

"Is Madison with you?"

"Um, no. Her mom is home."

"She is?" Poppy shot Killian a surprised look, saying to him, "I thought she was working tonight?"

Killian opened his mouth to tell her some excuse. An excuse he hadn't even formulated yet, but fortunately, Daisy answered for him.

"Oh, I'm sorry. I thought you asked me about Emma." She laughed, smacking a palm to her forehead. "I'm totally out of it from working on that project. Emma's mother *is* home—and Madison went there to eat."

Poppy nodded, clearly accepting her sister's excuse. Apparently, Madison hopped from friend to friend's on a regular basis.

"Well, we're having tacos. And Killian is joining us since Ginger is at work."

Daisy nodded, but when Poppy turned back to the stove, she narrowed a warning look toward him.

He frowned, not understanding what had irritated her.

From the other room, a song suddenly began to play. Killian recognized it as the rapid-fire refrain of REM's "It's the End of the World as We Know It."

The eighties were making a resurgence in Hell too.

"Your phone," Daisy said to her sister.

"I hear it." Poppy turned down the heat under the frying pan and hurried from the room. Killian heard her answer; then her voice faded as she moved into another room.

"What are you doing?" Daisy asked.

Killian shook his head, confused. "I'm befriending your sister. Like you wanted."

Daisy studied him for a moment. "Okay, that's good. I just didn't expect to find you back here today."

"Well, as you so kindly pointed out to me, I have to stay in that horrible apartment until the wish is granted. So I'm pretty inspired to get this done." And, of course, Vepar's appearance had also spurred him on, but he wasn't going to mention that.

"Okay," Daisy said. "Good. Just remember you can't decide *you're* into my sister. I want her to have a human boyfriend."

"Believe me, I'm not going to decide I'm into your sister." He waited for the absolute ludicrousness of that idea to hit him, but it didn't. At least, not with the certainty he thought it would.

No, he was here to matchmake . . . and not himself. At least, not for real.

CHAPTER 11

"It's going great," Daisy told her friends as they walked down the hallway toward Mrs. Maloney's apartment. "Killian stayed for dinner last night, and he was perfectly nice. Charming, even."

Emma looked impressed. Madison, of course, did not.

Daisy continued, talking directly to Emma. "I think Poppy was really getting comfortable around him. He even did the dishes."

Emma giggled at that. "A demon doing your dishes. That's pretty wild."

"It was," Daisy agreed, laughing too.

"I'm telling you, this isn't going to work," Madison said.

Daisy shook her head, frustrated with her negative-Nellie friend. "It is. He's"—she lowered her voice, even though the hall was empty—"a demon. He can make it happen."

"But even if he has promised that he wouldn't ever be interested in Poppy, what if she falls for him? You know, instead of falling for some other guy?" Madison asked.

Emma sobered. "That's true. He is really cute—you know in an old-guy, demon way. What if she decides he's her true love? You could end up with a demon as a brother-in-law."

Daisy had considered that last night—not that Poppy had

done anything that even hinted she liked him. In fact, she never got close to him. She definitely didn't flirt, but then Daisy wasn't sure Poppy even knew how to flirt.

"Well, he has to do what we say," Daisy said reasonably.

"But Poppy doesn't," Madison pointed out.

Some of Daisy's happiness faded. Why wouldn't Poppy fall for a guy like Killian?

She rapped on Mrs. Maloney's door and waited. After several seconds and another round of insistent knocks, the door jerked open and Killian stood there, wearing nothing but his black pants. Hair unruly from sleeping stuck out all over his head, and a night's worth of facial hair darkened his jaw.

He looked like a pirate. He looked pretty hot.

She grimaced. *Well, you know, hot for an old guy.*

He groaned. "Why are you here so early?"

"School." She pointed to her uniform and her book bag.

He didn't respond, except to continue scowling. Well, he was clearly not a morning person. Neither was Poppy.

Crap, she didn't want to consider similarities between the two.

"We just wanted to check in with you before we left. What's your plan for today?"

Plan?

Killian gritted his teeth. These girls were damned slave drivers. He hadn't slept for shit. In fact, he'd only just dozed off maybe an hour or so ago, and now they woke him because they wanted an *agenda*. He just wanted to crawl back between his flowery sheets and sink into oblivion.

"I was sleeping . . . so a plan wasn't really on my mind at the moment."

"Well, this will only take a second," Daisy said, clearly unconcerned that she was talking to a very irritated and frankly irrational demon. "We have debate at eight-fifteen."

Debate. Given the fact that this girl always had an answer and more than a little tenacity, he didn't think that was a class she really needed.

"So here's the thing. I don't want you to be interested in Poppy, but you also have to make sure she doesn't become interested in you."

He stared at her. This was what they had to talk about at such an ungodly hour?

Daisy looked at him expectantly, but he didn't respond. Honestly, he was afraid of what would come out if he opened his mouth. Besides, he thought his glower probably said enough.

Apparently not, because as usual, this slip of a girl stared back, unfazed.

"So be nice to her, but not too nice," she said.

This was getting absurd. Utterly, utterly absurd.

Madison flipped open her hot pink cell phone and checked the time. "We have to go."

"Have a good day," Daisy said with a smile. "Maybe you should take Poppy out to lunch or something. Someplace with lots of people. You know, a place where there are available men."

The girls hurried away, and again he was amazed by their lack of concern over his demonic status. Maybe what all the worried moralists said was true: Movies and TV had desensitized the youth today.

One thing was clear. If good wanted to put evil its place, just send in a group of teenage girls.

He turned back into the apartment, not even bothering to register any of the antiquated horrors. He was too tired. He beelined straight back to his old-lady bedroom, stripped off his pants and collapsed back onto the lumpy mattress that was probably as old as its owner.

"Be nice, but not too nice," he muttered to himself as the sleep that had eluded him most of the night finally took hold.

"Killian . . ."

He groaned. Damn, who was it now?

"Killian—wake up, my love."

My love? He struggled to open his eyes, but his lids refused to open as if they were adhered together. Finally, he cracked them, blinking to focus in the dim light.

Gradually, the form at the end of the bed came into view.

"Poppy?"

She walked closer to the bed. Actually walking didn't do justice to her movement. *Sashaying*—that was the right word. Her hips swayed as she came closer. Each movement was accented by the satiny material of . . .

"What are you wearing?" he asked, unable to keep the shock out of his voice.

She looked down at herself, then back at him. "Oh, this? Just something comfy."

Comfy was the T-shirts and jeans and worn sweaters he'd seen her in. This was a slinky chemise, colored deep pink, the warm hue bringing out the porcelain pinkness of her skin. The material showed off every lithe curve: the delicate angles of her shoulders, her small but perfectly rounded breasts, the subtle curve of her hips.

She continued to the edge of the bed, stopping to look down at him. The bed dipped under her slight weight as she sat down beside him, facing him. In a mesmerized daze, he watched as she reached out a hand to brush her fingers over his cheek.

Her touch smoothed over him, as warm and soft as fur. His body reacted instantly. His muscles tensed. His groin ached with need as he came to full, hard arousal.

"Killian," she whispered. "Killian . . ."

Her voice trailed off into a weird hiss, but even that didn't

detract from the sharp longing coursing through him. A longing that was so strong, so intense—

"Shit!"

Killian shot upright in bed, touching a hand to the piercing
pain that suddenly stung his cheek.

Poppy. Where was she? And why had she scratched him?
But instead of seeing her standing over him, he saw the sudden movement of something matted and dingy white shooting off the end of the bed, thumping to the floor and
skittering out of the room.

The fucking cat, he realized.

He looked around him again, still disoriented. Poppy wasn't
here. He'd been dreaming.

He lifted his hand away from his face to see smears of
blood on his fingers. That damned cat.

Falling back onto the mattress, he kept his hand pressed to
his cheek.

"Cats and teenage girls," he growled. "Pure evil."

He closed his eyes, trying to get some control over his
cloudy head. It had been a dream. Nothing but a dream.
Poppy hadn't come to him in a sexy negligee. She hadn't
stroked his skin, driving his senses and body wild. He was
not attracted to her.

All of it had been a strange figment of his imagination. A
dream created by the ridiculous orders of the adolescent girls
who ruled his life at the moment.

Who wouldn't have weird dreams under these circum-
stances?

"Just a crazy dream," he assured himself.

Which was all fine and dandy, but did not explain his still-
hard erection, tenting the floral comforter like an effin' may-
pole.

His eyes snapped open as the mattress shifted. The cat sat
at the end of the bed, looking decidedly smug.

"You are evil," he muttered to the hideous beast.

"That goes without saying," the cat answered.

Killian blinked, his dick instantly shriveling. Why hadn't he suspected this was Vepar all along?

"Did you scratch me?" Killian snapped. He didn't like Vepar on the best of days, but at this moment—let's just say he'd give serious thought to strangling the cat if that would kill Vepar too.

"No, I didn't," Vepar said, lifting a paw and inspecting it. "But I gotta say, I do kinda like this animal."

Killian didn't say a word, or even make any expression. He'd pushed his luck enough by being so terse.

Vepar sighed, his furry chest inflating, then deflating. "So . . . why are you still here?"

Killian sat up. "I haven't found this woman a mate. It's . . . it's taking a little time."

The cat's head bobbed, and Killian thought Vepar was going to be understanding—just a little.

"Well, you could just kill her."

"Kill her?"

"Sure. Kill her. If this mortal is dead, then you can't find her a mate, and you can get back to Hell and work, where you belong."

Yeah, that was more the response he should have expected from Vepar. He wasn't just a demon; he was an ass too.

"Killing her seems a little extreme, plus she's the only person the kid who conjured me has," Killian said. "I'll fix this quickly—and my way," he added.

"Fine."

Right away, Killian could tell when Vepar left the cat's body. Gone was the calm, intelligent air, replaced by a narrowed, wary stare, a twitching tail, and an attack posture.

But instead of another attack, the cat shot off the bed and skittered out of the room.

Killian threw back the covers and headed to the bathroom. Any lingering effects of his sexy dream were gone, so he opted for steaming hot water. He needed to get thinking clearly—and apparently he did need a plan.

He washed with quick efficiency, while his mind turned over the best way to find Poppy a soul mate. But as he finished rinsing, then stepped out of the shower to towel off, he still wasn't sure how to undertake such a task.

He wandered back to the bedroom and tugged on the clothes he was wearing for a third day. He hated to put them back on again, but he didn't have much choice. He needed a razor too. And a toothbrush. And some deodorant.

Wait, that could be a start. He'd ask Poppy to show him where to buy the items he needed. That would get her out of the house. Then they would go to—lunch. The girls had suggested lunch.

He smiled at himself in the mirror above the ornate, antique dresser, pleased that he had a plan. He wasn't going to see Poppy killed—that was for sure. Of course, Vepar always went for the most extreme solution. Even Satan would not approve of that. Killing was only allowed if the person was evil. Sort of damned-soul harvesting, if you will. And Poppy didn't have an evil bone in her body. Not even a slightly wicked one.

Good, he had a plan. But this time his smile faded as he really saw the scruffy, tired face looking back at him. He looked like hell. Well, Daisy needn't worry. There was no risk of attracting Poppy's interest. Between the dark circles under his eyes, unshaven cheeks and wrinkled clothes, he looked more like a vagrant than someone Poppy would consider a romantic interest.

That was good, right? Neither of them would be attracted to each other as per the orders of the adolescent boss girls.

Then he recalled how Poppy had looked in his dream and his intense reaction to her.

"A dream, buddy. Just a dream."

Sighing, he decided it was time to get to work. Plus, he was starving.

Brunch was close to lunch, right?

CHAPTER 12

The sharp rap on the apartment door startled Poppy.

Who could that be? Most days she didn't talk with anyone. She still had a few friends from graduate school. But they'd all be at work at ten-thirty on a Monday.

Maybe it was a courier with a new manuscript. Her boss, Donald, had called last evening to ask if she had time to pick up a little extra work. But usually Donald told her if he was sending something over.

She stretched as she stood. She'd been huddled over her current manuscript, trying to stay focused and on task.

Occasionally, other thoughts had crept in. How much she'd enjoyed having dinner with Killian last night. How odd it was that she'd talked to him about her parents. How distracting his smile was.

She shoved those thoughts aside over and over. Killian was a nice guy—nicer than she'd first thought. He'd been an interesting distraction. But now it was back to her routine. Her work, Daisy, the usual.

But all that sensible reasoning couldn't stop something in her chest from doing a little flip as she opened the door to find Killian standing on the other side.

"Hey," she said.

"Hey," he answered back, his eyes scanning her body before they locked with hers.

Again her body reacted, her heart jumping a little, her skin prickling with awareness. Even though she couldn't decipher what his sweeping look meant.

"I was wondering if you could show me someplace to pick up toiletries and a few clothes."

This time, it was Poppy's turn for her gaze to roam over him. He hadn't shaved, she could see that. And he was wearing the same clothes from yesterday. Actually, even from the day before that, now that she thought about it.

"What happened to your luggage?"

"Umm—the airline lost it."

She frowned. "You flew?"

Not many people flew from Connecticut to Boston. Heck, that probably took longer than it did to drive. But she supposed someone might.

Clearly he had.

"I actually flew here from Sweden," he said. "You know, visiting some family there. Some of my father's family."

"Oh, that's nice." Wait. "But you said your mother's family lived in Sweden."

He paused for a second, then nodded. "That's true. But some of my father's family moved there too. Once he moved there."

That made sense—she guessed.

"My father's brother actually married my mother's sister."

"Really?" Poppy said. "That's kind of romantic."

"Is it?" His completely confused expression was so male. Of course he would have never considered that romantic.

She laughed, until she realized he was staring at her, his expression strange. And unreadable. She sobered.

"So you need a store?"

He glanced down at himself, then made a pained expression. "Yes. That would be good."

She thought of the best place to send him. "Well, there is a strip mall one stop away on the T. On the red line. That should have everything you need."

He frowned. "Aren't you going to go with me?"

Poppy hesitated, thinking of that manuscript sitting only half completed on her desk. Playing hooky was so not her.

"Umm—Ginger can't go with you?"

Killian frowned, not answering right away. "She's sleeping. You know, because she worked—late."

"Right."

"So you aren't going to leave me on my own, are you?" He smiled then, that breathtaking smile she'd imagined more than a few times this morning.

She glanced back to her office as if somehow the actual manuscript would give her permission to take a little time off. Shocker—it didn't.

"Surely you can take an hour or so to help out a traveler in need."

She debated for a moment, then released a pent-up breath. "Sure. I can take a little while."

He smiled then, but when her eyes locked on to the handsome curve of his sculpted lips, he sobered.

She didn't quite understand his reaction, but she didn't allow herself to ponder it. She'd definitely been doing enough pondering about him as it was.

"Let me grab a sweater." She turned, leaving him in the doorway. She refused to look at the pages of manuscript as she hurried through her office to her bedroom.

She wasn't going to feel guilty. After all, she was helping a friend—well, an acquaintance—in need.

See, Killian told himself as he watched Poppy dash off, no sexy Poppy of his dreams. She was clad just as he'd expected in another T-shirt. This one sported an image of Dr. Seuss's Cat in the Hat. Along with her T-shirt, she wore a pair of faded jeans and fuzzy black-and-white socks. Her long hair was knotted messily on the top of her head.

Not a hint of the sexy vixen of his dream. And that, he told himself, was because dream Poppy was just that. Imaginary. A strange, unexplainable creation of his unconscious mind.

So he shouldn't give it another thought. Period. He would stay focused on finding her a man. That was the best plan for all of them.

"Okay. Ready." She returned to the door wearing a gray cable-knit sweater with big buttons. On her feet, she wore sneakers that looked more appropriate for a small boy.

Definitely not his type, he told himself as he watched her lock her door. Then she turned and smiled at him. He caught a glimpse of her dimple, and just like that, his body reacted, seeming to vibrate with awareness.

Okay, she was cute. Adorable, even—in a whimsical way. But still not his type. And adorable would make it easier to find her a match.

"Do you think we could stop and get a bite to eat first?" he asked.

"Umm—sure," she said, falling into step beside him. "Do you have anything in mind?"

Daisy did have a point. He needed to get Poppy somewhere where there were men to meet. He glanced at her, noticing how tendrils of her brown hair had escaped the barrette and curled against the pale skin of her neck. Something like a sharp jolt of electricity shot through him again, and he fought the urge to groan.

He *had* to get out of here. When he started finding women in bulky cardigans and little-boy sneakers attractive, it was getting pretty damned strange. He was starting to think the spell had actually addled his brain. Time to just pick some guy, control his thoughts—assuming he could—make him fall for Poppy, and then get the hell out of here.

"I want to go someplace busy."

She gave him an odd look, then said, "That would be Smiley's."

Smiley's. Of course, he'd be taking the cute, whimsical girl to a place called Smiley's.

As Killian stepped through the door, he realized Smiley's wasn't at all like what he'd been picturing. Surprisingly, the atmosphere was quite trendy in a bohemian coffee shop sort of way. Like a Starbucks meets an upscale diner meets a cool baroque salon.

A fire blazed in an ornate fireplace, the flames reflecting off the gilded walls and highly polished wood floors. Sofas upholstered in rich-colored velvets were situated in clusters here and there. Round tables and elegant chairs lined the walls.

Poppy led him to one of the tables, taking a seat.

"They have great omelets," she told him, opening her menu. "And delicious waffles."

He picked up his own menu but didn't open it. Instead, he perused the place. Definitely an assortment of men. Some in suits. Some more casually dressed. A few ate and read the paper. Others sat with their coffees, talking on cell phones or typing away on computers. This was definitely a trendy hotspot. There should be plenty of prospective true loves for Poppy here.

He noticed a man just a few tables away. He was dressed in business casual, a decent shirt with a tie. He had a briefcase open on the chair beside him and papers spread out on the table.

His hair was trimmed in a typical business-guy style, and he wore wire-rimmed glasses. His build was average. A good steady sort of guy. He could work.

But Killian's attention turned to another guy. He sat on

one of the sofas, reading the paper. This guy wore a simple button-down shirt with jeans and boots. Maybe a little more laid-back than the briefcase guy. That might be a better fit for Poppy.

Killian's gaze moved still to another man sitting by the fire, talking on his BlackBerry. The cut of his suit stated he had some money. Probably some power in his job. He was a little older than the other two. Hmm, that might be good for Poppy too.

Just pick one. The object here was to get this woman a boyfriend. Do it and be done.

But still he didn't choose.

Poppy frowned, watching Killian. He'd been the one to say he was starving, yet he hadn't even cracked open the menu. Instead, he'd been looking around, his attention going from one person to another. He'd tilt his head, narrow his eyes as if he was trying to decide something very important. Then his gaze would move on again.

"Are you all right?" she finally asked, after watching him for several minutes. "Didn't you say you were starving?"

He blinked at her, then seemed to come back from wherever he was.

"Yes. Yes, I am." He opened his menu, reading down the list of delicious breakfast and lunch items.

She returned her attention to her own menu. When she looked up again, his attention was no longer on the menu. Again he surveyed the room as if searching for someone.

But he couldn't be expecting to see anyone he knew. So what was he doing?

Then the realization hit her like ice water thrown in her face. He was searching for women to meet. A potential friend, lover, wife. Hadn't he told her that was what he wanted to accomplish in Boston?

Suddenly, Poppy didn't feel hungry either. Which was stupid, she told herself. He'd already told her that a relationship was something he very much wanted.

And it wasn't like this was some impromptu date between them. That was stupid.

She didn't want that anyway. As much as he wanted a relationship, she didn't want one.

She glanced at him. And definitely not with him.

Yet, before she could stop herself, she asked, "See anything you like?"

She tried not to wince at her tone, doubting he'd miss the annoyance there.

His attention turned back to her, but instead of giving her a look of speculation, or even just answering with his usual tactless honesty, he looked back to his menu.

"The waffles do sound good. That's what I'm getting." He set aside the menu. "What about you?"

She looked at him for a moment, trying to decide if he really hadn't been checking out women. Maybe he hadn't. And thankfully, he didn't seem to be at all aware of her peevishness.

She looked back to her menu, feeling a little silly for getting worked up. Couldn't the guy just appreciate the cool décor without her getting all offended?

"I think I'll have the waffles too. With fresh berries."

This time, when she looked up, Killian was staring at her. Again he had that intense look she'd noticed earlier. An expression she didn't understand at all.

"What was your old boyfriend like?"

CHAPTER 13

Before she could answer, a waitress arrived to take their orders. Poppy vaguely recalled ordering a coffee and waffles. She wasn't even sure if she'd asked for the fresh berries.

Killian ordered too, seemingly oblivious to her stunned reaction.

But as soon as the waitress left, he turned back to her, eyebrows raised, clearly awaiting her response.

"My old boyfriend?" Why would he suddenly want to know about Adam?

"Yes, you said you lived with him. What was he like?"

Poppy shook her head. She didn't know what to say. She didn't want to talk about him. Adam had been the love of her life. Her first serious boyfriend, the person she thought she was going to grow old with.

"He was . . ."

She wasn't going to talk about this.

"He was a nice guy."

"So you like nice?"

Poppy shrugged. "I don't think many women actually like mean."

Adam had been mean at the end. She hadn't liked that at all. No, not mean exactly. More like distant, cold, absent in the relationship. But she'd held on, hoping he'd change back to the man she'd loved and so terribly afraid she'd lose another person who was important to her. In the end, she'd had to let go.

"I guess that is true," Killian said, drawing her attention back to him, away from a memory she'd rather not recall. "But some women do like bad boys, right?"

"I guess." Why were they talking about this?

"But definitely not you?"

She stared at him. "Not really."

"And what about income? And age? Any preferences?"

Poppy didn't answer for a moment, studying his face. His expression was expectant, his eyes bright with interest, as if her answers were of the utmost importance to him.

"Why are you asking me all this?"

He straightened, for the first time in the conversation appearing a little uncertain, like maybe his line of questioning was odd.

"It's always nice to know what a woman wants in a man," he said, shrugging as if suddenly her answers weren't of much importance to him.

The waitress returned, placing steaming mugs of coffee in front of each of them. Killian took a sip of his, then turned, suddenly finding the painting on the wall above their table inordinately fascinating.

She added cream to her coffee until the dark liquid was pale brown. She reached for a couple packets of sugar. What had spurred on that line of questioning?

She stirred her coffee, puzzled. Then she realized what must have motivated him. Of course. How stupid of her. He'd been asking her about preferences, using her as a barometer to understand what women wanted in general. Maybe because of the loss of his own fiancée. And probably to understand what his new love interest might want.

He didn't want to make the same mistakes again.

"I like men who are intelligent," she said.

He immediately turned his attention back to her.

"And a good sense of humor is a must," she added.

"Okay," Killian said, nodding as if he was making a mental checklist in his head.

"And good looking never hurts," she said with a smile. He definitely had that one in the bag. "And interesting is good. You know, not just run-of-the-mill."

Killian listened to her list. Run-of-the-mill. That ruled out the guy with the average haircut and average build he'd been considering. The older man in the corner was definitely the best-looking guy in the restaurant. But there was one guy with longish hair who looked the most interesting. Damn, this was confusing.

"He has to like kids and pets. And have a great laugh."

Killian frowned. How the hell was he supposed to find out half this shit? What did he know about a guy's laugh anyway?

This was going to be impossible. A great laugh? Yeah, impossible.

"But I'm just one woman," she finally said, after taking a sip of her now very creamy, very sweetened coffee. "You will find a woman who loves all the things you have to offer."

Killian paused, the coffee mug halfway to his mouth. What woman? Then he realized she was referring to his declaration about wanting to find a wife.

He nodded, setting down his mug. "I hope you are right."

"I am. You're a catch," she told him with a smile, then reached for another packet of sugar.

He watched as she added the fourth sugar to her coffee, the spoon clinking on the ceramic.

"You think I'm a catch?"

She smiled then, that little dimple appearing. "Of course."

Something warm spread through his chest, a strange sensation that felt like pleasure, but more than that.

He didn't trust it.

He took a long swallow of his coffee, letting the burn of the hot liquid replace the other warmth in his chest. Then he looked back at the other single men in the restaurant.

The one on the couch with the goatee and boots. That was his choice. Done.

Focusing on the man, he sent his thoughts through the air like radio waves directly to the man's brain. The man immediately lowered his paper, frowning, a slightly confused look in his eyes.

Turn and look this way.

The man shifted on the sofa cushion. Well, apparently Killian's powers still worked—that was a relief. He couldn't understand why they didn't work on Poppy, but at least being able to control her love interest would make this crazy task only half as difficult.

Become aware of her.

Killian glanced at Poppy so the man would know whom he was supposed to notice.

The man turned further, craning his neck to see Poppy. She was in the midst of testing her coffee. She wrinkled her nose and reached for yet another sugar. Something about the action was really quite cute.

Find her cute. No, Killian amended, studying her pretty mouth and soulful dark eyes, *find her beautiful.*

The man stared at her, clearly not finding Killian's order too difficult to obey.

Come over and speak to her.

The man folded his paper and tossed it down on the table in front of him. Then he rose and headed directly to their table.

Killian watched his approach, wondering at the strange feeling of dread tightening the muscles in his shoulders and making his teeth clench.

"Excuse me," the man said.

Poppy looked up at the man, her dark eyes wide as if a strange man talking to her was uncommon and a little startling.

"I'm sorry to interrupt," the man said, offering a reassuring, friendly smile.

Poppy glanced at Killian, clearly confused by the man's attention.

"It's okay," she said, smiling, albeit weakly. Killian couldn't say why, but he was pleased to notice the dimple didn't make an appearance for this guy.

"Can I help you?" she said, her voice polite but impersonal.

The man looked flustered then, as if he wasn't really sure what he was doing either. Killian thought of sending him another mental nudge, but something stopped him.

"I—" The man gave her a pained smile. "I never just approach a woman like this. But I noticed you from where I was sitting over there." He gestured to the sofa. "And I just had to come over and speak to you. And—and see if I could—I don't know. Call you sometime."

Poppy stared at him, something akin to shock on her face.

"I mean, if that's okay," the man said. "I'm really not some weirdo."

Killian fought the urge to make a face. Like a weirdo would admit he was a weirdo. Then Killian narrowed a critical look at the guy. Was he a weirdo?

Suddenly he decided maybe this wasn't the right guy for Poppy. After all, as far as he could see, the guy had no sense of humor at all. And intelligence, well, there wasn't much sign of that either. And interesting was also right out the window with this one.

Then the man laughed nervously—a nasally twitter. Okay, if the great laugh wasn't even there, what was the point?

But before he could send the man a thought to gracefully—and quickly—leave, Poppy answered him.

"I'm sorry," she said, offering him a pained smile of her own. "I'm involved." She nodded toward Killian.

The man glanced at Killian for the first time since approaching the table. Killian tilted his head, giving him a cool smile by way of greeting.

"Oh. I'm sorry," the man said to Poppy, then looked back at Killian. "I'm sorry," he repeated to Killian.

"No problem," Killian said, finding it easy to go along with Poppy's story. "She is a lovely woman."

Killian saw Poppy look at him out of his peripheral vision, surprise in her brown eyes.

"Very lovely," the man agreed.

Okay, enough was enough.

Walk away now.

"Sorry to bother you." the man bowed slightly.

And don't talk to Poppy again, Killian added for good measure.

The man headed back to the sofa and his paper.

Poppy watched him go, then shot Killian a puzzled, yet amused look. "That was strange."

"You don't get men asking you out?"

She laughed as if the very idea was ludicrous.

"No." She chuckled again. Killian couldn't help noticing her laugh. Lovely. Sweet. A sound he could hear over and over. You know, if he ever considered laughter. Which he didn't. Well, you know, until she'd mentioned it.

The waitress arrived with their food, giving him something else to focus on. But not even food distracted him long.

He watched Poppy as she cut off a piece of her waffle with her fork, a small, secret smile still on her lips.

The man's attention had really pleased her. But he couldn't imagine she didn't get noticed all the time. Although, that man probably wouldn't have noticed her without Killian's mental prompting.

He watched her as she picked up a raspberry and popped

the small fruit into her mouth. A raspberry as ripe and red as her lips.

Killian stared at those lips. He couldn't believe she wouldn't get attention. He hadn't been lying when he'd said she was lovely. She was.

Then he glanced over at the man. He watched Poppy over the top of his paper. There was still keen awareness in the man's eyes. An awareness Killian found himself disliking. Very much.

Before he even realized it, a thought was fired from his head, sent out like a warning shot.

She's mine.

The man's gaze moved from Poppy to him, and Killian found himself staring back. Unflinching. Unapologetic.

The man looked away. And Killian felt relief, mingled with a very real feeling of possessiveness. A feeling he refused to overanalyze as he returned his attention to his breakfast.

CHAPTER 14

Of course, by the end of breakfast, he had analyzed his feelings—to death. And he'd realized that he was clearly confusing possessiveness with concern. He could admit that he'd come to rather like Poppy, which made it harder to just pick any old guy for her.

He didn't really care for concern as an emotion. Not his thing. But it was better than possessiveness. Possessiveness didn't even make sense.

"How about this store?" Poppy asked, pointing to another shop in the strip mall where they'd just picked up his toiletries.

The drugstore she'd taken him to was fine. He could get a functional razor, toothbrush and deodorant anywhere. But clothing? From a place called . . .

"*Old Navy?*" What kind of name was that for a clothing store? He wasn't planning to swab a deck any time soon.

Poppy smiled at him as he read the large sign over the glass storefront. "Why do I get the feeling that you've never set foot in this store before?"

"Probably because I never have."

"Well, I figured this would be a good place for you to just pick up a few essentials. After all, your luggage is bound to be returned to you eventually."

Leave it to her to be practical at all times.

He followed her into the store, realizing he had heard of this place—in television ads. Ads that used weird talking mannequins to sell their clothes. He was used to live models on runways selling him his clothing.

Ah well. When in Rome. Or Boston.

He picked up an orange-and-blue checked shirt, grimacing. Or in some cases, Hell on earth.

"How about this?" Poppy held up a faded brown T-shirt with a logo of a skull and wings across the front.

He must not have hidden his disdain, because she returned it to the pile, muttering, "Okay, maybe not," under her breath.

He wandered over to a rack of button-down shirts, rifling through them until he found a few that weren't too unpleasant. Next he went to a rack of jeans, also choosing a couple pairs of those. He wouldn't need much—after all, he had to have this job done as quickly as possible.

"See. You found some things," Poppy said, not hiding her self-satisfaction with her store choice.

"That remains to be seen," he told her.

She rolled her eyes, the action more cute and impish than derisive.

"The dressing room is over there." She pointed to the back corner of the store.

He headed that way, still not optimistic about this shopping trip. When he saw the employee working the fitting room, he felt even less sure.

"How many?" asked the young man, who looked as if he'd never met a hair dye he didn't like. Or a piercing gun.

"Too many," Killian muttered and the kid, clearly not very worried about the rules of his job, randomly plucked a red plastic card labeled with a white six and handed it to him.

Killian had more than six items, not that he was going to make an issue about it. He followed the kid to the closest closet-sized changing room, then quickly shut the door to block out the cockatoo boy.

Without any preamble, he tried on one of the shirts, which much to his surprise, fit pretty well and didn't look totally like he should be hanging out in the crow's nest of a ship.

The jeans fit well too, he realized as he studied both in the full-length mirror. He tilted his head to take a closer look at the shirt's collar, which didn't look quite right, but overall not too bad.

"So? How do they look?" Poppy called, clearly some distance away.

Killian smiled to himself. Leave it to Poppy to holler to him as if he were a small boy allowed to try on clothes by himself for the first time and she was his anxious mother.

He opened the door to show her.

"Well? You tell me?"

Killian strolled toward Poppy and her first thought was of a sexy, disheveled model sauntering down the runway. The white shirt he'd chosen fit his broad shoulders to a tee, his unruly hair just brushing the collar. The sides were tailored just enough to accentuate his muscled torso and flat stomach.

Nix that—probably washboard stomach.

His jeans were slung low on his narrow hips, and she had to push aside an image of how his muscled stomach, flat navel and hipbones would look above the waistband.

Good golly.

"Um—they look—fine," she managed, which was no small feat, considering she could barely pull in a full breath. It was just not right that a man could look so sexy.

He came closer. "I hate to admit it, but they're not bad."

"No, not bad at all."

She was pretty sure most men who shopped here didn't make the clothes look this good, though.

Lovely. He'd used that word to describe her at lunch. She realized he didn't mean it; he'd just been backing her story. But she could easily use that word to describe him now. Without hesitation, and in all honesty.

Whoa, girl. She needed to get a grip here. Sure, he was good looking. But she was dangerously close to drooling. And frankly, she just didn't go mushy over guys. Boy crazy wasn't a term ever applied to her. She'd only been crazy about one guy—and that had been nothing but a lesson in heartache.

The sudden thought of Adam sobered her as quickly as an ice-cold shower. She met Killian's eyes then, and offered him a little smile. She hoped it looked more sassy than she felt.

"I guess my suggestion wasn't so bad, after all."

He smiled back, his golden eyes flashing with amusement. "I'm not giving you any credit. I'm sure I'll never hear the end of it if I do."

Poppy managed to feign a wounded look. Even as her heart did little skips in her chest—her body reacting—again.

"And," he added, "while the shirt isn't bad, there is something messed up with this collar."

He tugged at one side, and Poppy noticed for the first time there was something odd about it. She stepped forward to look closer, then reached up to fiddle with it.

"It was just tucked under," she said as the one side unfolded to match the other. She patted it down, leaned back a bit to compare the two sides.

"Perfect," she said decisively, her smugness returning as she looked up at him.

As soon as their eyes met, Poppy saw something like awareness in Killian's golden gaze. A flicker like sparks ignited into flame. Suddenly she became painfully aware of how close they were standing, and that her hand remained pressed to his chest. She could feel the heat of his skin, the hardness of his muscles, the steady thump of his heart against the palm of her hand through the cotton of the shirt.

Helpless to stop herself, she moved her fingers, just a little, just a tiny caress.

"Um, it's not really kosher to get all cozy in the dressing rooms."

Poppy started, dropping her hand guiltily away from Killian, turning to find a boy, who looked not much older than a teen with multicolored hair and skinny jeans. He raised a pierced eyebrow at her.

"Oh, sorry," she managed to mumble, backing away from both of them. "I'll—I'll just wait out here." She gestured over her shoulder with her thumb toward the exit, still backing away. That was until she ran into a rack of unwanted clothes.

She caught herself on a pair of cargo pants that, thankfully, didn't fall off the hanger under her weight. Righting herself, she avoided both men's gazes and spun on her heel to hurry back into the store.

Once hidden behind a rack of hoodies, she closed her eyes and groaned.

"Not at all embarrassing," she muttered to herself.

A woman a few feet away glanced at her as if Poppy were mad. Poppy ignored the woman. Yes, she was the crazy lady talking to herself among the hoodies. What of it?

She deserved to have a moment of insanity. Actually, she'd already had that. She'd acted like a woman who'd never touched a man before. So classy. So poised.

And there was no way Killian had missed her reaction. After all, the androgynous fitting-room clerk had even seen her attraction. And he didn't seem like the type to notice much beyond the newest dye colors and piercing jewelry at Hot Topic.

Darn it . . . no, damn. Damn, damn, damn. How could she act so stupid?

Killian walked back to the changing room, stunned by what had just happened. And his reaction to it. She'd been merely fixing his shirt. A brief brush of her fingers. A small touch.

He looked at himself in the mirror, glad to see his shirttails hid exactly what that touch did to him.

He dug sex as much as the next demon—who by their very nature adored it: the gratification, the release, the pure unadulterated pleasure. But he also considered himself a demon with great control.

His sexual reactions were on his terms, just like all of his existence was on his terms. That was until he was conjured by teenage girls. Since then, nothing had been on his terms. And apparently that included his physical reactions.

He unbuttoned the shirt, shrugging out of it to inspect the place where Poppy's fingers had pressed against him. His chest burned as if she'd left an imprint there, her mark. But there was no physical sign. Nothing to explain the raw need her touch created.

Shaken, he tossed the shirt aside. He took his time changing back into his old clothes, using these moments alone to gather himself.

Why would he react that way to Poppy? He'd been with human women far more beautiful than she. He'd been with demons more beautiful. So what was it about this pint-sized human with brown hair, brown eyes, a boyish figure, and very definitely boyish shoes? He just didn't get it.

But you can't hide out in here forever.

"Did everything work out for you?" the cockatoo guy asked as soon as Killian stepped out of the fitting room. "Can I take anything?"

Killian glanced at the pile of garments draped over his arm. "I'm taking them all."

Killian didn't know if it was a store policy or not, but it seemed to him if a man got a hard-on in a pair of jeans while trying them on, he should be required to buy them.

CHAPTER 15

"I appreciate your helping me out today," Killian said as they reached Poppy's door.

"Sure," she said, not looking in his direction. "I hope you got everything you needed."

"I did," he said. "Thank you."

Well, this all sounded polite and nicey-nice, but in truth neither had said more than two words to each other since leaving the clothing store.

Awkward, but the usual ending to one of their outings.

Poppy had spent their shared silence trying not to analyze what Killian was thinking. Not that she had to deliberate too much to guess his thoughts.

She was sure he was embarrassed by the encounter between them. He'd have to have been blind not to see her reaction. And given how quiet he'd been as well, he was clearly uncomfortable with it too.

He probably thought she was some pathetic single woman desperate for affection. Lonely and needy and willing to throw herself at any eligible man. And though he said he wanted to settle down and have a real relationship, she wasn't naïve enough to think she'd be in the running for that position.

He wanted an elegant, sophisticated type with impeccable taste and a killer body. That was not Poppy.

She shopped at places like Old Navy—when she shopped, which was rarely. She had minimal curves and only got her hair cut when she remembered. She liked gourmet food, but almost always ate at home with her sister.

That was not the description of the woman she saw on Killian's arm.

Then she caught herself. Okay, so she wasn't what Killian would find appealing, but she wasn't lacking. She wouldn't demean herself that way. She'd done that, and it had gotten her nothing.

Besides, she didn't want a relationship anyway. Okay, she was attracted to the man. She'd have to be dead not to be. But her reaction in the dressing room didn't mean she wanted anything from him. Not really.

Several times on the way home, she'd opened her mouth to tell him just that. But every time, she stopped herself.

Even now, she considered explaining herself, but instead said, "Okay, well, have a good day. Say hello to Ginger for me."

"Oh. Yeah, I will."

She unlocked her door, only fumbling with the key once. Then she glanced at him, quickly, before opening the door. He regarded her closely, but his golden gaze was guarded, unreadable.

"Okay. 'Bye," she said again because she didn't know what else to say.

He nodded. "Good-bye."

Poppy closed the door, then stood in the hallway, still unsure of what to do. She glanced at the closed door, wondering if he was already gone.

A part of her wanted to go look. To stop him and talk out all this awkwardness, but another part told her to walk away. Go back to her life and not waste any more time worrying about an insignificant moment in an Old Navy dressing room.

Killian stood on the other side of the door, holding his bags of clothes and toiletries like some character in a movie kicked out of the heroine's apartment. Forced to shuffle away like a down-and-out loser. Of course, Poppy hadn't even let him inside to actually kick him out. Did that make him even more pathetic?

He remained there for a few moments, debating on knocking and getting Poppy to come back and talk to him. To discuss the thing that had happened between them back at the store.

But, instead, he turned and headed back to the elevators. He would have to smooth things over with Poppy, eventually. Otherwise, he'd be stuck here—with Vepar breathing down his neck. But maybe for now, they both needed a little time to forget their brief moment of attraction.

If that was even what it was. At this point he didn't know exactly what they had shared. In fact, he was starting to think that maybe he was the only one who had felt anything.

He'd watched her on their way home, and though she'd been quiet and lost in her own thoughts, she'd otherwise seemed unaffected.

Which was good, he assured himself as he made his way back to the floral hell. He needed to stay on task and get her a man. Juggling his several bags, he rooted around in his pocket for the key.

He unlocked the door and was assaulted by the musty old smell and wanted to groan. He had to figure out how to get back onto good terms with Poppy and get this stupid matchmaking task done. A mission that was never going to happen if things kept getting awkward between them.

"Of course," he said aloud to the dreaded apartment. "If you'd just let the guy from the restaurant ask her out, you'd be halfway home—maybe even all the way home."

He grimaced at the place he had to call home for now. Away from here. That would be—dare he say it?—Heaven.

But that guy hadn't been right. Poppy needed someone better than that guy.

"You didn't even know him," he muttered roughly to himself. Killian couldn't tell anything about him, good or bad.

This was an impossible task. Why had he been the demon conjured anyway? There were demons who could read minds. Read auras. Even touch a person and see that person's whole past. Wouldn't any of those have been a better choice than him?

He wandered into the bedroom, dropping his bags onto the floor. Then he searched the room for the fiendish thingy otherwise called a cat. Or Vepar. Which was even worse.

He looked behind the furniture, under the bed—being extra careful about that one—even in the closet. Twice he'd spun around in defense mode because he thought he'd heard something. He was starting to feel like Inspector Clouseau, awaiting an attack from his house servant Cato.

Cato. More like Cat-o. Evil Cat-o.

Okay, clearly his mind was scrambled. Again he was starting to feel like this place was having that effect on him.

When he was sure the room was clear, he shut the bedroom door and fell onto the bed. How was he going to find a man for Poppy? A decent man?

But his attempts to sort that out were soon driven away by other thoughts. Thoughts of how her little hand had felt touching him. Tiny hands that seemed to have the power to ignite him. To make him burn for more of her touch. Even the slightest caress.

Then his disobedient mind imagined what those hands of

hers would feel like on his bare skin. Stroking him. Down his chest, over his stomach, down, down to the flesh that ached for her.

He groaned, closing his eyes and allowing himself to indulge in his fantasy. Just for a minute.

Poppy did something that she rarely did. She gathered up the manuscript she was working on, the one she should have been working on all day, and took it to her bedroom. She needed to work, but she felt exhausted. Certainly more emotionally than physically, but either way her bed was calling to her.

She piled up several pillows and settled herself against them, arranging herself and her papers. Once situated, she reread the last part she'd been editing, then started in. She forced her mind to stay on task, finding the occasional typos or grammar mistake, as well as readying the format for the typesetters.

Her mind stayed focused for almost three pages. Then she found images of Killian replacing misspellings and missing commas. More precisely, images of how he'd looked in that shirt and how his chest had felt under her hand.

She gave up marking the page in front of her for a moment, letting her head fall back against the fluffiness of her down pillows. Closing her eyes, she allowed her thoughts to go where they wanted.

He'd been so strong and so warm against her fingers.

You shouldn't go there, she warned herself. But her mind wasn't listening any better than her body. She imagined what that kind of power and heat would feel like against her. Pinning her to the bed. Pressing her down into the mattress. Pushing deep into her body.

She pulled in a shuddering breath. She hadn't thought of such things in . . . well, forever. A longing so sharp, so intense, pierced through her, making her ache. But she didn't open her eyes. She didn't force the thought away. She could just fantasize for a few moments, couldn't she? Just a few minutes.

The sheets were tangled, the bed a rumpled mess. Sweat clung to their skin. Bare skin. Bare legs intertwined, as tangled as the sheets. Arms locked. Chests touching. Hearts beating in time. Pounding out a steady rhythm. Or maybe the rhythm was created by the even, deep thrusts. One body filling the other, only to pull away and then refill. Delicious friction. A deep, heavy fullness. Muscles tensing with combined pleasure. A sharp gasp. A moan. A relentless rocking toward ecstasy. Each thrust pushing closer to release, toward Heaven. Closer. Closer. Closer.

"Yes, yes! Oh, yes, Killian."

"Oh my God! Poppy."

Poppy flung her arm back over her head, panting. Sweat trickled over her flushed skin. More moisture pooled between her legs, the flesh down there pulsing with her release. She'd fallen asleep and had a dream.

A very, very graphic dream.

She knew she should be embarrassed. Mortified, really. She didn't have sex dreams, but the truth was, she was simply too weak to even muster concern. Her body felt heavy and sated—as if Killian had really been in bed with her, loving her.

Killian gasped, his whole body shaking from the intensity of his dream. A bead of sweat rolled from his temple, slowly down his neck, and even that tortured his overwrought skin.

A dream, he realized as he reached down to press his hand against his waning erection. The organ was still so sensitive, he gasped, imagining what it would feel like to be inside Poppy when he experienced that kind of release.

They both closed their eyes, allowing themselves to float.

It had only been a dream. A delicious, lovely and utterly erotic dream. This time when sleep returned, it was nothing more than engulfing black. Peaceful and warm.

CHAPTER 16

"Poppy?"

Confused, Poppy sat upright, looking around her. She was in her bedroom, her manuscript pages strewn across her duvet cover. Daisy stood in the doorway, her brows drawn together with confused concern.

"Oh, sorry," Poppy said, still feeling heavy and languid. "I must have fallen asleep."

"Are you all right?"

Daisy came closer, her dark eyes worried. Poppy wasn't the type to nap, unless she was sick. And even then, she wouldn't sleep through Daisy's getting home from school. Poppy never liked the idea that Daisy might not come home and no one would know for hours she was missing. Poppy was an unbridled worrywart. Daisy knew that.

"Yes," she reassured her little sister. "I'm fine. Just sleepy."

Daisy sat down on the edge of the bed, her eyes still reading her. Poppy, self-conscious, touched her hair, brushing wisps that clung to her warm skin back from her face.

"You don't look right," Daisy said. "You're all sweaty, and your cheeks are really flushed."

Poppy touched her face. She did feel hot, but she knew that was because of her dream and her own embarrassment.

"I'm fine," Poppy repeated, gathering up her work papers, then crawling off the bed. Her legs quivered as she stood, as if she'd really participated in the act of her dream. Even the sensitive spot between her legs felt different, heavy and moist as if Killian had really . . .

She blushed. But then she cleared her throat and forced a wan smile. "You know, maybe I do feel a little off. I think I'll take a quick shower."

She grabbed her robe off the back of the door and started down the hall toward the bathroom, only to stop when she realized Daisy was following right behind her.

She turned back to her sister, this time regarding Daisy closely.

"Is everything okay with you?" Poppy asked.

Her own residual reaction to her dream and her embarrassment disappeared as soon as she realized Daisy looked—anxious.

Daisy fiddled with her ring, one she always wore: a gold band with a garnet stone, her birthstone. A gift from their mother.

"Nothing's wrong," Daisy said with a smile, but Poppy got the feeling she still wanted to say more.

Poppy raised an eyebrow expectantly. She knew her little sister. Something was on her mind.

Daisy made a *what?* sort of face, but then asked, "So did you do anything today?"

For some reason that wasn't what Poppy had expected her to say. Not that asking Poppy about her day was so out of the ordinary. But there was a strange paradox between Daisy's fidgety body language and the casual—the almost *too* casual way—she asked that just didn't seem normal.

"Why? Should I have done anything?"

Daisy shrugged, again the movement a practice in mild indifference. But not total indifference. The ring was still being twirled. Daisy wanted to know something.

"I did go out to lunch with Killian," Poppy finally offered.

"Killian? Really?"

Around went the ring again. And again.

Oh, there was definitely more to this line of questioning than her sister was revealing. But Poppy simply nodded, waiting to see where Daisy's questions would go now.

"So you really like Killian. I mean as a friend."

"Sure," Poppy said, trying not to think about her other, more-than-friendly reactions to him.

"Did you go somewhere nice? Where did you go?" Daisy asked, her finger moved from her ring to her hair, twirling a strand by her temple. Another nervous habit.

"We went to Smiley's," she said.

"Oh, that's good." Daisy nodded, her expression approving. But Poppy got the distinct feeling it wasn't because Daisy loved the food there. What did Daisy expect to happen today?

Poppy nodded back, deciding maybe the best thing to do was just go take her shower. Maybe she was reading too much into Daisy's behavior.

"Well, I'll be out in a minute."

"Okay," Daisy said, turning to head into to the living room. But then she looked back. "Did anything—you know, interesting happen? At Smiley's, I mean."

Poppy didn't answer right away. What *was* she trying to find out?

"Not really," Poppy said, which wasn't exactly a lie. All the excitement, such as it was, had happened after lunch.

Just briefly her dream replayed through her mind.

"Did you have fun?" Daisy asked.

Poppy shrugged; this time she was the one to play casual. "It was fine. Just lunch."

"Oh, okay," Daisy said, her expectant look fading.

She left then, but Poppy got the distinct feeling her little sister had been disappointed.

"Why are you in bed?"

Killian sat upright, startled out of the warm cocoon he'd been lost in. What the hell?

Then he saw whom the demanding voice belonged to, and all vestiges of anything remotely dreamy fled.

Madison leaned against the doorframe, her arms crossed, her mouth set in its usual disparaging smirk. Emma stood behind her, nothing visible but her round face, huge eyes and pale Shirley Temple curls. It was a bit like a two-headed teen monster.

And neither was the female he'd want to find in his bedroom doorway. At least there was no sign of their ringleader. He supposed that was a small blessing. And they were perhaps better than either the cat or the possessed version of the cat.

"So did you take out Poppy today?" Madison asked, either not aware, or not concerned, with the fact he'd been asleep and wasn't fully awake now.

"I did," he answered, running a hand through his hair, trying to clear his head enough to comprehend what was going on.

"Where?" Madison asked, her tone as staccato and no-nonsense as a drill sergeant's.

He grimaced. He didn't remember, and he didn't want to think about it frankly. He'd been rather enjoying a nice, deep sleep after his highly sensual dream.

Talk about a buzzkill here.

"I don't know. Some coffee place that actually served food. The name didn't match the décor at all. It had good waffles and lots of gilded decorations."

"Smiley's. That is a good place." Emma nodded with approval.

"Well, clearly Poppy chose it," Madison said with her usual disdain.

"How would I choose it? Not from here. From Hell. Remember?" Killian said, irritated with himself that he was even bothering to be defensive.

Madison rolled her eyes. Emma's eyes grew wider, if that was possible. At least one of these girls was smart enough to be unnerved by an aggravated demon.

Small consolation, that.

"So did you find her a guy?"

Killian supposed he should be as pleased that they were as antsy as he was to get this mission done. But answering to sixteen-year-olds didn't please him. At all.

He was quickly learning that teenage girls had one-track minds. And they said it was boys who were the ones prone to that affliction. Well, he was here to tell the world, "Not so."

"There were guys, but do you really want me to pick just anyone?" he said.

Emma shook her head, while Madison spent more time considering the question.

"Shouldn't you just get a feeling or something about who would be the right guy for her? I mean there has to be a reason the spell chose you to come do this. Right?"

He couldn't agree with Madison more, but as of yet, he just didn't see any signs of why he was the chosen one.

"It's going to take a little time," he said. And he wasn't just referring to finding Poppy the right man. He'd have to somehow smooth over things too. But he wasn't about to tell the teenage harpies he had to re-befriend Poppy. Yet again.

"I'm working on it," he said instead.

"Not if you're sleeping," Madison pointed out.

Killian gritted his teeth.

"I'm working on it," he repeated, this time his voice low, taking on a growling quality.

A little of his demon showing.

Madison stepped back, bumping into Emma. Both girls looked stunned, scared. And Killian would like to say he felt bad, but at this moment—nope, he didn't.

Then Madison rallied, although he noted she didn't step back to her original position in the doorway proper.

"You aren't taking your time on this because you've got a thing for Poppy, are you?"

"Oh, hell no." All bodily reactions and dreams to the contrary, but they didn't need to know that.

"Okay. Just—just making sure."

The two girls turned then and hurried through the apartment. He heard the door slam moments later.

Killian stared at the door, not totally sure what the girls had wanted from that conversation. Was it to see if he was doing his job? Or to see what his intentions were concerning Poppy? After that dream, he wasn't sure about either one himself.

With a sigh, he swung his legs over the bed, only to snatch them back up just as a grayish paw shot out and curled toward his foot, sharp claws extended. The paw fished around a few seconds longer, then disappeared back under the bed.

"Damn beast," he muttered. The girls must have let the evil cat in when they opened the bedroom door. With another sigh, he vaulted away from the bed. Then he grabbed the bags with his new clothes and toiletries and headed to the bathroom, making sure the door was tightly closed behind him.

But just as he began to rinse his sudsy hair, he heard the bathroom door rattle. He pulled back the shower curtain, blinking through soap bubbles.

The knob rattled again. Great. Now the teen queens were attempting to interrupt his shower. Was there no privacy?

"Go away!" he shouted. "You can grill me more once I'm done."

He slammed the curtain closed and returned to the hot spray.

"I do rather like that one girl," a distinctly male voice said from just outside the bathtub.

Killian whipped back the curtain to find the cat sitting on the closed toilet lid.

"You know, the one with all the attitude. The Kewpie-doll blonde I could do without, though."

"Vepar," Killian muttered. "I find it hard to believe you don't have better things to do than possess a cat and pester me."

"I'm just checking to see if you are on task. Satan is getting testier by the minute."

Killian stepped out of the shower, unconcerned with his nakedness. "I'm working on it." Not as expediently as he could, but he was working.

"In the way that girl said? By falling for this mortal yourself?"

"Hardly," Killian said, reaching for a towel. "And do you mind—?" He gestured to his nakedness.

Vepar curled back the cat's lip in disdain.

"Hmm, I hope for your sake that's true. And I'm serious, you better speed this up. Or else," his coworker hissed.

Vepar disappeared again, leaving him yet again with the psycho beast. Killian wasted little time escaping the bathroom. He had too many important parts bared to risk another attack.

As he dressed, he realized, as much as he hated it, Vepar had a point. Between his awareness of Poppy, the erotic dreams, the beleaguering teen girls, the fusty floral apartment and the sometimes possessed, always evil cat, it was really time to get down to business.

Mission *Boyfriend for Poppy* was officially on. Whether Poppy liked it or not.

Whether he liked it or not.

Something terrible occurred to Poppy as she showered. What if Daisy had somehow set up Killian to ask her out? Her little sister had mentioned more than a few times over the past couple years that she thought Poppy should be dating. Daisy worried that when she went off to college in the next two years, Poppy would end up living alone.

"You'll be a crazy cat lady," she'd say.

"I'm allergic to cats," Poppy had pointed out, but her little jokes never convinced Daisy that Poppy wouldn't end up alone. Without even a cat.

That was it, Poppy realized, toweling off. Her little sister was playing matchmaker. And her chosen match was Killian, of all people.

Poppy pulled on her robe and headed to her bedroom. So her sister wanted to see her date Killian. Odd choice, but she supposed Daisy wasn't immune to Killian's amazing looks either. But that match wasn't going to happen.

And Daisy had to get that crazy notion out of her head. She considered telling her little sister just that. No. She didn't want to hurt or embarrass her sister. But she did need to nip this cockamamie idea in the bud.

Then the obvious solution came to her. Poppy would help Killian find a girlfriend.

If he was involved with someone else, Daisy would give up this silly plot. And Poppy would stop having dreams like she'd had today. After all, she was not going to be interested in an attached man.

So that was it. She'd play matchmaker herself.

Feeling better and more in control, she found a comfy T-shirt and jeans to put on and, as she dressed, she found herself smiling. Still she supposed it was rather flattering that Daisy thought Killian could be interested in her. But she ignored the warm tingle that idea sent through her.

"Well, we have one good thing here," Madison reported to Daisy, when they had assembled in the basement laundry room, a place they often went if all the authority figures were home. "Killian is not in the least bit interested in your sister. I asked him outright, and he acted like it was the craziest thing he'd ever heard."

Daisy lifted herself up onto one of the top-load washers, and nodded her head. "Yeah, Poppy isn't at all into Killian either. She acts like she barely notices him. So that is one thing we don't have to worry about."

"But I don't think we're making any headway on this boyfriend thing either," Madison said.

"No, Poppy sounded like the whole outing was pretty dull. Not that I think she'd tell me right away if she met someone. But I'm sure I would know."

"You would," Emma agreed. "She'd have a sparkle in her eyes. Or a secret little smile that only she understood."

"You gotta lay off the romance novels, babe," Madison said.

Emma made a face.

"No, I agree with her," Daisy said, referring to Emma. Although Emma did read an abundance of romance novels. Usually ones lifted from her mother's bedroom bookshelves.

Still, Emma gave Madison a *so-there* look, then said, "I think Killian has a point. He can't rush something like this. You don't want Poppy just dating any old guy. He has to be special. Isn't that the point?"

Daisy nodded. "Definitely."

She wanted her sister to find her soul mate, if that was possible. Could a demon find that for her? He did deal in souls, right? Of course, not exactly like this.

"Maybe we need to help him out," Emma suggested. "You know, tell him places where men she might like would hang out."

"That is a good idea," Daisy said.

Even Madison nodded.

Apparently, this wasn't going to be as simple as the *Jenny Bell* book made it sound. Their demon clearly needed a little direction.

CHAPTER 17

"What are you doing?"

Daisy peered over Poppy's shoulder, surprised. She wasn't surprised that Poppy was already up. Or reading the newspaper while sipping her morning coffee. Her older sister did that every morning.

It was the section of the paper that had Daisy taken aback.

Poppy was reading the "Things To Do" section of the *Boston Globe*. Even that wouldn't be terribly stunning, except instead of reading the family-related events—her usual points of interest—she was reading the "Nightlife" and "Singles" sections.

That implied that she might be planning to do something a normal single woman might do—like go out. Weird.

Maybe they wouldn't need to direct Killian, after all. Maybe Poppy was finally seeing she did need to get a life outside her little sister, her work and this apartment.

Daisy grabbed a box of Mini-Wheats, along with a bowl and a spoon, and seated herself beside Poppy so she could sneak peeks at what she was reading.

"I'm just seeing what's going on in the singles world," Poppy said with a smile.

This was amazing. Poppy was actually admitting she needed to go someplace where real, live, single men were?

Maybe this spell was working differently from how Daisy had expected.

Maybe Killian was just supposed to nudge her in some way so that she decided she herself wanted to date. Which, when Daisy thought about it, was probably a far better idea than letting a demon choose a boyfriend for her.

Daisy finished pouring her cereal and added milk.

"I've decided to help Killian find a romantic interest."

A little milk sloshed over the edge of her bowl as Daisy looked at her sister. Poppy's attention remained on the newspaper.

So that was it. She'd decided to help Killian with his earlier claim that he wanted to settle down. A wave of disappointment splashed over Daisy like the milk on the tabletop.

Oh, well. What was that old saying about spilled milk? If Poppy's matchmaking plan got her out—and meeting people too—then it worked for Daisy.

Poppy picked up one of the red pencils she used for editing and circled an event. Leave it to Poppy to be all systematic about her matchmaking. No wild schemes like conjuring a demon for her big sis.

"So what do you see?" Daisy asked, her mouth full of cereal.

"Well, there are a few interesting singles events this weekend. One is a speed-dating thing on Friday. And there's a singles dance on Saturday."

Daisy leaned in to look closer. "What about for tonight?"

Poppy searched. "There's a ladies' night at O'Malley's. That's just down the street. Oh, and there is a mixer at the Roger Klein Gallery Thursday night. From six p.m. to nine p.m. That might be good."

She circled both.

"You should go to those," Daisy said.

Poppy nodded. "The art gallery would probably be a good place for him to meet the type of women he's interested in."

"And you love art too," Daisy pointed out.

"Oh, I wouldn't go." She laughed as if the idea was the most preposterous thing she'd ever heard.

"Why not?"

"Well, for one thing, it's a school night."

"Not for you."

Poppy laughed. "True. But for you. And I don't go out while you're here at home, alone."

Daisy's hopes sank. Poppy was searching for events for Killian to attend. Without her.

Really, Poppy? Did you have to make everything so darned difficult?

"He won't go alone," Daisy said with total authority.

Poppy frowned at her sister. How could she be so certain of that? What did Daisy know about Killian anyway?

But she still found herself asking, "Why not?"

Daisy shrugged. "He just doesn't seem like the type."

What type was that? But instead of asking, Poppy said, "Well, then Ginger can go with him."

"You know Madison's mom. If she has a night off, she doesn't like to go out."

That was true. Ginger worked so much she didn't like to miss any free time she did have with Madison.

"Well, then you can understand how I feel about leaving you alone."

"You're with me all the time."

Poppy reached over and tugged Daisy's ponytail. "I like being with you."

Daisy smiled. "I like it too. But—"

Here came another of her sister's speeches on Poppy's ending up an old maid. And frankly, Poppy did not want to hear it. Not this morning, while she was imagining Killian with a stunning, interesting girlfriend. The image of Poppy old and alone was too easy to visualize at the moment.

"You know, I'll just give him this section of the paper," she said, cutting Daisy off with a smile, "and if he sees something he wants to check out, I'm sure he will."

Daisy looked like she wanted to argue, but she turned her attention back to her cereal.

"In fact," Poppy said, circling another event, "I'll walk down with you and give this to him."

"Walk down with me?"

"Sure, you are going to meet Madison, right?" Daisy always did.

"Yes. But—but I doubt Killian will be up yet. He's a night owl. You know, because of being a paranormal investigator."

"Was he investigating last night?"

Daisy nodded.

Poppy was surprised by that idea, which made no sense. He was here to do research, and he hardly had to report his goings-on to her.

"Well, I can always give it to Ginger."

"She might be sleeping too."

Poppy regarded her sister for a moment, realizing Daisy must be throwing out all these reasons why Poppy couldn't possibly give Killian this paper because she still harbored hopes of matchmaking the two of them.

Poppy offered her sister an indulgent smile, but said, "I'll walk down with you anyway. Just to see."

Daisy looked like she still wanted to argue, but then nodded. "Okay, but I've got to get some stuff together before we go down there."

She was immediately on her feet and practically dashing through the apartment to her bedroom.

Poppy frowned, puzzled by her sister's abrupt departure. She shrugged it off. Teens were nothing if not confusing.

A noise stirred Killian. A faint, repeated tapping. He ignored the sound, telling himself it was probably the pipes rattling . . . or the radiators knocking somewhere in the build-ing.

Then he heard another noise. A faint voice. At least he thought it was a voice. He levered himself up on his elbows to look at the bedroom door. It was still closed.

Then he heard the sounds again. A hesitant knock fol-lowed by a weak, "Mr. Killian."

He got up and reached for his jeans, tugging them on. Then he strode across the room, yanking the door open.

Emma squeaked in surprise, backing away several steps. Killian glowered at her. Did these girls just have a thing for waking him up?

Clearly, his disgruntled expression didn't help Emma's nerves. She gasped for breath like a beached fish. Great, all he needed was a hyperventilating teen on his hands.

"What is it, Emma?" He kept his voice low and calm. He also stopped glaring—well, as best as he could.

His demeanor seemed to help. After several more deep breaths, she managed to say, "Sorry to wake you up. But Daisy just texted me. Poppy's going with her to Madison's."

Killian shook his head, not following.

Then words started tumbling from the girl like a verbal flash flood.

"She's going to Madison's. Your pretend cousin's apart-ment. So you should be there. But you can't be there because Madison's mother is home this morning. And you're not really her cousin. But Poppy can't know that. So you have to cut her off. Somehow. But I'm not sure—"

Killian raised a hand to stop her. The poor girl was a mess—and in serious threat of brain damage due to lack of oxygen.

"I'll get dressed."

Emma nodded, her expression thankful that he'd some-how followed her panicked explanation.

He rushed back to the bedroom, pulling out one of the shirts from yesterday's shopping trip. Without fully unbuttoning it, he tugged it on over his head, then strode back to Emma.

They needed to hurry. If Poppy discovered he wasn't really Madison's cousin, then he might very well be stuck in this place for good. If Poppy found out everything she'd been told thus far was an elaborate lie, she'd likely never talk to him again.

As he followed Emma, he didn't allow himself to ponder why the second of those concerns seemed to bother him more than the first.

"Wait. I've got something in my shoe."

Poppy turned to see Daisy drop to the hallway floor and pull off her black oxford.

"Come on, Daisy. You are going to be late if you don't get moving."

"I know," her sister said, but continued to fiddle with the insole of her shoe. She tried it on, then shook her head and off it came again.

Since they'd left the apartment, this was Daisy's third stop. First she'd decided she'd forgotten her apartment key. That holdup hadn't seemed out of the ordinary, though. Daisy did forget her key a lot. But after taking everything out of her book bag, she'd realized the key was around her neck, on a cord Poppy had bought her for just that reason.

Next, she'd had to stop because her shoe was untied, which for some unknown reason required her to almost totally unlace her shoe, so it could be relaced and finally tied.

And now this problem.

Poppy tapped the folded newspaper against her leg, watching as Daisy continued to fiddle with the shoe.

But before she could hurry her along, a chime sounded

from Daisy's backpack, announcing an incoming text message. Daisy dropped the shoe and fumbled in the side pocket of her bag for her phone. Funny, she could always find that.

"Daisy! You don't have time—"

Her sister lifted a finger, silently telling her to wait just a second as she read the text.

"It's just Madison checking to see where I am."

Poppy smacked the paper impatiently against her leg again. "I wouldn't wonder."

Daisy, the girl who'd done nothing but dawdle this morning, shoved her foot back into her shoe, grabbed her backpack, rose and then practically speed-walked toward Madison's apartment.

Poppy followed, shaking her head, totally not understanding what her little sister was doing this morning.

When they reached Madison's apartment, both she and Emma waited outside.

"There you are," Madison called much louder than necessary.

"Yes, I'm finally here," Daisy said, her voice just as loud.

But before Poppy could ask them why on earth they were talking that way, the door behind Madison opened, and Killian appeared. He was barefoot, clad in a pair of the jeans he'd purchased yesterday and a pale blue shirt with the same cut as the white one. Half the buttons had been left undone, revealing a glimpse of muscular chest. His hair was unruly from sleep, and a night's worth of facial hair darkened his chin. He'd clearly just tumbled out of bed.

Poppy swallowed, willing her gaze elsewhere, then forcing herself not to recall her erotic dream.

"I thought I heard someone out here," he said, glancing over his shoulder, then shutting the door firmly behind him.

"I think most of this floor heard someone out here," Poppy said, giving the girls a searching look.

"Sorry," Daisy said, keeping her voice to a near whisper now. "See you tonight."

Without waiting for an answer, the girls hurried toward the elevators.

Poppy frowned, watching them scamper away, still feeling like something had gone on here that she didn't understand.

"Come on," Killian said, gesturing down the hallway toward her apartment. "Gin . . . ger is still asleep, and I don't want to wake her."

"I think you might be too late," she said, but followed him down the hall. He smiled over his shoulder at her, and she tried not to give any credence to the strange flutter in her chest.

It's nothing. Nothing.

Once around the corner from Ginger's place, he stopped and pointed to her hand. "What's that?"

Poppy glanced down, confused. Then she saw the reason she'd come here in the first place.

"Oh, this is for you." She handed the paper to him. "It's a list of singles events going on in the area. I thought, since you are interested in meeting someone, this might be a good idea for you."

He scanned the ads, then nodded. "This is a good idea."

She smiled, although the gesture felt forced, and she couldn't understand why. Wasn't this her plan? Didn't she want him to be involved with someone so she could get her silly attraction to him under control?

"There's one tonight." He glanced up from the paper. Her eyes met his and held. As if to make a point—a point she could have done without—her body reacted. His golden gaze was like a physical touch, reaching out, stroking her skin. Making her body hum with awareness. With longing.

She managed a nod. "Yes, I saw that."

Duh, she was the one who circled it, after all.

"Great. I'll pick you up at seven."

CHAPTER 18

Killian started walking away, hoping it was going to be that easy. No such luck.

"Wait," she said, before he was even a few steps away. "What? Seven?"

He turned back to her, and she shook her head. "I'm not going with you."

He returned to stand in front of her again. "You've got to go with me."

"Why?"

He frowned as if the answer should be totally obvious. Not that he expected the look to sway her. But he needed to buy himself a moment, because he didn't have an answer to that one either.

Finally, after another I-should-think-this-would-be-evident look, he said, "If I go alone, then I'm that creepy guy, hanging at the bar, sipping the same watered-down drink, watching women. Making them uncomfortable."

"I doubt any woman would feel that way about you," she said, although her expression didn't indicate whether that was a compliment or not.

"Really?"

If he was hoping for an outright compliment—which he was—she wasn't biting.

"Why don't you ask Ginger? I'm sure she'd go with you."

"You know Ginger," he said, hoping that was vague enough to make sense to her. Since he didn't know Ginger at all.

Poppy sighed. "Yeah, I know she doesn't like to go out when she has time with Madison."

"Exactly."

Poppy looked down at the floor, tracing the carpet design with a sock-covered toe. Finally, she said, "I don't see how having another woman with you is going to help you meet women."

Well, that wouldn't be his strategy if he was really looking to meet women, but he wasn't, so . . . "The women will see me hanging with a female friend and just assume I must be a good guy," he said.

Poppy's eyebrows drew together. "How will they know I'm only a friend?"

"They just will." As soon as the words were out of his mouth, he realized they were pretty insulting. But did that matter? She wasn't going to be with him. She was going to meet someone herself. That was the goal.

Eye on the goal.

They would just know.

Poppy told herself not to be offended. After all, she didn't want to be seen as his girlfriend. She didn't want to go at all.

"I can't go," she told him, starting to move away from him. She needed to get away. She didn't like where any of her thoughts and feelings were going at the moment.

"Well," he said with a big sigh, "I guess if you won't go, I won't either."

No! That wasn't good. She needed this man to be involved with someone for her own sanity.

She paused, struggling with the urge to growl in frustration. But instead she said, "Fine, I'll go."

Killian smiled. A breathtaking, stunningly beautiful smile.

Oh, she so needed him otherwise involved, and a night out was hardly a huge sacrifice to see that happen. Like it would take him more than a night to find a woman.

"See you at seven," he said again, and headed down the hall. She watched him leave, then hurried back to her apartment.

Once inside, she told herself to force all thoughts of Killian and tonight out of her head. She had work to do.

Without further thought, she went to the kitchen and filled her favorite oversize mug with coffee. She added her usual abundance of cream and sugar.

Mug in hand, she went to her desk. She sat down and set the cup to her right within easy reach. Then she tidied up the chapters still askew from her attempt to work in bed. The papers clacked on the desktop as she lined up the edges, then she placed them directly in front of her. She lined up her red pencils. She liked to have three of them. That way if the tip broke, or got dull, she didn't have to stop to sharpen it. She just reached for another.

With everything situated, she could now work. And not think about—anything else.

She took a sip of her coffee, picked up her pencil, then focused on the last portion of the manuscript she'd read, *Title Risk and Insurable Interests.*

She tossed down the pencil.

Really! How could he be so darned certain she'd be only seen as his friend by other women? Was she not attractive enough to be his girlfriend? Not interesting enough? Did they really look so unlikely to be together?

Okay, she knew that she wasn't his usual style. She looked down at her baggy, ripped jeans. Jeans she wore because she worked at home, and what was the point of getting all dressed up to sit at a desk in her own place? They were comfy. And her shirt—she grimaced slightly as she realized that she was wearing her vintage Atari T-shirt—which was admittedly a little geeky. But she'd had the tee for years. Adam had been into vintage video games, so she'd bought it because she knew he'd like it.

She sighed. Okay, maybe she should part with this particular shirt. But overall her clothing was practical for her life. And she didn't have a life that merited designer clothes.

Then she touched her hair, knotted on top of her head in her usual messy bun. But again, that was just sensible. She hated her long hair getting in her face when she worked.

And makeup. Well, there was no point at all in bothering with that.

So she didn't sport the female equivalent of his style. But would a whole room of women honestly rule her out as his girlfriend?

She groaned at herself. Why did it matter? He was attractive, so she was naturally attracted to him, but she didn't want him.

"He's arrogant. Just look at the 'friends' comment. And he's shallow. Look at how Old Navy threw him. And he can be totally rude."

And you, my friend, are totally talking to yourself.

She was willing to bet crazy cat ladies always talked to themselves. She grimaced. Maybe Daisy had a valid reason for concern. Maybe she did need to get out there and meet people. Maybe half her reason for being so attracted to Killian was because he was actually the first man she'd done something with since . . . well, in a really long time.

Maybe tonight was the perfect time for her to meet some single men too. It certainly wouldn't hurt her to mingle with them. To remember how to be comfortable around them. Then she wouldn't focus all of her thoughts on a man who was so not *her* type. Yeah, why was she worried about being his type? He wasn't hers.

"And we'll see who's mistaken for the friend."

*   *   *

Poppy came out of her bedroom, tugging on the form-fitting turtleneck sweater. Now she remembered why it had sat in her dresser, unworn, for so long.

"Wow, you look great."

Poppy looked up from frowning down at the snug garment.

"You really think so?"

"Trés chic," Daisy said, and Poppy noticed her sister was working on her French homework.

"Nice." But Poppy did smile. Daisy went back to conjugating *obliger*—to make someone do something. Which seemed apropos, although Poppy had no idea who was making whom go on this outing tonight.

Or what had made her decide to wear these clothes. She also wore a new pair of jeans, which just reminded her why she loved her old, worn ones. She felt more like a trussed chicken than a fashionista.

"Don't look so miserable," Daisy said. "You look fabulous."

Poppy appreciated her sister's compliments, but somehow they made her want to back out of this whole night even more. What if Daisy was just being kind and she looked . . . well, silly?

"Are you sure you are okay with me going out?"

"I'm fine," Daisy said, shaking her head as if she knew Poppy was looking for an excuse to stay home.

A knock rattled the door, startling Poppy. She hesitated, tugging at her sweater again.

"Go answer the door," Daisy told her with an encouraging smile.

Poppy nodded, then strode down that hallway in a pair of boots she'd only worn once, the heels clacking on the hardwood with an assertiveness she didn't feel. Taking a calming breath, she opened the door.

Killian stood on the other side, looking like he had just walked off the set of a modeling shoot. He just wore jeans and the white shirt from yesterday, but he still managed to look stunning. His hair was still a little damp from his shower, flipping at the ends in an attractively tousled way. And he'd shaved, leaving only a patch of hair under his lower lip. The look accentuated his sculpted lips and added a little edginess to his beauty. He looked sexy and naughty and . . .

She was staring.

Her eyes moved up to meet his, only to discover he was doing his own inventory of her. His golden gaze roamed over her until she had to brace her muscles to stop the shiver his heated perusal created.

"You look fantastic." His voice was low, velvety and so sexy.

She pulled in another breath, losing herself to a shiver. "You too."

He smiled then, and her limbs turned to jelly.

It was the lack of oxygen from her tight clothing, she told herself. But then she managed to get enough to her brain to invite him in.

Killian told himself to stop staring, but as he followed Poppy down the hall, his eyes were locked on her. Or more accurately, at this moment, her rear end.

The jeans she wore were dyed dark blue and fit her to a tee, the material emphasizing her legs and the curve of her perfect little butt.

When they reached the living room, he managed to tear his stare away, but he wasn't certain it was before Daisy noticed the direction of his look.

She gave him a glance he couldn't quite read, but then smiled. "You two look ready for a fun night."

Killian nodded, not that he was sure what this night would be like. As he glanced back over to Poppy, he knew with her looking like that, he wasn't going to have any trouble finding her a boyfriend.

"Daisy, really, if you are nervous being alone, I can stay home."

Killian could hear an almost pleading quality in Poppy's voice, but he knew she was begging the wrong person. Daisy was a girl with a mission.

"I'm almost sixteen, Poppy. I will be fine. And if I need anything I can go to Madison's or Emma's or any of the neighbors'. Plus, I could just call you. You'll only be a couple blocks away."

Poppy nodded, but she was noticeably disappointed. "I know." Then she seemed to brace herself as if she was getting ready to go get a root canal rather than going out to a ladies' night.

"Let me just get my coat." She disappeared from the room.

As soon as she was gone, Daisy set her schoolbook aside and scooted across the couch to get closer to him.

"I think your plan is a good one," she whispered.

Killian frowned and shook his head, not sure what plan she was referring to.

"That you are taking your time finding her a guy," Daisy said. "She hasn't been with anyone since her last boyfriend. She really thought he was the one. But he wasn't all that."

Rather than making him feel good, Daisy's comment bothered Killian. Poppy was still pining for her ex. The guy didn't deserve that kind of mourning as far as Killian was concerned.

Apparently, Daisy felt the same. "Adam was a musician, and he thought he was so cool, but he was really just a pretentious jerk. He really, really hurt her."

Poppy hadn't said that when she'd spoken of him, but he'd gotten that impression anyway.

"This time, I want her to have someone really good for

her. Someone who will treat her the way she deserves. Someone perfect."

Killian nodded, although he didn't know anything about perfect. Perfection wasn't what got people into his world. Imperfection, shortcomings and failings were what he understood.

But if Mr. Perfect was out there, then Poppy deserved him.

As if on cue, Poppy walked back into the room. She'd added a tailored gray peacoat and a red-gray-and-black plaid scarf to her outfit.

The combination of colors made her skin look as flawless and pale as a china doll's. Her eyes looked dark and soulful. Her brown hair was down, glossy and straight. She looked . . . ethereal . . . he pulled in a slow breath. Maybe perfection did exist, he realized.

"Ready?" she said.

He straightened. "Yes."

Daisy rose from the sofa to follow them to the door.

After they stepped out into the hallway, Poppy turned back, mouth open, but Daisy cut her off, "I'm fine. Go have fun. And don't worry."

Poppy hesitated, then nodded, but she couldn't contain one last maternal worry.

"Make sure you lock the door."

Daisy rolled her eyes but smiled. "I will."

Killian didn't move once the door closed, knowing Poppy wouldn't leave until she heard the dead bolt click into place.

It did, and he placed a hand on her arm. She started at the touch, but didn't pull away.

"Ready to do this?" he asked

She nodded, but he had no doubt she wanted to say, "no." Instead, she said nothing as they made their way out of the building.

Once on the sidewalk, he looked up and down the street. "Which way are we headed?"

"This way." She pointed to the right, and they fell into step, although he noticed he had to modify his stride more than usual. For the boots, he realized, as he watched her picking her way around the cracks in the pavement. They looked great on her, but clearly they weren't comfortable.

"So what exactly happens at a 'ladies' night?' " he asked, deciding maybe taking her mind off her feet might help.

She glanced at him, surprise clear in her eyes. "You've never been to a ladies' night at a bar?"

He shrugged. "Maybe, but I wasn't aware of it if I was."

"Well—" She glanced at him again, but her thought was cut short as her heel slipped in a crack and her ankle twisted. Instantly, Killian caught her, catching most of her weight before it could land on the turned ankle.

She clung to his arm, accepting his help. That was until she was able to balance herself. Then she dropped her hands from him.

"Sorry," she said, her cheeks flushed. "This is why I wear sneakers. I can't even manage three-inch heels."

"I couldn't either," he assured her. Then he offered his elbow. She stared at his proffered arm as if it were a snake ready to strike. But after a moment, she looped her arm through his.

At least his touch was better than a twisted or broken ankle. The lesser of two evils, as they say.

"So," he said once they started walking again, her body much closer than before. He could feel her heat and smell something deliciously spicy like cinnamon on her skin, "You were going to tell me what happens at a ladies' night."

She didn't answer for a moment.

"Well, I haven't been to a bar for years," she said. "But usually they have half-price drinks for the ladies. No cover charge for them if there's a band. Maybe some discounts on food."

"And that's enough to draw in women?"

Poppy actually found herself laughing at his dry query. Which surprised her, because she was altogether too aware of him being so close. Her shoulder brushed his arm as they walked. Their arms entwined. Her fingers rested on his forearm.

"It isn't the discounts that lures them in," she said. "It's the hope of meeting someone like you."

"Me?"

"A hot, single guy looking for a real relationship," Poppy said, then realized she'd said too much. And Killian didn't miss it.

"So I'm hot, huh?"

Like he ever doubted it, but she was saved from having to answer. "We're here."

She gestured to the bar, which appeared to be relatively busy. Not packed, but then it was early yet. As she recalled from her younger days, things didn't really get hopping at the bars until after nine or so. She dropped her arm away from his, walked into the small courtyard area where café tables and chairs were set up in the warmer months.

But before she reached the concrete steps that led up to the entrance, Killian's hand was back, cupping her elbow.

She glanced at his hand, raising an eyebrow. "I'm just going up some steps, I should be fine."

He smiled. "Better safe than sorry, right?"

"But aren't you afraid we'll be mistaken for a couple?" Then she stopped and gave him a pointed look. "Wait, you said no one would make that mistake, didn't you?"

CHAPTER 19

Why had she said that? Her comment sounded petty and jealous. Or worse yet, like some sort of challenge.

But it was out now, so all she could do was focus on why they were here. Finding him a woman. And maybe—maybe, chatting with a few men herself.

She looked around the pub, surveying the place. She'd walked by many times, but had never been inside. The atmosphere was quaint with brick walls and molded tin ceilings. A long bar made of glossy stained wood took up most of one wall. There were tables and chairs littering the rest of the room. At the far end was a spot for a band to play.

But the only music was from a CD jukebox mounted on the wall in the far corner.

And there was one thing there was no shortage of—women.

A large table surrounded by women was centered in the middle of the pub. And they had already spotted Killian, eyeing him like predators stalking their prey, hopeful and hungry.

Several leaned closer to say something, clearly about him. Then they smiled, white teeth and glossed lips glistening in the low light.

Poppy knew this was why he was here, why she was here with him, but she still found the ladies rather disturbing.

She glanced at him and found he was looking around, seemingly oblivious to the stir he was causing.

Then he touched her arm.

"Table or bar?"

Poppy blinked. He really hadn't even noticed the pack of women licking their chops and getting ready to bring him down like a felled buck.

"Umm . . ." she said, noticing that the nearest empty table was dangerously close to the women.

"There are two seats right there." She pointed to a couple of vacant stools at the end of the bar. "How about the bar?"

They would be a safe distance away from the waiting vultures.

He nodded and led her toward them. This time, he placed his hand on the small of her back, and even though she wore her jacket, she would swear she could feel the heat of his hand.

Imagination, she told herself, even as she shivered from the sensation.

"Cold?"

Not at all, but she nodded. "A little."

Relief flooded her as she slid onto the barstool and away from his touch.

A bartender appeared.

Killian gestured for her to order first.

She was usually more of a coffee and tea drinker, but she did have the occasional wine with dinner. And tonight seemed like a good time for wine too. If she was going to have to watch scads of women vie for Killian's attention, then she needed something to take the edge off.

"A pinot noir."

The bartender listed a few brands.

"The first one," Poppy said with a slightly embarrassed smile.

"And I'll try the pale ale," Killian said. He smiled when the bartender left. "Not a wine aficionado, huh?"

She smiled back, still feeling a little self-conscious. "Not really. I usually buy whatever wine has the prettiest or most interesting label."

Killian chuckled, the sound rich and low. An amazing laugh.

"Yeah, I don't know much about wine myself. I'm more of a scotch drinker."

"Scotch—" She shuddered. "Now that I couldn't handle at all."

He laughed again, and Poppy was willing to bet the women at the table behind them would swoon at the sound of it. Poppy certainly felt a little light-headed.

And then there was his smile. *No!* This was exactly why she was here. So he could find someone, and she could forget how amazing his smile was.

The bartender returned with their drinks, and she took a large gulp of the wine. Not her usual way of enjoying a glass of vino, but her nerves were already frayed. And they just got here.

"So, I think you have your pick tonight," she said, turning on her stool to face the rest of the room. He did the same.

"Mmm," he answered, but she couldn't tell if he was impressed with the selection or not.

Then she remembered his aversion to blondes. Well, four of the ten were out of the running right off the top. And one had light brown hair with highlights, so Poppy wasn't sure if she'd make the cut or not.

They were all pretty, though. And well dressed. Well, one of the brunettes was wearing something that looked a little trashy and desperate in Poppy's opinion, but maybe Killian liked that look.

Poppy slid him a glance to see which one captured his attention, but he wasn't looking at the table. He perused the bar instead.

Maybe none of the women were to his liking, which was too bad, because they were very much liking him. A couple of them stretched their necks like turtles, trying to catch his eye.

"Excuse me."

Poppy looked over to see that a woman had come up on the other side of Killian. A sneak attack like a gator lunging out of the water to pull down a drinking deer.

Okay, maybe her animal analogies were getting a little out of control, but Killian was causing quite the reaction and the women here were definitely on the prowl.

The woman beside Killian was pretty. Prettier than a gator, to be sure. About the same age as Poppy with long, wavy hair. Auburn, which was good. Gray-green eyes. A black wrap dress that was sexy and stylish at the same time.

Poppy suddenly felt a bit frumpy in her sweater and jeans. But at least she wasn't wearing one of her T-shirts.

"I'm sorry to interrupt, but you look so familiar to me."

She smiled to reveal perfectly white teeth. Definitely bonded. And as far as pickup lines went, well . . .

"Sorry," Killian said, offering the woman a quick, impersonal smile. "I'm sure we haven't met."

She pursed her mauve-painted lips, thinking. "I was sure we had. Are you from around here?"

He shook his head. "No."

Poppy had to admit she was enjoying this. Killian must not be interested in this one, because he definitely wasn't giving her the reception she wanted. Unless he didn't realize that he could have said they'd met on the moon, and this woman would have gone along with it.

The woman tilted her head, batting her eyes. "I just know I've seen you somewhere before."

Killian opened his mouth, and from the look on his face, Poppy suspected his next comment wasn't going to be even as polite as his last ones. So Poppy spoke first.

"You probably recognize him from television."

The woman's eyes widened with dawning excitement, acknowledging Poppy for the first time.

"Television?" she said, her attention coming right back to Killian.

Killian was paying total attention to Poppy. He narrowed his eyes at her before the woman began her barrage of questions.

"What do you do on TV? Do you have your own show? Have you been in movies?"

Killian shook his head. "I'm not really—"

"He's not really one to brag," Poppy finished for him. "He's got his own show about the paranormal. He's a paranormal investigator."

The woman raised her perfectly tweezed brows. "Really? That's such an interesting job."

"Isn't it?" Poppy agreed.

Killian shot Poppy an aggravated scowl. Poppy smiled back.

Oh, Poppy was enjoying this way too much.

Killian glared at her, and her smile only widened. That cute little dimple in her left cheek appeared. Some of his irritation faded. She really was lovely. Pale skin, those dark eyes that drew him in. And that smile. That impish smile.

"Tell her about your research, Killian," she said, her eyes sparkling like dark smoky quartz.

He narrowed a glare at her again, then turned back to the redhead beside him. Really, the woman was quite attractive. She definitely filled out her clothing perfectly with ample breasts and flared hips.

But as he looked at her, he found himself thinking about smaller breasts and subtler curves.

Damn it. He was doing it again. He could not be attracted to Poppy.

Yet he couldn't stop himself from glancing at her again. She still grinned, clearly amused by his discomfort at dealing with this woman.

Well, maybe he should show her. Would she be so amused if he turned all his attention to Jessica Rabbit here?

"I am in Boston to research places where there are reputed hauntings. For a television show I'm developing."

The redhead nodded, her grayish-green eyes wide with interest.

"That's exciting."

"Yes," he said. "I had a show that was very popular in Sweden. It was one of the top-rated shows every week it aired."

"Really? And you are from Sweden?"

He nodded. *"Ja."*

Quickly the conversation with the redhead took off, although he was only half aware of what she was saying. The other half was fully attuned to Poppy.

Poppy sat listening and, at first, he didn't think she was bothered by the interaction between them. But gradually, he noticed Poppy start to fidget. Her foot tapped on one of the rungs of the stool. She looked around. She checked her cell phone. Once he thought he heard her sigh.

Finally, she interrupted them.

"I'm running to the restroom. Would you mind ordering me another pinot noir?"

Killian nodded, acting as if he could barely drag himself away from the redhead's scintillating conversation.

But as Poppy slid off the stool and started toward the back of the bar, he couldn't stop himself from watching her. The subtle, lissome sway of her hips, the delicious curve of her backside.

His body reacted, and he had to shift on his seat.

"So is she a friend?" the redhead asked, the question almost comical given what he was feeling at the moment.

He looked back to the woman. "Yes. She is."

The woman, whom he thought was named Lisa. Maybe Liza. Liz? Whatever her name was, she smiled.

"Well, she's a lucky woman to have a friend like you."

Killian frowned. What did that even mean?

He glanced toward the back of the bar. Poppy was gone.

He suddenly wondered why he'd been bothering to talk to this woman. To make Poppy jealous? That wasn't the goal of the night.

Right now, he just wanted to get rid of this woman.

"Actually," he found himself saying to the redhead, "Poppy is my girlfriend."

"She is?" The woman didn't look convinced.

"Yes."

The redhead placed a hand on her hip. "A man like you? With a mousy little thing like her?"

Killian stared at the woman, stunned by her tactlessness. Which was something, given whom she was talking to.

He didn't even hesitate.

Go away. And don't come back.

The woman blinked, but then mumbled some reason to excuse herself, although she clearly didn't understand why she was doing so.

Killian nodded, then turned back to the bar before she had even walked away.

Good riddance. He was here for Poppy. And he would stay focused on his task from now on.

* * *

Poppy walked into the women's room, fighting the urge to kick the door of one of the bathroom stalls. Why had she actually encouraged that woman?

Now she was going to spend the evening listening to those two chatter and laugh, while she sat there like some dull little wallflower. And all because she thought she was going to somehow make him uncomfortable.

Did people who looked like those two ever feel uncomfortable?

She wandered over to the mirror and stared at her reflection. She turned her head one way, then the other. She knew she looked better than she usually did. But when compared to people like Killian and that woman out there—well, she was just a plain Jane at best.

She studied herself a moment longer, then she opened her purse and pulled out a tube of clear lip gloss. She dabbed some on her lips, rubbing them together. She fluffed her hair, wishing the fine tresses had more body.

Ah, well, tonight wasn't about her anyway. This was Killian's time to find a new love interest—so encouraging him to chat with other women was exactly what she needed to do.

Maybe she'd find some guy to chat up, not that the idea appealed to her much. But she straightened her posture and lifted her chin.

This wasn't about her, but she wasn't going to look like some pathetic tagalong of Killian's. She was going to smile and laugh too.

As she stepped out of the ladies' room, she saw Killian. He was hard to miss. He was like a golden angel. His light brown hair reflected gold highlights in the low lamplight. His skin was warm and golden too. And although she couldn't see his eyes from here, she knew their color as if she'd looked into them all her life. A golden amber. Molten and beautiful.

Suddenly, Killian was blocked from view, and Poppy collided with someone or something.

"Oh!" she said, her hands shooting out to balance herself. Hands at her hips did the same thing, and she registered it was a *someone* she'd run into.

"I'm sor—" she started, looking up to see a man with a bald head, wire-rimmed glasses, a goatee and blue eyes that Poppy hadn't seen for years, but still recognized as if she'd just seen them yesterday.

"Sorry," he said, then those blue eyes grew huge behind his glasses. "Poppy? Poppy Reed?"

Chapter 20

"Eric," Poppy said, although she knew she didn't sound as thrilled as he did.

"Oh, my God." He grinned. "It's been like, what? Four or five years?"

She nodded, managing a tight little smile. "Yes."

Eric hugged her then. She stiffened, then lifted her arms to return the embrace.

"So are you still playing?" she asked when they parted, having hugged the guitar on his back as well as him. Which, if he was the same Eric, was appropriate. His guitar had been as much a part of him as his arms and legs.

His grin widened. "Oh, yeah. When I can. There's not as much free time now as there was in our good ol' college days."

Poppy nodded, noticing he looked older. The boyish looks she remembered had been replaced by a squarer jawline and more defined features.

Did she look different to him? She felt different. But she'd felt different for a long time now.

As if he were following her train of thought, he said, "You look great, Poppy."

"Doesn't she?"

Poppy looked away from Eric to see Killian standing beside them. He stood several inches taller than Eric, and his build was much bigger, much more powerful. A sense of safety that she didn't quite understand instantly washed over her.

"Um, Killian, this is an old college friend, Eric. Eric, this is—" What title did she give Killian? "This is my friend, Killian."

Killian nodded at Eric, then almost as if it were an afterthought, offered his hand. "Nice to meet you."

Killian shook the man's hand, not feeling in the least bit pleased to meet this person. In fact, when he'd first watched the guy bump into Poppy and seen her shocked expression, he'd risen, ready to come over and step in.

Then recognition and a small smile had appeared on her face. And there had been the hug. So he'd sat back down. But only for a few minutes.

Something about Poppy's demeanor had called to him. She wasn't comfortable with this guy, and now up close, he could practically sense her emotions in the air. A subtle wafting of dismay mixed with melancholy.

Had this man hurt her in the past? Was this the ex? No. No, Eric wasn't the right name.

"I can't believe it's really you," Eric said, shaking his head, smiling fondly at her. "Adam just mentioned you last week."

Adam. That was the ex's name.

Beside him, Poppy swayed, just a quick rock from foot to foot, but Killian moved closer. Just in case.

"He—he mentioned me?" she finally gathered herself enough to say, the hesitant words dripping with hope.

Something in Killian's chest twisted. A strange pain he didn't understand. He disregarded the feeling, focusing on Poppy instead.

She didn't look well. Her already pale skin faded until it appeared almost translucent. He placed his hand on the small of her back, wanting to give her support, simply needing to touch her for his own sake. She stiffened, just a bit, then sagged against his hand.

He rubbed her lower back, noting that Eric saw the touch. A strong surge of possessiveness filled Killian.

He didn't like seeing Poppy so upset. He wanted to help her. That's all.

Eric's eyes moved back to Poppy, another ready smile on his lips. "Of course, Adam mentions you."

Poppy swayed again.

"He's actually playing a gig this weekend," Eric added. "You should go. I know he'd love to see you."

Another slight weave.

Killian fought a grimace. My, wasn't ol' Eric cheerfully oblivious. Totally unaware of the effect his words was having.

Then still merrily unaware, Eric looked around as if suddenly remembering why he was here.

"Speaking of gigs, I better set up," he said. "You're going to stay and listen to me play, right?"

Poppy nodded, although Killian wasn't sure if she'd really heard the question or just realized a response was expected of her.

"Great! I'll come join you for a drink on my break."

Again, Poppy nodded.

"Nice meeting you," Eric said to Killian.

Killian dipped his head in response, then waited until the man walked away

"Poppy?"

She blinked up at him as if she'd forgotten he was even there. Seeing this guy had really shaken her. He rubbed her back again to soothe her. He tried to ignore the idea that it might also be to make her aware of him.

"Sorry. I'm just a little—" She laughed, although the sound was brittle, humorless. "I'm just a little surprised, I guess."

No one, with the exception of maybe clueless Eric, could miss that.

"Come on, I got you another wine."

Poppy allowed Killian to lead her back to their seats, taking comfort from his hand, steady and strong, on her lower back. She slid up on the stool and reached for the glass of wine he'd ordered her. She polished off most of it in one gulp.

Behind her, Eric started strumming a song she knew very well. A song that he'd played back in their college days. The strains of the music acted like a trigger, setting off an explosion of memories in her head.

Sitting in bars like this, watching Eric play with another musician. She closed her eyes and she could hear the other guitarist's amazing voice. His classical guitar training shone through, even on pop songs. His wild, unkempt hair and Byronic good looks. His love of art and creativity and learning.

Adam.

The talks they'd had. The plans they'd shared. All the things they were going to do. Traveling around Europe, living in different cities, not caring if they existed hand to mouth, just living on love and the art they would create.

She finished off her wine and waved to the bartender, gesturing to her empty glass once she'd caught his attention.

When the third drink arrived, she took another long swallow.

"Whoa there," Killian said from beside her, startling her. How did she keep forgetting he was here? He wasn't exactly forgettable.

He took the glass from her, placing it in front of himself. She didn't argue, mainly because the wine was almost gone anyway.

"What's going on?"

Poppy frowned at him, pretending she didn't have a clue why he was asking such a thing. "What do you mean?"

He raised an eyebrow, his expression the very definition of sardonic. "You would not be on the top of my list of lushes."

"Lush?" Poppy laughed. She wasn't a lush. Never had been. "I don't think three drinks—really two drinks and a half—constitutes lush status."

Killian's gaze moved over her face, studying her, but then he nodded. "No, I suppose not. But it just doesn't seem like you."

Like her. She almost snorted at that. *Like her.*

Which her was he talking about? The her who was going to have a wild, adventuresome life with the man she loved? Or the her who pined for the man who'd walked out years ago? The her whose life revolved around her little sister? The her—

"Tell me about Adam."

Killian's quietly asked question knocked the breath out of her like a sucker punch to her gut. She hadn't seen it coming, but she should have. Killian was pretty straightforward and rarely subtle.

"Umm," she started. What did she say? That he'd left her because . . . because she wasn't enough for him. Did she admit that?

She couldn't. Not to this man, who already saw her in the same light.

No. No. Killian just wanted and needed a different type of woman. That wasn't the same. But wasn't it? Wasn't it exactly?

"Adam was—" Poppy stopped as a woman appeared beside Killian. Not the woman who'd been here when she'd left for the restroom.

Poppy looked around. What had happened to her, anyway?

Well, whatever. This was a brunette with a short pixie cut and big baby-blue eyes. The kind of eyes a man could get lost in—wasn't that the cliché?

"Hi." She smiled, leaning in right between the two of them, so Poppy had to lean back to avoid being bumped.

"My friends over there"—she gestured to the table of women—"and I have a bet going. Are you a model?"

"No," Killian answered, his tone curt.

"Really, because I could swear I've seen you somewhere before."

Poppy snorted. "You better get a more original line than that. He's already heard that one tonight."

Poppy snapped her mouth shut. Had she really just said that?

She giggled a little, until she realized both Miss Blue Eyes and Killian were staring at her. Blue Eyes looked annoyed. Killian looked—amused. His golden eyes flashed with silent laughter.

Poppy suppressed her own laughter. Well, mostly. A slight snicker escaped.

"I'm sorry." The brunette shifted so she was standing closer to her. "I don't believe I was talking to you."

"Oh, I realize that." Poppy smiled, undaunted by the other woman's irritation.

"Then maybe you should mind your own business."

Poppy blinked. Hadn't this woman seen that she was here with Killian? Didn't she see him walking her back over here? Didn't she see them talking? Hadn't she seen his hand on her back? Given how they'd all been watching him since he got here, Poppy knew she had. They all had.

Something inside her snapped. This was another person telling her that she wasn't good enough. *No*. Not this time.

"Oh, he's my business," Poppy said. She knew it was probably the wine talking. But at this moment, it felt pretty darned good. No, pretty damned good.

"Oh, really?" the woman said, eyeing her like there was no possible way she was telling the truth.

But before Poppy could reply, Killian tapped the woman's

shoulder and when she turned to look at him, he said, "Yes. Really. Come here, baby."

Then before Poppy realized what he intended to do, he reached over and pulled her, stool and all, closer to him. The move brought her against him and effectively nudged the brunette out of the way.

Poppy looked from Killian to the woman, then back to Killian. This was silly. She started to giggle.

Killian smiled too, then he murmured, "Come here."

For a split second she didn't understand. Her stool was already bumped right against his. Then his hand came up to catch her chin, and his head descended.

He kissed her.

CHAPTER 21

Poppy remained still, stunned. Killian was kissing her. His lips moved over hers. Gently teasing her. Unhurried. Wonderfully soft and strong at the same time.

But her lack of response didn't last long. He felt too good. A small moan escaped her, and she looped her arms around his neck. She kissed him back, all the emotions of this night coming out in her reaction to him.

He moaned too and deepened the kiss. His tongue found hers, brushing, tasting. The intimacy of the touch made her shake with need. God, he felt so good.

She sank her fingers into his hair, feeling the silky strands twining around them. His hold on her face was so sensual, so possessive. His thumb tugged at her bottom lip, opening her to him. And he tasted her more.

It was wild and erotic, and she knew she was acting out of control. But she didn't care. She wanted to surrender to this.

But then he was gone. She swayed, her eyes still closed, her body limp with desire, her breathing short, disjointed pants.

"Poppy?"

She opened her eyes, trying to focus. Killian was still only inches away. She fought the urge to lift her lips to his again.

"I'm sorry," he said. "I shouldn't have done that."

His words jarred her like a bucket of ice water dumped over her head. Why not? It had been wonderful. Perfect.

"But she's gone."

She blinked again. Who? Then reality truly hit. He'd just kissed her to get rid of that woman. The kiss had been fake. A charade.

She straightened, although she still felt like she was reeling.

"Good," she said with more composure than she felt. Inside, every muscle quivered like Jell-O. Even as she told herself to just shake it off. The kiss wasn't real. Killian hadn't felt the same things she had.

She managed to look out at the barroom. The table of women gaped at her, and even in her embarrassment and hurt she realized some of them looked at her with surprise, but others appeared almost impressed. Except the brunette. She'd returned to the table but sat with her back to them.

Maybe Poppy should have had a sense of smugness, but she just felt stupid. Stupid and offended. And hurt.

Beside her, Killian shifted and she realized she was still basically wedged between his legs. Carefully, because her legs wobbled as if she was on stilts, she stood and moved her bar stool.

Space would help. God, she hoped it would help.

"I shouldn't have done that," Killian repeated, and she found his apology angered her.

But her voice was quiet and even as she said, "No woman wants an apology like that."

Killian nodded. She was right. He'd way overstepped his bounds, and how could a simple "I'm sorry" make up for that?

His only thought had been to make a point to that rude

woman. Both women had been overbearing and disrespectful to Poppy. Something she didn't deserve from anyone.

Of course, his kiss had been both of those things too.

But she'd been so feisty with the woman. It was utterly adorable—and arousing. He frowned at his own thoughts.

And if he was being honest, putting that woman in her place wasn't why he'd kissed Poppy. He'd just wanted to kiss her, and then once he was, all he'd been thinking about was how amazing Poppy felt in his arms. And how he just wanted more of her.

But his loss of control hadn't been fair to her.

He started to apologize again but caught himself.

Poppy reached for the wineglass in front of him, but she didn't make eye contact as she did so. She finished off the last bit, then clutched the glass in her hand, watching her friend play guitar. But he didn't think she was even seeing him.

He polished off his beer and signaled to the bartender for another.

"Want another wine?"

She shook her head, changed her in mind in mid-shake and nodded. "Sure. Why not?"

This time when the bartender brought her the wine, she sipped it. Still watching her friend.

Which allowed him the chance to study her. Poppy surprised him. That kiss surprised him.

The Poppy he'd seen was usually so reserved. No. Reserved wasn't the right word. That implied she was distant, cold. That wasn't Poppy. She exuded warmth and kindness. She was just—guarded. Yes. That was the right word.

But not in her kiss. She'd responded to him with her whole being. With utter abandon. Even the thought of it got him hard. Not that that bad boy had fully dissipated from the actual event.

Unfortunately, Poppy's guard was back, like a force field

that had shot up as soon as the kiss had finished. Definitely designed to keep him out. And he did not like it. Not now that he'd tasted her vulnerable passion.

In the dim light, he could see her lips appeared a little pinker, a little swollen from their kiss. He could still taste her on him. The tang of wine, the sweetness of her. The heat of her passion.

He couldn't think about her this way. He was here to do a job. A job that would get him home. He wasn't from this world. And he didn't want to be. He wanted to get this stupid task done and just leave.

Do it now. Pick a man now. Stop all this nonsense before something more happens.

He looked around the room. More men had arrived, but he didn't even attempt to manipulate one of them. He couldn't.

Then he glanced toward the guitarist. Maybe he'd be a good fit. Eric and Poppy had once been friends. That would be a plus, right? He was a musician, which he knew Poppy liked. And maybe it would get back at Adam in some way. Adam deserved that as far as Killian was concerned.

But he still did nothing.

Instead he returned his attention to Poppy.

"You were really great with that woman."

Poppy looked away from Eric, surprised by Killian's sudden announcement.

"Really? Why do you say that?"

Killian grinned, the effect utterly breathtaking. "You were so sassy."

Poppy found herself smiling too, despite her earlier humiliation.

"She was pretty awful."

"Totally awful," Killian said.

Poppy laughed. She knew it must be the wine, but at his words, she just felt lighter. Definitely the wine.

"I don't think you'd have a hard time finding someone to date here," she added, her smile fading a little. Along with some of her sudden pleasure.

Because he was here to meet someone. She had to remember that. The kiss had been a—a prank, really.

"I'm not impressed with the women here," he said. Then his eyes locked with hers. "Well, except one. And I came with her."

Poppy's heart jolted and her breath caught.

"You're a really good person," he said, giving her a fond smile.

Some of Poppy's delight vanished, and she released her pent-up breath. The tone of his voice, the look on his face. Even his words. All of it stated he considered her a great friend.

Which was fine, she assured herself. That was good. Very good.

"So tell me about college," he said, the sudden shift of topic confusing her for a moment. Or was it the wine? Most likely both.

"College?"

"Yeah, you said your majors were children's literature and illustration. What did you want to do with those degrees?"

Poppy giggled then. "They don't sound like very useful degrees, do they?"

Killian smiled. "That isn't what I was saying, but you must have had a plan of how you were going to use them."

"I did," she said with a reminiscent nod. "I was going to write and illustrate children's books."

"So why aren't you doing that?"

His direct question caught her off guard. Most people

never asked what she'd done in college. And those who did just accepted that her plan was a pipe dream, and she'd needed to be more practical.

"Well, I had to get a job that paid a little more regularly."

He nodded, but then said, "Couldn't you do both?"

"I—I tried," she said. "But it was like my creativity shut down. No stories. No pictures in my head. Nothing. It was like my artwork seemed frivolous after I lost my parents. And I lost . . ."

She stopped herself, wishing she could just pull everything she'd said back inside and simply say, "No, I couldn't do both."

But the words were out, and now Killian studied her as if he was trying to see deeper inside her mind.

"He really hurt you, didn't he?"

Poppy, even in her wine haze, didn't have to ask who *he* was.

She nodded slightly.

"Hey."

They both turned to see that Eric had joined them.

"Hi," Poppy said, managing to sound normal, even though her thoughts were still on her conversation with Killian. "You sounded great."

Eric smiled. "Not too bad, I guess. But not as good as Adam and I did in the day."

She forced a smile back. Adam. It was a night of Adam, wasn't it?

Then she felt Killian's hand on top of hers. Instead of pulling away, or just allowing the touch, she turned her palm toward his and linked their fingers.

This wouldn't make any sense later, when her head was clear. But right now, she just accepted his comfort.

She half expected Eric to raise an eyebrow at the touch, but he didn't even seem to notice. Instead he asked if either of them wanted a drink, then stepped up to the bar to order one for himself.

When he returned, they still had their fingers joined, and though the touch made her nerve endings hum with awareness, it also gave her peace. A sense of calm.

She even managed to chat with Eric, talking about what he'd been doing. He was married, with a two-year-old son. He worked for a large law firm in midtown. She told him about her sister and her work. All the while Killian continued to hold her hand, a quiet presence that somehow made her feel composed, grounded.

"Well, I have to get back up there," Eric said, jerking his head toward the makeshift stage. He leaned in to hug her again, and Poppy released Killian's hand to return the hug. The loss of his touch instantly left her feeling set adrift.

"Good to see you too, Eric," she said.

"Really," Eric said as he pulled away. "Come see Adam this weekend. My wife and I will be there. And a few other members of the old gang. It would be a great time to catch up."

"Oh," she shook her head, "I don't—"

"We'll be there," Killian said, the first full sentence he'd said since Eric had walked up.

Poppy gaped at him. Killian smiled back at her, his expression serene.

"I'd love to meet your college friends," he said.

She still stared at him, unable to comprehend why he was doing this.

No. She wouldn't go.

"Great," Eric said, pleased and somehow oblivious to the silent exchange between the two of them. "Samson and Delilah's. It's a new bar down on the Back Bay. Eight-ish."

"We'll be there," Killian repeated.

Eric strolled away, and Poppy stood too. She glared at Killian.

"What the hell do you think you are doing?"

But she didn't wait for his answer. She turned, her heel catching on an uneven floorboard as she did. She wobbled, but righted herself and managed to flee the bar. And the man who clearly thought her life was a joke.

CHAPTER 22

Killian dashed out onto the sidewalk, making a frantic search in both directions. He saw there was no slight woman with glossy brown hair, teetering away as quickly as her high-heeled boots would allow.

"Shit."

He'd tried to make a quick exit, throwing a couple twenties on the bar, more than enough to settle up the tab. He'd been rushing toward the door, when the bartender called him back. Poppy had left without her jacket and purse.

Then at the door, the rude brunette, who must have witnessed Poppy's abrupt departure, cut him off. He'd gotten rid of her, *again*, this time using his abilities to send her on her way.

He swore again, both at the hindrances that had slowed him down and because he couldn't see Poppy. He didn't think she could have gotten very far. Between the wine and the boots, her progress would have to be pretty slow. He'd be lucky if he didn't find her sprawled on the concrete with a broken ankle.

That image spurring him on, he strode down the sidewalk toward the apartment building. Surely she wasn't so tipsy she'd taken off in the wrong direction.

One block later, he found her. She sat on the steps of a row house, one boot already off as she tugged at the other one.

At least she was clearheaded enough to realize her ability to negotiate these sidewalks was not good. Of course, walking in stocking feet wasn't a great plan either.

"Put your boot back on," he said softly. "I'll help you."

Poppy glared up at him, and he could see tears glistening in her dark eyes. Smudges of mascara darkened her cheeks.

"Oh, I think you've helped enough, thank you very much."

His chest tightened. Jerk. That's what he was.

He looked around, not sure how to handle this. Was he used to crying? In his line of work? Of course. But he had his mind control to handle that. And the ones crying, well, they didn't deserve comfort. Neither of those things applied here.

Poppy deserved comfort. She deserved the right words. He knew she'd never gotten them in the past when she'd so desperately needed them. And unfortunately now, she was stuck with him.

He sat down on the step beside her, even though from her stiffening posture he could tell she didn't want him there. And certainly not this close.

As if to punctuate that thought, she shifted away from him and began pulling at her boot again.

He placed a hand on top of hers, his larger one completely covering her tiny one.

"Please stop. Please," he said, an almost desperate quality to his voice, only because he didn't quite know what else to do.

Apparently that worked, because her hand stilled. Reluctantly, he pulled his hand away. He liked the softness of her skin. Too much.

He knotted his own fingers together, his elbows resting on his thighs.

"I didn't mean to upset you," he said, not sure where he

was going with this, but deciding that following his gut was the best strategy.

"Why did you say we would go?"

He could see her staring at him from the corner of his eye, but coward that he was, he didn't look back. Her teary eyes ate at him.

But her question was a good one. And deserved a good answer.

He decided just to state the facts as he saw them. He had no doubt they would be the wrong facts. After all, what did he know or understand about these kinds of emotions? But here he went, right or wrong.

"I know this Adam guy hurt you. But this is how I see it—" He pulled in a breath, preparing for her to stomp away before he could get half the explanation out.

"He was a selfish jerk," he said, "who left because things got too difficult. For him. Instead of thinking about the struggle and sacrifice you were going through, losing your parents, taking care of your sister, giving up school, he just thought about how the change affected him."

He paused, waiting. But Poppy remained seated. Totally motionless, in fact. He glanced at her. She stared at the boot in her hand, and he wondered if she was even listening to him. Maybe she was just thinking of ways to injure him with the three-inch heel.

At the risk of said heel to the face, he kept going. "He should have stood by you. Helped you. He should have been there to ease your pain, not add to it. Clearly, he still causes you pain, and I just can't see letting him hurt you any longer. No man is worth that. Especially one who'd walk away when you needed him."

Again he waited, prepared for her to go, or yell, or . . .

She released a shuddering breath, then sniffed.

Oh, damn. More tears. He'd do better with yelling.

"So how's seeing him going help stop the pain?"

Her voice was low, barely above a whisper, so he had to lean closer to hear her. Their shoulders brushed, and a jolt of longing shot through him like a violent zap of static. How could he want her, even now when things were so far from sexual between them?

But he forced himself to focus on her question. It had merit. A lot of merit. And he did have an answer for it.

"Because you will walk in there, head high, and show him you're fine. That you don't need him. Letting him know you've moved on could be the best catharsis."

She didn't speak for a moment.

"But I haven't moved on."

Killian supposed in her mind she hadn't. She was still raising her sister. She was still working at a job she didn't love instead of working on her art. She was still alone. But he saw her as someone who showed the world she was strong and could handle anything. She was clearly tougher than this idiot Adam.

"You have. You've kept your family together. You've been one tough cookie." She looked at him then, and he gave her an encouraging smile. "But we can make the moving on seem bigger."

She raised an eyebrow. "What do you mean?"

"Well . . ."

Why was he offering to do this? Because this guy deserved to see that someone else got the amazing woman he gave up.

"You won't be there alone," he said, then made a show of straightening his collar and making himself presentable. "You'll be there with your fiancé."

Poppy studied him. Was he really suggesting himself? Her heart skipped a few beats at the idea. Why? What he was offering was just another charade.

"Just like the kiss."

Killian frowned. "What?"

She shook her head, which only made her thoughts more confusing and the sidewalk spin. She touched a hand to her temple. Wooziness filled her head like fog, clouding her thoughts, making it hard to think straight.

"Are you okay?" Killian asked, placing a hand on her back.

She shook her head. "Too much wine."

"Okay," he said, taking the boot she still held from her limp fingers. "Let's get you home."

He lifted her foot onto his knee, and the sudden shift made her topple back against the steps' railing with a soft grunt. She lay there, eyes closed, willing away the vertigo that only seemed to be getting worse.

"Are you okay?"

When she opened her eyes, Killian leaned over her, his eyebrows pinched together with worry. His eyes golden even in the low light. He really was all golden and beautiful.

She reached up to run her finger along his jawline. She could feel stubble, a rough and sensual friction against her fingertips.

"You'd make a nice fiancé," she murmured more to herself than him.

He remained still, letting her stroke him.

"You are very beautiful," she whispered.

Killian caught her hand then and lowered it to her side. He straightened and began working on getting her boot on. She remained lounging back against the railing as she felt his large, strong hand on her ankle, lifting her foot, slipping the boot on.

"It's like you are Prince Charming," she said, then giggled.

"Hardly." She could hear the derision in his voice. Derision that was clearly aimed at himself.

She levered herself up, still feeling light-headed, but able to focus. Well, occasionally there were two of him, but that wasn't really a bad thing.

"You don't think you are the gallant type?"

He looked up from zipping her boot. "Definitely not."

"Are you a cad? A scoundrel?"

He smiled at that, the slight twist of his lips making him look deliciously roguish. "Now that would be more accurate."

He held out his hand to her and she placed hers in it without hesitation. He helped her to her feet, making sure she stood slowly. Clearly, he did not trust her to maintain her balance. She swayed. Probably a good decision. Looping an arm around her, he anchored her against his side. She fit right in the crook of his arm and shoulder, and she couldn't stop herself from resting her head against his chest.

Their progress was slow, because walking seemed to be terribly tricky.

"So why would I marry a scoundrel?" she asked once she'd gotten the rhythm of their gait.

"That is a good question," he said, and while she couldn't take her eyes away from the sidewalk—at least not without the real risk of breaking something—she could still tell he was smiling.

"Although," he added, "scoundrels can be a lot of fun."

Poppy didn't doubt that. Despite the ups and downs of the evening, she had to admit it was the most fun she'd had for a long time.

"Especially that kiss."

"You liked the kiss, huh?" he said.

She giggled at her admission. Well, she had discovered one thing tonight. Wine made her very loose-lipped.

"It was nice," she said, although her fuddled mind wanted to say much more than that. But somehow she kept the other comments reined in. Words like: *Wonderful. Delicious. Erotic. Again, please.*

"I liked it too."

Forgetting her need to focus, she glanced at him.

He smiled back, although that beautiful smile didn't last long, as she tripped and he scrambled quickly to catch her.

She wondered if Killian ever missed.

"Careful," he said, slowing his pace even more.

She nodded and was relieved when she saw the front door of their apartment building. He helped her up the steps and straight to the elevator.

Once inside, she leaned in the corner, wishing she could just slide down the wall and sit. She wanted to sit. She leaned her head back and closed her eyes.

Her jumbled thoughts moved on to other things she'd like to do. Take off these boots. Lie down. Sleep.

She opened her eyes, just a little, but enough to see Killian standing nearby, watching her.

She'd like to lie down with him. Sleep with him. Do more than sleep with him. He was her fiancé, after all.

She giggled.

"What?" he asked, confused but smiling.

She shook her head, which wasn't good. She splayed her arms out to her sides to balance herself. Again Killian was right there, hands on her waist, holding her up.

"You are drunk, imp." She could hear laughter in his deep voice.

"Imp?"

He smiled. "You are definitely an imp."

"I picture imps having big ears."

He chuckled. "Well, you are a cute imp. And your ears appear to be regular size."

She smiled up at him, only to realize how very close he was. His body nearly pinned her in the corner of the elevator as his hands remained at her hips.

Her breasts suddenly ached, feeling heavier, fuller. Her nipples felt sensitive against the satiny material of her bra. And the delicious ache crept lower and lower, centering between her thighs until she felt swollen and needy, her body begging for release from the slow, building yearning.

"If you are going to be my believably wicked scoundrel fiancé, shouldn't you practice doing things that are naughty and depraved?"

Had she really just said that? She had. And it felt good.

Killian hesitated for a second, but his gaze locked on her parted lips. He nodded.

"Yes, I suppose I should."

He lowered his head, his lips brushing slowly over hers, his large body pinning her against the cold metal of the elevator wall.

She moaned. Heaven.

Killian told himself he shouldn't. But Poppy looked so adorably wanton, her arms spread against the elevator wall. Her eyes half closed, sultry. Her pink lips parted, inviting.

He had to steal a taste. But now, a quick sample seemed impossible. Their kiss had turned into a slow, long savoring of each other. Her lips clung to his, his body rolling against hers. Their movements unrushed, but no less filled with desperate hunger.

Then one of her hands left the wall to stroke his back, running up and down its length until she found the hem of his shirt and slipped her fingers under the cotton.

Small fingers shaped to the muscles of his back, smoothing over his hot skin.

He groaned, that simple touch igniting him. He pinned her harder to the elevator wall. One of his hands left her waist, sliding down her outer thigh to hook his hand around her knee.

He lifted her leg so it was curled around the back of his thigh and he was wedged tighter against her. Their bodies ground against each other. And the slow, sensual kissing took on a frenzied passion.

With his hand still anchored beneath her knee, his other hand found the hem of her sweater, snaking underneath, caressing the velvety skin of her stomach. Up higher and higher to tease the underside of her breast.

He cupped her, feeling the hard prod of her erect nipple through lace. He flicked his thumb over it, and she gasped into his mouth. He did it again and received another gasp.

Her breath become his own. One. One.

He froze, something akin to fear dousing the desire coursing through him.

This wasn't right. Not with her drunk. Not with him here to find her a man. And especially not with his being a demon.

She deserved better.

He eased her leg down and stepped away from her, careful to make sure she didn't fall.

She swayed but remained on her feet.

"I think we should get you home."

She pouted, her expression utterly cute, but he forced himself to ignore that fact.

"I liked what we were doing."

He smiled despite himself. She was so going to regret this in the morning. If he thought otherwise, he'd be tempted to take her to his fussy, floral bed. Very tempted.

Instead, he wrapped an arm around her shoulders, trying to keep the touch as impersonal as he could. Not an easy task considering what they'd just done.

"I think you'll like getting some sleep just as much."

"Mmm-mm." She shook her head.

He chuckled.

He walked her to her apartment, fishing in her purse for her keys, as well as keeping her balanced against his side. Not an easy feat.

Once the door was unlocked, he helped her inside, relieved to see Daisy wasn't in the living room. He didn't want to explain why her older sister, her highly responsible, often laced-down older sister, was sloshed.

Without too much difficulty, he maneuvered Poppy to her bedroom. It was a pale green room with an antique four-poster bed and a simple, cream-colored duvet.

"Lie down, baby," he said, half-setting her onto the bed. She fell back, her legs still hanging off the edge. He scooped them up, spinning her so she was fully on the mattress. He fixed the pillows. Then debated on whether he should try to undress her.

The erection in his pants told him that was probably a bad idea—at the very least an experiment in torture.

Instead, he placed a throw blanket from the foot of the bed over her.

"Sleep well, baby." He placed a kiss on her forehead.

She nodded, with a sweet little smile on her lips, sleep already creeping over her.

He watched, all amusement and pleasure disappearing. He couldn't get involved with this woman.

But even as he told himself that, his gaze roamed down her body, silhouetted by the blanket. Her delicate hands resting on her stomach. Her lovely face.

No. He couldn't do that to her.

He turned and left the room, heading for the door. Then he stopped and returned to the hallway. Poppy would want him to be sure Daisy was okay.

He guessed that the door past Poppy's was Daisy's room. If the BEWARE: FALLING OBJECTS sign with a stick figure getting hit with things that looked like . . . ducks? was any indication.

He knocked lightly, deciding just opening a teenage girl's bedroom door was probably not a good idea. He listened, then tapped again. Still no answer.

He could hear faint strains of music, but no actual response.

Carefully, he turned the knob and peeked inside. A lava lamp glowed on her bureau and cast the room in pink. He could make out the faint light of her iPod speakers. A song played low.

And Daisy was curled in bed, covers up to her chin. A book was opened beside her on the mattress. She rolled over, her face toward him, but she didn't wake. In her sleep, she looked like a little angel.

Too bad he knew the difference.

Then he smiled to himself. Not that he couldn't respect someone who went for what she wanted. He was that way too.

He closed the door and walked back down the hall, pausing outside Poppy's door. She hadn't moved, and he could hear her even breathing.

He watched her for a moment.

He always went for what he wanted. But not this time. This time he'd walk away. No matter how hard it was.

CHAPTER 23

"Whoa, I guess you had fun last night."

Poppy tried not to grimace at her little sister, which was difficult, because her head pounded. And she felt like an idiot—on so many counts.

She wandered over to the coffeemaker, very pleased to see Daisy had already made some. Daisy loved coffee as much as she did, and Poppy supposed if that was her little sister's biggest vice, they were doing okay.

Although this morning Poppy was learning the payback on vice was hardly worth it. She prepared her coffee, the clinking of the spoon against the ceramic mug ricocheting through her head like gunshots.

Finally, she collapsed onto one of the kitchen chairs and stared at the steaming coffee, not even attempting a sip. Now even her favorite morning beverage didn't appeal. In fact, the usually wonderful scent reeked to her. Like rotten garbage mixed with turpentine.

She nudged the mug away.

"So?"

This time, Poppy did grimace at her sister. Daisy couldn't possibly expect details. Not right this moment, anyway.

But her obvious misery wasn't going to deter Daisy.

"So you did have fun, right?"

Poppy managed a slight nod. No sudden movements. No . . . sudden movements.

"Did Killian have fun too? Did he meet anyone?"

Let's see. He'd definitely met a drunken floozy in the elevator. She dropped her head to rest on her hand, her elbow sliding across the table under the weight.

God, she'd never known her head could hurt this badly. Like her brain no longer fit in her head and was pulsing directly against her skull. The pain almost obliterated her embarrassment. Almost.

"Did you meet anyone?"

Poppy managed another minute headshake.

Then Poppy's complexion must have taken on a thoroughly green hue, because Daisy seemed to take pity on her and stopped asking questions.

Of course, her cereal sounded unusually crunchy this morning.

Finally, Daisy rose and placed her dishes in the sink.

"Can I get you anything?" Daisy asked as she picked up her school bag.

"No," Poppy managed, then had to swallow several times to tamp down the nausea. God, she was an idiot.

Daisy pursed her lips as if debating what to do.

"Don't worry about me," Poppy said, mustering enough energy to sit up. "I think I just have a bug or something."

Daisy nodded, although Poppy was pretty sure she wasn't really buying the flu excuse.

"Go on," Poppy said, even managing a little smile. "I'll be fine."

"Okay. Text me if you need anything."

Poppy nodded.

Someone knocked on the apartment door.

"Probably Madison," Poppy said, swinging her book bag onto her shoulder and waving as she left the kitchen.

"Have a good day," Poppy called after her. Then she let

her head drop to the table, her temples pounding, her stomach roiling.

Dear God, just let me die now.

Daisy opened the door, a smile on her face, which disappeared as soon as she saw Killian standing there.

"Expecting someone else, huh?" he said wryly.

Daisy glanced over her shoulder, then stepped out in the hall.

"What happened to my sister?"

Killian's own smile slipped. He couldn't imagine that Poppy would share anything about their kisses with her little sister, but what else could have Daisy looking ready to kill?

"What's wrong with her?" he asked, deciding to play dumb.

"She's way hungover."

Ah, yeah. He would have guessed that if his guilty conscience hadn't taken him in the direction of their kisses.

"She ran into one of Adam's old musician buddies."

Daisy's expression instantly grew much less ferocious. "Oh."

Killian nodded in agreement. And in truth, seeing Eric *had* contributed quite a bit to Poppy's imbibing. Killian might not have helped, but Daisy did not need to know that.

"So, I'm going on the assumption that there was no matchmaking last night?"

He shook his head. "None. But I'm starting to know Poppy better." Much better. Intimate details about her—like her feel. Her taste. Her smell. "So it will be easier to find the right guy."

"That's good," Daisy said. "It sucks she ran into that guy. No wonder she looks so upset and miserable."

More guilt landed square on his chest.

"I'll go check on her."

"That's nice." Daisy made a face that stated she was impressed. Man, she so wouldn't be if she knew the truth.

Daisy's bag chimed. Her cell phone was receiving a text.

She didn't even bother to check it. "That's Madison. I'm running late. See you later."

Daisy smiled and dashed off. Killian watched her go, smiling slightly. It was sort of amusing how quickly and easily she'd just come to accept him. He was an effin' demon.

Somehow he didn't think Poppy would accept that tidbit of information with such aplomb.

But he wasn't here to tell her about his real self.

When he entered the apartment, he expected to find Poppy lying on her couch. But the living room was empty. The office?

No. The bedroom was empty too. And he could see into the bathroom, but he doubted she was down there if the door was open. So that left the kitchen.

When he walked in, Poppy sat at the table, her head face-down on her crossed arms. Then she heard his footfalls, and she raised her head, a wan smile on her pale face.

When she realized it was him, her smile vanished, and her face looked even sicker, a whitish-gray color.

The second less-than-thrilled greeting of his morning.

"I thought you were Daisy."

"I figured. You look like hell."

"Thanks," she said flatly, then let her head fall back down on her arms.

He smiled sympathetically. Not that he'd ever been sick or had a hangover. But he could see it wasn't pleasant.

He'd also read about remedies for hangovers. He read everything. One of the things he'd read said that something in eggs could help a rough morning after.

He crossed to the fridge, checking the shelves for an egg container. Finding it, he placed the carton on the counter, then gathered some butter and some bread. He crouched, searching a cupboard next to the stove for a frying pan.

"What are you doing?" she finally asked, barely turning her head to look at him.

"Making you some breakfast. It will help."

She made a noise that sounded distinctly like a gag, then fell silent again.

He found the pan he was looking for, other pots and pans clattering as he pulled it out.

"Must you be so loud? 'Cause that *isn't* helping."

He winced. "Sorry. I'll be more careful." He set the pan down gently on the burner. Then he returned to the cupboards to find a bowl to whisk the eggs. There were more *clanks* as he pulled down a small mixing bowl.

Poppy groaned.

He suppressed a chuckle, knowing that noise would be especially unappreciated.

He went to her side and leaned down, slipping one arm under the crook of her legs, while the other came around her back. Before she could stiffen or pull away, he lifted her, holding her up against his chest.

"W-what are you doing?" she sputtered, her eyes wide and her hangover momentarily forgotten.

"I'm moving you to the living room. There is no point in your being out here."

He carried her carefully, making sure not to jar her too much. She didn't struggle, which he was sure was because she just didn't feel well enough to do so.

He placed her on the sofa, arranging some of the pillows at the end, so she'd be propped up a bit, then helped her ease back against them. He left her to go grab the throw he'd used with her last night from the bedroom.

When he returned, he noticed a tinge of color had come back to her face, and her eyes were locked on the blanket in his hands.

"You put me to bed last night." It wasn't a question, just a sudden realization.

He nodded, wondering what else she'd forgotten. "You were pretty—tired."

She gave him a wan smile at his description of her behavior. He tucked the blanket around her for the second time in less than twelve hours.

"Just rest."

Killian disappeared back into the kitchen, and Poppy closed her eyes, listening to him work.

Was it possible to feel miserable, embarrassed, and oddly happy all at the same time? Because somehow she seemed to be managing it.

What was wrong with her? Last night had been a disaster. A crazy, pathetic mess. He'd kissed her. Not once, but twice. And neither time should make her feel good. Once to dupe that woman and the second time, because in her drunken mind it had been reasonable to throw herself at him. More forward and shameless than either of those women at the bar could ever hope to be.

She groaned. This was awful.

She remained still, her head throbbing. Her whole being was mortified by her behavior. Yet, she did like that he was here.

In the background she heard him puttering around her kitchen, trying to keep his movements as quiet as possible.

Why would he even be here after the way she'd acted?

She didn't understand. She would have expected him to flee from her as fast as his long, muscular legs could carry him.

Then his legs—his whole body—flashed in her mind.

The memory of the elevator returned to her. His body against hers. His mouth. His hands on her. The passion she felt. She could swear she'd felt passion coming from him too.

But then she'd thrown herself at him. And he'd responded. What guy wouldn't? Like she'd been in any state to know what he was feeling. He'd probably felt obligated to return her kiss.

But that didn't explain why he was here now.

As if on cue, Killian came in to the living room, carrying two plates.

He set one on the coffee table for her, then took a seat in the old rocker that had been her great-grandmother's. Something about seeing his large, powerful frame on such a delicate piece of furniture seemed almost amusing. If she could bring herself to laugh.

"Try to eat some," he told her, digging into his own.

She sat up a little, reaching for the plate. As soon as she got a good whiff of the eggs, her mouth started watering and her stomach clenched.

Do not vomit in front of this man, she told herself. She'd already filled her quota of embarrassing deeds for the week. Heck, the year.

She breathed in slowly through her nose and out through her mouth several times until the nausea passed. Then she tentatively pierced a bit of the scrambled egg on the tines of her fork and nibbled it.

The texture was not pleasant, but she forced herself to chew and swallow. Again. And again. She took a bite of toast, the bread gummy in her mouth, but again she made herself eat it.

By the time she'd finished half the plate, she was surprised to discover her stomach no longer churned.

She let out a slow breath, this time due to a full stomach rather than nausea.

"Are you okay?" Killian asked, uncurling his large frame from the rocker, his plate empty.

She nodded. "Yes. That made me feel much better. Thank you."

"Least I could do." He smiled, and something flashed in his eyes that she didn't quite understand. But it looked a lot like regret.

Some of her pleasure at feeling better vanished.

"Done?" he asked.

She nodded, holding her plate out to him. He took it, his eyes now not meeting hers.

More concern swelled up in her chest. Why did she get the feeling that Killian was going to tell her something? Something she might not want to hear.

He carried the dishes into the kitchen, but he was soon back. This time, he didn't take a seat in the rocking chair, but perched on the arm of the sofa. He looked down at his linked hands, and Poppy could tell he was working up to something. Something big.

"Poppy," he said, his voice a low, velvety rumble. He had the richest, deepest voice. A voice she could listen to for hours. But right now, she didn't want to hear what he was going to say. She just knew she wasn't going to like it. Not at all.

"I wanted to talk to you about last night. I realize I was way too forward."

CHAPTER 24

Here we go.

She'd known this was coming. But Poppy remained quiet and tried to keep her face impassive.

He was going to tell her that the elevator kiss had been a silly moment that should never have happened. They'd just gotten caught up in the craziness of the night.

She already knew that, but she didn't want yet another apology. An apology that was essentially a polite way of saying, "I'm not interested in you. I never could be. Don't make anything out of it."

So she wouldn't. She'd just remain calm, indifferent. She would shrug off his words, and he would never know that the apology had any effect on her. She wouldn't give him that satisfaction.

Remaining stoic was her best defense. It had been her only defense all these years.

He looked up from his hands to meet her gaze. "I owe you an apology."

And there it was.

Her face felt stiff, as if there was a mask over it. She just waited, wondering what wording he would use in his attempt to make this apology seem kind and thoughtful. Rejection for the better good. But for the better good of whom?

"I don't want you to feel forced to go see your ex this weekend."

Wait? What? Wasn't he going to talk about how he shouldn't have kissed her? That it had been a mistake? A huge mistake?

"And though I'd love to see the guy's face when he sees you and realizes you are doing great and"—he made a humorously derisive face—"that you are engaged to a fantastic guy, I shouldn't have said anything. It wasn't my place."

Poppy stared at him. There had to be more to this, right? Was he regretting offering himself up as her faux fiancé? That had to be it.

After a moment, when he clearly felt ill at ease with her silence, he added, "I put you in an awkward position where it will be uncomfortable if you go, and uncomfortable if you don't. I'm sorry."

"So you don't want to go?" she asked, still sure the fiancé suggestion had to be the real problem.

"Oh," he answered instantly, "I want to go. I think this Adam guy needs to see what he lost. But I shouldn't have made that decision for you."

Truthfully, she hadn't given that portion of the evening a single thought. Her mind had been stuck on other parts of the night.

"So you aren't going to apologize for kissing me?"

Confusion marred his features now. "I did apologize about the kiss at the bar, but you told me not to do it again."

Ah. That's why he wasn't saying anything about the kiss in the elevator. He figured the same rule applied to that one too.

"So you do regret the kiss in the elevator?"

He frowned, shaking his head. "I don't regret either kiss."

He didn't? Now she was thoroughly bewildered, and apparently that was evident on her face, because Killian added, "I didn't apologize for the kiss in the bar because I regretted it, just for how I did it. Without asking you, or even giving you a clue to what my plan was."

"Oh." That was all her muddled mind could manage.

"And the only thing I regret in the elevator is the fact you were so tipsy. Because I knew you might be unhappy about it later."

"Oh," she said. Well, this wasn't at all what she'd expected.

Killian studied Poppy's dazed expression, not sure what she was thinking.

During the night, he'd come to a conclusion about Poppy Reed. More than she needed a boyfriend, she needed to remember who she was, the things she loved and that she was a very desirable woman.

At the risk of sounding like some new-age relationship guru, if Poppy got back to who she was, then she'd be ready to meet this true love Daisy wanted for her.

He'd also decided forcing Poppy to deal with Adam before she was ready wasn't the right way to do that. Maybe she just needed to get comfortable with men and be herself. Maybe the past needed to stay in the past for now.

"I'm starting to think we both have things we need to work through. You need to—"

Poppy nodded, finishing his sentence for him. "I need to deal with Adam, and you need to come to terms with Agnetha."

Agnetha?

But he nodded, "Exactly." Who or what was an Agnetha?

"I'm sorry," she said, giving him a pained look. "Madison told me about your fiancée."

Of course. Another brilliant story from the minds of teens. So now he had an ex-fiancée. At least he assumed she was an ex. It really would be nice of the girls to share these little facts of his pretend history *with him*.

"I hope it's okay that I know. Madison told me because I was confused by your dislike of blondes."

He disliked blondes? Then he remembered the food court and his rejection of the tall blonde.

"Oh, sure, it's okay," he said.

So this was the story the girls had come up with to fix that snafu. He didn't like blondes because of a blond fiancée. He supposed that was as good an excuse as any.

Poppy reached forward and touched his hand. "It must have been very hard."

He nodded, looking down at her hand on his. "Yes, it was."

So, girls, what awful thing happened? Did she die? Did they realize they weren't suited? Maybe she left him for another man?

"And to leave you for the minister."

. Or for a man of the cloth. Of course. Couldn't these girls ever come up with a normal story?

"Yes, that was very hard." He nodded, looking down, feigning pain. "And makes you question your faith."

Poppy squeezed his hand, her dainty fingers feeling good against his.

"They also told me about how you lost your show too. Seeing her every day, you had to leave—I'm sure."

Ah, yes, his Swedish paranormal show that he apparently worked on with his ex-fiancée, Agnetha.

"What was your show called?" she asked.

Shit. He didn't know. But neither did she, so he could just make up anything, right?

"Umm, *Paranormal . . . Time.*"

"*Paranormal Time?*"

"Well, that's a loose translation from Swedish." He paused, suddenly afraid maybe this wasn't the Swedish television show they were talking about. Did he have another show? A non-paranormal one?

But Poppy nodded as if his response made perfect sense.

"But yes," he said, moving back to the point of this whole conversation, "I think maybe we both need more time to work through how to date again. How to have any sort of relationship."

Poppy didn't say anything for a moment. Then she squeezed his hand and released him.

"I know you must still have things to work through," she said as she shifted back against the pillows. "Look at me, the mere mention of Adam, and I wind up acting like a fool and sporting a hangover."

Killian nodded, glad his tactic had worked.

Poppy yawned, and she let her head fall back against the pillows. She blinked, then blinked again, and he could tell she was exhausted.

He was too. All this emotional-sharing crap really drained a person. And a demon too, apparently.

"Why don't you nap?" he said softly.

She widened her eyes as if doing so would suddenly cast off her sleepiness.

"I need to get to work. I have just a couple chapters left to edit in a law text."

"Okay, well, stay still and let me get it for you. You can work on the couch today."

She looked as if she was going to argue, then nodded. "The chapters are on my desk, and I need the red pencils that are there too."

He nodded, heading off to her office. The first thing he noticed was her desk. Beautiful and antique, he noted as he gathered the items she needed. Then he went to the bookshelf beside her desk to find a large hardcover book she could use as a makeshift writing surface.

He pulled one out, flipping it to read the cover. The book had no title or author printed on it. Curious, he flipped the book open. Inside were drawings. Vivid, magical images created in colored pencil. Some in ink.

Poppy's illustrations. Worlds of fairies and dragons and princesses and castles. They were amazing.

He looked back to the bookshelf, realizing there several more books like this one. Hundreds and hundreds of pictures Poppy had produced, images from her own mind.

"Are you finding everything okay?" she called from the other room.

He carefully replaced the sketchbook and grabbed another one, a hardcover about jewelry making, and returned to her.

"Yes," he said with a smile. "I think I got everything."

He handed her the items, then watched as she got herself situated. Once done, she looked up at him, one brow lifted in silent question.

"I'm just going to go clean up the kitchen," he told her.

"You don't have to do that."

He shrugged. "I want to. Cleaning helps me think. You know, about this new show idea."

"Okay," Poppy said. "But I can clean it up later. You cooked, so I should clean."

"Nah," he said. "I've got it." Plus he didn't want to go back to that apartment. He'd much rather stay in Poppy's bright, homey place. And if he was being honest, in her presence.

"Go ahead and work. I'm fine."

Poppy did as he said and turned her attention to her editing. As she worked, she could hear Killian moving around the kitchen. Dishes being washed, cupboards being opened and closed. Unlike earlier, she found the noises pleasant. Comforting. Nice.

She finished a chapter, then allowed herself to drop her head back against the couch cushions and just listen to him cleaning.

Her thoughts drifted, thinking of what he'd said about both of them needing time to let go of their past relationships. He was right.

She should be over Adam, but she'd just never dealt with her loss. Maybe it was time.

Then she thought about Killian's kisses. And her reaction to them. It might have been the alcohol, it probably was, but she didn't recall Adam's kisses affecting her like that.

Passionate, all-encompassing, earth-shattering kisses. Even just the memories made her breathless.

Of course, there hadn't exactly been many kisses since Adam. None to be exact. So maybe any kiss would have thrown her body into overdrive.

One thing was for sure: She did need to let Adam go. She needed to stop holding on to the past. She felt a closeness with Killian over this. He understood her hurt over Adam, because he'd lived through heartbreak too.

"Are you feeling okay?"

Poppy opened her eyes to see Killian leaning in the doorway, wiping his hands on a dish towel, concern burning in his golden eyes.

She smiled, then said with certainty, "Yes, and I want to go to that gig."

CHAPTER 25

"He's been here the past few evenings," Daisy whispered, peering around the corner from the hallway to spy on her sister and Killian in the living room. They sat on the couch, one of them on each end, watching television.

"Well, he said he was going to get to know her," Madison said, watching them with her.

Emma snuck occasional peeks too.

"But how's he going to find her Mr. Right, if all they do is hang out in our apartment?"

Killian said something to Poppy and she laughed. Her reaction seemed real and carefree. Daisy loved hearing her laughter. She loved seeing her sister having fun. She was just worried.

She nudged Madison, then gestured for both girls to follow her back to her room.

"I think they're falling for each other," Daisy said, once they were in the room with the door shut.

"Nah," Madison said. "You already told him that he can't let that happen. And he has to do what you say. The book was clear about that."

Daisy nodded. "True. And he has done everything else we told him to do."

"They are just becoming friends," Madison said, flopping

down on Daisy's bed. She began flipping through the newest *Seventeen*.

Emma sat down in the fuzzy hot-pink beanbag in the corner, reaching for the English homework they were supposed to be working on. But she just opened the book, letting it rest in her lap.

"I think it's nice they are becoming friends," Emma said with one of her small, dreamy smiles. "Poppy doesn't seem to have many, and they actually get along well."

Daisy couldn't argue with that. Her sister was sort of friends with Ginger and Emma's mother, Sara. And she did have a few friends at work, but really she'd cut herself off from the world since their parents had died. She supposed a pal was good for Poppy. And she did seem to genuinely like Killian.

"But isn't she going to be sad when he goes back to—you know?" Emma dipped her head toward the floor.

Madison rolled her eyes. "We'll just tell her he moved back to Sweden."

Daisy smiled, shaking her head. "That works."

Maybe Sweden wasn't such a bad place to say he was from after all. Poppy wouldn't very well go visit him there.

"And let's face it," Madison said in her pragmatic way as she flipped through the magazine, "once Killian finds Poppy her soul mate, she'll be all into that. She won't even care about him anymore. If she even does now."

Daisy supposed that was true. She probably was worrying for no good reason.

A knock rattled the door, and all three girls froze.

After a moment, Daisy's heart rate went back to normal, and she opened the door.

Poppy stood on the other side. Her eyes moved over Daisy, then her gaze shifted past Daisy to her friends.

"What are you girls doing?"

Daisy and the other girls exchanged looks.

"We're just working on our English papers," Daisy said, her voice surprisingly calm, even to her.

To back up Daisy's words, Emma held up her copy of the book they'd read: *Much Ado About Nothing*.

Daisy really hoped that was what she was feeling about her sister and the demon. Then she noticed Poppy had changed from her usual jeans and T-shirt to a cute skirt and sweater.

"Why are you dressed up?"

Poppy looked down at herself. Now she was the one with the decidedly guilty expression.

"Killian and I have decided to go out for a bit. We're going to check out that art gallery show."

The *singles* art gallery show.

Daisy's concern flitted away like her attention to the term paper she claimed they were working on. Things were okay. Killian was on the task, and Poppy was agreeing to go out. It was all good.

"Will you girls be okay for a bit?" Poppy asked, her guilt replaced by that searching look of hers.

Daisy nodded right away. "Sure. We'll just be here working."

Poppy considered that, then raised an eyebrow at Madison. The girl pushed away the magazine and held up her copy of Shakespeare too.

Poppy's gaze moved from one girl to the next until it returned to Daisy. She nodded. "Okay. Make sure you get those papers done. We won't be late."

"We will," Daisy assured her. "Have fun."

Daisy closed the door, then turned to grin at her friends. She didn't have anything to worry about. The quest for a soul mate was still full steam ahead.

When Poppy walked back into the living room, Killian couldn't miss the strange expression on her face.

"Is everything okay?" he asked.

"Yeah," she said, although the affirmation wasn't exactly convincing. "Sometimes I get the feeling those girls are up to something."

Oh, they were. He could attest to that. They were conjuring demons. And somehow Killian didn't think Poppy would approve.

But he couldn't explain even if he wanted to, which he didn't. He had a strict order he couldn't tell her he was a demon. And telling her about the conjuring would be outing himself.

Not that Poppy would believe him anyway.

"I'm sure they are just talking about boys or something," he said instead. "Isn't that what teenage girls do?"

"You're right. They probably are," she said, but again Killian didn't get the feeling she quite believed that excuse.

"So are you ready?" Distraction seemed like the best tactic.

For many reasons.

"Yes." She pulled in a breath as if to cast aside her current worries. But her mind managed to move right to another concern.

"Do you think this looks okay?"

Killian had thought her outfit looked more than okay as soon as she stepped into the room.

She'd changed into a white skirt with big red flowers. Poppies, appropriately enough. The skirt stopped just above her knees to reveal bare, shapely calves. With it, she wore a black camisole top and a bright red cardigan. The style suited Poppy. Still comfortable and casual, but fashionable too.

She looked beautiful.

But instead of telling her that, he simply said, "It's nice."

The expectant glitter in her eyes faded, and he got the feeling she'd been disappointed by his reaction. But before he could say anything else, she busied herself with getting her purse and a jacket.

Killian watched her bustling around, wanting to tell her what he really thought of the look. And knowing full well he shouldn't.

In fact, his thoughts had been going lots of places they shouldn't over the past few days. He'd been hanging around because he hated being in the flowery apartment, and he was avoiding Vepar. Plus, it did make sense to get to know Poppy better. At least, that's what he'd been telling himself. And sometimes he even believed it.

But that fact was he liked being around Poppy. He liked her smile and her laugh. He liked her sense of humor. He even liked her sense of style. The girl could rock a *Sesame Street* T-shirt like no one else.

In fact, it was when he started finding that look sexy that he decided they needed to hit the singles circuit again.

So he'd suggested going to the singles reception at the art gallery. He was doing far too much liking himself, and not enough finding other guys to like her.

Time to matchmake. Whether he wanted to or not. He'd been surprised when she'd agreed. And maybe a little disappointed too.

"Okay," she said with a smile, "I'm ready."

He nodded, holding out a hand for her to lead the way to the door.

He was ready for this too.

"Um, wow. This is . . ."

Poppy nodded, not even needing Killian to finish his thought. They stood among a bunch of strangers looking at photos of people. . . .

Well, there was no delicate way to say it. Having sex.

Having sex in an artistic, black-and-white, avant-garde sort of way, but sex nonetheless, and quite graphically too.

"Maybe I should have read the ad more closely," she said, not able to take her eyes off the photo in front of her showing a couple engaged in . . .

She tilted her head. Fellatio? Cunnilingus? Truthfully, she wasn't really sure of the genders of the people involved. But it still managed to be very intimate and very erotic.

She glanced at Killian. He stared too, until a waitress clad from head to toe in shiny black vinyl walked past with a tray of champagne. He snagged two of the flutes, handing one to Poppy.

"I think we're going to need this," he said, taking a large gulp.

She sipped hers, agreeing with him, but not willing to have a repeat of the other night. The elevator incident flashed through her mind. No, she didn't want a repeat of that, even as her body started to ache at the memory.

She took another sip of the pale gold liquid. Killian wasn't as restrained. He guzzled his.

"We can go if you want." Poppy said, once he'd finished his drink.

He shook his head. "No, this is fine. I'm sure we can meet some interesting people here."

As if to validate his theory, a man wearing a corset, tight leather pants and a top hat walked by.

"But if you try going home with him, I'm going to have to stop you," Killian said, eyeing the man dubiously.

"I think we're good on that one."

They shared a smile.

"I'm going to get another," Killian said, lifting his glass, scoping the room for a waitperson. He spotted another, easily visible due to the shiny PVC garb.

"I'll be right back," he told her, almost as if he were afraid to leave her alone.

"I'm fine." Which was true. She'd been startled by the initial realization of what the art exhibit consisted of, but really some of it was quite amazing. And not in just a shocking way.

She wandered along the wall, stopping to study some of the shots. Several were pretty scandalous, maybe even bordering on pornographic, while others, like the one she was in front of now, were actually very beautiful. A glossy photo of a couple clearly joined in intercourse, legs and arms entwined, rapture on their faces. It was really quite powerful. And very erotic.

Much to her dismay, Poppy felt her nipples pucker and harden at the sight. She glanced down at herself, glad her cardigan covered the evidence of her arousal.

She looked around for Killian. He'd gotten another glass of champagne and was now talking to a tall, buxom blonde.

A surge of something far too akin to jealousy shot through her.

Don't, she told her wayward emotions. He wasn't interested in her, and that was okay. She could admit that maybe she did have a mild crush on the man, but she knew he wasn't her type. And he'd been open about his lingering feelings over his ex.

She snuck another look at him, his expression polite but uninterested. This wasn't going to be the woman to stir his feelings again either.

She was blond.

Poppy turned back to the photo, telling herself the slight weakness in her muscles wasn't relief. Nope. Not at all.

She smiled, allowing herself a moment to admit it totally was. She didn't want Killian interested in a woman like that.

She wanted him interested in someone like . . .

Don't go there.

Instead she focused her attention back on the art, on the couple tangled in passion. An image of being entwined with Killian flashed in her head. His body on top of hers, her legs wrapped around his waist. Their bodies connected as intimately as any man and woman could be.

"It's quite powerful, isn't it?"

Poppy jumped, snapped out of her daydream. Heat crept up her cheeks as she realized a strange man was standing next to her, watching her.

"Um"—she cleared her throat—"yes, this one is very powerful."

He nodded, turning his attention back to the black-and-white photo. She wandered on to the next picture, and the man followed. Her first reaction was to be unnerved, but then she told herself that was silly. This was the point of the evening—to mingle. To meet single men, which meant actually talking to them.

"Have you seen this artist's work before?" she asked him, her voice sounding a little higher than usual because of her nerves.

He smiled, and she noticed he was quite good looking, with straight teeth and dark hair. He appeared to be in his mid-thirties. The gray shirt he wore brought out the steel color of his eyes. Both his shirt and pants looked expensive, but she wasn't sure. Killian would know.

She mentally pushed Killian aside, forcing herself to pay attention to this man.

"No, I can't say I have," he said; his voice was gravelly and held a hint of some sort of accent. "My name is—Parve."

Parve. That was unusual.

"I'm Poppy," she offered, then opened her mouth to ask where he was from, but he spoke first.

"Poppy, that's an unusual name."

Killian had made that same observation just the other day, and she'd shared that her mother had adored wildflowers. That she considered them a symbol of beauty and survival.

She'd even told Killian what her mother had said so many times while hugging both her and Daisy.

"Love is like wildflowers; it's often found in the most unlikely places."

But to this man, Poppy just smiled and agreed.

"So, Poppy, are you really here alone?"

She hesitated, finding his question odd. This was a singles event, after all.

He must have sensed her misgivings, because he promptly added, "I'm sorry, it's just that I saw you come in with another man."

Oh, of course. Killian was pretty hard to miss. Apparently even to other men. The competition, she supposed.

"Oh, we are just friends."

Parve nodded, but she got the distinct feeling he didn't quite believe her. She supposed it was pretty hard to imagine that she wouldn't be interested in a guy like Killian.

She shot a longing look toward Killian. And really, wasn't she? Just a little?

"We're just friends," she repeated to the man in front of her.

Killian glanced past the blonde chattering at him. He wasn't listening, but the occasional nod seemed to be enough to keep up his side of the conversation.

How could he focus when Poppy was talking to that guy? A guy he hadn't sent to her.

He was supposed to pick out the man for her.

Yet, what difference did it make? The goal was to find her a man. It didn't matter how. And he did need to get back to his world.

But still, he couldn't stop watching her talking to that man. Something wasn't right. His skin prickled with wariness, but he couldn't pinpoint why.

Poppy laughed at something the man said, and again suspicion raked over Killian.

"Isn't that funny?" the blonde said with a loud laugh, drawing him back to their conversation, such as it was.

"Very," he said automatically, but his gaze went right back to Poppy.

The blonde began blathering on again, the words little more than white noise.

The man said something else, then touched Poppy's arm.

Killian's muscles tensed like a dog with its hackles going up.

"So you're from here, then?"

Killian blinked at the woman. "Ah—yeah. I mean no. I'm from—Sweden."

"Sweden!"

He nodded, his eyes back on Poppy again. Now she strolled away with the man, talking to him as if they'd known each other for years.

Killian gritted his teeth. Why was he even here if she was going to find her own man? The strange possessiveness he'd experienced other times returned, this time stronger than ever.

And again, he felt like something wasn't right about that guy.

"Ah, so that little thing has caught your attention," the blonde said, following Killian's stare.

Killian fought the urge to glare at the woman, somehow irritated that she'd noticed where he was looking.

He shook his head. "We came here together. We're just friends."

The blonde laughed, the sound tinny and harsh. "*Friends* is not what's in your eyes. You look ready to eat her up."

CHAPTER 26

"We are just friends," Killian repeated, even as he stepped away from the blonde, edging in Poppy's direction.

"Okay," she said, the one word thick with doubt.

She smiled, disappointment clear in her heavily made-up eyes, but she didn't try to stop him. In fact, she just repositioned herself beside another man a few feet away.

Killian turned his attention back to Poppy, who had walked to the other side of the room; only flashes of her bright red cardigan allowed him to make out where she was.

He strode in that direction, intent on speaking with her, only to catch himself when he was a few feet away. He stopped, lingering, half shielded by a potted ficus.

See, this was good, he told himself, peering between the branches. She was supposed to be meeting someone. That was the point of this evening.

So why didn't it feel right?

The two continued to talk. Poppy didn't appear to stiffen or pull away when the man placed a hand on her shoulder. But Killian felt his own muscles tighten. Like a lion ready to rear up and attack.

Poppy laughed again, and Killian clenched his teeth. Then a group of chatting singles a few feet away caught his attention. They were watching him. One man raised an eyebrow, clearly aware of and amused by Killian's spying. The woman next to him looked less amused, and more bothered. Killian offered a tight smile and stepped out from his hiding place.

What was he doing? He was acting like a jealous husband stalking his wife. Or maybe ex-wife was more accurate, since she had every right to be talking to another man.

Of course, if he was Poppy's husband, he wouldn't have let her get away to begin with.

He paused at that thought. Okay, he was losing it. This guy wasn't *another* man. That implied Killian was her man—which he wasn't. And why was he even thinking things like keeping her versus letting her get away?

Stop it, buddy. Just stop.

The man's hand slid from Poppy's shoulder all the way down her arm as he leaned in to say something. His mouth was close to Poppy's cute, little seashell ear. Close enough to smell her cinnamon scent. Close enough for his lips to brush against the pale skin of her neck. Right away distrust flared, along with his possessiveness. Whether he was being irrational or not, something about this guy made him very uneasy.

Without another consideration of what was right or wrong, what he was here to do or not do, he sent his thoughts to the man.

Get away from her.

The man glanced in his direction as if he'd heard Killian's demand, but he didn't drop his hand. In fact, he curled his fingers around her wrist, staking a claim.

What the hell?

Tell her you have to go.

The man said something to Poppy, but didn't move. He glanced again in Killian's direction, a slight smile on his lips, something glinting in his eyes. Something that looked like—smugness.

This wasn't right. Killian knew something was wrong. He started toward them, and only then did the man move away from her. He shot Killian one last look, then disappeared into the crowd.

When Killian reached Poppy, the man was gone. And Poppy looked decidedly embarrassed. She crossed her arms and glanced around as if looking for the guy.

Killian's satisfaction faded. What if Poppy had been truly interested in that guy? What if she'd wanted to get to know him better? What if he was her soul mate?

No. Something hadn't been right. It was as if he'd heard Killian but didn't have to obey. And he was sticking to his gut on this one. His own desires hadn't motivated him. Well, much.

"Hey. Who was that guy?" he asked.

Poppy didn't look at him right away, her arms still crossed tightly around her. But eventually she shot him a sidelong glance that didn't shield the hurt in her dark eyes from him.

"Just some guy. Obviously no one important."

"What? What did he do?" He frowned. Had that jerk hurt her somehow? If he had, Killian would find him and beat the shit out of the guy.

"Nothing. It doesn't matter."

Killian could see her shield, her wall, fall back into place. She was hurt and shutting him out.

Was she simply upset the man had left?

Because the last thing Poppy needed was to doubt her appeal. Her ex had already made her do that for years, she didn't need to feel like other guys found her lacking. Especially since it had been very—almost too—obvious that guy had been interested in her.

Until Killian sent him on his way—if he even had. And his gut still told him something had been amiss with that man.

But maybe he wasn't really gone.

"Is he coming back?"

Poppy laughed, the sound tight, not at all like her usual joyful giggle. "I doubt it."

"Well, then clearly he's an idiot."

Poppy forced a smile. "Right."

"He is." Then, even though he knew he shouldn't, he reached out and took Poppy's hand.

She hesitated at the touch, her fingers tense against his, but then slowly they curled to squeeze his back. Suddenly, the edginess that had been keeping him rigid and agitated disappeared. He'd done the right thing coming to her.

Poppy tried to understand what had just happened in the last ten minutes. First she'd thought that Parve had been genuinely interested in talking with her. He'd been almost too intense but, overall, she'd found him likeable.

He'd laughed and asked questions. He'd touched her several times. She hadn't dated in many years, but weren't those all signals that he liked her?

Then as if some switch went off in his head, he'd walked away, barely saying good-bye, much less giving her an excuse for his sudden change of attitude.

Had she said something offensive? He'd been asking her about her life. Where she lived. About her career. A little more about Killian. That last subject she'd avoided, but she didn't think she was rude about it.

Perhaps she had bad breath or something, but that still didn't merit such an abrupt departure. She fought the urge to place a hand up to her mouth to test her breath.

And now, here was Killian. At her side. Holding her hand. Maybe it was her imagination, but she could have sworn Killian seemed relieved when she'd accepted his hand.

Maybe Killian was just relieved to be rid of the blonde he'd been talking to. Poppy supposed that could be it. But that still didn't explain why Killian was holding her hand.

Was he just feeling bad for her? Poor rejected Poppy.

She tried to pull her hand away from his hold, but he squeezed, keeping her fingers entangled with his.

"You don't have to hold my hand," she said to him, suddenly sure his touch was spurred by pity. She didn't want or need that.

"I want to."

He stroked his thumb across the back of her hand. The touch was light, barely even there, but the feathery caress still sent a shiver through her body.

He wanted to hold her hand. He'd said he'd wanted to kiss her too, but he'd showed no signs of wanting to do it again over the past few days.

"You're kind of confusing," Poppy said suddenly, nearly biting her tongue for blurting that out.

But Killian just chuckled. "I know."

She frowned at him. Well, that wasn't helpful at all. In fact, it was just more confusing. Shocker.

But she didn't say anything. Instead they just walked silently, looking at the photos. The photos that depicted intimacy in various and erotic forms.

Killian paused in front of one of the photographs. This one was taken from above, most of the picture showing a woman with her head flung back in ecstasy. But out of focus beneath her, Poppy could see the form of a man's large hands holding her hips and his head between her thighs.

She was straddling him and he was . . .

She looked away, heat burning her cheeks and neck. More heat pooled between her legs, which made her blush even hotter. Killian's thumb brushed across the top of her hand again, the tiny caress stirring every nerve ending to life.

Her skin, her breasts, between her thighs. Her whole body ached.

She looked at the picture, no longer seeing the models. Seeing herself. Killian's hands at her hips, his head between her thighs.

She released a shuddering breath. The image was so vivid. She hated to admit it, but she wanted it. So, so much.

As if realizing she was swiftly becoming overwrought, Killian led her to another photo. This one was blown up larger than the rest. This one too was mainly of a woman, naked. Her arms flailed out to her sides. Again there were male hands on her hips, but no other part of the man was in the picture.

Even so, there was no mystery as to what the man was doing to her. Poppy imagined herself the woman in the photo with Killian kneeling in front of her. His mouth on the most intimate part of her, parting her, tasting her. Making her beg for more.

Without turning her head, she shifted her gaze to peek at him. He wasn't looking at the photo. He was watching her. She met his eyes then, seeing desire in their golden depths like flames flickering to life. Igniting them both.

He didn't say a word as he led her away from the exhibit, through the crowd to a set of stairs that led to an upper balcony. She didn't ask him where they were going, her mind too clouded with need, her body aching to the point she wanted to cry out.

At the top of the stairs, he looked around and then as if he knew exactly where he was going, he urged her toward a gray utility door. The door opened into a stairwell. Again he didn't hesitate. He climbed the steps until he reached a landing and another door, this one metal. It scraped open as he shoved the bar that served as the handle and stepped through it.

Cool air washed over her flushed skin, and she realized they were on the rooftop. Light from the city illuminated the asphalt and created dancing shadows among the pipes and vents.

He stopped, not releasing her hand as he used his foot to kick a brick between the door and the frame, leaving it ajar.

She watched, even that moment of practicality not pulling her out of her desirous daze. Her mind seemed to be on an endless loop, where all she could think about was wanting this man. Common sense and thoughts of what might happen later just didn't matter at this moment.

Killian tugged her hand, directing her farther away from the door. Then he spun her around in front of him, walking her backwards until she was pressed against the wall. She put her hands out to steady herself, the bricks rough under her fingertips.

Killian looked at her, his gaze roaming her face. Then his head descended, his mouth capturing hers, wild, possessive. Both their movements were greedy, desperate.

Killian lifted his head, hunger making his eyes glitter. "I've wanted to do that all night."

She'd wanted him every moment they'd been together, she realized.

She touched his face, her fingers stroking his jawline. The gentle touch just served to inflame him more. His mouth returned to hers, his possession total, as he nudged her lips open and tasted her.

Poppy didn't know how long they remained that way. Mouths moving over each other, hands grazing over one another's bodies.

He left her again, and she whimpered, reaching out to pull him back, but he just smiled at her. A naughty, breathtakingly sexy smile. Then, as if in slow motion, he sank down to his knees.

She felt as if she were watching from somewhere outside herself as she stared down at him. He placed his hands on her ankles, slowly inching them up the outside of her legs. His palms large and hot, his fingers strong, shaping to her.

Her head fell back against the bricks as she just allowed herself to feel him. His touch moved over the curve of her calves, the slight dip of her knees, the softness of her thighs, the flare of her hips.

His hands stilled briefly, his motionlessness torture. She wanted him to continue, to caress her more. Then his fingers moved, toying with the waistband of her panties. Teasing her with his intent, with the promise of more caresses—deep intimate touches. He hooked his fingers under the elastic and slowly pulled them down.

She lifted her head to watch as he maneuvered them over her feet and dropped the small bit of lace and silk on the ground beside them.

She could feel the swirl of cool air under her skirt, the invisible touch almost painful on her hot, moist flesh.

She shouldn't be doing this, she thought in a moment of lucidity. But the thought was quickly lost as his hands returned to her legs. This time, he moved up the front of them, his thumbs brushing against the inside. Slowly, painstakingly, he headed upward, with steady, sensual pressure spreading her legs apart.

She gasped when his hands reached the apex of her legs, his thumbs just barely nudging the swollen flesh between her thighs.

"Pull up your skirt for me, baby," he said, his voice low, raspy with need.

Her fingers fumbled with the material of her skirt as if she was crumpling paper rather than soft cotton, her desire making her clumsy. But she managed to inch the skirt up, baring herself to him.

"Damn, you are so beautiful," he muttered roughly.

She let out a strangled cry as he pressed his mouth to her.

CHAPTER 27

Killian moaned as he tasted Poppy's wet heat. Using his thumbs, he spread her open to him, sinking his tongue deeper, savoring her. With each flick, each swirl, she gasped and writhed. Her hand came down to rest on his head, her fingers tangling in his hair, tugging him tighter against her. She strained against his mouth, her body begging for release.

But he didn't give that to her. Not right away. He wanted to relish this. To taste her, to feel every quiver and shake of her body. To memorize her texture and heat against his tongue.

He couldn't remember anything as erotic as the feeling of this woman moving against him. She responded to each slight touch.

And he responded too. His cock pulsed against his jeans, mimicking her trembles and shudders. He wanted to be buried deep inside her sweet body. Damn, he did. But he also wanted this.

He wanted to please her. To be on his knees, worshipping her with his mouth. A demon worshipping at the altar of a pure, innocent soul. He'd never wanted anything more.

Her trembling became more intense, and he could tell she was getting close. He flicked his tongue faster against her, until she seized, her body tensing under him. He moved his hands to her hips, holding her as her knees buckled with the intensity of her release.

But still he didn't leave her. He continued to lave her, accepting her orgasm as his reward.

"Killian," she whimpered as her arousal began to build again.

"Give me another one, baby," he murmured against her wet, swollen flesh. She writhed, her fingers pulling at his hair.

He loved her reaction, wanton and unguarded. So different from the Poppy who usually held her emotions in check.

She came for him again, this one quicker, shorter, but no less intense. He stayed with her until she sagged against the brick wall, spent. Then he rose, his lips glossed with her. He kissed her and she returned the embrace without hesitation, her arms coming around his neck.

"Feel good?" he asked her.

She nodded, her eyes heavy, her body limp. He wished that he could just lift her into her bed and crawl in beside her. Holding her until they both slept.

He paused at that thought, the tenderness of it.

Sex was one thing. But to want that kind of intimacy? That unnerved him.

Even in her sated state, she seemed to sense the shift in him. She righted herself, using the wall to regain her balance. She quickly brushed down her skirt, her sleepy bliss replaced by flustered awkwardness.

He didn't want that.

"Poppy," he said, but she cut him off.

"We'll just blame this on the photos," she said, bending down to snatch up her panties. Her movements were jerky as she struggled to tug the tiny piece of clothing over her ballet flats and up her legs.

"I think it was more than the photos," he said, but she didn't seem to be listening as she straightened herself.

"We should probably go." She wouldn't meet his gaze.

Nor did she wait for a response, heading to the door, although her escape was probably not as speedy and graceful as she'd have liked. He could see her legs were still shaky.

He caught up with her, putting a hand to her back to steady her. She flinched slightly at the touch, and he felt exactly like the cad she'd dubbed him the other night.

They made their way back to the exhibition floor. Killian left Poppy waiting by the doors as he went to gather her coat and purse from the coat check.

As he walked back toward her, there was no missing her slightly mussed look and the blush coloring her skin. She looked like a woman who'd been well loved. Unfortunately, she also looked like a woman who was painfully embarrassed by that fact.

Neither spoke as they headed back to the T. As the train began to move, the clatter and rock of the car just seemed to emphasize the silence between them.

Killian couldn't stand it.

"Poppy," he said, turning on the hard, narrow subway seat to look at her. She fiddled with the strap of her purse, refusing to look at him.

"Please look at me," he asked.

She met his gaze, her dark eyes filled with embarrassment and something that looked far too much like pain.

He wished he hadn't taken her up on the roof. But his need for her had overwhelmed him. Now he just wanted to pull her against him and soothe away the hurt he saw in her eyes.

"Don't you dare apologize," she warned.

Her words startled him, and he couldn't stop himself from smiling.

"I'm not going to," he assured her. "I loved every minute of it."

She blushed, her gaze dropping back to her purse. She plucked at a loose thread on the stitching of the strap.

He caught her chin, bringing her gaze back up to him.

"I'm just a little shocked at my behavior," he said, which wasn't strictly true. It was more his emotions than his actions.

"Me too," she said softly, then added, "I mean my behavior too. You know, not yours. I don't know if that's your usual behavior or not. Not that I'm saying . . ."

She just let her sentence trail off, realizing her point was sort of made, and further explanation wasn't helping.

He smiled slightly, finding her adorable.

Her gaze dropped to his lips, and instantly he was aroused again. How did she have this effect on him? He was good at self-control. Well, he usually was.

They both fell silent again, remaining that way the rest of the trip home.

This wasn't supposed to happen. He'd been told in no uncertain terms that he couldn't become involved with Poppy. Nor could he allow her to have feelings for him. He wasn't sure what her feelings were, but he sure as hell felt he was having them for her. Funny, the one rule he wouldn't have minded having to follow was the very one he'd managed to break.

This was not good.

But Killian wasn't going to let them leave each other without saying something. They'd had too many nights end this way.

"Poppy," he said, catching her wrist to stop her as she strode toward her apartment door. "I—I really like you."

Poppy fought the urge to cringe. *Really like you.* To her, that sounded like the beginning of a "I like you, but we should really just be friends" conversation.

Instead of waiting for him to continue, she decided she'd rather beat him to the punch.

"I like you too, Killian. And I understand this was just something that happened. Spurred on by the erotic photos, maybe even fueled by the idea that we both want a relationship."

Killian nodded, although she didn't get the feeling he agreed. But then again, she couldn't read what he was thinking. Those golden eyes of his could be beautiful—and inscrutable.

But she didn't let her uncertainty slow down her words. She was going to deal with the rejection in her own way, not wait for him to do it.

"We are both young—and I know I haven't—" She hesitated, feeling awkward admitting her lack of intimacy over the years. "Well, things just—happened. I don't think we need to dissect it, do we?"

Killian shook his head, but again she wasn't sure he necessarily agreed with her.

"We just had some fun." She paused. "Well, I had fun."

Killian smiled then, and she had no trouble assessing that particular look. In fact, the hunger in his eyes made her insides zing back to full awareness of him.

"Oh, I definitely had fun," he said.

She nodded, but a smile didn't quite reach her lips. She could pretend she was cool and collected about this, but she couldn't be lighthearted and flirty. Not right now.

Never, if she was smart. Dabbling with a man like Killian, thinking she could have casual sex, and not start feeling too much, was dangerous business.

"So it's all good," she said with a decisive nod. "It was a fun and unexpected night. I'm fine. You're fine."

His smile faded at her tone, but again he nodded.

"As long as you're fine."

She managed a small smile. "I am. Good night, Killian."

She turned then and unlocked her door. She didn't look back as she stepped inside.

Unfortunately, she had little time to gather herself.

Daisy popped out of the kitchen. "You're home early."

Poppy tried to muster the same calm she'd always managed over the past four years, hiding her true feelings, keeping her emotions in check. But tonight that composure was just somewhere out of reach. She attempted a carefree smile, knowing it fell short.

"The showing only went until nine. And it was—pretty dull."

Daisy nodded, but Poppy could tell she was trying to read her expression. Poppy forced another smile.

"I got my paper done, and I was just getting a snack before heading to bed. Want some?" Daisy held out a bowl of popcorn.

"No thanks." The truth was Poppy couldn't think of eating. Her stomach was churning with nerves, confusion and something that still managed to feel like excitement.

Daisy took her popcorn and headed into the living room, collapsing on the couch. She curled her legs under her and reached for the television remote. The theme music to a popular sitcom filled the apartment.

"Are you going to watch *Big Bang Theory* with me?" Daisy called out to Poppy.

Move. Answer her. Don't give Daisy any reason to question your behavior and worry.

"Yeah," she said, "I'm just going to—go change."

"Hurry. It's a new one."

Poppy walked to her bedroom. She closed the door and pressed her back against it. She allowed herself a moment to fall apart.

Running a shaky hand through her hair, she closed her eyes.

"What are you doing?" she whispered to herself, her voice trembling as much as her hands.

She should have put a stop to the encounter. She should have told him no, that she wasn't interested in him that way.

"But you are," she murmured, for the first time really admitting it, even if it was only to herself.

It could only ever be to herself.

Nothing good could come out of a relationship with Killian O'Brien, even if that was what he wanted.

Nothing good at all.

She wandered around her room, not quite sure of what to do. Tonight had been so surreal, she somehow felt out of place just dropping back into her normal world.

She sat on the bed, only to stand up again. She walked over to her dresser, rifling through the drawers, only to pause, clothes forgotten in her hands.

This was no big deal. Just a casual sexual encounter. Adults did that. Didn't they? Casual trysts that didn't mean a thing.

She looked down at her hands, realizing she clutched several garments. What had she been looking for? Pajamas. That's right, pajamas.

And she couldn't hang out in here indefinitely. Daisy wanted her to watch their favorite show. She pulled out a pair of plaid cotton pajama bottoms and a T-shirt. Quickly, she changed into them and braced herself to act normally.

She could hear Daisy's laughter as soon as she opened the door. The sound should have pleased her. It usually did, knowing that Daisy was thriving, happy. But tonight, it just made her feel guilty and ashamed.

Was her behavior tonight the example she wanted to set for her little sister? Not that Daisy would ever, ever know about it. But Poppy knew, and she couldn't believe how easily she'd let Killian do whatever he wanted. No, that wasn't fair. She'd wanted it too. So very much.

"Poppy, you're missing the whole show."

She joined Daisy, curling on the couch too.

"Sheldon cracks me up," Daisy said, popping some of the buttery popcorn in her mouth.

Poppy smiled, and tried to follow what was going on, but her mind kept wandering back to that rooftop and the feeling of Killian's touch. His body against hers. His mouth. And his very naughty tongue.

"That was a good one," Daisy said, dragging Poppy out of her erotic memories.

Poppy shifted, pulling her legs in tighter to herself. The show was over, and she couldn't recall a single word of it. Heat crept over her cheeks and neck. She ran a hand through her hair, hoping the action would distract from her surely red cheeks.

"It—it was good." She smiled.

Daisy studied her for a moment, then sighed. "I guess I'd better get to bed."

Poppy nodded. "It is getting late."

Daisy picked up her popcorn bowl, bringing it into the kitchen. She paused on her way back through the living room.

"Did you have any fun at the art gallery?"

More embarrassment burned her face, but she managed to shrug. "Yes. It wasn't too bad."

"I'm glad," Daisy said, then headed off to bed, a little bounce to her step.

Poppy fell back against the cushions, relieved Daisy seemed to think everything was fine. Maybe she'd behaved more normally than she'd thought.

Daisy closed her door and rushed over to her nightstand. Her cell phone lay among the piles of books and hair bands and pens and papers.

She flipped the phone open, and her fingers began flying over the character pad.

He did it! Poppy def met some-1 2nite. Killian did it!

She hit send, and the text whisked through the atmosphere to find her friends' phones.

She dropped the phone back to her nightstand and crawled into bed, a smile on her face. She'd really started to think this conjuring idea was a bad one.

But Emma had been totally right. Daisy had been able to tell as soon as Poppy stepped into the apartment that something had happened tonight. She'd looked all flushed and dreamy. She hadn't seen a bit of her favorite show. She was thinking about someone. A man. Daisy could just tell.

She turned off her light, then hugged her pillow, grinning to herself. Poppy was going to find happiness, finally.

Daisy just knew it.

CHAPTER 28

He was on his knees. She looked down at him. Their eyes held. Locked. Words flowed between them. Hunger. Need. Lust. But so much more than that. Words that shouldn't be there, but were. Gentleness. Caring. Affection.

He rose, their eyes never leaving each other's.

Slowly, he leaned in, bring his lips to press against hers. Kissing her. Tasting her. She savored him too. The embrace was unhurried, thorough, encompassing. A true melding of beings. Of souls.

Time didn't seem to exist, they just were. One.

Finally they parted, eyes searching each other. Heat and emotion swirling there.

Then words were said aloud.

"I love you."

Poppy gasped, sitting up straight in her bed. She pressed a hand to her chest, her heart crashing against her rib cage like a panicked bird trapped in a cage. Like she'd just woken from a horrible nightmare.

But it hadn't been a nightmare. Not exactly. More like . . .

She pulled in several more breaths, trying desperately to calm herself. It was just a dream.

She fell back against her pillows. Just a dream.

Just a dream in which she told Killian that she loved him.

Killian's eyes snapped open. He didn't move, although his heart raced as if it were trying to escape his body. His breathing sounded rapid and harsh in the silent darkness.

He'd been dreaming. A very vivid, very real dream.

The words that had come from his lips echoed through his mind in time with his heartbeat and his breathing.

I love you. I love you.

He'd told Poppy he loved her.

"Wow," Daisy said when she shuffled into the kitchen the next morning in her Hello Kitty slippers. "You look like you didn't sleep too well last night."

Poppy looked up from the chapter she'd been editing, knowing full well she looked exhausted. After the dream, sleep had never returned. By three a.m., she'd given up and decided to get some work done.

"Yeah, I couldn't sleep," Poppy said, "and there didn't seem to be much point just staring at the ceiling."

Plus, staring at the ceiling gave her way too much time to reflect on the significance of her dream.

Of which there was none, she assured herself. For the umpteenth time. Dreams were just crazy workings of the subconscious mind. They didn't have to mean anything at all.

And really, why would she even give it much thought? Loving Killian. That was silly. She barely knew him. So he'd hung around her place a few days. And they'd gone on a couple ill-fated outings. And . . . some other things.

She should be laughing about the dream, not flipping out about it.

Daisy joined her at the table with her usual cereal and milk.

"So are you still going out tomorrow with Killian?" she asked as she poured—cornflakes this morning—into a bowl.

Poppy paused at the sound of his name. "Umm, no. I don't think so."

Daisy stopped, half a gallon of milk in her hand, poised mid-pour. "Really?"

Poppy shrugged, confused by the displeased expression on Daisy's face. "Well, I'm not sure, but I do have a lot of work to do. So I thought I'd probably just stay in."

Daisy looked unimpressed. She finished preparing her breakfast, and Poppy had the distinct feeling she was irritated.

"And I'd like to go do something with you," Poppy added, hoping to appease her annoyance. Annoyance she didn't understand.

"I'm going with Emma and her family this weekend. Remember, we're going to her grandmother's place on the Cape?"

"Oh, right." No, Poppy hadn't remembered that, but she had agreed weeks ago Daisy could go. And even though Poppy really wanted her sister's company this weekend, there was no way she could tell her she couldn't go now. That wouldn't be fair.

"So you should really go out this weekend," Daisy said, her tone bordering on—bossy.

Poppy put down the red pencil she held and regarded her sister closely. Going out was becoming really important to her.

She sighed. "Well, maybe I will. You know, now. Because you are going to be away."

Poppy still had no intention of doing so, but a half-truth was better than a continued debate with a fifteen-year-old. Talk about an exercise in futility.

Daisy took a bite of her cereal, looking neither as if she believed Poppy nor as if she was appeased.

Poppy sipped her coffee.

After a moment, Daisy blurted out, "I thought something happened last night."

Poppy's heart stopped. But she managed to look up calmly at Daisy. "Why did you think that?"

Daisy shook her head. "I don't know. I just thought something had."

"No," Poppy said, trying to appear perplexed by her sister's notion.

Daisy returned her attention back to her breakfast.

"Like what?" Poppy found herself asking. Did Daisy still have some false hope that she'd become interested in Killian? Even after Poppy had made it clear that wouldn't happen?

Instantly, the incident on the roof and then the dream flashed through Poppy's mind.

Yeah, she'd made that clear all right. Maybe to Daisy, but apparently not to herself.

"I thought you might have met someone."

Someone. Not Killian, just a random, faceless someone.

Poppy found herself nodding. "I did."

Daisy's head popped up, her dark eyes searching Poppy's. "You did? Really?"

Poppy nodded again.

"I knew it," Daisy exclaimed, a huge grin replacing her sullen irritation. "What's he like?"

She shouldn't be doing this.

"He's nice," Poppy told her. "A—professor."

"Really?" Daisy's smiled widened, if possible. "Like Dad? That's a good fit for you."

"Well, we just met. So, you know, I don't want to make too many assumptions, but yeah, it could be good."

Daisy jumped up. "Well, I think it's great. You gotta go out this weekend." She hugged Poppy. "I'm late, but I'm really happy for you."

"Thanks."

As soon as Daisy bounced out of the room, Poppy's strained

smile faded. Why had she told her sister that? There was no professor. There was just a tawdry encounter on a rooftop with a man who would never really be interested in her— well, you know, beyond "like." But she'd hated her sister's disappointment.

And Poppy supposed it would be easy enough to get rid of a nonexistent professor. She just didn't want Daisy to worry about her. Even for a weekend.

"Have a good day," Daisy called to Poppy as she headed to the apartment door.

"You too," Poppy yelled back, then pulled in a deep breath.

Twirling the pencil on its tip, she wondered how she was going to have a good day. Not with all these worries haunting her.

Killian was just stepping into the lobby of the apartment house when Daisy and the girls came off the elevator. Daisy grinned, dashing up to him. And much to his surprise, she hugged him.

"Thank you!" she said, squeezing him.

He hesitated, and then his arms went around her thin form. He hugged her back.

Daisy embraced him a few moments longer, then stepped back to beam up at him. "I knew you would do it."

He nodded as if he understood.

"I could tell last night when Poppy walked through the door that it had finally happened." Daisy practically danced with happiness.

Killian glanced at her friends. Emma smiled too, a small, wistful smile. Madison for once didn't look completely unimpressed. But still he had no idea what was going on.

"I'm really happy with your choice," Daisy said, giving him another quick hug. Then the girls hurried out of the lobby, rushing off to school in a flurry of giddy, girlish chatter.

Killian watched them leave, trying to understand what had just transpired. She knew what had happened last night and she was thrilled?

Somehow he had a hard time believing that Poppy would share all the details about what had happened. But she must have told Daisy something.

Killian walked into the elevator and pressed the number for Poppy's floor. He leaned against the wall as the elevator shuddered to life. The wall against which he'd kissed Poppy.

He'd spent most of the night walking around Boston, thinking about everything that had happened over the past week. Trying to understand. Understand why he'd been conjured here. Why he hadn't been willing to find Poppy a man, any man, and leave. Why was he attracted to her? More than attracted. His body ached for her.

As he'd walked and walked, one thing started to become clear to him. He was supposed to be with Poppy.

Not as her soul mate. He'd have to have a soul for that. But maybe as a stepping-stone. All along he'd had this sense she needed to move on. She needed to rediscover herself. To mend some of the wounds caused by Adam, and her parents' deaths.

He had to help her do that before he could do this job. He couldn't think of any other reason for everything that had happened. Including the sex. She needed to rediscover herself sexually too.

He considered sex pretty damned important. But then, he was a demon, so he would. But as he walked, and thought about the events of the art gallery, he also found himself thinking about those photos. Captured moments of human sexuality.

And he realized that Poppy needed to learn to open up to that side of herself just as much as any of her other sides.

Sex was important. And she needed to feel confident about that to move on too.

So he was going to talk to her right now about his plan. And it was a good one.

Poppy answered the door on his second knock. She was still in her pajamas. The T-shirt clung to her slight frame, and he struggled, not letting his gaze wander downward to appreciate the way the fabric hugged her pert breasts, more revealing than any silk teddy.

"Killian."

He couldn't tell if she was pleased or not to see him. Her dark eyes regarded him, wide, maybe a little uncertain.

He understood that feeling. Maybe for the first time in his existence, he wasn't sure about his next actions. But he didn't see any point in standing there, hemming and hawing. He knew this was part of what he was here to do.

"Poppy, I think we should have an affair."

CHAPTER 29

Poppy hadn't known what to expect from Killian's early morning visit. But she was fairly certain that announcement wasn't it.

No response came to her boggled mind as she stared at his expectant face. All she could do was gape at him as if he'd sprouted horns and turned into one of the demons he'd described to her from his paranormal research.

He waited a few seconds, then realized she wasn't going to speak.

So he continued, "I know that sounds kind of abrupt and crazy, but I really think it would benefit us both."

Oh, she could well see the benefits. At least the physical ones. But . . . she just couldn't wrap her mind around the fact that he'd even suggested such a thing.

"You see," he started, and suddenly a moment of awareness reached into Poppy's scrambled brains. She grabbed his wrist and tugged him inside the apartment. It wasn't likely that any of her neighbors would venture by, but if they did, she didn't really want them hearing Killian's theories on why they should become lovers.

Call her old-fashioned.

She continued to tug him with her until they reached the living room. Then she dropped his arm like he was on fire.

She moved across the room as if more space would help her think straight.

Killian watched her for a moment. Waiting again, she supposed, to see if she'd say anything, but really, still no words were coming to her. Well, none that she could string together into a comprehensible sentence.

"Poppy, I know this sounds crazy," he said, taking a step toward her, then stopping, "but it's clear we're both very attracted to each other."

Poppy realized her eyes must be the size of saucers. She was attracted to him. Absolutely. And she couldn't deny a part of her was thrilled that he was saying he was attracted to her too. But the way he was approaching it was more like a business arrangement than a love affair.

"You see," he continued, "we've both been too hurt from our past relationships to jump right into something committed again. In fact, I think that would be a disaster."

She waited.

"But," he said slowly, "I don't think we can ignore our physical attraction. And maybe we could help each other gain some confidence again."

By some miracle, she found her voice. "You didn't seem particularly insecure last night."

Killian actually smiled at that. Apparently he didn't find this proposition strange at all.

"Believe me, you are the only one who has been able to make me react like that."

Poppy's heart fluttered at his admission. Was that true? He didn't do things like that on a regular basis?

"I—I've never done something like that."

Killian's smile broadened, making him stunningly beautiful. His eyes glittered, filled with pleasure and what Poppy thought looked like possessiveness.

Her whole body reacted, skin tingling.

"So you can see, we have something special happening between us." He closed the space between them, stopping inches from her.

"I don't know if this is wise," she said, even as she wanted to press herself against him and let him kiss her senseless. In fact, senseless sounded wonderful. No more thinking, just feeling. Just letting go.

But she managed to finish voicing her concern. "I still think there is the potential to really get hurt."

He nodded. "I've thought about that too. But we have started this great friendship, so if we are just up front with each other, then things should be fine. We need to learn to trust again."

She still didn't answer. To her, this sounded like a recipe for disaster.

"I don't think we're going to be able to ignore the attraction here." His eyes caught hers, holding them. Heat flared between them.

No, she couldn't argue with that, but she just wasn't sure.

"So what do you see as the final outcome?" she asked.

He shrugged, the muscles of his shoulders rippling under the cotton of his shirt. "We have fun, keep it light, learn how to be comfortable being ourselves and being with someone else."

She studied him for a moment. His eyes were filled with sincerity and hopefulness. He really thought this idea could work.

"I don't know," she finally said. "I've never seen myself as a casual affair kind of girl."

"No," he agreed immediately. "But this isn't exactly casual. We're friends. We will remain friends no matter what. I'm suggesting . . . I don't know, a relationship with training wheels."

Poppy raised an eyebrow at that analogy. She was more inclined to see it as a relationship on a unicycle. On a tightrope. Someone was bound to fall hard.

And she was afraid it was going to be her.

She crossed her arms around herself, then moved to sit on the sofa. What did a person say to a proposition like this? Part of her wanted to say yes. Unequivocally yes. But another part of her, the rational part, the part not driven by her libido, knew she should absolutely say no.

The couch dipped as Killian joined her, his knee so close, it nearly brushed hers. Just the possibility of an innocuous touch like that and her body pulsed with longing.

Saying no would be so difficult. But saying yes could lead to much harder times ahead.

Even as she thought that, her head nodded as if the other part—the libido part—was answering without her consent.

Killian paused. Had she agreed? Even though he'd thrown the idea out there, he realized he hadn't expected Poppy to agree. Of course, he wasn't sure that slight nod was truly agreement, much as he wanted to see it that way.

"I—I just don't see how." She paused, clearly struggling with the idea. "I just don't see how this works. I mean, I'm not comfortable with you just showing up to—hook up."

That wasn't how he'd imagined it either.

"I think we simply go on like we have been, except when it seems appropriate to both of us, then we . . ."

This sounded kind of weird now that he was saying it out loud.

"We . . ." How did he say this with any finesse?

"We fool around," she supplied.

"Yes."

Damn, what must she be thinking? About this suggestion? About him? That he was some weird lecher or something.

He sighed. Perhaps laying it out like this wasn't the brilliant idea he'd thought it was while wandering the streets of Boston in the wee hours of the night.

Maybe he should have just let an affair happen on its own.

Or not happen. Now he was back to not being so sure why he was here.

"Okay," she said, standing.

He waited for her to ask him to leave. Or to tell him that it was the most offensive proposition she'd ever heard.

Instead, she walked toward the kitchen, pausing to ask, "Would you like a cup of coffee?"

Wait, the "okay" had been her answer. She'd agreed.

"Um, sure," he said after a second. "That would be great."

She nodded and disappeared into the kitchen, and he fell back against the couch cushions. She'd agreed. She'd agreed to an affair.

His cock leapt in his jeans as if in an attempt to give him a high five.

And he groaned. What was he doing?

Poppy took down a mug from the cupboard, then stopped, bracing her hands on the edge of the countertop. What was she doing? She felt like she'd just made a deal with the devil. An affair with Killian?

Could she really do that?

She snorted quietly to herself. Oh, she could do it. Last night proved that. But could she do what he was suggesting? Sex without attaching to him? Nothing more than friends?

She couldn't deny that she had chemistry with him. And clearly he felt the chemistry too, or why else would he suggest the arrangement?

She pulled in a calming breath and reached for the coffee carafe. She refilled her mug and then poured his. As she stirred in her cream and sugar, she realized one thing. The fact they were going to have sex, or rather more sex, was kind of inevitable.

So maybe having an up-front, discussed agreement was better. She would go in with her eyes wide open and enjoy this for what it was. And maybe she needed to take a risk and do something a little wild.

See, there already was a change in her. A change that might let her open up to other opportunities in the future.

She picked up the mugs and carried them back to the living room. Killian lifted his head from the back of the sofa as she entered.

Lines pulled at the sides of his mouth. She hadn't noticed them before, and she wondered if he was already regretting his suggestion.

Then he smiled when she held out the cup to him. His fingers brushed hers as he took the handle. Jolts like electricity snapped between them.

No, she decided, this wasn't wrong. It *was* inevitable.

"So what's the plan?" she asked, feeling nervous.

He took a sip of his coffee, looking the picture of calm, which seemed hardly fair, then said, "Well I know you need to work today. So I'm going to actually let you do that."

She frowned. She did need to work, but this didn't sound like the setup to a torrid affair to her.

"Then," he continued, "you are going to get all dressed up."

"Dressed up how?"

He smiled, the curl of his lips utterly naughty. "Are you expecting me to ask for a corset, stockings and high heels?"

She shrugged, offering him a look that stated she had no idea.

"Well, I'm definitely not opposed to that, but tonight, you are going to get dressed up in your best dress. The high heels are optional, because I know you hate them. For both outfits," he added, his naughty smile widening.

She couldn't help smiling back. "Thank you."

"Then I'm going to come pick you up at six."

She waited for him to continue, but instead he took another sip of his coffee. He set the mug down on the table and stood.

"Wait," she said, when she realized he was planning to leave. "That's it?"

He grinned, his golden eyes flickering with inner light. "Impatient, huh?"

Poppy blushed. Did she seem too desperate? She probably did.

Then he walked over to her, reaching to take the coffee cup from her hands. He placed it on the table, and turned back to her, taking her hands, his larger ones enveloping them. He pulled her to her feet.

Their eyes locked, and she could see desire flashing in his eyes' depths. Heat filled her.

He leaned in and kissed her. His lips clung to hers. A sweet, lingering, wonderful kiss.

He pulled away slowly as if he didn't really want to end the embrace, but he did, his gaze returning hers.

"I want to stay, but I'm going to leave. You work. I'll—work. And we will have tonight."

She nodded. Waiting did seem wise, even though her body thought it was the dumbest idea ever.

He kissed her again, this one a quick peck.

"See you at six."

She nodded, still speechless.

He left the apartment, and she remained rooted to the spot.

Six. Part of her was eager and excited. And part of her was terrified.

This was going to be a long day.

CHAPTER 30

"You are attracted to her."

Killian frowned, looking around, wondering if he was somehow hearing his own voice, aloud.

Then the mangy white cat leapt up onto the kitchen counter.

"Vepar," he muttered. "You really need a hobby."

"A hobby like your little mortal perhaps?"

Killian gritted his teeth. Damn, he really disliked this jerk—a dislike that was intensifying with each of these unorthodox visits.

The cat paced the kitchen counter, its mangled tail flicking.

"Poppy is her name, right?"

Killian didn't answer, not seeing any point. Why was Vepar here? Killian knew he did have to go back to Hell at some point, probably sooner rather than later, but that wasn't Vepar's call.

"She's quite lovely. I can see where she'd be a delightful little hobby."

Killian immediately tensed, glaring at Vepar. "When have you seen her?" He'd assumed Vepar knew Poppy's name from him, not that he recalled saying it, but there was no way he should have seen her. Not if he'd only been possessing this awful cat.

Then Killian recalled the man from the art show.

"You were there last night."

Vepar pulled back the cat's lips in a sneer. "I was. She was delightful. And so tempting. But I doubt Satan would be as understanding."

Killian growled low in his throat and lunged for the cat. Vepar jumped away, darting past Killian's legs and out of the room.

"Satan would love to hear about the dalliance that's keeping you from your work, now wouldn't he?" Vepar called from somewhere in the living room.

Killian stood in the middle of the living room, scanning the room for grayish-white fur.

"Vepar, you stay away from her. Or I'll—"

"You'll what? Satan is not pleased. I'd be more worried about that, if I were you."

Vepar purred, the sound loud and oddly perverse. Then the room fell silent.

Killian growled again. Was Vepar telling the truth? Was Satan that angered by Killian's absence? Killian didn't quite believe him. But at the same time, Vepar had been at the art gallery. That was why Killian hadn't been able to use his mind control, and that was why he'd sensed something off about that man. The guy had been possessed by Vepar.

"Just kill her," Vepar's earlier words echoed through Killian's head. Would Vepar do that? He would if Satan ordered it.

The only thing Killian knew for certain was Poppy had to be guarded.

Poppy made a frustrated sound low in her throat as she tossed down the mascara wand and reached for a tissue. So far, getting ready for the evening had been nothing but an exercise in frustration.

Much like the day in general. Killian had been mostly true

to his word, letting her work, although he'd stopped by twice. Just to say hi, he'd said, but she'd sensed a tenseness about him.

Maybe he was honestly as nervous about all this as she was.

She swiped at her watering eye and the smudge of black that now marred her cheek. And her nerves were taking their toll. So far she'd managed to cut herself shaving, burn a lock of her hair with the curling iron, and now poke herself in the eye with the mascara.

She looked worse than when she started getting ready.

"What are you doing?"

Poppy looked in the bathroom mirror to see Daisy behind her. She had on a baseball cap and Windbreaker. A backpack was slung over her shoulder.

"Getting more makeup in my eyes than on my lashes."

Daisy smiled, excitement on her face, which Poppy knew wasn't related to her trip with Emma. "You look great."

Poppy didn't feel like she looked great.

"What time is he picking you up?"

"Six," Poppy said, although the *he* Daisy was referring to wasn't the *he* who was actually coming. Poppy didn't feel good lying, but she wasn't about to tell Daisy she was going to all this fuss for a date with Killian. Poppy still suspected Daisy had wanted to matchmake her and Killian, and she didn't want Daisy getting any false hopes about that.

She certainly couldn't explain that she was just having a fling with the man. No, Daisy would never know about that.

"Okay, well I have to head down to Emma's. They are leaving in like fifteen minutes or so."

"What time is it?" Poppy asked.

"Only five-fifteen. You have plenty of time." Daisy grinned again like a kid finding out that Santa had left the very gift she'd asked for under the Christmas tree.

A pang of guilt tightened Poppy's chest. But she took a deep breath and forced the remorse aside. After all, she was taking steps in the right direction.

Sort of, anyway.

Poppy turned as Daisy stepped into the bathroom. They hugged, and Poppy kissed her cheek.

"Be good."

Daisy rolled her eyes. "I'm always good."

"I know," Poppy said, not holding back an ounce of the love and pride she felt for her little sister. Daisy was a great kid. She probably would have been no matter what, but Poppy allowed herself a moment of satisfaction. She had done a good job raising her sister thus far.

"Text me when you get there," she told Daisy, hugging her again.

"Of course."

"Actually, text me when you get on the road too."

Daisy shook her head. "Don't be such a worrywart. Just enjoy your evening." She started to leave the room, then paused. "You haven't even told me this guy's name."

The question caught Poppy off guard. She hesitated, then she spotted the shampoo on the edge of the tub. Herbal Essence.

"Herb," she said automatically.

Daisy wrinkled her nose. "Herb? That's not a hot name."

Poppy made a face. She couldn't disagree.

"Well, have fun with Herb. I hope he's cuter than his name."

"Oh, he is," Poppy assured her. Killian was much cuter than the imaginary Professor Herb.

Daisy left then, off for her weekend of seaside fun.

What kind of fun was she going to have tonight? Poppy wondered as she returned to the mirror to repair the damage done earlier.

*   *   *

Killian had lurked in the hallway outside Poppy's door most of the day—making sure Vepar, in any form, didn't appear at her apartment. Now Daisy was gone, and he couldn't wait any longer to see Poppy. Both to be sure she was safe and also just to see her.

Since his run-in with Vepar, he'd debated going back to the original plan of just finding Poppy a man and returning to Hell—tonight if possible. But he still wasn't sure. Something kept telling him he had to stay. Something beyond this spell.

One thing was for sure, he had to keep Poppy safe.

He pounded on the door with more force than necessary, his nerves and protectiveness making him agitated, anxious.

What was taking her so long? He lifted his hand, ready to knock again, when he heard the knob rattle. Then the door opened to reveal a Poppy he'd never seen before.

And all other worries left his mind, as his gaze roamed over her. She looked . . . gorgeous.

She wore a Chinese-style dress with a high collar and ornate cloth buttons. The black brocade with bright red flowers brought out the paleness of her delicate features and the darkness of her wide eyes. Her brown hair was swept up into a loose chignon, tendrils escaping to frame her face. The dress stopped mid-thigh, revealing a long expanse of shapely legs and tiny feet encased in strappy black heels.

Her weight shifted from one of her small feet to the other, and Killian realized he was doing nothing but staring. He looked up at her face, only to realize she was staring at him too.

Once he'd formulated this "affair plan," he'd purchased some new clothes just for this date. A Kenneth Cole suit coat, black tie. He'd also bought a Kenneth Cole shadow stripe dress shirt, which he wore with jeans. He'd even bought a new pair of black shoes. Bruno Magli.

He suspected not a single thing Poppy wore was designer, but her look blew him out of the water.

She obviously didn't agree.

"You look amazing," she said, smiling tentatively. Just a hint of the dimple he found so appealing appeared. A little tease.

"I think 'amazing' is the word that applies to you," he told her. Then, for the first time, as if it was totally natural and truly his right, he kissed her. Right in the open doorway.

Poppy stayed in his arms for a few moments. Then, groaning, she pulled her lips away from his. But she rested her forehead against his chest.

"If we keep doing that, all the work of dressing up will be for nothing."

Killian smiled, dropping a kiss onto the top of her head. He liked knowing she was struggling not to just head straight to the bedroom too. But he followed her lead, and with hands on her hips moved her away from him.

He smiled at her. "We'd better go now then. Or we never will."

She nodded and disappeared back into the apartment to grab a black wrap and her purse.

Killian rested his head on the doorframe, willing his body to calm down. How could he be feeling like this? He had a crazy demon stalking Poppy. He had been gone from Hell for nearly a week. Gone from the place he considered home. And possibly, Satan was really pissed at him. Yet all he could think about was this woman. This little slip of a mortal.

He was losing his mind. But right now, he wanted nothing more than to follow her inside, close the door and ravish Poppy on every bare surface in the house. And just pretend nothing else existed except the two of them.

"Ready," she said, returning to the door. He straightened and forced his brightest smile.

He nodded. He would figure out how to best protect her, but after tonight. Tonight was theirs.

* * *

Once out on the sidewalk, Poppy lifted her flushed face toward the evening breeze, thankful for the cool air.

One kiss and she was burning for the man. If she'd been a little more forward, she would have suggested forgetting the outing and just heading to bed. But she wasn't that forward. Yet.

Silly girl, her aroused body told her. And she couldn't argue. But she managed to rally and get her body under control. A bit.

"Where are we headed?" she asked.

He took her hand, linking his fingers through hers. "You just follow me."

She smiled at his self-assured tone. "So you know your way around now, huh?"

"Well, considering I just spent a whole night walking around the city, I kind of gave myself a crash course."

"Find any new ghosts?" she asked, wondering how many nights he'd been up wandering the spookier parts of historical Boston.

He gave her a look that she couldn't quite decipher, and she noticed he tensed. The same tenseness she'd sensed during his visits today.

"None that we're going to think about tonight."

She got the definite feeling his response had a double meaning, but she didn't understand it.

He led her to the T, and after several stops and a line change, Poppy realized they were headed for Beacon Hill.

"Where are we going?" Her curiosity was killing her.

"You'll have to just wait and see."

They walked another block, and then Killian stopped. Poppy looked around. "Are we here?"

He nodded. "We're here."

Poppy frowned. Most of the buildings along this street

looked like brownstone apartments. Spring flowers had started to bloom in some of the flower boxes. And though it was beautiful, she couldn't see why they were here.

She finally gave up, raising a quizzical eyebrow. "Why are we here?"

He chuckled, the sound low and rich. He grabbed her hand and pulled her toward one of the brownstones. As they walked up the concrete steps, Poppy noticed a sign painted on the frosted glass of the front door in scrolling green lettering.

A Garden in Every Childhood.

"What is this?" Poppy asked.

"Go look." He pushed open the door for her to enter.

She glanced at him, and he gave her an encouraging smile.

She stepped inside and realized it was a gallery. But unlike last night's gallery, there was nothing "adult" about this exhibition. Instead of a world of the erotic, she was suddenly enveloped by an atmosphere of enchantment.

She walked farther into the room, her senses overwhelmed by color and texture and whimsy. Paintings of various sizes hung on the walls. Some done in watercolor, some in pencil, some in oils. All depicted fantasy worlds. Fairies, dragons, magical lands.

Poppy turned slowly, taking in everything until she'd come full circle back to face Killian.

"What is this place?"

"It's a gallery that sells fantasy artwork. Some of the art here is from children's books. A lot is just made specifically to sell."

She gazed around her again, moving to look more closely at an amazing painting of a pond scene with flowers and water lilies and iridescent water nymphs waltzing on the water's surface, leaving rippling patterns in their wake.

The one beside it was a darker pencil drawing of an irritable-looking ogre in his lair. The detailing of his scaly skin, his tattered clothing, the annoyance in his eyes—sheer magic.

She turned back to Killian, stunned. "How did you find this place?"

Killian shrugged, a smug little quirk to his lips. "I just happened upon it during one of my research trips."

In truth, he really didn't know how he'd found the tiny gallery himself. He'd been walking, his mind totally consumed with Poppy. And his dream. And what he'd said to Poppy in his dream.

Yet something had drawn him out of those thoughts, just in time to notice this particular townhouse and that particular, almost unreadable sign on the door.

He found himself climbing the steps to inspect the sign closer. When he'd been able to read the name, and realized it was a gallery, he'd immediately thought of Poppy's artwork. Even before he'd peeked through the window. Even before he saw it was indeed a gallery of fantasy and fairy-tale artwork.

But as soon as he'd peeked inside, he knew he had to bring Poppy here.

In fact, this place had triggered the idea of an affair too. He supposed whimsical fairy-tale images were an odd segue into that train of thought, but seeing the art got him thinking about Poppy getting her confidence back. About her artwork and herself.

He started to think that was why he was really here. And why he was so attracted to her. He was meant to have a fling with this woman. He was meant to give her back her groove.

He should be doubting that. He should be worrying about getting Daisy's wish granted, getting out of here and keeping Poppy safe. That was what a wise demon would do, but he wasn't. Again, it was as if he couldn't. He had to carry out this wish in a certain way—and that way required his staying here.

Now, watching her smile with amazement and admiration

at the painting in front of her, he felt certain he was doing the right thing.

"These pieces are amazing. I love them." She beamed at him, flashing that dimple that for some reason he found to be both so adorable and so sexy.

She meandered to another painting, mesmerized by the details. Then she looked at him again, and though her lips were still curved into a smile, he sensed hesitance in her dark eyes.

"This—this is like the kind of artwork I used to do."

"I know."

She gave him a querying look. "I know I told you I wanted to illustrate children's books, but I didn't think I told you my work was like this."

"No, that's true. You didn't." He paused, wondering if she'd be annoyed by the fact he'd seen her work. Then he decided lying wasn't an option—not when he couldn't tell the truth about so many other things. Besides, he wanted her to realize her work was amazing.

"I accidentally saw it that day when I brought you your copy edits so you could work on the couch. I'd been looking for a book you could use as a makeshift desk, and pulled down one of your sketchbooks."

Poppy nodded, but he couldn't really read her reaction. Did she consider that a breach of privacy? Was she upset?

"I was so impressed," he said. "You are very talented. As talented as these artists, if not more so."

Poppy looked back at the painting in front of her, an oil of a fairy town built on the limbs of a giant oak. Lightning bugs served as streetlights. Leaves and acorns were fashioned into houses. Fairies flitted here and there.

"Do you really think so?" She didn't look in his direction as she asked.

"I do. You are amazing."

She looked at him then, hope glittering in her eyes. She

really didn't quite believe him, but she wanted to. He could see that.

He reached for her hands then, pulling her to face him.

"You have no idea how amazing you are." He kissed her then, a sweet, soft kiss, maybe a little worshipful too.

"In every way," he murmured as they parted.

Her cheeks colored like pink glaze on white porcelain, but he wasn't sure if the blush was because of his words or his actions. Either way, she'd see how wonderful she was. He'd be sure of that.

After the kiss, they wandered around the gallery, hand in hand, stopping to admire and to discuss. Poppy seemed to favor colored-pencil drawings. She liked lots of detail and color. Killian did too.

Once Poppy had looked her fill, he suggested they go eat.

Poppy seemed almost relieved at that idea, and Killian didn't think it was because she was starving.

"Are you nervous about what might happen later?" he asked with a naughty grin.

"Maybe." She cast him an apprehensive look.

He stopped walking down the sidewalk, drawing her to a halt too.

"There's no pressure here," he told her. Although he wouldn't lie to himself that he was hopeful there was going to be a "later."

He kissed her, keeping this one brief, so as not to shatter her nerves completely.

"Thank you," she said with a small, still unsure smile. But he did notice her gaze returned to his lips, and he chose to see that as a good sign.

But instead of kissing her again, which was what he wanted to do, he started walking again.

"Sushi, here we come."

Poppy glanced at him, this time her expression a different kind of uncertain. "Sushi? Really?"

CHAPTER 31

"It's really not bad," Poppy said.

Killian laughed. "Not exactly rave reviews."

"I do like it," she insisted. "At least what I managed to get to my mouth." She wagged her chopsticks at him. She'd not been terribly successful with her utensils. Of course, the two glasses of plum wine might not have helped.

"You did great," he assured her.

She knew he was lying, but she appreciated his attempt to allay her embarrassment.

"And I do love the décor," she said, settling back against the cushions to take in the lovely rice-paper partitions and ornately carved woodwork. They sat in their own private booth, which had also made her ineptness with her chopsticks a little less harrowing.

"I love the décor too," he said, and she knew he wasn't referring to the restaurant at all. Her cheeks burned, even as her heart skipped at his compliment.

"I really like the privacy—so I can do this," he murmured as he leaned in to steal a kiss. She leaned in too, loving how he felt and tasted. The embrace intensified, their passion exploding as easily as gasoline ignited by a mere spark.

But she broke the kiss before it could get too passionate, too out of control.

"Shy?" He gave her a teasing smile.

"A little."

He glanced at her mouth longingly, but then he took a sip of his sake.

"I still cannot believe you speak such fluent Japanese," Poppy said suddenly, trying to get her lust- and plum-wine-dazed mind back onto a different topic.

"You shouldn't be so impressed—I can only speak a little."

"It's still amazing. Do you speak other languages? You know, besides Swedish."

He nodded. "I have a basic knowledge of several languages: French, Russian, some Italian and Spanish. A little Portuguese too. Even some Hungarian."

He stroked her leg under the table, his fingers toying with the hem of her skirt. She caught his wandering hand, trying to keep her thoughts appropriate for a restaurant.

He grinned, but kept his hand still under hers.

"And Swedish."

His smiled faded just a bit. "And Swedish, of course."

"How did you learn them all?"

"For my work," he said.

"So you've traveled all over the world to do your paranormal investigations?" She supposed that made sense. There were ghosts and spooky stories everywhere.

He nodded. "Yes."

With his free hand, he reached for his sake, taking a deep sip.

Poppy took a sip of her drink too. The wine was sweet and a little syrupy, but she liked the plum flavor.

"All the traveling must have toned down your Swedish accent," she realized. "In fact, you really have none."

He turned to her then and said, *"Om lopp JAG icke gör det har en Svensk accent. Jag er en demonen, inte en smula Svensk."*

"That's the first time I've heard you speak Swedish." Poppy's dark eyes glittered, clearly excited to hear Killian speak in his "native" language. "What did you say?"

What did he say? That no, he didn't have a Swedish accent, because he was a demon, not a Swede. But Killian couldn't tell her, by Daisy's orders, except in a language Poppy couldn't understand. Still the incomprehensible admission felt good somehow.

Instead he said, "I just said 'I don't speak Swedish much these days, so I have lost my accent.' "

She nodded, taking another sip of her wine.

"I recognize the words *Swedish* and *accent.*"

He smiled. Great, was he going to spend the night teaching her Swedish? Which he could do. Demons could speak all languages. But those weren't really the type of lessons he was hoping for tonight.

"I also heard something that sounded like *demon.*"

He paused, his drink halfway to his mouth, his lustful thoughts evaporating. Damn it, he shouldn't have said that.

"Um, yeah, that is the Swedish word for—for paranormal. I actually said, 'Since becoming a paranormal investigator, I don't speak Swedish much anymore.' "

She nodded, willingly accepting his explanation. Then she laughed. "That's kind of strange, isn't it? I mean since your paranormal expertise is in demonology."

He smiled, the gesture strained. "Yes, isn't that strange?"

Poppy sipped her wine again, but then pushed it away. "That's good but very sweet."

Killian was relieved at the change of topic. "Perhaps you'd like some tea."

She nodded, smiling at him again, that lovely dimple peeking out at him.

"I should keep my wits about me; it would seem you could seduce me in several languages."

"*Äsch, JAG ja hoppas så.*"

She smiled, but eyed his naughty grin suspiciously. "What did you say now?"

He leaned in until his lips just barely brushed against hers, then murmured, "I certainly hope so."

He kissed her, this time until they were both senseless with desire.

When the waitress returned, they barely managed to end the kiss. But Killian did have the wits to pull away, knowing Poppy wasn't totally comfortable with their public displays of affection . . . or rather lust.

Killian asked the waitress for the check, and when he turned back to Poppy, true to form, her cheeks blazed bright red.

"I think I should go to the restroom before we leave," she said, clearly trying to gather herself.

He smiled, loving her sweet shyness just as much as her wanton abandon.

She slid out of the booth and headed toward the back of the restaurant. Killian glanced around for the waitress. He wanted to pay and get Poppy home. His cock pulsed against the denim of his jeans, clearly in total agreement.

Poppy stepped into the restroom, glad for the coolness of the large, tiled room. She hadn't really needed to use the bathroom, but she needed a moment to collect herself. At this rate, Killian would have her naked on the subway on the way home.

She braced herself on the sink, trying to get her raging libido under control. After a moment, she reached for a paper towel and dampened it and pressed the square over her heated cheeks and neck.

Behind her, she heard the door open. A tall woman with dark hair entered, joining her at the sink rather than going to the stalls.

She rifled through a satchel purse, finally retrieving a silver tube of lipstick. She leaned over the sink, getting closer to the mirror to apply the makeup. Then she stopped, seeming to notice Poppy for the first time.

She lowered the lipstick and smiled at Poppy from the mirror.

"I hope you don't mind my saying this," she said, her voice oddly husky, "but aren't you the lucky lady?"

Poppy smiled, but knew she couldn't keep the confusion off her face.

"Your man," the woman said. "He's something else."

Poppy started to say Killian wasn't her man, but caught herself. Why not let this woman think he was hers? He was for now anyway.

"He is pretty amazing," Poppy admitted.

"Too good to be true."

Poppy couldn't deny that. She nodded, turning to toss the wet paper towel in the trash. When she turned back, the woman was still watching her, but this time there was a very strange look on her face.

"Be careful with a man like that," the woman said, her smile suddenly looking more sinister than friendly. "You could think he's going to show you Heaven, then you end up in Hell."

The woman laughed. A strange, guttural, crazy laugh that echoed eerily off the tiles.

Poppy forced a smile and backed away from the sink. She nearly ran to the door, but she couldn't stop herself from looking back as she exited. The woman still stood by the sink. Her body was that of a female, but Poppy could have sworn the reflection in the mirror was that of a man.

"Did you pay the check?"

Killian grinned at Poppy's anxiousness, pleased to see that she was as ready to move on with the evening as he was.

Until he noticed the paleness of her skin and the emotion flashing in her eyes. Definitely not desire. Definitely fear.

Instantly, he was up, looking past her toward the back of the restaurant.

"Are you okay? Did something happen?"

Poppy shook her head—a little too quickly. A little too adamantly. "No. Everything's fine. I just want—I just would like to go home."

He studied her a moment longer, then again glanced over her shoulder.

"Of course." He rose and moved to wrap a protective arm around her. She sank against him, and he could actually feel she was trembling.

Something had happened in the restroom. And he had no doubt it was Vepar. What the hell did he want?

By the time they got back to her apartment, Poppy had made up her mind that she'd imagined the incident in the restroom. It had to have been the wine. The lighting. Her own overstimulated body. Probably a combination of all of the above. But here in her cozy living room, the whole event seemed, well, silly.

But of course, now that she was here, alone with Killian, a whole different kind of nervousness filled her.

She glanced at him. He leaned on the hallway doorframe, almost as if he was afraid to enter the living room with her. Their arousal had simmered all night, and now that they were alone, maybe he was having second thoughts.

As if to corroborate, he remained where he was and asked, "Poppy, are you sure?"

She stared at him for a moment. She was nervous, but she wanted him too much to let her nerves stop her.

She nodded, just a slight bob of her head, but that was enough for him.

"Come here." His voice was rougher now, almost guttural.

She hesitated for only a moment, then walked toward him, watching his expression as she got nearer. His golden eyes burned with desire. Hot, hungry. The same emotions that blazed inside her.

Her body vibrated with need as she stopped just inches from him. She raised her face to him, knowing that uncertainty also mingled with her need for him. But she hoped something else was clear in her eyes. Trust.

She trusted him.

CHAPTER 32

But even as she offered her trust, she was scared.

Killian loomed over her like a ravenous lion, his golden eyes flashing with burning hunger. But that wasn't what scared her. She somehow knew he'd do whatever she asked. He'd stay; he'd go. He didn't frighten her.

She was what scared her. She was frightened of what would happen once she spent a whole night in his arms, once he was deep in her body, making her his. But she was just as frightened of telling him no and letting him walk out the door.

Could she handle this? She closed her eyes for a moment, willing herself to stop being so nervous, so scared to take any risks.

Then she felt his hands cupping her face. Large warm hands, making her feel delicate, and protected. She opened her eyes and met his gaze.

"Poppy." Her name was like a prayer on his lips. His eyes searched her face, concern replacing some of the yearning.

"I—I want you so much," she admitted. Her heart raced, a mixture of desire and fear.

"I want you too."

His hands still held her, and his lips came down, pressing to hers. Not a wild kiss of passion. Not one of persuasion.

Just a gentle brushing of his lips against hers. First at the corners of her mouth, then directly on the center.

"We'll do whatever you want," he told her against her lips.

She nodded, knowing that was her answer. She was doing this. She had to do this, or she would regret letting him leave for the rest of her life.

She reached up and caught one of his hands. Without a word, she turned and led him to her bedroom. The room was shadowy, the only light that from the living room. But she didn't reach for her lamp. She found the dimness comforting.

She turned back to him, and this time, she was the one to press her mouth to his. Her lips trembled against his, her fingers quivering as she touched his unruly hair, the strands as soft as his large body was hard.

He reached up to curl his fingers around one of her hands, then lifted his head, bringing their joined hands between them. Gently, he feathered kisses over each of her trembling fingers, his eyes still locked with hers.

"You don't have any idea how beautiful you are, do you?" he whispered.

She shook her head.

"Well, I intend to show you. And you'll never doubt it again."

She almost believed him. She wanted to believe him.

He shifted then, his movement so quick, she barely registered it until she was lifted high against his muscular chest. Not even time for a surprised cry, but her arms did come up around his neck to balance herself.

He strode to the bed, settling her in the center. She lay back against the softness of her duvet, watching as he straightened.

After a few moments, he touched her again, running a hand from her knee down to her ankle, where he paused at her shoe. With nimble fingers, he worked the buckle open.

The shoe thumped to the floor. His hands moved to the other leg, skimming downward again, knee to ankle; then he unfastened that shoe.

"Did I tell you how sexy your shoes looked?"

She shook her head, not sure what he'd said or not said. All she could focus on was this moment.

He curled his hands around her foot, his thumbs pressing into the arch, the pressure so erotic, she almost cried out. He massaged her foot for a moment, then repeated the action on the other foot, and this time she couldn't contain her whimper.

"Feel good, baby?"

She nodded, closing her eyes. He continued to knead her foot, the touch more sensual than she could have imagined. Then his hands moved to her ankle, her calf, up to her thigh.

Then his hands were gone. She whimpered again, opening her eyes. He smiled down at her.

"Want more, baby?"

"Yes," she whispered, her voice rough with desire.

He massaged up her other leg, stopping just short of the place that ached most for his touch.

Instead, he held out a hand to her. Mindlessly, she accepted it, and he hoisted her to her feet, her rubbery legs barely supporting her. But he anchored her against his broad, hard chest, while the other hand worked on the zipper at her back.

"I love this dress," he murmured, his lips close to her ear, his breath brushing her hair, tickling her skin. "I told you that, right?"

She nodded again, although she still didn't recall what he'd told her. She thought to tell him she couldn't remember anything beyond this moment, but her tongue refused to work.

Then he was pushing her dress down her body, and all thought was gone. She stood before him in just her black lace bra and matching panties.

This time he was the one to make a noise deep in his throat as his gaze skimmed over her body.

"Damn, you are so, so beautiful."

In that moment, she felt beautiful.

He caught her around the waist and brought her body up against his, her skin sensitive to the material of his clothes.

A brief moment of lucidity made its way to her dazed brain. "You need to undress too."

He smiled down at her, the curve of his lips lopsided and sexy. "Oh, I'm going to, don't you worry."

He stole a quick kiss, then spun her in his arms, the twirl making her dizzy. But she liked the feeling of her bottom pressed against his groin. She could feel his erection and instinctively rubbed against it.

He groaned and pressed her down onto the bed, his weight coming down with her. But all too quickly, he was gone again. She started to roll over to see where he'd gone, but his voice stopped her.

"Stay on your belly."

She obeyed, resting her head on her arms, waiting. She could hear the brush of material against material and realized he must be undressing. She ached, wanting to see him. She turned her head as much as her prone position would allow, but she couldn't see him. Not from that angle.

Then the mattress shifted under his weight as he joined her.

She moaned as his strong hands cupped her shoulders, rubbing the muscles there. They worked over the muscles of her back, pausing at her bra to undo the hook. When it fell away, he began his massage again, moving lower and lower.

His fingers reached her panties, wasting no time to slide them down and off her legs. Then Killian rubbed her bottom, squeezing the cheeks, a fingertip tracing the line that ran between her thighs toward the point that pulsed for his touch.

"Like that?"

She nodded vigorously. She'd had no idea someone massaging her bottom could be so erotic. Then he slipped one of his hands down past her bottom to the swollen aching flesh just below. His fingers parted her, circling the entrance of her vagina, teasing her.

"Oh, baby, you are so wet."

She thought for a split second that maybe she should be embarrassed at her prone, helpless position. At his comment about the intensity of her arousal.

Then his fingertip found her swollen clitoris, and all concerns fled, chased away on a rush of total ecstasy. She gasped and wantonly lifted her bottom to offer him better access.

And he rewarded her, staying on that engorged nubbin, while he filled her with a long finger, sinking in and out, mimicking what she wanted him to do with another part of his anatomy.

"Are you going to come for me?" His words were more a coax than a question.

"Yes," she gasped. "Yes."

He continued the motion, each thrust bringing her closer to the thing he requested. Then as her muscles began to spasm around the finger deep within her, he pushed on her clitoris.

And instantly her release hit her, a hard, sudden impact, knocking her breath from her with its intensity.

He continued to stroke her until the orgasm slowly rippled into small tremors. Carefully he withdrew his hand from her and eased her over onto her back.

She gazed up at him from heavy, hooded eyes.

"How was that, baby?"

She smiled up at him. "Wonderful. But now I want you inside me."

Killian fought back a moan at her demand. He wanted to be inside her too, but tonight wasn't about him. This was about Poppy and making her understand what a desirable, amazing woman she was.

She watched him, from those sleepy eyes, waiting. Then she levered herself onto her elbows.

"Come here," she whispered, a soft, sweet command.

He leaned over her, and she kissed him. Her lips were as soft and sweet as her voice. One of her hands came up to cup the back of his head, and she pulled him down with her.

"I want to feel you deep inside me," she murmured against his ear as she spread her legs, begging him to move between them.

That was a plea he couldn't deny. Hands on either side of her head, his shifted himself over her, bringing his hips into alignment with hers.

But he didn't enter her. Instead, he rubbed his erection against her, between her lips, against her wet heat. She gently pumped her hips too, slanting herself to better feel him rubbing against her.

He watched her expression, seeing her clearly despite the shadows moving around them. She was so gorgeous, her hair coming loose from the twist on the back of her head. Her pale skin flushed with desire. Her eyes sparkling.

He kissed her, needing to taste and feel that beauty with every part of him. Her hands clung to his shoulders, small fingers digging into his skin.

"Please," she begged against his mouth. "Please, I need you inside me."

He kissed her again, positioning himself, just nudging the head of his penis inside her. But Poppy was too impatient for slow. Her hands left his shoulders to grab his hips and with a powerful pull, she brought him fully into her wet, tight heat.

He cried out at the strength of his reaction. Ecstasy shot through him, making his muscles and his breath seize. He had to remain still, not just to allow her to adjust but to get back his control.

"Poppy," he moaned, and she writhed in response. He braced his hands on the mattress, and slowly he pivoted his hips, testing both his restraint and her ability to accept his size.

"You are so tight," he gritted through clenched teeth. Damn, she was going to push him over the edge in seconds flat.

"You are so big," she said back, straining against him.

He started to ask if he was hurting her, but her small wiggles and the lifts of her hips made it impossible to talk. So instead he focused on keeping his movements smooth and steady and not too deep.

But Poppy was having none of that. Her hands cupped his buttocks, fingers digging into the muscles there as she urged him in harder and deeper.

With a growl, he gave in to her insistence. He thrust into her, filling her over and over until they were both panting. Both filling the air with mindless moans and cries.

As Poppy got closer, her head thrashed from side to side against the covers. She bucked up against him, screaming out her orgasm.

He followed her, shouting out her name, keeping himself buried inside her, her muscles squeezing him, his cock pulsating in rhythm.

Damn. Damn.

CHAPTER 33

Poppy couldn't imagine that she'd so easily fallen asleep with Killian in her bed, but when she came back to awareness, sunshine flooded into her bedroom. She blinked, looking around her.

Killian was sprawled next to her, his large, muscular body taking up more than his fair share of the bed. She rose up on her elbow, admiring what she hadn't had the patience to admire last night.

Killian was beautiful all the time, but in his sleep he was almost painfully so. There was a sweetness to his face, like an angel fallen to earth. Lashes that most of the female population would kill for were splayed against his angled cheekbones. Waves of hair shone brown and gold and nutmeg against her pale green pillowcases. Perfect sculpted lips and a chiseled jawline. He was a breathtaking combination of pure beauty and pure masculinity.

Of course, his body was nothing but masculine magnificence. Tall with lean muscles, he had the body of a swimmer, with broad shoulders and tapered hips. His skin was golden and smooth, although fine golden hair covered his forearms and legs. Slightly darker hair whorled around his belly button, then into a line that disappeared under the corner of her duvet, the only bit of blanket that covered him in his sleep.

And she didn't think that had to do with modesty. Killian didn't strike her as the type to be worried about his nudity.

Using that as her justification, she reached for the edge of the blanket. Carefully she lifted it, peeking underneath at the part of his anatomy that had been inside her, but she'd had yet to really see.

Even soft and nestled amid curling, tidy pubic hair, his penis was large. But then she'd been aware of that fact last night too, as he'd filled her so fully that she'd been sure she would burst. In fact, as she stretched out her legs now, a pleasant soreness reminded her of just how well endowed he was.

She smiled to herself, realizing it was that secret kind of smile where only she knew what had occurred to bring it to her face. She flopped back against the pillows, curling on her side to watch Killian sleep.

He really was amazingly attractive. By far the handsomest man she'd ever seen. How had she gotten so lucky? She didn't know, but she wasn't going to question it. After all, this was supposed to be fun. Not too much analyzing allowed.

So she didn't question herself when she brushed a fingertip over his mouth, tracing the almost pouty curve of his lips. Then she snuggled against him. Even in his sleep, he curled an arm around her, tucking her close to his side. She smiled that secret smile again and let her eyes drift closed.

This was a nice way to wake up and a nice way to fall asleep too.

She moaned in her sleep as a large hand stroked over her skin, fingers plucking gently at her nipples, warm lips trailing kisses along her shoulder and neck.

Poppy opened her eyes, realizing this time she wasn't just dreaming. She looked down at herself, watching Killian's hand skimming over her body. Caressing her breasts, then down over her belly and between her thighs. She arched as he swirled a finger over her clitoris, and a broken gasp escaped her.

"Are you sore?" he murmured, his mouth right beside her ear.

"No."

He continued to tease her clitoris with light, sweeping brushes of his finger, gently bringing her to full arousal. When she was squirming for more, her breaths coming in short, whimpering bursts, he raised her leg and angled her so he could slide his huge erection between her thighs. He rubbed against her, spreading her open, then with low moans of his own, he entered her. Slowly, steadily filling her.

She gasped, arching her back, loving the feeling of him stretching her. Rocking her toward her release with long, unhurried thrusts.

"You feel so good," he whispered against her ear. "I fit like I was made for you."

She couldn't argue that, even if words would come. He did feel like he belonged there, deep inside her, sliding in and out, in and out.

Then his fingertips were back, stroking her. Rubbing that tiny sensitive spot that had the ability to make her scream. To suddenly make her moves frantic, desperate.

"There's no rush, baby." He kissed the side of her neck, then reached around to hold her chin, tilting her head to kiss her. His kiss was as thorough and leisurely as his lovemaking.

One hand returned between her thighs, while the other played with her breast, teasing her nipple. And still he kissed her.

The combination was too much, all those delicious sensations, catapulting her toward her climax. She tensed, waves of ecstasy flooding over her, so it was hard to catch her breath.

And still he didn't stop, touching her until yet another orgasm shook her. Then another.

Finally, holding her tight against him, his arm wrapped around her middle, her back to his chest, his hips slanted between hers, he began to drive into her deeper, harder. His speed picked up until she could feel his own release wrack his body.

He cried out, clutching her tightly to him.

Gradually, his hold loosened, but he didn't let her go. He again pressed kisses to her shoulder, and once he'd relaxed, she rolled over to face him.

"Good morning," he said, pressing a sweet, lingering kiss to her mouth.

"Good morning." She smiled back, then lifted her head to check the clock on her nightstand. "Yep, we just made morning still. Eleven fifty-six."

He glanced over his shoulder at the clock too. "Well, no wonder I'm starving."

"Oh," Poppy said, sitting up, bringing the sheet with her. "I can make you something to eat."

As she was about to stand, Killian snagged the sheet, causing her to topple back against him. Then he rolled her under him, so she was pinned between his weight and the mattress.

They both dissolved into laughter at the silliness of his behavior.

"So does this mean you don't want me to make something?"

He shook his head, grinning down at her, his face so handsome, his smile so naughty.

"Not if it means you have to get out of this bed."

"Ah, so you're keeping me here all day?"

He raised an eyebrow, pretending to consider the idea. "And maybe all night too."

He kissed her, even though she was giggling. Or maybe because she was.

"Well, not all night," she said once they parted. She was

still grinning at him, loving how carefree and silly they could be with each other.

"Really? You need a break, huh?" His look was smug as if to say he knew she couldn't handle that much time in bed with him.

She giggled again. "I don't need a break. But tonight is the night we make my ex realize exactly what he's been missing."

Killian's smile withered like a cut flower left out of water. Then he recovered, although this smile didn't quite reach his eyes.

"That's right. Tonight is Project Adam. I don't know how I forgot."

Poppy studied him, trying to understand his response. He seemed disappointed, and maybe even a little irritated, which made no sense since this had been his idea all along.

He rolled off her, flopping onto his back. She remained beside him for a few moments, hoping some of the easy happiness between them would return. But he just remained still, staring up at the ceiling.

Her gut reaction was to feel awful. To feel his guardedness was her fault, but she caught herself. She couldn't understand what he was thinking unless she asked. And hadn't he said they needed to be open with each other? Keep things clear and honest.

She sat up, hesitating when she saw his distant expression.

"Killian, are you upset about something?"

Confusion clouded his eyes as if he was coming back from some faraway place, but then he recovered, shaking his head and offering a smile. Again that smile didn't quite reach his eyes.

"No. Not at all."

She must have not looked as if she believed him, because he broadened his smile. "I'm fine."

She debated questioning him further, but before she could decide, he touched her cheek.

She met his eyes and held his gaze for several moments. Then he smiled again. It was still not like the smiles of earlier, but better, less strained.

He tugged her down beside him, kissing the top of her head as she snuggled close to his side.

They stayed that way, quietly enjoying each other.

"Do you really believe in all the paranormal phenomena you study?" Poppy asked suddenly. For some reason her thoughts had gone back to the experience she'd had at the Japanese restaurant.

Killian's hand, which had been idly brushing over her back, stilled. He didn't answer for a moment, and then she felt him nod.

"I do believe in some of it, yes."

She nodded too, but didn't say anything.

"Why?" he asked.

She considered just letting the topic go, but then decided if anyone was going to believe her story or give an explanation for it, Killian was the person. After all, he made his living dealing with the supernatural.

"I—I just had a weird experience in the bathroom at that restaurant last night." She told him about what had happened and what she thought she'd seen.

Killian didn't say anything for a moment, and she wondered if maybe she'd made a mistake sharing the story.

Then he said, "If anything like that ever happens again, tell me right away."

His tone was serious, very serious.

She lifted her head to look at him. "Do you think it will happen again?"

He studied her for a moment, his expression intense, even a little worried. Then he shrugged, all intensity gone, and she almost wondered if she'd imagined the other reaction.

"Not likely, but I like to know about these things."

She nodded, confused. Was he worried or not? Or was he just interested because of his work?

"You know, I think I am hungry," he said suddenly as he cupped his large hand around the back of her head and pulled her down to him, kissing her. "And I need to keep my energy up."

She laughed. "Having trouble keeping up with me, huh?"

"Well, you are an imp. And they are notoriously energetic. And insatiable."

She rubbed a hand over his chest, appreciating all his hard muscles and hot smooth skin. Her roaming hand headed lower. And lower.

He cocked an eyebrow, then glanced down at where her hand was going. "See, insatiable."

She grinned, but stopped just below his belly button. "Pancakes? Or a ham and cheese omelet?"

He blinked, then grinned. "Insatiable tease."

She smirked back, but continued to swirl a fingertip around his flat little navel, the coarse hair tickling her.

He caught her tormenting hand, bringing it up to his lips. He pressed a lingering kiss to her knuckles, then each finger, and just like that the teasing tables were turned.

He nipped the pad of the finger that had been circling his belly button, then said, "Definitely an omelet."

She frowned, too lost in the erotic sensations of his mouth on her hand to follow.

"I'll have a ham and cheese omelet," he clarified with a smug glint in his eyes. "I need some protein to keep me going."

She made a face at him, but said, "Omelets it is."

She crawled off the bed, swathed in her version of a sage-colored, ill-fitting toga, and trundled toward the kitchen.

"Want help?" he called.

"Nah, just rest," she said, poking her head back in the doorway. "You'll need that too."

She giggled as she headed to the kitchen.

Killian listened to Poppy shuffling through the apartment, her sheet trailing after her. But once she was in the kitchen and the noises turned to the clatter of pots and pans, his smile disappeared. He stared at the ceiling.

What was he doing? She had encountered Vepar last night. There was no doubt. And to top it off, he was more upset about tonight's plans. That shouldn't be. He wanted her to finally see Adam and deal with her loss of her former boyfriend. Wasn't that the point of all this? Didn't he accept that eventually she would be with another man? That she deserved to move on?

But nothing was going as he'd expected. He'd really believed sex with Poppy would be great—which it was. Beyond great. The best of his existence, if he was being honest.

But he'd expected it to just be sex.

He grimaced at his own thoughts. *It is just sex. There isn't an option for it to be more.*

Not with Vepar out there, being a lunatic. Not with Killian himself being a demon.

He had to find her a human man. Someone to really love her. Not just have sex with her. He had to.

But even as he told himself that, a small portion of himself held back, unwilling to let go just yet.

He listened to Poppy again, the sounds of domesticity somehow as appealing as everything else about her. Slightly off-key singing filtered through the apartment too, and he imagined how she looked in her sea of sheet, well satisfied, her hair tousled, singing—the Rolling Stones. At least he thought it was the Rolling Stones.

She was truly, amazingly adorable.

And he was feeling that he was in too deep.

But as if her out-of-tune song was the melodic call of a siren, he found himself being drawn out of bed. Called to her.

He couldn't seem to get enough of her. But as long as he remembered this was just for a brief amount of time, then he would manage to complete the mission he was here to do.

Poppy smiled as she stepped into the shower, the hot water like Heaven on her aching muscles. Today had probably been one of the best days of her life.

She and Killian had spent the entire day together—mainly in bed. Well, and on the kitchen table and on the rug in front of the TV. He'd called her insatiable, but in truth, their desire for each other was unquenchable.

She'd never experienced that kind of need for someone. It was exhilarating and a little frightening all at once.

She closed her eyes and let her head rest on the tile wall, water beat on her back, lulling her. Bed beckoned her, but this time for sleep. Maybe they should just stay home and finally rest. After all, did it really matter if she made some point to Adam? A point he probably wouldn't even get?

She was pretty sure he hadn't been as torn up about their breakup as she'd been. Strike that, she was positive he hadn't been. But, she realized with a smile, after a day of being satisfied again and again by Killian, her heartbreak over Adam seemed years away. And pretty darn insignificant.

She opened her eyes as she heard the doorknob to the bathroom rattle and twist. She opened the shower curtain to see Killian standing there, naked. Amazingly, beautifully naked.

"Can I join you?"

She smiled, knowing the gesture was lazy. "Sure."

He stepped into the water, closing the curtain, shutting out everything but them and the wonderfully hot water.

"I'm so tired," she murmured, moving right into his arms

and resting her head on his chest as if it were the most natural thing to do.

Even now, after all they'd shared today, her comfort level with him still startled her. He was physical perfection. The kind of man who had always made her feel, well, plain. But she didn't feel that way with him.

His muscular arms came around her, a cocoon of Killian and water. She moaned.

"This feels like Heaven." She sighed.

He was silent for a moment, then she felt his head nod against the top of hers. "I think you might be right."

She stood, half-dozing in his embrace. How long she didn't know, but eventually he released her and reached for the bar of soap. He lathered a washcloth, then began to rub the slick material over her, soft and soothing.

She sagged against him, her back to his chest as he continued to wash her, his touch so gentle and wonderful, she whimpered. The terry cloth stimulated her nipples as he moved over them, around them, then down her belly.

Unbelievably, her body reacted, and when he brought the cloth between her thighs, she spread for him, telling him silently she wanted him again.

She felt him smile against the curve of her neck and shoulder.

"Not this time, baby," he murmured. "You're too sleepy and sore. And we'll never make it out tonight if we do."

She wanted to argue and say that was fine with her, but instead she just nodded. Then she turned in his arms and again, rested her head on his chest.

"You're right," she said. And for the rest of their shower she tried not to want him. A near impossible feat, but one she somehow managed.

Killian released her and stepped out of the shower.

"I'm going to go get some clean clothes, but I'll be back down here in five."

She nodded, remaining under the warm spray, too relaxed to move.

"Stay right here and I'll be back."

"Okay." She didn't have to be asked twice.

Killian toweled off and threw on yesterday's clothes. Then he snagged Poppy's keys. He wasn't leaving her in an unlocked apartment, even for a few minutes.

Then he hurried back to his place—oddly he was actually beginning to think of the fusty apartment that way.

"Vepar!" he yelled as soon as he entered. He yelled again, looking for the cat in the living room, then the bedroom. No sign of it. Or Vepar.

"Damn you." What was that psychotic demon's game? He didn't know. He just knew Vepar seemed intent on something.

Just kill her.

Vepar's words echoed in his head again.

That couldn't be his real goal, could it?

CHAPTER 34

As they stepped into the loud, crowded bar, Killian again asked himself why he had turned down Poppy's sweet shower offer. He could have made love to her, and then let them both fall into a deep, sated sleep. And avoided this outing altogether.

That way she'd be safe. And he wouldn't have to meet the man she'd wasted so many years mourning.

But here they were.

Maybe he could seduce her and get her back to her place. Then he caught himself. His mission wasn't about himself. It was about Poppy and her happiness.

But it was getting harder and harder to remember that. All he could think about was being with her himself. It was almost an—obsession.

Why did he want this mortal woman so much?

She shifted by his side, a hint of cinnamon reaching his nose like the warm spices of home. Her heat radiated over him like morning sunlight. Her face was ethereal, pure, lovely.

He paused. What was wrong with him? He was getting all—poetic, flowery—nauseating.

His gaze slid to her again. She looked beautiful—sweet and sexy all at the same time in a pair of jeans, a simple, fitted black top with a crocheted, bright pink scarf and black ballet flats. Her hair was loose around her shoulders, glossy and flyaway.

"You look amazing," he found himself saying as if the thoughts just couldn't stay contained in his head.

"Thank you." She smiled, although he could see in her dark eyes that she was nervous.

Those nerves bothered him. They told him she still cared about this Adam guy. But the bigger question was why did he care that she cared? She was a project—why couldn't he remember that?

She scanned the crowd, even rising up on her tiptoes to see the stage. Then she shrugged.

"I don't see him."

A feeling altogether too much like relief spread through his chest. He pushed the feeling aside and gestured to the bar. "Let's get a drink."

She nodded, still scanning the room.

He weaved his way through the crowd, a mixture of younger and older patrons. The area around the bar was packed, but he caught Poppy's hand and edged his way through, need for a drink making him more determined.

"Well, he still draws in a big crowd," Poppy said, as she squeezed through a group of thirty-something women.

Killian nodded, not pleased by that comment either.

He made it to the bar, waving to a bustling bartender who ignored him.

Wait on me now.

The bartender stopped in mid-order and walked over to Killian.

"Hey," the patron the bartender been helping yelled down that bar at him.

Go away.

The man promptly left the bar, drinkless, rejoining his

group of friends, who were none too happy that he returned empty-handed.

"What can I get you?" the bartender asked Killian, who looked at Poppy.

"Pinot noir, please."

"A double of Glenfiddich."

Not the year and the quality of the whisky he had at home, but tonight it would suffice.

Beside him, Poppy still searched the crowd.

Oh, yeah, it would do for tonight.

The bartender returned with the drinks, and Killian opened a tab. He took a long draught before handing the wine to Poppy.

"See him?"

She shook her head. "Maybe he didn't end up playing here tonight after all."

Could they be that lucky? He took another gulp of the scotch whisky.

Killian gritted his teeth more at his own stupidity than the burn of the liquor. Why was he being so ridiculous about this? He wasn't seriously involved with this woman. They were hanging out and having sex. He had no ties to her, and it wasn't as if he could have more with her anyway.

"You're a fuckin' demon," he muttered to himself, but Poppy frowned at him, her dark eyes sparkling with curiosity.

"What did you say?"

But he was saved from having to answer as a man jostled into her. Both turned to apologize, but then neither said a word.

The man spoke first. "Poppy."

"Adam," Poppy said.

The man—Adam—hugged her then. Poppy remained stiff

in his embrace for a second, then returned the hug, her arms going around his shoulders.

Killian watched, his jaw aching from how tightly he was clenching his teeth. He took a sip of his whisky, but even that didn't stem his desire to gnash his teeth.

Finally they parted.

"Eric told me you might come," Adam said, his gaze roaming over her, eating up the sight of her.

Poppy smiled, her eyes actually alight with some emotion that looked far too much like happiness for Killian's taste.

"Yes. I was so surprised to see him."

"I'm so surprised to see you," Adam said, touching her arm. Then he gestured across the bar. "Come sit with us. Eric and his wife are over there. And a couple of my friends."

"Okay." Poppy started to follow him, then stopped, suddenly remembering Killian was there.

"Oh Adam, this is my fr—"

Before she could finish, Killian moved forward to extend his hand. "Fiancé. I'm Poppy's fiancé. Killian."

Out of the corner of his eye, Killian could see Poppy's shocked expression, but he ignored her, offering Adam his most charming smile.

She's mine.

Adam blinked, some of his joy at seeing Poppy evaporating. "Killian. Nice to meet you."

Damn right, buddy, she's mine.

Killian waited for his conscience to tell him he was behaving idiotically, but it didn't.

"Over here," Adam said as he led them to a less crowded part of the bar to the right of the stage.

When they reached the table, Eric greeted them too, then introduced them to his wife, Karen, and the two other women at the table, Nancy and Gina.

Killian noticed Poppy blanch, just a bit, as Gina was introduced. Adam pulled up chairs and the two of them joined the others.

"So Poppy"—Karen leaned to be heard over the buzz of the bar—"you went to college with Adam and Eric?"

Poppy nodded. "Yes."

"We actually dated for what . . ." Adam looked at Poppy for the answer. Then at Killian a bit more warily.

"Almost three years," Poppy said with a polite, social smile.

Killian took another sip of his drink. Hell, even he knew that. As he set down his drink, he noticed that Gina was watching Poppy through narrowed eyes. But when she realized Killian was watching her, she smiled. The animosity he'd seen there switched to something that looked remarkably like interest.

Killian looked away, to chat with the other woman, Nancy, a music teacher at a local high school. And also with Eric, who overall seemed like a pretty decent guy. Killian definitely liked him better now than the last time he'd met him.

"Well, Eric and I need to get back to work here," Adam announced to the table, but Killian noticed his look lingered on Poppy.

The two men went to the stage and began tuning up. With Adam's attention otherwise engaged, Killian had the liberty of studying the guy. And in truth, he found it hard to understand why Poppy had held a torch for him.

Adam was pretty much average. Average height, maybe 5'10" or 5'11". He had brown hair and similarly colored eyes. His build wasn't particularly muscular, but not heavy.

He was pretty much like any guy anywhere.

But hadn't he kind of thought the same thing about Poppy when he first met her? Killian glanced at her. She was chatting with Eric's wife, her features animated, her charming dimple showing. She pushed her hair away from her face. He noticed the way her hand looked as she did so, and the flow and shimmer of her chestnut hair.

She was so far from average, he just couldn't recall how he could have ever come to that conclusion.

Poppy stopped talking to the other woman as Adam began to play. Her eyes fastened on the man.

Did she see someone beyond average right now too? Then she looked at Killian and smiled. A happy smile. Her attention returned to the man on the stage.

Yeah, she did.

Did she see her soul mate?

Poppy had to admit this was the kind of night a scorned woman fantasized about. She was sitting at a table with her ex, with the woman her ex had left her for, and Poppy had a totally hunky, utterly charming new boyfriend. Strike that, fiancé.

Yeah, this was pretty sweet, and she didn't really care if she was being petty.

Of course, as she watched Adam up on the stage, she couldn't quite imagine why she'd let him affect her life for so long. He was a good-looking guy with thick hair and a nice smile. But somehow he seemed like a faded memory of the person she'd loved all those years ago.

She glanced at Killian. Of course, any man would seem pretty washed out when compared with Killian. Beautiful, golden Killian. Even now her body hummed with the recollection of all the amazing things the man beside her had done to her in the last twenty-four hours.

She took a sip of her wine, smiling that secret smile again. Then she noticed Gina watching her, a frown tugging at the woman's full lips.

Poppy wanted to giggle at her annoyed expression. Poppy's secret smile wasn't a secret to Gina. And Gina was jealous.

Good, Poppy thought. She didn't want Adam back from Gina, but she was glad the other woman was envious of her. That made up for the hurt Poppy had suffered, knowing Adam was in Gina's bed. That while Poppy struggled alone, heartbroken, Gina and Adam had had each other.

"Darling," she said, leaning against Killian as she spoke. "Would you mind getting me another wine?"

"Sure."

She smiled, then kissed him. He seemed a little startled by the gesture, but quickly rallied, kissing her back, quite thoroughly.

"Can I get anyone else another drink?"

"I'll take a dirty martini," Gina said, smiling at Killian. The other two women declined.

After he left the table, Karen and Nancy let out appreciative sighs. Gina just shot her another resentful glare.

"Where on earth did you find him, Poppy?" Nancy watched Killian cross the room toward the bar. She shook her head, impressed at the sight.

"I met him through one of my sister's friend's parents. He is her cousin."

"If only my sister's friend's parents had cousins like that," Nancy said with a smile.

Poppy laughed.

"And you can just see he's mad about you," Karen said. "I can't think of the last time Eric looked at me the way Killian looks at you."

Poppy's smile slipped just a bit. If only those looks were real. If only . . .

She shoved the thought aside. She was going to enjoy this for what it was.

"Killian would probably tell you that I had him falling at my feet the very first night we met."

Karen and Nancy sighed again, and Gina looked as if she wanted to be ill.

Yes, tonight was pretty sweet.

Killian would like to say that he was enjoying the evening as much as Poppy seemed to be. She chatted with the other women. Well, not so much Gina. But something about Gina's clear animosity toward her seemed almost to please Poppy.

Even though Poppy had never said anything about Adam's leaving her and getting involved with another woman right away, he deduced Gina was that person.

And from the looks Gina kept throwing him, Killian got the impression she'd like to repeat history. He ignored her. Gina was not his type.

He'd definitely developed a rather strong attraction to petite, pixielike women with dark eyes and dimples.

"I'm going to find the restroom," Poppy said, flashing that dimple temptingly at him. Her cheeks were flushed, and he could see the wine had gone to her head a bit.

"I'll join you," he whispered so the rest of the table couldn't hear him. He felt safe with her near him. Vepar might be nuts, but he had enough sense not to approach Poppy with Killian at her side.

"You had your chance at bathroom sex earlier. As I recall you turned me down."

"Stupid, stupid me."

She laughed again, then stood, excusing herself.

He'd let her go, but follow. He didn't want her to become aware that he was nervous about her being alone. That would lead to questions he couldn't exactly answer.

After a few seconds, he excused himself to quickly make his way toward the restrooms. Then he leaned against the wall to wait. He'd give Poppy five minutes before he entered the ladies' room—rules and politeness be damned.

"So," a female voice said from close beside him, and he looked to see Gina standing very close indeed. She'd followed him, he had no doubt. "I heard Poppy telling Nancy that you are from Sweden."

Killian stepped away from her, not liking the hungry look in her eyes.

"Yes, that's right."

She raised an impressed eyebrow. "That's pretty exotic."

He shrugged. "Not really."

"It is to me," she said with a laugh, touching his arm.

He looked down at her hand, then decided to just ignore her advance. "I'm going to have another drink. Can I get you anything? Another dirty martini?"

She considered, then said, "Actually, what I'd really like now is a screaming orgasm."

Killian stared at her for a moment, stunned she'd said that. Of course, what mortal women did in bars really shouldn't shock him anymore.

"So you and Poppy," she said, clearly having no intention of continuing on to the restroom. "It's hard for me to imagine."

Killian frowned at the woman, disliking her more by the minute. "Why's that?"

"Poppy was always such a little mouse. Timid. Quiet. And you seem like the type to want a bolder, more self-assured woman."

He pretended to consider her words, then simply said, "Nope."

Gina looked shocked by his casual rejection. She glanced around as if she intended to flounce away, but instead she leaned against the wall, making herself at home.

"Really?" she said, doubt in her catlike eyes.

"Really. I quite like my Poppy. Although she's far from a timid mouse. She's caring, sweet and funny. Very talented. And believe me, she's bold and self-assured where it counts."

"I'm self-assured where it counts too." She laid a hand on his chest, fiddling with one of the buttons of his shirt. Then she stopped, her attention moving to a place just beyond his shoulder.

When he followed Gina's gaze, he saw Poppy standing in the doorway of the ladies room. Her pale face was a sickly white, her eyes wide.

"Poppy," Gina said as if pleased to see her. "Killian and I were just chatting."

Poppy nodded, but didn't say a word. She started toward them, her eyes looking anywhere but at Killian and Gina.

Killian fell into step beside her.

"That was nothing," he assured her, and Poppy instantly nodded, flashing him a quick glance that didn't hide her hurt or doubts.

"Oh, I know." Her voice was airy, but he knew she didn't feel as unconcerned as she sounded.

Poppy's stomach clenched. It was like history repeating itself. Adam had said that very same thing about Gina all those years ago. *That was nothing.*

Poppy had found them flirting outside one of the bars where he'd played regularly. The two of them were standing close together. Gina touching his arm. His shoulder.

That was nothing.

Adam left her not a week later for Gina.

And now Gina wanted the man Poppy had now. But she didn't even really *have* this man. Dread filled her.

"I forgot something in the restroom," she told Killian, spinning on her heel, not waiting for his response. "I'll meet you back at the table."

"He's not yours," Poppy said to her reflection in the ladies' room mirror as if saying it aloud would make her heart feel different. It didn't work.

But they were only having a fling. He'd told her he was interested in settling down . . . but obviously not with her. She was only affair worthy. Whereas Gina could be just the type Killian wanted to really date.

God, she felt sick.

But she had to pull herself together. She had to remain cool. She'd known this was one risk of agreeing to this relationship.

And she couldn't hide in here all night. She had to go back out there and act as if the interchange she'd seen between Killian and Gina didn't matter. Didn't shake her confidence. She wouldn't give Gina that satisfaction again.

She braced herself, fixing her hair, applying more lip gloss. Then she opened the restroom door. She half-expected to see Killian waiting for her. Instead, Adam stood there.

Disappointment washed over her.

"Hello, Adam."

Adam smiled, and she noticed his front teeth overlapped slightly. Had they always been like that?

"Poppy, it's so great to see you. You look fantastic."

She forced a smile. "Thanks, Adam."

"You know, I've thought about you so much over the years," Adam said, shifting closer to her.

"Have you?" She didn't believe him.

"Yes. I often regretted how I handled things. I sort of panicked when your parents died. The idea of having a kid around, of essentially becoming a parent . . ."

Poppy didn't say anything.

"I wanted to contact you. To see you again."

"But you didn't," Poppy said.

"No, I was a chicken. I'm sorry."

Poppy stared at this man in front of her. Adam. But not the Adam of her memories. She didn't even know this guy.

"Poppy, seeing you tonight, I know I can't lose you again."

She gaped at him. Was he serious? Did he really think she'd take him back? After what he'd done? Leaving her when she'd needed him most?

"I'm sorry, but you lost me years ago."

"It doesn't have to be that way. I could make everything up to you. Poppy, you are so lovely. Seeing you, I just know I made a terrible mistake."

Poppy almost wanted to laugh. She'd fantasized about this very thing. Adam standing in front of her, willing to leave Gina the way he'd left her. Begging her to take him back. Acknowledging he'd made bad choices.

"Poppy, I think I've always known you were my soul mate."

Soul mate. The phrase hit Killian like a sucker punch to the gut. Adam was Poppy's soul mate. Maybe his whole time here had been leading up to this moment.

Poppy would be reunited with the love of her life, and he'd go back to Hell. He waited for that idea to please him, but instead he still felt like he couldn't breathe.

He watched as the two shadows merged. Coming together in a kiss. He watched, a sickening dread rising in his chest. He'd leave now. He knew it, without ever getting to tell Poppy what she meant to him.

Suddenly the smaller of the shadows jerked and the other shadow moved back.

"Adam! What are you doing?"

"I had to kiss you. I've been thinking about it from the moment I saw you."

Poppy made a noise, a muffled whimper.

"Adam."

"Poppy."

Killian frowned, instantly sensing something was different.

The sound of Adam's voice. The energy in the air. Something wasn't right.

Killian moved to peer around the corner. Adam held Poppy in his arms. Poppy didn't struggle, but nor did she look pleased.

"Just tell me the truth," Adam said in that voice that wasn't quite right. "Do you love Killian O'Brien?"

There was no hesitation.

"Yes." The one word, so certain, so true. "Yes. I love him."

CHAPTER 35

Killian stepped into the hallway.

"Adam, you'd better let her go."

Adam shot him a sneer of a smile. A smile Killian recognized instantly. Vepar.

"I think our boss will be very interested in this," Vepar said. "You wasting your time with a lovesick human."

Killian saw Poppy gape at him, trying to comprehend what was going on.

"Why are you doing this?" Killian demanded.

"Because I can. Because I think it's time for Satan to see who is the worthy demon. The one who deserves more power."

Killian shook his head. That was what this was about?

Again Poppy stared at Killian, terrified. She struggled in Vepar's grip, but he held her easily.

"Let her go," Killian said, his voice a low growl. "Clearly this is between us."

Vepar laughed and tightened his hold; a whoosh of air escaped Poppy's lungs.

"You can't even get yourself out of a magic spell. You aren't even trying. Instead, you are dallying with an insipid little mortal. While I work. While I bring more damned souls to Hell. Why would Satan favor you?" Vepar spat.

Killian stared at his coworker. He was doing all this just for job advancement. He was simply spying to report back to Satan. Nothing but a lowly tattletale.

But then Vepar stunned him. With lightning speed, he moved his hands from Poppy's waist to her throat. He snaked his hands around her fragile neck, squeezing.

Poppy made sickening gasps, her fingers clawing at the hands choking her, desperate for air.

Killian leapt to grab Vepar/Adam, his own hands going for the other demon's throat. Killian slammed him repeatedly against the wall. Over and over until he released Poppy. She collapsed to the floor, and Killian prayed, yes, prayed, she'd just fallen unconscious.

When Killian let go of Vepar/Adam's neck, he too crumpled to the floor. Behind him, Killian heard the gathering of a crowd, but he didn't look toward them. He rushed to Poppy's side, checking her pulse. She was okay. Breathing. Alive.

He scooped her up against his chest and shoved his way through the crowd. He saw Eric in the sea of faces and called to him to check Adam. Then he left the bar.

He didn't really recall the trip home, his attention centered solely on Poppy. She was okay, but she'd never understand or accept what had just happened. Who he was.

When he finally got her to her apartment, he took her straight to bed. Carefully, he placed her in the center, then sat down beside her, watching her. Afraid she wasn't really okay.

After a few minutes, maybe hours—he didn't really know—her dark eyes fluttered open, and she stared up at him.

"What—what happened?" she whispered, her voice hoarse.

He didn't speak, waiting for her memories to return.

"Are you okay?" she finally asked, and he couldn't tell if she recalled anything. Then she added, "Did you and Adam get into a fight?"

She didn't remember—not clearly anyway.

"Yeah, we did, but we are both okay."

Poppy nodded, closing her eyes again. "No reason to fight over me."

Killian watched her rest, then murmured, "You are the *only* thing I would fight for."

She smiled slightly, but didn't answer.

Within minutes, Poppy's breathing became even again. He just listened to the soothing sound. Had he ever just listened to someone breathe? He didn't have to strain his memory over that one. The answer was no.

Yet at this moment, he felt this was the only place he could be content. Okay. She'd used the word *Heaven* to describe their shower earlier, and he'd thought perhaps she'd been right, not that a demon had any idea about what Heaven was.

But now he really understood Heaven. It was a place where Poppy was safe and alive and still . . .

I love him.

He heard her saying those words she'd said to Adam—when Adam had still been Adam. And he knew she'd meant them. He could just—tell.

Love. Yet another thing he'd never contemplated. Love—not a foreign concept to demons, but to him, yes.

She roused then, nestling among her pillows. She smiled sweetly at him, and something in his chest tightened. A painfully full feeling.

"Time for bed?" She still didn't remember. But she would.

"For you, yes." He brought her thick duvet up, tucking it around her.

"You aren't coming to bed?" Her face fell like a child being told she couldn't have a toy or a piece of candy.

"I will in a minute. You just rest."

"Now," she said with languid bossiness.

He chuckled. And he was so tempted to hold her, just for a moment.

But he couldn't. He didn't feel that he deserved to hold her. Not after the events of tonight. Not when she would eventually be repulsed by him.

"In a bit. Rest."

She sighed, then murmured, "You'd never fall for Gina, would you?"

He almost laughed, amazed that was all she'd retained of their crazy night.

"Not in a million years."

She smiled again, and he did allow himself to lean in for one last kiss. Her little hands came up to cup his face, the touch both sweet and sensual at the same time. Just like her.

He pulled away, telling himself he had to leave. Gather himself. Get real.

But instead of leaving, something urged him to stay. He walked around to the other side of the bed, watching her. Then he eased himself onto the mattress, just lounging beside her, arms crossed. Not touching her.

He'd stay just a little longer, until he decided what he had to do.

Small hands touched his body, slipping inside his shirt over his skin. His sleep-quieted body hummed to life. Every nerve ending centered on that touch. Phantom lips joined in, hot, moist, feathery kisses following the path forged by roaming hands.

He pressed his head back into the pillows, arching his body in response to both caresses. He just wanted more. More.

And more came. Hands teasing down past his navel, down lower, lower. He moaned as fingers curled around his rigid cock. Then the hand began to stroke. Up. Down. Up. Down. A slick palm and fingers squeezing over his shaft. Over. And over.

He moaned again. The motion stopped, even though the

hand still held his turgid flesh. Then another sensation hit him, as powerful and jarring as a battering ram. Yet such a tiny thing.

A breath. A hot puff of air against the oversensitized skin of his erection. His cock pulsed in response.

Another fiery breath, then a single, body-wracking lick up the length of his penis.

His own loud, harsh groan woke him. Another dream. Another one, so realistic, so amazing. Even now, so real.

"Hi."

Killian lifted himself on an elbow to find Poppy kneeling by his hip, her small, delicate hand holding his erection. A thumb stroked the sensitive underside.

He closed his eyes, releasing a shuddering breath. When he opened them again, Poppy was still there. No figment of his imagination. No specter in a dream.

She smiled, and in the dim light, he could see the indent of her dimple.

"Lie back," she told him, lightly moving her hand over him.

He did as she asked, falling back against the mattress, and was instantly driven mad.

Her tongue lapped up his length again and around the head. His hips rose up of their own volition. He was like a puppet, her hands, her mouth making him act on her demand.

She licked him again, then slowly brought his length into her mouth. Her movements took on a new speed, a new intensity. She sucked and licked and swirled her amazing little tongue until he felt ready to burst.

He groaned, the sound broken, raspy. She hummed in response, the sound vibrating all around his cock. He groaned again, one of his hands knotting in her hair, the other in the bedding at his side.

In tune with his reactions, Poppy began to bob her head, faster and faster, her mouth making love to him.

His release hit him, ripping through his entire body, tensing his muscles to the point of pain. Then nothing but bliss, total, mind-blowing ecstasy.

Poppy stayed with him, riding out the entirety of his orgasm, only moving when he tugged her up to lie by his side, half on the bed, half on him.

"That," he managed to mumble between gasps, "was amazing."

She grinned, clearly quite pleased with his reaction and with herself. He caught the back of her head with his hand, pulling her in for a kiss. He could taste the saltiness of himself on her lips.

That possessiveness he so often felt around her returned, stronger than ever. She nestled in against his side, idly circling a fingertip around his nipple.

"I thought that was just a dream. At first," he told her.

Poppy angled her head to smile at him, then returned her attention to her swirling finger.

"I've had dreams about you," she said after a moment. Her voice was quiet, maybe even a little shy.

"Have you?"

Her head nodded against his chest. "A couple, actually. And last night, I had the strangest one."

He watched her expression, intent. "Tell me."

She shook her head. "It was silly. But I have had other ones too. Sexy ones."

She told him about those, dreams he already knew, because he'd had them too. Shared dreams.

"I've had the same exact dreams," he said suddenly, knowing he shouldn't admit it, but needing to tell her. Compelled to tell her.

She raised her head again. "The same? Exactly?"

He nodded.

"How can that be?"

He shook his head, even as he answered her silently: *Because I'm a demon.*

He kissed her. They kissed for minutes, hours, he didn't know. He was just lost in her, in every facet of her being. Gradually their kisses fueled a deeper exchange, but this time their lovemaking was unhurried, sweet and slow. Hands touching each other in gentle, exploring brushes. Small kisses scattered over each other's bodies.

Until finally, he pressed her back against the mattress, slowly entering her. A small gasp escaped her as he filled her completely, then just remained deep inside her. Feeling every nuance of her body under his.

Then eyes still locked, he began to move. Their fingers linked above her head, and he loved her with his whole body, never breaking their gaze.

And when both their climaxes finally came, they still remained totally in tune with each other. The moment was more sensual, more powerful than anything Killian had ever experienced.

Poppy's hand came up and touched his cheek, the caress sweet, loving. Her dark eyes searched his.

"I had another dream—one in which I told you I loved you. I *am* in love with you," she said, her voice so quiet he wasn't quite sure that he'd heard her correctly. Then she kissed him, and he felt all her love in that single moment.

She smiled at him when they parted. Then she moved to curl against him, her back to his chest. He held her close, the thrill of her words warring with pain.

She loved him.

They stayed like that until the sun was starting to rise in the sky and her breathing was even again.

Then carefully, he eased himself out of bed. As silently as possible, he dressed. He leaned over and kissed her. Tiny kisses on her eyelids, her nose, her lips.

Then he stood, backing away from the bed, and he said the words that he knew he couldn't deny any longer. The words that would damn him.

"I love you too."

Almost instantly the room spun, Poppy disappearing from his view as he was sucked away in a swirl of pitch black and blood red.

CHAPTER 36

Poppy stretched, then opened her eyes, expecting to see Killian's sleeping face on the pillow next to her. Instead, she was greeted by an empty bed and a flood of confusing, frightening memories.

She pushed herself upright, still wanting to find him, despite what she thought she knew.

"Killian," she called. The apartment was silent. "Killian."

She got out of bed, pulling on just her panties and a T-shirt that had been flung on the back of her bedroom chair. She padded into the living room. The apartment was still and empty feeling.

"Killian?"

Almost instantly she knew he was gone.

She went back to the bedroom, realizing all traces of him had disappeared as if he'd never existed. Had he?

She walked back to the living room, then to the kitchen. No signs. Maybe she'd imagined him. Her—demon lover.

She walked back to the bedroom and dropped on the edge of the bed.

Yes, he was gone.

*   *   *

By afternoon, Poppy realized she couldn't just accept that Killian, whatever he was, hadn't been real. God knew the heartbreak she was feeling sure felt real. Painfully real.

And maybe what she thought she'd remembered wasn't accurate. She had no memory of getting home, or anything after her brief talk with Adam. Maybe she wasn't remembering the rest of the night accurately either.

So she went to the one place she could think of to find Killain. With resolve, she knocked on the door. Then waited. And waited.

Again her determination flagged. But she knocked again.

Another few moments, then the doorknob wiggled. Poppy pulled in a calming breath.

"Poppy."

Poppy deflated. "Ginger. I—I'm sorry to wake you."

The other woman pushed sleep-tousled hair away from her face and fought back a yawn.

"That's okay." She frowned, her eyes going from drowsy to concerned. "You didn't hear something from the girls, did you? Is everything okay?"

"No," Poppy said quickly. "No, nothing like that. I was actually looking for Killian. Is he here?"

Ginger's frown deepened. "Killian?"

"Yes. Your cousin."

Her neighbor stared at her for a moment, concern returning. "I don't have a cousin named Killian."

Poppy's stomach dropped, a horrible sick feeling rushing through her. "Umm—are you sure? Tall, very handsome, from Sweden?"

Ginger smiled. "Well, he sounds like a good cousin to have, but he isn't my cousin."

Poppy looked around, suddenly not sure what to do or say. Killian wasn't Ginger's cousin.

"Are you okay?" Ginger asked, her smile dissolving into a worried motherly look.

"Yes—yes." Poppy attempted to gather herself. "I—I guess I misunderstood. I'm sorry to have bothered you."

She looked around again, trying to get her muddled brain together enough to walk away.

"I'll talk to you later," she said to Ginger, forcing her feet to move, hurrying down the hall back to her apartment.

She heard Ginger call something after her, but she couldn't register the words.

She made it back to her apartment, stepping inside. She collapsed against the closed door, her mind whirling.

What had she just experienced over the past week? She just didn't know.

"Hey," Daisy called as she stepped into the apartment. "I'm home."

She was greeted by silence. Dropping her bags in the hallway, she headed toward the living room.

Poppy sat in the rocker, her face stony.

Daisy's heart sunk.

"Hey," she said tentatively. "What's wrong?"

"Who is Killian?"

Daisy felt the air being sucked out of her chest.

"Who is he, Daisy? Because I know for a fact he isn't Ginger Cobb's cousin. She'd never heard of him."

Daisy scrambled, trying to think of what to say. God, she shouldn't have gone away this weekend. She should have known they couldn't leave a demon here unsupervised.

"He—he is . . ." Daisy couldn't think of a single reasonable explanation. "He was just a guy."

Poppy stood, her movements abrupt, agitated.

"Just a guy?" She laughed at that, the sound harsh, brittle. "Did you hire him, Daisy? Was he a—a paid escort or something?"

"No!" Daisy shook her head. "Nothing like that."

Poppy ran a hair through her hair, her dark eyes glittering as if she was painfully close to tears.

"Then what?" Poppy's voice sounded frantic.

Daisy fought her own urge to cry. Her plan wasn't supposed to go like this. The demon was just supposed to find Poppy a boyfriend. Nothing more.

"Who is he?" Poppy demanded when Daisy stood there, speechless.

Daisy gave her a pained look, close to tears herself. "You wouldn't believe me if I told you."

"Try me."

"He—he's . . ." How could she tell Poppy this? Her sister would think she was nuts.

Poppy widened her eyes, waiting.

Daisy could tell her sister that she had hired Killian. As a matchmaker. But she knew Poppy wouldn't just accept that. She'd want to know where Daisy had found him. What agency or whatever he worked for. All sorts of questions that Daisy wouldn't have answers to. The hole would just get bigger and bigger.

So before she realized what she actually planned, Daisy blurted out the truth. "He's a demon."

Poppy opened her mouth, then snapped it shut.

Daisy waited for her sister to yell, to tell her to stop making up stories, even to look shocked. But instead she looked almost resigned, hurt.

Daisy could feel tears rolling down her cheeks, and she just started talking, spilling the whole truth.

"You know those books I love? The Jenny Bell ones—" She didn't wait for an answer. "Well, they have spells in them. So Madison, Emma and I decided to try one. It was supposed to conjure a demon who would fulfill a wish. We thought it would be fun."

* * *

Poppy stared at her sister. This was madness. Utter madness.

Yet she said, "So you did the spell, and Killian appeared."

Daisy nodded, tears streaking her cheeks. "We didn't actually think it would work."

Poppy collapsed back into the rocker. So the strange memories of demons and Satan were true.

"I swear, that is the truth," Daisy said. "I swear."

"I know."

"You do?"

Poppy nodded, but she suddenly needed to be alone. She needed to process. "Go to your room. Please."

Daisy gave her pleading look. "I'm sorry. It wasn't supposed to be like this."

Poppy nodded again.

Daisy turned to leave, when Poppy stopped her.

"What was the wish?"

Daisy blinked back more tears. "He was supposed to find you a boyfriend. Your soul mate."

Souls. That was Killian's trade. He worked in souls. And never had he really thought much about his own. Or whether he even had one.

Now he knew he did. But it had been left with Poppy when he'd been sucked back to Hell. And now he just felt empty. Hollow.

He tossed down the controller to his Xbox and reached for his scotch. He took a sip and looked around at his ultra-modern apartment. All the luxuries he could want: a huge TV, surround sound, expensive leather furniture, toys, gadgets—he had them all.

But all he kept thinking about was a small apartment with eclectic décor, no expensive perks and the most perfect person he'd ever met.

He kept thinking of Daisy's comment about wanting someone perfect for Poppy. He'd wondered then if perfection existed.

Now he knew for certain it did. And he'd lost it forever.

After he'd gotten back to Hell, Satan had called both him and Vepar to his court. There he'd punished Vepar for attempting to kill a pure human, banishing him to the Ninth Circle of Hell to work in the molten lava mines. And he'd punished Killian too, forbidding him to return to the mortal realm.

"You've more than used up your vacation time," Satan had told him in his thunderous voice.

Still, Killian had tried right away to transport himself back to her, knowing if he only got to see her one more time it would be worth it. But he couldn't do it. In the same way he'd been trapped in the human dimension, he was now trapped here.

He polished off his liquor, then reached for the bottle on the glass coffee table, refilling his crystal glass.

He'd been back here for days. A week, a month, he couldn't recall now. One day rolled into another, an endless abyss of weltschmerz—not Swedish but close enough. and all he knew for sure was he had eternity ahead of him. Eternity without Poppy.

He realized he'd never really understood the implications of being damned to Hell until now.

He polished off another glass of scotch, which did nothing to squelch his pain, no matter how many glasses, how many bottles, he drank.

He stretched out on the sofa, closing his eyes. Poppy instantly appeared to him. Dark hair and eyes. That sweet smile. Her infectious laugh. Her small, gorgeous body against his.

Did she even know he loved her?

* * *

"We should just redo the spell," Madison said.

Daisy shook her head, sneaking another peek at her sister. Poppy sat in her bed, pencil in hand, doing something in a black bound book.

"We don't even know how we got him last time," Daisy whispered. "What if we get another demon?"

"She fell in love with him," Emma said with a sigh that was somewhere between wistfulness and regret.

Daisy agreed. She didn't understand how she'd missed it, but yes, she knew Poppy had fallen in love with Killian. Poppy hadn't said so, but Daisy could just tell. Her sister acted like she was okay. She never even talked about him. What was there to say, really?

All Daisy knew was that she felt awful.

"I got the new Jenny Bell book," Emma said, sitting on Daisy's bed, "but I don't even know if I want to read it."

Daisy knew it was irrational to take out her frustration on the book—after all they were the ones who'd tried the spell— but she kind of agreed. Jenny Bell didn't seem so great anymore.

Poppy picked up a red pencil, shading in what she'd just drawn.

She paused and studied the drawing. Pretty good. Sighing, she set the book aside. Then she headed to the kitchen for another cup of coffee.

In the hallway, she could hear her sister and the girls talking quietly in Daisy's room. They all had been very reserved around her these days, clearly remorseful about what had happened.

Poppy considered speaking to them, in an attempt to let them know she was fine, but she didn't.

She wasn't fine. Not totally. But she was trying.

A demon. Killian was a demon. Leave it to her to fall for a demon. The idea should have scared her. The very idea that demons existed should have terrified her, but it didn't. Killian might be a demon, but he was also the best man she'd ever met.

And it did explain his appearing in the apartment that first night. And why, several times, she'd overheard the word *demon*. And in Swedish, Killian had even used a term that definitely sounded like demon.

She took a sip of her coffee. Yeah, leave it to her to fall for a demon.

But whatever had happened, Killian was gone now. She had to accept that and move on. It wasn't as if she didn't know how to do that. Loss was a part of her life.

And he'd probably never loved her anyway. Did demons even know how to love?

CHAPTER 37

"Daisy! Daisy!"

Daisy stopped and turned, nearly getting run over by several other students on their way to class. Behind their glaring and muttering was Emma. She ran toward Daisy, her blond curls bouncing.

"We can bring him back. There's a way to bring him back."

"What?"

"Killian. We can bring him back. The new Jenny Bell book has a spell."

Daisy made a face and shook her head. "No way. I've messed up enough stuff."

"But Poppy loves him."

Daisy shook her head again. "What if it makes things worse?"

"Can they be worse?"

"What if Killian doesn't love her?"

Emma made a face is if Daisy was just being silly. "Of course, he loves her. He wouldn't have gone back to"—she shot a look at the floor, which was actually above the cafeteria, a hell of sorts, Daisy supposed—"if he wasn't her soul mate."

Daisy wasn't sure about that.

"It's worth a try. But he can't stay unless he's willing to sacrifice something big."

"Like what?"

Emma made a face. "He has to pick what that is for himself. But what other choice do we have? Poppy is miserable."

Daisy sighed. "All right."

What did she have to lose? Actually, she didn't want to think about that.

Daisy arranged for Emma and Madison to spend the night the following Friday.

Daisy tiptoed to Poppy's room, listening. Her light was out, and the room was quiet. She snuck back to the living room, where Madison lit several candles.

"This one is more complicated," Daisy said, looking at the circle Emma had made on the floor with salt.

"It will be worth it," Emma said. She brushed off her hands, excess salt flying, then reached for the book.

"Okay," she said in a whisper. "Stand around the circle, and each hold a candle."

The girls moved around the circle, spreading out until they were equidistant from each other. They held up their white candles.

Emma, who still held the book in one of her hands, began to read the incantation.

"To everything—turn, turn turn."

She gestured for the girls to turn.

"Counterclockwise," she reminded them. "Three times."

They did, coming back to the middle.

"There is a season—turn, turn, turn."

They rotated three times again.

"Isn't this some old hippie song?" Madison asked, her usual skepticism in place. "I think my mom listens to this. Or maybe my grandmother."

"Shh," Emma hissed, but Daisy thought Madison had a point.

"There is a reason—turn, turn, turn."

More spins.

"A purpose to all things above and below us."

Emma raised her hands, still trying to see the book, which was now above her head.

Daisy just hoped she didn't spill wax on her head.

"We evoke the powers of all around us to do as we bid. Gather and bring us the one we request. Energies of all, bring Killian O'Brien. And should he choose to sacrifice, then he shall receive the thing he desires most. And in doing so, happiness shall prevail."

Daisy hoped so. Happiness was all she'd ever wanted for Poppy.

"Come, Killian O'Brien, come."

Killian tugged off the shirt of his uniform. Another day's work done. Nothing but an eternity more to go.

A job he was finding unbearable. Vepar could have it. Before, he'd just done his work, never thinking much about the damned souls he was escorting to their appropriate place in Hell. He never thought about who they were, or what they'd done to get there. He just did his job.

Now he often wondered what wrong choice they'd made. What they would do differently now if given a chance, if they'd realized what the outcome would be?

And he thought about the fact that he had no choices. He was created here, and he would stay here. Tortured in his own way.

He wandered into his bathroom, a white-tile-and-chrome affair, stark and cold. He turned on the shower, then turned to grab a fresh towel from a closet.

As he was about to place it on the towel rack, his vision

closed in on him. Just slightly and just for a moment. He blinked.

Weird.

He turned to test the water.

Again, his vision narrowed in. Like briefly peeking through a keyhole. Grabbing for a towel, he wrapped it around his hips. Maybe he needed to go sit down for a second.

He reached out for the wall again as another wave of dizziness hit him. What was going on?

Then his vision blackened completely and his head began to spin. He flailed out his arms, feeling as if he were falling like Alice down the rabbit hole toward Wonderland.

"It's him!"

Killian blinked and gradually his eyes came back into focus. In front of him stood . . .

"Daisy." He blinked again. She was still there when he opened his eyes. "It's really you."

Utter joy filled him. He looked around him and saw Poppy's apartment with its mismatched furniture and knickknacks, Madison with her haughty looks, Emma blushing as usual.

He could hug them all. But he kept searching, trying to find the one he wanted to hug first.

"Where is she?"

As if she heard him, Poppy's bedroom door opened.

"What are you girls . . ." Her words trailed off as she saw him. She blinked, too, as he just had.

She didn't move, just standing there, staring as if he was a figment of her imagination.

He stared, eating up the sight of her, hair tangled from sleep, wearing pink polka-dot pajama bottoms and one of her vintage T-shirts. This one had the Byrds on it.

"Poppy," he said. He wanted to walk toward her, but something held him back.

"Sorry," Emma said, "you can't leave the circle."

He looked down, realizing he was indeed inside a circle of some sort of white granules.

When he looked back up, Poppy was coming toward him, her movements slow, unsure.

She paused a couple feet away. They just stared at each other.

Finally, she said, "Are you really a demon?"

He hesitated, then nodded. "I am."

She nodded as if that was the most normal thing in the world.

"But he's your soul mate," Daisy added, then made a face as if she realized being a soul mate with a demon was less than ideal.

Poppy didn't say anything for a moment, then sighed. "I know."

"You do?" Killian said, stunned. He'd expected disbelief, anger, disdain. Anything but quiet acceptance.

"Yes," she said, "but I don't see where we go with it."

"I don't know either," he admitted.

"But we do," Daisy said.

Both Killian and Poppy looked at the girls.

"This spell will give total happiness," Emma said with one of her dreamy smiles.

"But you have to make a sacrifice. Something big," Madison said with a slight smirk.

"But then you can be together," Daisy said with a hopeful grin.

Killian and Poppy exchanged looks.

"Is that what you want?" he asked.

Poppy stared at him for a moment, then nodded. "Yes."

He released a pent-up breath, relief washing over him. "That's what I want too."

"But what can you sacrifice?" she asked. "Definitely not your designer clothes."

She looked pointedly at him, and the girls giggled. Then he remembered for the first time he was wearing only a towel. Thankfully, it covered the crucial bits.

He smiled too, but then sobered, thinking, realizing he didn't have much. He had wealth, but that didn't seem so important now. He had stuff, but that would be no sacrifice to leave behind. Nothing was more important that her, and he'd do anything to be with her.

He shrugged, feeling helpless. "I don't know what I have to sacrifice, but I know I would die for you."

As soon as he said the words, darkness enveloped him again.

Poppy watched as Killian collapsed to the ground. She vaguely heard the girls' cries and gasps, but all she could focus on was Killian.

She ran to him, falling on her knees beside him. She touched his face, his hair. His skin was cold. His skin a terrible gray color.

"No," she cried. Liquid dripped onto his motionless face and she realized vaguely it was her own tears. She moved to cradle his head in her lap.

This wasn't fair. She'd lost enough, not Killian too. Not him. Not when she'd just gotten him back.

Then she felt him shudder. At least, she thought she did. No, maybe it was her own body, heaving, wracked with sobs.

Then she felt him move again.

"He just moved," one of the girls said as if to confirm her own wishful thoughts.

"I saw it too."

Poppy cupped his cheek, turning him toward her. "Killian. Killian?"

Just when she'd thought they'd all imagined the movement, his eyes fluttered open. His beautiful golden eyes.

"Poppy," he said, his voice raspy.

More tears spilled down her cheeks as she kissed him. He reached a hand around her head and kissed her back.

Behind them the girls cheered.

When they parted, Poppy said, "Don't do that again."

Killian smiled, albeit weakly. "I don't plan to." Then his expression grew serious. "All I've wanted was to get back here to you, to tell you I love you."

She smiled, more tears filling her eyes. "I love you too."

EPILOGUE

Cheers rose up around them along with Abba's "I Do, I Do, I Do," an homage to Killian's first "fiancée." The newly married couple turned to beam at their guests.

"So when we came here that first day," Killian said, referring to the park, "you never guessed you'd be marrying me."

Poppy leaned toward Killian and whispered, "No, I didn't. But then I never guessed I'd be married to a demon either."

"Ex-demon," he said as he always did when she mentioned being in love with a demon. He stole another kiss, to all of their wedding guests' approval.

Daisy appeared, hugging them both. "You look so happy."

Poppy squeezed her sister, who looked beautiful in her red bridesmaid gown. "Thanks to you."

Daisy's brown eyes were a little teary, even as she grinned.

Madison and Emma, Poppy's other bridesmaids, came forward to hug them too. Emma, of course, got emotional, but even too-cool Madison looked a little *verklempt*.

"Well, I can see why you were looking for this guy," Ginger said, coming up to congratulate the new couple. "And believe me, none of my cousins are this handsome." She winked at Killian.

Killian smiled back. "Thanks, Ginny."

Ginger looked a little confused, but let the nickname go. Killian had that effect on women.

"Mrs. Mahoney," Poppy greeted the older woman who was with Ginger, "I'm so glad you made the wedding. I wasn't sure if you would. When did you get back?"

The old woman nodded. "Got back a couple days ago. Strangest thing. I swear someone was staying in my apartment."

"Really?" Poppy glanced at Killian, who managed to look totally innocent.

The old woman nodded. "Yes, things were moved all around, and Sweetness hasn't been acting right since I got back."

"That cat is Satan. And I would know," Killian muttered as soon as the old lady tottered away. "And even her dress is covered in flowers."

"Behave." Poppy kissed him.

"I'm not that much of an ex-demon."

Another guest approached the couple. This was Mr. McCarthy, Poppy's boss from the legal publishing firm.

"Frank," she said. "I'm glad you could come."

He smiled, hugging Poppy and then shaking Killian's hand. "I hear we are celebrating more than a wedding today."

Poppy grinned. "Yes. Little Red School House Press offered to buy my book. Thank you so much for mentioning me to the editor."

Poppy had received a call yesterday from an editor who wanted to publish her first children's book, *Lily and the Demon.*

"No problem. Congratulations to you. Both."

Killian hugged Poppy to him, his pride clear for all to see.

"Married to my soul mate and a published author," she sighed. "Life is perfect."

"It is," he agreed.

She couldn't help asking, "But don't you miss being immortal?"

He shook his head. "Not at all. Even if we only had one hour, I'd take that over an eternity without you."

Poppy smiled at him, knowing he meant it. She also knew life was too precious to spend time guarding herself against hurt and loss. She'd done that, and had been lonely and sad.

Now she planned to live every moment. With her family by her side.

If you liked this book,
try Rebecca Zanetti's FATED,
in stores now . . .

"Mama! Mama, wake up." Tiny hands clutched at Cara's worn nightshirt, shaking with all their might.

Cara's eyes flew open, and her heart hitched in her chest. Terrified blue eyes speared her through the dusk of the morning. The little girl must have had another nightmare. "Janie, sweetheart, what?"

"They're coming. They're coming now, the bad men. We have to run." Janie's breath came in sharp gasps before she let out a high-pitched sob.

Cara shook her head, reaching out to enfold her daughter in a hug. She slowed her own breathing, the need to comfort her child overwhelming her. Poor Janie. Not another nightmare. She reached for her reading glasses on the table only to realize she'd fallen asleep with them on. Again. The newest edition of *Botanical Magazine* hadn't been the barn-burner she'd expected.

She smoothed Janie's hair down while silence echoed around them. Now more than ever, she wished Simon had lived; maybe he could have soothed their daughter's fears. She flipped on the antique pink Depression-glass lamp. "It's okay, sweetheart. I'm sure it was just a bad drea—"

A loud crash came from the other room, and Cara yelped. The sound of splintering wood propelled her to action. She leapt from the bed, yanked Janie into her arms, and sprinted for the master bath, barely missing the potted fern in the corner. Her heart slamming against her ribs, she locked the door and rushed toward the small window. She failed to unlock it before the thin door burst open behind her.

A broad hand stopped the door from clanging against the wall. At least six and a half feet of muscle-packed male filled the doorway.

With a cry, she dropped Janie to her feet and dodged in front of the four-year-old. The air caught in her throat, and her ears started to ring as adrenaline spiked through her blood. This was not happening. She yanked her head to the side and forced herself to accept the situation. Accept that she needed to fight. She dragged oxygen into her tight lungs and searched the tiled counter for a weapon—her tweezers probably wouldn't harm anybody.

She pushed Janie back against the wall. Retreating a step, she held one hand out to ward off the threat. His size made her gulp. Brown eyes raked her from his hard cut face, and raven-black hair reached his collar with a freedom that disavowed any ties to the military—although he wore the requisite flack boots and dark jeans under a bulletproof vest. She'd seen the gear on a Discovery Channel special about soldiers.

The energy emanating from him stole her breath.

"Get out," she said, shielding her child. Trying to shield herself from the feelings he threw at her. Anger, passion, and urgency all swirled together, mixing with her own panic and making her light-headed. Her knees wobbled, and her head began to ache. She usually blocked better than this. Or maybe his emotions were just that strong.

"We need to go." His tone was water over sharp rocks, as if he was trying to gentle a naturally rough voice. Then his eyes dropped to her faded nightshirt to see the image of Einstein surrounded by shopping bags, QUANTUM SHOPPING. His top lip quirked up, and a dimple winked. Her heartbeat slowed in response. Then he stalked a step closer, his hands at his sides, and her gaze flew to the gun on his hip, to the several knives secured in his vest.

Her heart leapt back into action. "You have the wrong house." She glared up at his implacable face—a face cut from granite with a jaw made to take a punch. She'd have to jump to even come close.

The scent of spiced pine and male infused the room.

He shook his head. A pit the size of a large rock settled in her stomach as adrenaline slammed the room into sharp focus. Her breath came in short pants, and her scientific mind sought an answer. A way to take his massive frame down. She stamped down on the rising panic when nothing came to mind, and again searched for a weapon, spotting the tiny Fittonia "White Anne" in the terra-cotta planter. She couldn't throw Annie at the man; the plant would never survive.

The intruder took another step to peer over her shoulder. "It will be okay. We have to go." His large hand encircled Cara's bicep before dragging her into the bedroom. Fear seized her vocal cords for a moment, and her mind scattered. Should she tell Janie to run? Could she slow him down long enough?

Then, with a muffled curse, he dropped her arm. A low growl emanated from him as he peered at his hand. He wiped it on his pant leg and grabbed her again. What had been on her shirt?

The phone near the bed caught her eye, and she lunged for it. He jerked her back, his hand warm and firm on her arm. Cara dug her feet into the carpet, but their forward momentum didn't slow, so she tried to yank away as he pulled her toward a basket of clothes at the foot of the bed.

"Janie, follow us," he tossed over his shoulder.

Cara coughed out air. He knew Janie's name. This wasn't random. Fear choked her again. "How do you know her name?"

He pivoted until she smacked flush against him. Heat filled her, surrounded her. His hands settled on her arms, and his determination and intent beat at her. Damn it. She couldn't block him—she sucked as an empath. Then he lowered his head.

"I know both of your names, Cara. Listen. My name is Talen Kayrs, and I won't hurt you. I'm here to help." Determined eyes captured hers while he gave her a moment. "Take a deep breath. I can feel your power. You can find the truth here. You know I won't hurt you." His voice rumbled low. Soothing.

Her body softened from his tone even as her mind rebelled. Her breathing evened out. Danger radiated out of the man, but she could sense no intention to harm her. Or Janie.

Janie tugged on her waist. "It's okay, Mama. We have to go. They're coming."

Cara stepped to the side and nodded. "Fine. We'll leave. We can follow you." If she could just get Janie to the car—

He grinned, flashing even white teeth. "You can't lie worth spit. You have one minute to throw on clothes." The sound of his rough voice shot nerve endings alive through her skin. But not from fear. He turned toward the door.

"No." She again tried to wrench away while her body tingled where it met his.

"Then you go in your pajamas." He grabbed the basket of clothes in his other arm while he towed her into the hallway. "Keep up, Janie." The little girl stumbled behind, keeping her hands glued to Cara's waist.

"Wait, no, Mama," Janie cried out, pulling on her mother. "I need Mr. Mullet." Her voice rose to a shrill sob.

Talen whirled around and squinted over Cara's shoulder.

"Mr. Mullet?" He eyed the living room entrance and then focused on the little girl.

Cara pressed a hand against his chest, settling her stance to protect her child. "Mr. Mullet is her stuffed bear—she doesn't go anywhere without him." If Janie could leave the room, Cara could really fight.

Talen raised an eyebrow, his gaze thoughtful. "Hurry, Janie. Get the bear—we have to go."

Quick as a flash, Janie darted from the room. Dark eyes met Cara's, and she wavered, then shot her knee upward to his groin, simultaneously punching her fist toward his face with a fierce grunt.

He shifted, allowing her knee to connect to the muscle of his upper thigh while his arm shot out to stop her punch. His broad hand enclosed her fist inches away from his chin, and the slap of skin on skin echoed around the room. The basket of clothes remained safe in his free arm.

Pain lanced through her leg, and fear cascaded down her spine. Panting out breath, she waited for retaliation. If he hit her, he'd knock her out. What about Janie?

Talen tilted his head to the side, his hand warm around hers. "Is your leg all right?"

He asked about her leg? Seriously? She'd just tried to turn him into a eunuch. "Fine," she hissed through her teeth.

"Hmmm," he said, twisting his hand to grasp her wrist and yank her into the living room. "You might want to work on not broadcasting your intent with those pretty blue eyes next time." Mere politeness colored his tone, not an ounce of anger to be found.

Cara stumbled, truly off balance for the first time that evening.

"I got him, Mama," Janie chirped, running into the room with the stuffed bear and her worn blankie. "We can go now."

The front door hung drunkenly split in two. At the sight,

Cara began to struggle again. With an exasperated sigh, Talen dropped the basket of clothes, shifted her to the side, and lifted Janie into his arms.

"No!" Cara cried out, reaching for her daughter before pounding on his broad back. Pure instinct moved her to protect Janie, and rage choked her as she beat on his dark vest.

"Get the clothes and move it," he growled over his shoulder. He crossed the front porch, heading toward a black Hummer idling at the curb.

Cara threw herself against the man holding her child, knocking over the basket. Clothes scattered across the wooden planks.

"Let her go, you bastard!"

He may not intend harm, but he had no right to kidnap them. She clutched one arm around his massive neck as her knees dug into his spine. She jerked hard against his windpipe. A rush of anger slammed through her body, pushing out the fear.

Even with her struggling on his back, his long strides continued toward the vehicle unhampered. He yanked open the rear door, placed Janie in a booster seat, and buckled her in with quick motions. Cara moved to jump off him, only to have him close the door, grab her arm, and pull her around. Two strong hands held her aloft. Hard steel met her backside when he stepped into her, his face lowering to hers. "Stop fighting me."

His strength was unbelievable. Her own vulnerability beat into her as she realized her nightshirt had risen to reveal pale pink panties. The cool night air rushed across her bare legs. Dark denim scratched the tender skin of her inner thighs, and she opened her mouth to scream.

One swift movement, and his mouth covered hers. Hot, firm, and somehow restrained. The effort of his restraint belted into her. He fought to control himself. Heat slammed through her. A roaring filled her ears, and her breath hitched.

Her heart slowed, and time stopped. For a brief moment, *his* heartbeat echoed throughout her body to a spot below her stomach.

He growled low and his mouth moved over hers, no longer silencing her, but tasting. Exploring. One thick arm swept around her waist and pulled her into him; the other lifted to tangle a hand in her hair. He tugged, angled her head more to the side. He went deeper.

She moaned as his tongue met hers. He explored her mouth like he owned it. For a moment, he did. She forgot everything. There were only his lips on hers, demanding. Promising. His heat warmed her as she returned his kiss, pushing closer into his hard body, forgetting reality.

Pure strength surrounded her. Hot. Dangerous. Tempting.

Here's a peek at
INVITATION TO RUIN,
the debut novel from Bronwen Evans,
out now!

That evening, the entourage walked into the Cavendishes' ballroom and joined the queue waiting to greet their host and hostess. As they descended the stairs, the whispers behind twitching fans started. Melissa could well imagine what the other guests were saying. She had her arm through Lord Wickham's, and on his right, so did Cassandra.

She knew the men were praising Lord Wickham's skill in keeping the ravishing beauty on his right as his mistress, while marrying the plainer, quiet, demure cousin on his left. A raving beauty to bed for pleasure and a wife to bed to provide the much-needed heirs.

Melissa lifted her head high and kept her eyes looking directly ahead, hoping her cheeks had not colored. Never had she wished so fervently for the floor to open up and swallow her. Cassandra played up her part and was spitefully pleased with the ton's interpretation of events. To reinforce the perception, Lady Sudbury stroked her hand down the arm of Anthony's jacket until he bent his head and let her whisper something in his ear.

At his gruff laugh there was a surge of activity; the array of fans were fluttering wildly.

This evening was going to be torture.

The line of guests shuffled forward until, with the pleasantries completed, they could move fully into the ballroom. Letting go of Anthony's arm, Melissa began scouring the room, trying to see if Anthony's mother or brother were present.

"Are you looking for anyone in particular?" he asked, his voice radiating about as much warmth as a snowflake.

Melissa turned to look at him. Her traitorous breath caught in her throat. How did he do it? She tore her gaze away from the intoxicating sight of him, trying to quell the fluttery sensation developing in her stomach. He was so handsome this evening. The white on black ensemble set his physique off to perfection. The material was tight enough to be considered indecent. Yet Melissa would wager every woman in the room longed to run their hands over the ebony velvet. She longed to feel the hidden strength beneath the soft fabric, the urge as overwhelming as the man himself.

This evening, in his finery, he screamed Lord of Wicked. His silver-gray eyes seemed to deliberately issue an open invitation, a temptation sent to make her sin. Every married woman in the room envied Cassandra, while the young debutantes were miffed they'd not been as brave as Melissa and caught him in matrimony. Her legs felt as if she'd just ridden at full gallop all day. She didn't dare return his avid gaze. She wasn't brave or courageous or fearless enough to accept— yet. She let a satisfied smile curve her lips. But she was his.

He leaned nearer, the tantalizing scent of expensive cologne mixed with raw maleness made her dizzy, and as he placed his large hand at her back, guiding her toward a chaise upon which Lady Millington sat, she wondered if tonight would be the night she'd finally swoon.

"Remember my warning. I trust you will conduct yourself appropriately. You are to be my wife."

The sudden bolt of awareness flashing down her side—the side he'd touched—had nothing to do with the anger his harsh warning provoked. She could sense him, hard, strong, and very male, a potent living force beside her.

His nearness was pure pleasure. She glanced at his face, but he'd already turned to see to Cassandra.

He must have felt her gaze though, because his eyes swung back to her. He saw her studying him intently, and his gaze grew direct; his eyes searched hers.

Her lungs seized.

The introduction for the first waltz cut through the hypnotic moment. She heard Cassandra stir. *Please do not disgrace me by dancing the first dance with Cassandra.*

His eyes still held hers, and perhaps he read the desperation there. His fingers closed about her hand, and he lifted it fleetingly to his lips. He then elegantly bowed, his eyes never leaving hers. "My dance, I believe?"

She let out a huge breath, gratitude beaming from within her smile. At that precise moment he truly was the most wonderful man in the world, her knight in shining armor. She inclined her head and let him draw her to the floor.

Her body responded as soon as he gathered her close and steered her into the swirling throng. Her chest felt tight, and her skin came alive. She became a young giddy schoolgirl, taut with anticipation, expectations. This man would soon be her husband. She remembered his naked body lying next to her, and her gaze dropped to his groin.

Even in his nonaroused state he was large; she could see the bulge quite clearly. A sweet tremble filled her being. What would it be like to have him make love to her properly, to feel those large hands caress her naked skin?

She swallowed. This man wasn't going to stay her imaginary lover. He would become her husband. Since their last dance together, everything had changed. The planes of his face seemed harder, more chiseled, more austere. His body seemed more powerful, and there was something in his eyes as they rested on hers—something . . . was it regret? Whatever it was, her instincts recognized enough to make her shiver—either in fear or anticipation, she wasn't sure which.

Without thinking she uttered, "How did you get your scar?"

His countenance changed immediately. She could feel his muscles tighten beneath her hands, and he almost led them straight into the path of another couple.

"Is that why you did not wish to marry me? You find my face repulsive?" His words were uttered harshly, and her face heated in mortification. She had offended him.

She made sure she looked him straight in the eye. "I find the scar interesting. It gives your face character." She paused, not sure if she should utter what she really thought, but given his reaction she decided she owed it to him. "Besides, you would be too extraordinarily handsome without some slight imperfection. It makes you look more human and less godly."

Typical man. He was trying to stop the smile hinting at the edges of his lips. "I'm no saint, and my behavior is far from that of the Lord Almighty."

She blushed. "No. I meant like a Greek or Roman god."

She saw he was pleased with her compliment.

"And which god do you believe I take after?" Now he was teasing her.

"When you are trying to be dark and mysterious, then I believe Ares, God of War. When you smile I think of you as Apollo, the God of Healing."

His brow creased and his smile vanished. "Healing? Ironic really, for if anyone needs healing it is me."

"How so?"

He straightened and pulled her closer. He seemed to realize he'd said too much. "Never mind." He changed the topic. "I have made the wedding arrangements. Mother is organizing the event. We will hold the ceremony and wedding breakfast at Craven House. I hope that will be suitable?"

She wondered if he had deliberately changed the topic so as to avoid answering her question. She decided not to push the subject in full view of the gossiping ton. But later when they were alone she would press for her answer. How had he got the scar, and why did he need healing?

Don't miss A SENSE OF SIN,
the second novel from Elizabeth Essex,
in stores next month!

Del had not known who she was when he first laid eyes upon her, but he instinctively didn't like her. He distrusted beauty. Because beauty walked hand in hand with privilege. Unearned privilege. And she was certainly beautiful. Tall, elegant, with porcelain white skin, a riot of sable dark curls and deep dark eyes—a symphony of black and white. She surveyed the ballroom like a queen: haughty, serene, remote and exquisitely pretty. And beauty had a way of diverting unpleasantness and masking grievous flaws of character. No, beauty was not to be trusted.

Her name was confirmed by others attending the select ball at the Marquess and Marchioness of Widcombe's. It wafted to him on champagne-fueled murmurs from the hot, crowded room: "Dear Celia," and "Our Miss Burke." And the title that everyone seemed to call her, "The Ravishing Miss Burke," as if it were her rank and she the only one to wear that crown.

The ravishing Miss Celia Burke. A well-known, and even more well-liked local beauty. And here she was, making her serene, graceful way down the short set of stairs into the ballroom as effortlessly as clear water flowed over rocks in a hillside stream. She nodded and smiled in a benign but uninvolved way at all who approached her, but she never stopped to converse. She processed on, following her mother through the parting sea of mere mortals, those lesser human beings who were nothing and nobody to her but playthings.

Aloof, perfect Celia Burke. *Fuck you.*

Yes, by God, he would take his revenge, and Emily would have justice. Maybe then he could sleep at night.

Maybe then he could learn to live with himself.

But he couldn't exact the kind of revenge one takes on another man: straightforward, violent and bloody. He couldn't call Miss Burke out on the middle of the dance floor and put a bullet between her eyes or a sword blade between her ribs at dawn. No.

His justice would have to be more subtle, but no less thorough. And no less ruthless.

"You were the one who insisted we attend this august gathering. So what's it to be? Delacorte?" Commander Hugh McAlden, friend, naval officer and resident cynic, prompted again.

McAlden was one of the few people who never addressed Del by his courtesy title, Viscount Darling, as they'd know each other long before he'd come into the bloody title and far too long for Del to give himself airs in front of such an old friend. And with such familiarity came ease. With McAlden, Del could afford the luxury of being blunt.

"Dancing or thrashing? The latter, I think."

McAlden's usually grim mouth crooked up in half a smile. "A thrashing, right here in the Marchioness' ballroom? I'd pay good money to see that."

"Would you? Shall we have a private bet, then?"

"Del, I always like it when you've got that look in your eye. I'd like nothing more than a good wager."

"A bet, Colonel Delacorte? What's the wager? I've money to burn these days, thanks to you two." Another naval officer, Lieutenant Ian James, known from their time together when Del had been an officer of His Majesty's Marine Forces aboard the frigate *Resolute*, broke into the conversation from behind.

"A private wager only, James." He would need to be more circumspect. James was a bit of a puppy, happy and eager, but untried in the more manipulative ways of society. There was no telling what he might let slip. Del had no intention of getting caught in the net he was about to cast. "Save your fortune in prize money for another time."

"A gentleman's bet then, Colonel?"

A *gentleman's* bet. Del felt his mouth curve up in a scornful smile. What he was about to do violated every code of gentlemanly behavior. "No. More of a challenge."

"He's Viscount Darling now, Mr. James." McAlden was giving Del a mocking smile. "We have to address him with all the deference he's due."

Unholy glee lit the young man's face. "I had no idea. Congratulations, Colonel. What a bloody fine name. I can hear the ladies now: *my dearest, darling Darling.* How will they resist you?"

Del merely smiled and took another drink. But it was true. None of them resisted: high-born ladies, low-living trollops, barmaids, island girls or *señoritas.* They never had, bless their lascivious hearts.

And neither would *she*, despite her remote facade. Celia Burke was nothing but a hothouse flower just waiting to be plucked.

"Go on, then. What's your challenge?" McAlden's face housed a dubious smirk as more navy men, Lieutenants Thomas Gardener and Robert Scott joined them.

"I propose I can openly court, seduce, and ruin an untried, virtuous woman." He paused to give them a moment to remark upon the condition he was about to attach. "Without ever once touching her."

McAlden gave a huff of bluff laughter. "Too easy, in one sense, too hard, in another," he stated flatly.

"But how can you possibly ruin someone without touching them?" Ian James protested.

Del felt his mouth twist. He had forgotten what it was like to be that young. While he was only six and twenty, he'd grown older since Emily's death. Vengeance was singularly aging.

"Find us a drink would you, gentlemen? A real drink and none of the lukewarm swill they're passing out on trays." Del pushed the youths off in the direction of a footman.

"Too easy to ruin a reputation with only a rumor," McAlden repeated in his unhurried, determined way. "You'll have to do better than that."

Trust McAlden to get right to the heart of the matter. Like Del, McAlden had never been young. And he was older in years as well.

"With your reputation," McAlden continued as they turned to follow the others, "well deserved, I might add, you'll not get within a sea mile of a virtuous woman."

"That, old man, shows how little you know of women."

"That, my darling Viscount, shows how little you know of their mamas."

"And I'd like to keep it that way. Hence the prohibition against touching. I plan on keeping a very safe distance." While he was about this business of revenging himself on Celia Burke, he needed to keep himself safe—safe from being forced into doing the right thing should his godforsaken plan be discovered or go awry. And he didn't *want* to touch her. He didn't want to be tainted by so much as the merest brush of her hand.

"Can't seduce, really *seduce*, from a distance. Not even you. Twenty guineas says it can't be done."

"Twenty? An extravagant wager for a flinty, tight-pursed Scotsman like you. Done." Del accepted the challenge with a firm handshake. It sweetened the pot, so to speak.

McAlden perused the crowd. "Shall we pick now? I warn

you, Del, this isn't London. There's plenty of virtue to be had in Dartmouth."

"Why not?" Del felt his mouth curve into a lazy smile. The town may have been full of virtue, but he was full of vice. And he cared about only one particular women's virtue.

"You'll want to be careful. Singularly difficult things, women," McAlden offered philosophically. "Can turn a man inside out. Just look at Marlowe."

Del shrugged. "Captain Marlowe married. I do not have anything approaching marriage in mind."

"So you're going to seduce and ruin an innocent without being named, or caught? That *is* bloody minded."

"I didn't say innocent. I said untried. In this case, there is a particular difference." He looked across the room at Celia Burke again. At the virtuous, innocent face she presented to the world. He would strip away that mask, until everyone could see the ugly truth behind her immaculately polished, social veneer.

McAlden followed the line of his gaze. "You can't mean— That's Celia Burke!" All trace of joviality disappeared from McAlden's voice. "Jesus, Del, have you completely lost your mind? As well as all moral scruple?"

"Gone squeamish?" Del tossed back the last of his drink. "That's not like you."

"I *know* her. Everyone in Dartmouth knows her. She is Marlowe's wife's most particular friend. You can't go about ruining—*ruining* for God's sake—innocent young women, like her. Even *I* know that."

"I said she's *not* innocent."

"Then you must've misjudged her. She's not fair game, Del. Pick someone else. Someone I don't know." McAlden's voice was growing thick.

"No." Darling kept his own voice flat.

McAlden's astonished countenance turned back to look at Miss Burke, half a room away, now smiling sweetly in conversation with another young woman. He swore colorfully under his breath. "That's not just bloody-minded, that's suicidal. She's got parents, Del. Attentive parents. Take a good hard look at her mama, Lady Caroline Burke. She's nothing less than the daughter of a Duke, and is to all accounts a complete gorgon in her own right. They say she eats fortune hunters, not to mention an assortment of libertines like you, for breakfast. And what's more, Miss Burke is a relation of the Marquess of Widcombe, in whose ballroom you are currently *not dancing*. This isn't London, you are a guest here. My guest, and therefore Marlowe's guest. One misstep like that and they'll have your head. Or, more likely, your ballocks. And quite rightly. Pick someone else for your challenge."

"No."

"Delacorte."

"Bugger off, Hugh."

McAlden knew him well enough to hear the implacable finality in his tone. He shook his head slowly. "God's balls, Del. I didn't think I'd regret having you to stay so quickly." He ran his hand through his short, cropped hair and looked at Del with a dawning of realization. "Christ. You'd already made up your mind before you came here, hadn't you? You came for her."

Under such scrutiny, Del could only admit the truth. "I did."

"Damn your eyes, Delacorte. This can only end badly."

Del shrugged with supreme indifference. "That will suit me well enough."

They called it blackmail, though the letter secreted in Celia Burke's pocket was not in actuality black. It had looked innocuous enough: the same ivory-colored paper as all the other mail, brought to her on a little silver tray borne by the butler, Loring. It would have been much better if the letter had actually been black, because then Celia would have known not to open it. She would have flung it into the fire before it could poison her life irrevocably. The clenching grip of anxiety deep in her belly was proof enough the poison had already begun its insidious work.

"Celia, darling? Are you all right? Smile, my dear. Smile." Lady Caroline Burke whispered her instructions for her daughter's ears only, as she smiled and nodded to her many acquaintances in the ballroom as though she hadn't a care in the world.

Celia shoved her unsteady hand into her pocket to reassure—no, not reassure—*convince* herself—the letter was still there. And still real. She had not dreamt up this particular walking nightmare.

She released the offensive missive and clasped her hands together tightly to stop them from trembling. She had no more than a moment or two to compose herself before the opening set was to begin.

Blackmail. The letter, dated only one day ago, was clear and precise, straight to the point.